VIKING RAIDER

Heide Katros

Historical Romance

New Concepts   Georgia

Be sure to check out our website for the very best in fiction at fantastic prices!

When you visit our webpage, you can:

* Read excerpts of currently available books
* View cover art of upcoming books and current releases
* Find out more about the talented artists who capture the magic of the writer's imagination on the covers
* Order books from our backlist
* Find out the latest NCP and author news--including any upcoming book signings by your favorite NCP author
* Read author bios and reviews of our books
* Get NCP submission guidelines
* And so much more!

We offer a 20% discount on all new ebook releases!
(Sorry, but short stories are not included in this offer.)

We also have contests and sales regularly, so be sure to visit our webpage to find the best deals in ebooks and paperbacks! To find out about our new releases as soon as they are available, please be sure to sign up for our newsletter (http://www.newconceptspublishing.com/newsletter.htm) or join our reader group (http://groups.yahoo.com/group/new_concepts_pub/join) !

The newsletter is available by double opt in only and our customer information is *never* shared!

Visit our webpage at:
www.newconceptspublishing.com

Viking Raider is an original publication of NCP. This work has never before appeared in book form. This work is a novel. Any similarity to actual persons or events is purely coincidental.

New Concepts Publishing
5202 Humphreys Rd.
Lake Park, GA 31636

ISBN 1-58608-677-4
(c) copyright 2004 by Heide Katros
Cover art (c) copyright 2004 Eliza Black

NCP books are available at special quantity discounts for bulk purchases for sales promotions, premiums, fund raising, or educational use. For details, write, email, or phone New Concepts Publishing, 5202Humphreys Rd., Lake Park, GA 31636, ncp@newconceptspublishing.com, Ph. 229-257-0367, Fax 229-219-1097.

First NCP Paperback Printing: 2005

Printed in the United States of America

CHAPTER ONE

Hedeby, Scandinavia 845

Talon Herjolfson raised powerful arms, their bulging biceps encircled with costly silver bands, toward the heavens. "May the great all-knowing Odin grant us his blessing!" he roared from the bow of his warship *Raider*. "May he give us strength to distinguish ourselves on the battlefields, so when we die we may enter Valhalla in glory." Icy, aquamarine eyes briefly connected with each warrior.

"Valhalla and glory!" his men shouted in unison, their sentiment echoed by Ragnor Lodbrok's crew, who watched spellbound from the sister ship *Seadragon.*

Talon waited until the warriors quieted. A wry smile tugged at the corners of his generous mouth. The fervor of both crews pleased him, but he intended to push their spirit to fever pitch. Closing his eyes, he threw back his massive head with its thick white-blond mane. The cords in his strong, sun-tanned neck bulged against the strain. Taking a deep breath, he let loose a blood-curdling war cry. Before the last note was carried away by the soughing winds, the rest of the men echoed his whoop, creating an eerie howl that rivaled the caw of the gulls overhead. Talon paused again until the din died down.

"Two days hence, as we travel ever southwest, we will go ashore in the lands of the Franks!" he shouted. "We have it on good authority that the people there are rich ... richer even than the English monks." A note of disdain crept into his booming voice. "It seems only fair that the Franks should surrender a portion of their wealth. If they refuse, we will fight for that which should be ours!" His gauntleted fist slashed through the air accompanied by a roar of approval from the warriors. "We'll take no prisoners and we won't leave anything of value behind. What we can't take with us, we will burn ... If you find a likely wench, take her quickly, then slit her throat." He glowered down at his crew, his massive arms akimbo and his muscular legs braced slightly apart for balance. "Let the world know that we are Vikings, warriors of the sea, and we are not to be trifled with!

In time they will learn to pay homage to us and give us our due without a fight." This time the howl of appreciation from the men was deafening. Talon's eyes narrowed to hide his satisfaction. The crews were ready. Raising his gauntleted hand, he brought it down in one fell swoop, the signal to slip the mooring.

As one twenty elite warriors leaned into their oars and the craft pulled steadily away from the dock. Once they reached the open sea, they would unfurl their solitary sail and allow the wind to catch it. Craftily mounted precisely in the middle of the ship, this single sail gave them the unique ability to travel in either direction without turning around.

On shore a large crowd of well-wishers watched in silence as the two vessels eerily silhouetted against the blood red backdrop of the setting sun sliced swiftly through the undulating waves. A raucous cheer went up when Talon's black sail adorned with a lone silver gauntlet caught the breeze alongside Ragnor's red sea dragon in a field of white. A few seagulls accompanied the two crafts; their short shrill whoops sounding as if they too were caught up in the excitement of the moment.

Only when the ships were but small specks against the darkening horizon did the crowd disburse. As they headed for their homes they were immersed in their own thoughts and fears. The warriors would be gone less than a fortnight, but since they would engage in battle, the women who stayed behind never knew whether they would still be wife or widow when the ships returned.

The second night brought the Vikings within sight of the coast of what would some day be called Normandy. Talon stood at the bow of the *Raider*, his keen eyes skimming the barely discernible outline of the shore against the background of the dawning horizon. They would make land before the sun was fully up. Grimly, he recalled other raids, when they had surprised their targets in the wee hours of the morning. He remembered the fear his horde of howling warriors inspired when they came charging into the towns ere the sun was up rather than attack at a later hour.

Talon chuckled at the thought of how the French would try to flee before his heavily armed men and how little chance they had of escape. A white-toothed grin split his handsome, sun-kissed features as he signaled to his second in command. Asgard came quickly to stand next to his friend and strained to identify what

Talon was pointing out to him.

"It won't be long before we will have to cease all talk and the men will have to ply the oars to the rhythm of silent cadence."

"When do you want to lower the sail?" Asgard inquired anxiously, his own eyes fixed on the ship up ahead. Now that battle was imminent, the tension aboard had grown tangible as each warrior contemplated how he might distinguish himself this very day.

"I will raise my arm as soon as I see the *Seadragon* lower her sail. Go among the ranks and tell the men again that once I lift my arm, I expect complete silence. Only with the added advantage of surprise will we meet with the least amount of resistance."

Asgard's brow lifted slightly in question. "The men will be disappointed. They are looking forward to a good fight."

"Never fear, my friend, the French are a hot-blooded lot." Talon chuckled in wry amusement. "They will not meekly hand over their possessions like the English monks."

He saw it then. The *Seadragon* started to lower her sail and Talon raised his arm to follow suit with the *Raider*. "Tell the men that they will need to give their full attention to the oars," he cautioned. "The river Seine is said to have as many curves as a well shaped woman."

Asgard laughed into his beard at Talon's crude comparison and slapped him resoundingly on the shoulder. They were tall, rugged men and almost of an equal height, both standing above six feet. Where Asgard had a bushy beard and thick mustache, Talon was clean-shaven by choice. A choice that often garnered him vulgar jokes about the supposed lack of his manhood.

There never was any doubt about his sexual prowess, since the women back home made no secret over their feelings for him. His bed was never cold at night and he had plenty of options. Indeed, even his strongest detractors would not deny him his handsome looks.

Talon's square jaw sported several small battle scars that added to his mystique. He rarely smiled, but when he did, his wide, finely sculptured mouth would reveal even white teeth. His nose was strong and set amid high, flat cheekbones. Thickly lashed, wide-set aquamarine eyes, that crinkled in the corners from the steady squinting against the sun, and the straight slash of darkly golden brows redeemed his otherwise forbidding demeanor.

His friends, as well as his crew, merely teased him about his clean-shaven features, because it was as good a reason as any to provoke a rousing fight. When Talon had enough of their jibes, he would take their good-natured bait and either challenge them to hand to hand combat or a sword fight, which was exactly what they tried to arouse with their unfounded criticism. However, his gauntleted hand was never mentioned or made fun of. And no one was more aware of the deformity the glove hid than Talon himself.

Talon rarely thought of his given name anymore. The name Gundar had fallen by the wayside, when an accident at the smithy reduced his left hand to an ugly claw at the tender age of ten. At the time his disfigurement loomed like a pall overshadowing his future, but nothing was more painful than his sire's rejection.

"I want no cripple for a son," Holgar Herjolfson proclaimed, when he was told of the accident. His father never found it in his heart to retract his harsh words. Not even after Talon distinguished himself in battle time and again, fighting with a vengeance to prove himself as worthy as any man with two good hands.

When the Viking ships finally crunched to a jarring halt in a sandy cove just North of the city of Rouen, the sun was still struggling to top the horizon. The sails had been furled several leagues from shore as the warriors rowed the rest of the way. It was cool. Dew sparkled on the leaves of the shrubs and trees that dotted the shoreline, but the beauty was lost to the invaders who only cared about concealment.

Not a word was spoken as the men quickly unfastened their shields from the gunwales and checked their weapons. Their battle axes at the ready, broad swords hanging from heavy belts hugging their hips and wicked wide-bladed knives tucked in the cross garters of their fur boots, they looked a deadly lot. Talon allowed his gaze to drift over each warrior before he nodded with grim satisfaction.

As his eyes locked with Asgard's, he quirked an amused brow at his friend. "You look like a denizen straight from Hades," he quipped in a hoarse whisper. "Your hair stands away from your head in salt encrusted spikes and your clothes didn't fare much better." His shoulders shook in silent mirth when Asgard rewarded him with a baleful glare.

"And you look just as lovely as a maid on a spring day?" Asgard jeered. "You should take a gander at yourself in that river yonder. You look like old Loki himself. Your hair is frosted with salt and your wolf's skin seems to stick to you as if you had grown it on your own hairless hide."

At mention of his hairless chest, Talon's hackles rose and he stepped closer to his friend, glowering, his wide shoulders hunched in preparation of a scuffle.

"Hey, you two fighting cocks," intervened Ragnor. "Save your strength for the real enemy. The French will try to defend what's theirs."

A muted roar of approval from the rest of the men did more to quell their urge to fight one another than Ragnor's warning. They stepped apart, rueful grins replacing their scowls.

The eagerness of the assembled warriors to attack showed plainly on their rugged faces. Adrenaline coursed through their veins and added to their brute strength as they chafed in their tracks anticipating Talon's signal.

With Ragnor and Talon in their lead, they hacked their way through the dense brush and silently marched toward the city of Rouen, where the citizen were just getting ready to face another day. Many of them would never see another.

As the warriors approached the town, a collective murmur of satisfaction passed through the ranks. The gates were already thrown wide. Several farmers had left before daybreak to till the land, never guessing that they would be among the few lucky ones who would live to tell of the Viking attack.

CHAPTER TWO

Danielle D'Arçenau stood poised at the very edge of the cliffs that formed the Northern border of Honfleur-sur-mer, her family's estate. Beneath her the North Sea slammed with mesmerizing regularity against the age-old granite promontory, spewing salty spray more than twenty feet into the air.

Danielle watched through tear-blurred eyes as the sea slowly receded. Rubbing her arms to ward off an inner chill, she tried to imagine if she would feel a great deal of pain, when her body hit those craggy rocks that lurked just beneath the surface. No, she could never take her own life. Somehow everything would work out. It had to. It simply had to.

Exhausted from a night of weeping and railing at her misfortune, she sank to her knees and buried her face in her delicate white hands. She still refused to believe that her brother Jean-Jacques, the third Marquis D'Arcenau, would actually go through with the plans he had divulged to her last night.

In her mind she had played the scene over and over until she was sure she would never forget that horrible moment in time. Honfleur was the only home she had ever known. Why couldn't she accompany him to Paris? What had possessed him to choose Gaillard? The cloister was located in a desolate area, way out in the country. She balled her fists and pressed them against her mouth. *Mon dieu*, she would die of boredom.

Bitterly, she reflected that never in her life had she been as miserable as she was today. Not even when her beloved father died not too many months hence. And for the dozenth time she recalled every torturous detail of the evening before.

Minette had just served a dessert of warm apples with a honey sauce, when Jean-Jacques asked her to join him in the study as soon as she finished. He excused himself, declining his own serving of the sweet treat. Thinking back, Danielle reflected sourly that he had certainly not declined another goblet of wine.

Assuming he had some small diversion in mind for her, she gobbled her dessert and followed her brother down the long hallway to the room that had not so long ago been occupied by her beloved papa. She rapped her knuckles against the heavy gilt-edged door and did not even wait to be asked to enter. Undisguised curiosity and an expectant smile flitted across her delicate features as she slipped into the room.

"Here I am, brother. You wanted to speak to me?" she inquired almost breathlessly, her question ending on a lilting note.

Jean-Jacques stood by the fireplace, one arm resting negligently against the mantel, a glass of fine port in his well-manicured hand, an air of utter world-weariness about his person. His hooded gaze swept Danielle in cursory dismissal as he lifted the finely cut goblet and took a deep swallow of the dark red liquid.

His saturnine expression stopped Danielle cold in her tracks just inside the door. When Jean-Jacques continued to keep her standing, she audibly cleared her throat and then tapped her foot on the shining parquet floor in tacit exasperation. Since even that did not evoke any response from her brother, she walked boldly up to him, her hands balled into small fists at her sides.

"Jean-Jacques you asked me specifically to meet you here but a few moments ago." Her green eyes glittered with suppressed anger and her tone of voice left little doubt of her annoyance. "Either you tell me why or I am leaving this very minute." She tossed her head for emphasis and the silken curtain of midnight hair rippled in elegant waves about her small head before it settled just above her slim waist.

Jean-Jacques' fleshy lips compressed into a thin line to convey his displeasure over her impertinence. His pale blue eyes narrowed contemptuously as he tried to stare her down. Finally, with a long-suffering sigh, he motioned with his glass toward the leather sofa across from him. "Sit already, sister dearest. The lack of my asking has never stopped you before." The last was uttered with a sneer.

Danielle took Jean-Jacques' crudeness in stride. She was used to his mood swings when he was into his cups. By the look of it, her brother was definitely no longer sober, a condition that had become more obvious since dear Papa had died.

Jean-Jacques raked his pale hand through his thinning brown hair and smacked his lips. He cocked his head to one side and his gaze became downright malevolent. "My dearest sister," he continued matter-of-factly, "I have decided that it would be in your best interest, if I sent you to the cloister of the Good Sisters of the Benevolent Shepherd until such time when I have found a suitable husband for you."

Danielle gasped and her hand fluttered toward her throat to clutch at the finely wrought gold brooch that adorned the high-necked collar of her gown. She was in desperate need to hold on to something in view of that particular news and the sharp edges of the brooch inflicted enough pain to her tender palm to keep her from blurting out her innermost feelings.

"Why would you find it necessary to send me to the nuns, Jean-Jacques? You cannot mean it," she stammered in wild confusion, trying hard to stay calm.

"I cannot recall a single instance when I would have displeased you or given you one moment of trouble, since dear Papa passed on." She reverently crossed herself in memory of her father, but deep inside her a raging fury built over her brother's gross injustice. She knew she would have to think quickly or her fate would be sealed forever.

Danielle had no intention of spending her youth on her knees in some damp cloister amid some old dried-up women. Danielle had dreams of having a husband who adored her, of children and laughter, not the drone of constant prayer and doing charwomen's work. Nor did she want Jean-Jacques choosing a husband for her. No, she simply would not have any of that, she thought rebelliously.

Acting demurely and with feigned submission, she regarded her brother from beneath heavily lashed lids. She couldn't chance to look him straight in the eye for fear that he might discover her loathing for him in their depths. Instead she hurried to apologize.

"I am sorry, Jean-Jacques, I did not mean to erupt in such an unladylike manner, but your announcement comes as a shock to me. Surely, you must have a good reason for wanting to banish me to a cloister and I trust you will tell me why."

Jean-Jacques was momentarily caught off guard, wondering if she knew something of his discovery. He hesitated, holding his breath, anticipating that she might say something more. Gripping the wine goblet, he waited.... No, she could not possibly know. She was an impulsive chit. She would have confronted him with the evidence now carefully hidden in his chambers, but in view of those damning papers he felt it best to send her away. He needed time to ponder the consequences.

Pleased that Danielle did not seem to have any idea of his real reasons, he pushed himself unsteadily away from the mantel and closed the space between them, staring suspiciously down at his sister not quite trusting that she might not know after all.

"Ah, *ma petite*, I am so sorry, but I feel there is little choice. I have urgent business in Paris and I simply cannot take you with me."--Why, he would never tell the chit the truth. It was imperative that he liquidated as many assets as possible before the solicitor came snooping around. Couldn't leave it to chance that the old Marquis might have left a copy of his will somewhere. Jean-Jacques was still in a state of shock over the contents.

There had been nothing accidental about his find. He'd snooped, because he was deeply in debt. He was in desperate need to know how much he stood to inherit. The old Marquis had been a frugal man, sometimes downright miserly. Jean-Jacques was sure that he'd put away a good amount of coin and he meant to have control of it. He'd felt almost giddy when he found the parchment until he read that he'd been born on the wrong side of the blankets as the old man so glibly referred to his illegitimacy. Apparently, he was nothing more than the offspring of a night's passion between the master of the house and a chambermaid. Why, the old Marquis even dared to question the credibility of that particular claim.

Ever since Jean-Jacques found the documents, he wondered over and over again, if their mutual father thought it a joking matter or whether it was simply his way to garner vengeance for reasons only known to him? Why did he raise Jean-Jacques as his legitimate son? Why did he allow him to believe that he was the rightful Third Marquis D'Arceneau of Honfleur-sur-mer, only to leave instructions to toss him out by the ear after his death? It made no sense. Jean-Jacques felt entitled, because his sire had raised him to enjoy the finer things of life. The devil take his soul!

Jean-Jacques interrupted his own musings, when Danielle fidgeted in her seat. Acting, as if he had never paused, he continued with a dismissive wave of his hand. "One, we do not have a suitable chaperon, Danielle, my dear. Two, I plan to ride hard and make camp along the way. None of it would be acceptable for a young woman of your breeding. Aside from that, you will only spend at most two months with the good sisters."

"Two months!" Danielle screamed in anguish, unable to contain her feigned acceptance any longer. "Surely, you can't be so cruel as to subject me to a dreary life like that for any length of time?" Crossing her arms over her breasts, she stamped her small foot rebelliously. Her mouth formed a becoming moué and the first tears gathered in her expressive eyes. "I will not go, Jean-Jacques," she stated firmly and her delicate chin shot upward in defiance. "I will not go and you can't make me."

Jean-Jacques chuckled in wry amusement. "Can't I now, *ma petite*? And who pray tell is going to stop me?" His brow lifted in disdainful question. By the time the family solicitor came around with a duplicate of the will, and Jean-Jacques was sure that there would be such a document, he would have secured his future. And of course Danielle would never know. She could rot in the nunnery for all he cared. She was nothing but a meddlesome female, always in the way. No, he intended to take all and Danielle be damned.

Danielle knew she had lost. She collapsed against the back of the brocade covered settee, suddenly too weak to hold herself upright. Fumbling for a lace-edged handkerchief, she dabbed at her eyes. No longer did she question the fact that she was going to be forced to go. She knew no one would stop her brother. He was the rightful Marquis D'Arcenau now that papa was gone. There was no fight left in her voice, when she asked the obvious. "What is going to happen to me, in case you should not return?"

Feeling a little more benevolent now that he had victory so well in his grasp, Jean-Jacques smiled down at his weeping sister. Drinking another large gulp of wine, he elaborated further on his devilish scheme. "Ah, *petite*, I plan to leave a goodly sum with the sisters and instructions to allow you to leave, if I don't return for you when the two months are up. Of course, you will not be able to come back to this estate alone, you know. I will appoint a suitable guardian for you in that case with the stipulation that he marry you in good time."

Danielle was about to protest that he could do that before his leave taking. It would be better than being shut away in a cloister. Her protest died on her lips when she heard his next pronouncement.

"I will instruct the good sisters to turn you over into the capable hands of the Earl of Montvignon."

Danielle felt the bile rise in her throat and fought valiantly against disgracing herself. His announcement left her speechless with disdain for the man who called himself her brother. She took several deep breaths and rose shakily to her feet. With all the dignity she could muster, she no longer hesitated, but looked him straight in the eye. "You are utterly contemptible, brother. It makes me ill to think that I am related to someone who would stoop so low as to choose a man who is not only older than my dear departed father, but is rumored to have the pox on top of that." She lost all control then, feeling that she had nothing to lose. So with the vehemence of all the fury and absolute contempt she felt, she spit on his polished riding boots.

Jean-Jacques was momentarily stunned by his sister's behavior. Raising his chin, he glared at her with narrowed eyes, while his nostrils flared in repressed fury. The corners of his mouth turned downward with unequivocal spite as he carefully shifted his wine glass to his left hand.

"You filthy little imbecile," he hissed, a fine spray of spittle issuing from his mouth. "How dare you soil my person in such vulgar fashion? You will pay for this insult make no mistake about it," he hissed, then slapped her face with the open palm of his hand with such force that her head snapped back.

Danielle should have seen it coming, but in all her seventeen years, no one had ever laid a hand on her. Her eyes stung with unshed tears and the pain of the vicious blow, but Danielle was beyond giving in to self-pity. Gulping several deep breaths, she held her ground. Cradling her throbbing cheek with her hand, she gritted, "This would best be your one and only time that you do me bodily harm. I swear that I will kill you, if you should ever try it again."

Danielle did not give Jean-Jacques the chance to test her mettle, but turned on her heel and ran from the study all the way to her chambers. Once there, she threw herself across the counterpane of her bed and cried until she thought her heart would break.

Danielle thought she had no more tears left, but after she replayed that horrible scene in her mind once again, she found that she could still cry.

In her wretched state of mind and the constant roar of the breaking waves, she did not hear the approaching footsteps. Emile, the old butler, was almost upon her before she noticed him. Ashamed to be caught weeping, she turned her face away. She tried, but did not quite succeed to keep the catch out of her voice. "Yes, Emile, what is it?"

"I beg your pardon, *mademoiselle*, but the master would like for you to return to the manor at once." There was sympathy in his old reedy voice and it proved to be Danielle's undoing.

"Oh, Emile," she cried, turning her tear-stained face toward him, no longer caring that he should see her that way. "What am I to do? Did Jean-Jacques advise you of his plans for me?"

The old butler dropped his gaze in embarrassed silence, enough proof to Danielle that he knew all about it.

"I am sorry, Emile," she whispered, painfully aware that she had overstepped her bounds by confiding in the old servant and ever more aware that she would have nowhere to turn for help. Defeated, she slowly followed the old man down the path.

Her heart sank when she saw the family carriage waiting under the *porte cochère*, a small chest and a leather satchel loaded atop and the driver already in his seat. Her hand flew to her mouth to stay the anguished scream from bubbling over. She twisted her head to question the old butler, but Emile had fled into the house, unable to stay and witness his young mistress and her distress.

Jean-Jacques sauntered down the steps at that moment, a thin cigar in one gloved hand and a silver-headed cane in the other.

He was elegantly dressed in fawn breeches and morning coat, his travel cape slung negligently across one shoulder.

"There you are," he exclaimed as if Danielle were a wayward child who was late. He swept her with an insolent gaze. "You look positively windblown, my dear, but that cannot be helped right now. Besides, where you are going your looks won't matter, will they?" he added maliciously.

Abruptly, he grasped her upper arm in a viselike grip that made her wince and jerked her within inches of his face. "Climb into that carriage at once, before I make you regret it," he ground out viciously from between gritted teeth.

Danielle was too stunned to even think. Fighting tears, she opened her mouth to protest his rough treatment, but Jean-Jacques' fingers only dug deeper into the tender flesh The sharp twinges of pain running up and down her arm, made her realize that any resistance on her part would prove futile. Docilely, she allowed him to lead her to the carriage. Applying pressure to the small of her back he shoved her unceremoniously into the dark interior.

Stumbling, Danielle scooted to the far side of the velvet-covered seat and pressed herself into the corner. Her eyes were wild with fear and apprehension. *Mon dieu* what had happened to her brother? Jean-Jacques never before displayed such a violent streak and she feared for her very life at this moment.

Jean-Jacques carelessly threw his cigar into a nearby planter before he followed his sister into the carriage. He settled himself across from the frightened girl and let out an amused chuckle. "You do resemble a regular shrew, my dear. Thanks to your unkempt appearance I won't have any trouble convincing the good sisters that they will need to keep a wary eye on you and that you are sorely in need of discipline." Again he laughed and the sound of it made Danielle cringe.

He is quite mad, she thought. She'd better not say anything more to him or it might drive him over the edge. Let him think that she was thoroughly frightened and ready to obey him in anything he asked.

"Don't think one moment that you have me fooled," he snapped suddenly. "I know you are scheming something against me, little sister. You are far too quiet."

At first, she didn't respond. Then she blurted, "Is it my dowry, Jean-Jacques? Are you in need of the money for some reason?"

He regarded her with something akin to admiration. "I would

never have credited you with having such astute ideas, little sister." He leaned closer and Danielle could see that he was clearly enjoying himself. He waved his gloved hand negligently through the air, then settled his elbow on his knee and rested his chin atop his fist. "Of course, one can never have enough money and I would not object to having the sum papa has settled on you," he drawled, "and I might still have it, if I can find the right husband for you. One who will be willing to forgo the dowry in return for a woman who is untouched."

Danielle's stomach turned in revulsion as she followed his train of thought. "Would you really stoop so low as to sell me to the highest bidder?" she bit out.

Jean-Jacques chuckled obscenely. "Oh, I would not put it quite so crudely, my dear. You see you are a little past your prime and you have to admit that there haven't been suitors knocking down our doors at any time. But, yes, there are men who are willing to forgo beauty and youth in return for being the one who, shall we say makes a woman of you?" He chortled loudly at his own jest and Danielle became more convinced than ever that he was slightly demented or deeply into his cups.

"Of course such men would prove to be older, but think of all the experience they can bring to your marriage bed, my dear." He stopped short of elaborating further, caught up in his own lascivious thoughts.

Danielle dug her hands into the velvet cushions in an attempt to keep from getting sick. In the end the swaying of the carriage, combined with Jean-Jacques lewd descriptions of what she could expect from marriage at her age, were her undoing. Before she could warn her brother, her stomach emptied itself right in front of his feet.

Shuddering, Jean-Jacques pulled his boots away from the ill smelling pool of bile and quickly reached for a small pomander of roseleaves and cloves and brought it to his nose. His pale blue eyes filled with malice. "You filthy slattern! I have a good mind to leave you to the tender mercies of the nuns forever." He grabbed for his cane and for a split second Danielle thought he would hit her with it. Instead he rapped against the top of the carriage and bade the driver to stop.

Jumping nimbly to the ground, his face a grimace of disgust, he turned back to the ashen girl. "Wipe the filth from this carriage so we may continue on our way!" he ordered.

Danielle looked helplessly about her. She had never been asked to do menial work, but she realized that Jean-Jacques might beat her if she did not clean the mess on the floor. She scrambled unassisted from the carriage and picked up bunches of dry grass. Only when she had cleaned the spot to Jean-Jacques' satisfaction, did they continue on their journey.

CHAPTER THREE

The guards at the gates to the city of Rouen blinked at the sudden appearance of some forty heavily armed ruffians, who seemed to have sprung from the very bowels of hell. The men gaped in open amazement at the grotesque shapes, which hardly resembled any human forms they had ever laid eyes on.

"*Mon dieu*, Davide, do you see what I see? It eez like no people I ever saw." One guard exclaimed in awe as he pointed toward the approaching horde of men. He stared at the crude garments made of animal hides and their odd cross-gartered boots, thinking that they seemed oblivious to the chill in the air, since their massive arms were bare and their tunics reached only to mid thigh.

The man named Davide nudged his partner into action. "Don't gape, Henri. Let's close the gates!" he screamed just as the first shrill war whoop of the Viking warriors rent the still morning. By that time it was already too late. Pitifully outmatched, the two gatekeepers defended their ground and tried to fight the invaders.

Ragnor and Talon stood side-by-side and fought one of the hapless guards, while Asgard and Leif took on the other. It was not much of a fight, but swift and bloody and served to stir up the blood lust in the rest of the warriors.

Even before the two guards were dispatched, the rest of the Vikings stormed past their leaders, their lips drawn back in a feral rictus, their urge to kill riled beyond reason.

The citizens of Rouen were still rubbing sleep from their eyes, when they heard the first gruesome battle cries dispel the serenity of the early morning. Brave husbands and fathers grabbed their weapons and took to the streets, while their wives and daughters hid under beds and inside armoires. Just as Talon had predicted, the French were no match against the onslaught of the Vikings.

The fighting lasted little more than an hour and by then the sun had scaled the horizon and shone down on the carnage that strewed the hard packed earth throughout the conquered city. The stench of blood hung heavily in the morning breeze and still the Vikings yelled their battle cries and searched for survivors.

Talon wiped the sweat from his eyes and stared down with a bleak smile as he pulled his sword from his latest victim. The smell of clotting blood clogged his nostrils, but the sight of the dead and dying evoked a sense of power in him and in sheer exhilaration he threw back his head and let out a piercing yell. Some of his men took up his chant, a terrifying sound that sent renewed shivers through those who were still hidden and hoped to escape the slaughter.

Talon climbed up on the city fountain so all his men could see him. His teeth reflected whitely against his sun-bronzed skin as he addressed them, his blue eyes sparkled.

"You have done good work! Break up into units of two and search every house. Bring all the valuables you can find and pile them right here in the middle of the town. Make sure that you are not ambushed and cut anyone down who should stand in your way! Leave no witnesses behind. When the farmers return by nightfall, they will be witness enough."

The warriors disbursed in quick compliance and once again there were screams of terror and anguish as they ruthlessly rummaged through the houses and killed those who had not hidden well enough.

The sun was standing high in the horizon by the time the Vikings finished wreaking their havoc upon the city of Rouen. Each man was loaded down so heavily with booty that their steps would falter as they made their way back to their ships. Black wisps of smoke billowed behind them as the flames licked eagerly at wooden structures. Soon all of Rouen would be on fire, creating a huge pyre for those who had died trying to defend the city.

The warriors were in high spirits when they got back to the boats. Like a bunch of wayward children they compared their plunder. "Hey, Olaf, how do you like my hat?" Leif wanted to know as he donned a delicate little bonnet that was meant for a woman.

Olaf was too entranced with a wide red sash to find any interest in Leif's devilment. The true treasures of gold and silver were forgotten in light of the unfamiliar pieces of clothing and ornaments.

"This calls for celebration," announced a jubilant Talon. "From this day forward we will inspire awe among friend and foe alike. Let's break out some of the flasks of wine and toast our good fortune."

"Hear! Hear! To good fortune! May the all-knowing Odin continue to smile upon us!" they roared as they lifted purloined tankards and flasks.

They drank themselves into a stupor; no longer worried that anyone would discover them there in that sandy cove. They had fought hard and accomplished what they had come for. The Vikings needed riches to solidify their dominance and they would not stop to raid and pillage until that goal was met.

Drunk with wine and victory, they slept most of the afternoon away. Only the rumbling of their empty bellies made them stir long enough to build a fire and roast some of the hastily slaughtered fowl. Once sated, they drank some more and lay down again to sleep the night away.

Talon was too keyed up to sleep. He had eaten sparingly and the liquor he had consumed earlier no longer seemed to have any effect on him. Even a dip in the river did not cool him down. He prowled about the makeshift camp. Driven by an inner restlessness, he casually kicked Asgard's booted foot.

"Do you feel like scouting about the area?" he whispered to his friend.

Asgard hauled himself up and braced himself on one elbow as he blinked owlishly at Talon. "What is there to scout?" he asked sourly.

Talon shrugged. "Who knows? Maybe we missed something when we headed straight for Rouen. There could be another little village nearby and we could find us some wenches."

At the mention of wenches, Asgard brightened visibly and got nimbly to his feet. "Time's a wasting, Talon! Let's go!"

CHAPTER FOUR

A half moon bathed the countryside in an eerie light. Smoke hung still heavily on the air, irritating their nostrils with its acrid smell. Hardly a nocturnal animal stirred, and when Talon spoke it was in hushed tones. They had walked more than a mile without encountering so much as a hovel or winter barn.

"Maybe this wasn't one of my brighter ideas after all," grumbled Talon.

"Give it a chance, my friend. Now that I am up, I have found my second wind and I am not ready to turn back. Let's just go a little further."

They trudged on. Talon completely discouraged, but Asgard in high spirits, if for no other reason than to aggravate his friend. Talon was about to gripe some more, when a dark structure suddenly loomed against the horizon before them. It seemed as if it had sprouted from the ground, but then they realized that it had lain hidden behind a gently sloping hill, partially concealed among a copse of trees. Built of rough stone it blended into the shadows, making it almost impossible to distinguish at first sight.

Asgard elbowed Talon. "Now, what do we have here?" he asked drolly. "Do you think we found the lodgings of a nobleman or by chance a little monastery?"

Talon had already quickened his step, a feral gleam in his bright eyes. "Whatever it is, let's check it out. If we meet with great resistance, we can always retreat and come back on the morrow with the rest of the men. On the other hand, if we find a comely wench, we'll share and while the night away together."

Asgard grinned hugely at that prospect. They quickly fanned out and approached the high stonewalls from different directions. There seemed no one stirring within, so they met at the sturdy wooden gate and nosed about for a way inside.

"There is a postern gate in back, but it would mean that we would have to wade through muck and I don't like the prospect of that," offered Asgard.

Talon pointed to the large limb of an oak that reached nearly to the top of the wall. "How about trying it that way? We climb that tree and try our luck with jumping toward the wall?"

Asgard cocked his head to the side as he thought on that a minute. "If we miss, it'll be a long fall to the ground."

"Ha, you are getting soft, Asgard. First you complain about a little muck and now you are afraid of a few bruises. Next time I'll go on a raid, I'll take one of the women in your stead. At least she can spread her legs if I have a need."

Asgard's meaty fist closed about Talon's tunic and he dragged him so close that they almost touched noses. "You mewling little runt," he retorted good-naturedly. "I'll bet you any trinket from my share of the booty that I will have an easier time closing the gap between the branch and the wall than you will."

"You are on," chuckled Talon, quickly grabbed for the lowest limb and swung himself upward.

Within minutes they sat companionably side-by-side in the tree and stared into the inky depth below. "Nothing seems to be stirring. If there were a cur around, surely it would have sounded an alarm by now."

"Well, do you want carry out that bet we made or do you want to sit here blathering about the ifs and buts all night?"

Talon punched Asgard's arm in playful fashion and without another word launched himself into the dark void toward the wall. A muffled grunt heralded the fact to Asgard that his friend had made contact and that it was now his turn to jump.

Straddling the high rampart, they rubbed their raw chafed hands against their tunics, muttering ugly curses.

"Damned wall," muttered Asgard. "I think I took a layer of hide off my palms."

"Your hands and my knees. No wonder they have only a sturdy oak door and no dogs to warn of intruders. This wall is deterrent enough."

In unison they pulled their knives from their cross garters and clamped them between their teeth before they jumped noiselessly to the ground, their fall cushioned by a thick layer of rotting leaves. Their eyes cutting vigilantly from left to right, they crept forward.

The main building was old, moss covered, and in ill repair. An iron studded door loomed in the recesses of its domed entrance. The handle gave under their cautious probing and it swung open on well-oiled hinges. They hesitated, warily eyeing a long corridor of flagstones, worn smooth from years of wear and care. Apart from some moonlight spilling through a delicate lead-paned window at the far end of the hallway, it was dark. However, the meager light did reveal a narrow room with rough-hewn wooden benches and an equally plain altar.

"By Loki and all the hounds of Hades," hissed Talon. "By the looks of this we have risked our necks and scraped our hands and knees raw for nothing. There is not even so much as a valuable chalice to claim. The resident monks must have taken a vow of poverty."

He meant to keep his voice to a whisper, but the disappointment of being in a monastery and a poor one at that rankled Talon. Instead his deep voice reverberated against the bare walls like thunder.

A small, yet definitely feminine gasp answered them back and stopped the Vikings in their tracks. A fiendish gleam rose in Talon's eyes as he jabbed his elbow into Asgard's side.

"All may not be lost yet. There seems to be a female about. I pray to Odin that she is not too old or ugly. After all the tribulation I had to go through to gain entrance to this place, I certainly deserve something to soothe my soul and my manhood."

Straining to see in the gaping darkness of the room, Talon remarked, "Well, as luck will have, there are two of them, though they resemble a pair of crows." Pointing them out to Asgard, he whooped with glee. "See those twin shadows trying to escape at the far end? After them!"

The two men took no chances, brandishing their knives they stayed in hot pursuit of their quarry, their nostrils flaring with the anticipated delight.

Danielle and Sister Celeste knew they were running for their lives. Her heart beating painfully in her chest, Danielle headed for her cell. As she hurried down the familiar hallways, she called to the other nuns to beware.

"We have intruders! Hide! Hide!" she warned as she ran, her voice filled with the panic she felt. She told herself everything would be all right. How could it not? She and Sister Celeste had done their penance for dawdling in the garden instead of weeding. That was the reason they were up past midnight, saying their last atonement prayers.

As soon as Danielle reached her cell, she realized that she had made a huge mistake. She was trapped. To hide under the bed would be useless, since there was no other furniture in the room, apart from one chair, a small table, and a banded box, which held her spare clothing.

Faced with the reality of her error, Danielle collapsed dejectedly onto the chair to await her fate. Maybe it would be better to die a quick death at the hands of the prowlers than to pine her life away behind the walls of this cloister. She had long despaired of ever leaving. Jean-Jacques had promised to come and fetch her after two months, but that time had been up weeks ago. Her pleas to be released and her pledge to allow the nuns to keep whatever money her brother had left with them fell on deaf ears.

"You were given into our safekeeping, Danielle, I cannot

simply let you go. In time you will come to like it here. You may want to become one of us," the old Mother Superior told her each time she brought up the subject.

Staring straight ahead, Danielle sat stiff-backed on the wooden chair and stoically waited for the intruder to find her.

Despite her acceptance of her fate Danielle gasped when the door to her cell suddenly crashed open. The force bounced it off the wall with an ominous thud. She barely took notice of the noise over the thunderous beating of her heart. Her gaze riveted momentarily on two large fur boots, standing slightly apart. *Bon dieu*, they almost looked like animal feet. Leather strips criss-crossed them in the oddest fashion all the way up to some badly skinned knees.

Swallowing against her fear, she boldly allowed her eyes to wander ever upward. What did she have to lose? Her gaze lingered briefly on bare heavily muscled thighs that disappeared beneath a short fur tunic. For a moment she forgot to breathe as she contemplated the implications of her discovery. Lord have mercy that meant the man was naked underneath. Dipping her head she tried to hide her mortification. Oh, she would be spending hours on her knees doing penance for even thinking such naughty thoughts.

In for a penny, in for a pound, she thought irreverently and lifted her head higher. She repressed a shiver of revulsion when her gaze lit on the dried up legs of a wolf dangling from one broad shoulder… and then … Emerald eyes clashed with intense aquamarine ones. A curious spark passed between the two adversaries, filling the air with a bizarre electricity. It died as quickly as it ignited.

Danielle's heart slammed against her breast as stared in mesmerized fear. Her courage flagged and she pressed a slim hand to her mouth to stifle a moan of dismay. Mother of Mary, this was not just an ordinary prowler. This huge, powerful brute was a Viking if her guess was right. Fascinated she watched the display of hard muscle that rippled with a life of their own each time he inhaled. His presence left her feeling oddly disembodied. Mercy, he was magnificent, sleek as a mountain lion and probably more dangerous.

Talon gaped at the beauty before him. Bathed in soft candlelight, she was wondrous to behold. He had never seen a maid so creamy of skin or with such an abundance of hair the color of midnight. He'd expected her to scream and plead in face of the menace he represented, but she sat there boldly staring him down. A sliver of admiration for her courage spiked through him. For a long moment he simply stood and gawked until he noticed the disdain in her unusual green eyes. Fury shook him out of his reverie. He had come to take his pleasure on this wench and this unfamiliar feeling inside him would not stop him from his original plan.

Purposefully, he strode further into the room, his presence overpowering in the tiny space. With exaggerated care he slipped his knife into the top of his boot. Insolently, he slid his narrowed gaze over Danielle's slim form. Grunting his satisfaction, he reached for her, intent on throwing her on the nearby cot. Instead she stopped him cold, addressing him in surprisingly well-pronounced English.

Danielle's hackles rose. She inched back as far as she could and speared him with a frigid gaze. Gripping the edges of her chair with shaking hands, she addressed him in meticulously pronounced English. "How dare you intrude into my chamber without invitation?" she snapped in undisguised hauteur.

Talon withdrew his hand, a golden brow quirked in surprise. "You speak the English tongue rather well."

Danielle's chin shot up as she answered him in a most condescending manner, "My mother was English. She insisted that her children would learn her mother tongue. My sire, however, was French, so I have had the benefit of both languages."

Danielle deliberately spoke as if the man before her were dim-witted. Unfortunately, her arrogant tone struck a sour note with Talon and without further preamble, his large hand continued on its intended path and buried itself among the folds of her simple high-necked bodice. His face descended to within inches of her own, the smell of him savage, yet tantalizing.

"I am a Viking!" he announced with equal arrogance and barely concealed hostility. "I take what I want, when I want it. And at this moment I want you," he growled, his handsome face a veritable thundercloud. Seconds later the sound of tearing fabric echoed loudly in the tiny room.

Danielle gasped in indignation, but even as her breath whooshed through her parted lips her firm white breasts spilled forth. Shocked beyond words, Danielle stared stupidly at the twin globes, then back up at the man who dared to expose them to his view. She felt faint with terror.

Talon licked his lips at the delicious fare offered his hungry gaze. He felt himself harden beneath his tunic and all reason left him. Scooping Danielle from her chair, he dropped her unceremoniously on the narrow cot. With practiced motion he shoved her skirts over her head and quickly knelt between her thrashing thighs.

"Hold still, my little wildcat," he warned. "I'll have you fight or not. It will be easier on you, if you don't fight me until I am inside you, but it makes me no never mind. I have all night."

"Let go of me, you brute!" Danielle screamed, the sound of her voice muffled beneath several layers of petticoats. She was not going to give in without a fight. Struggling free of the voluminous skirts, she beat at his muscled chest with both fists.

Talon laughed at her puny attempt to deter him from having her. Pinning her down with one massive leg, he quickly tucked the ends of his tunic into his belt. He was buck naked underneath and fully aroused. Still grinning and without effort he captured her wrists in his gloved hand, holding them high above her head.

Danielle gaped, shocked by his nudity, but fascinated by the beautiful proportion of his body. Angry tears gathered in her eyes as she realized the futility of her struggle. Allowing herself to go limp, she sniffed back the tears, while she desperately searched her brain for a different tactic. Exhaling a shaky breath, she whispered, "Sir Viking, if you are half the man you seem to be, why then are you going to force yourself upon me? Why not find a willing maid to bed? Fair as you are of face, I should think you would not have such a hard time of it."

Talon's hand stilled, his lust waned at her taunt. The wench was right. Never had he found a need to force his attention on a woman. Of course, this one provoked a man beyond sanity.

"You have a point, demoiselle, but where may I ask will I find a willing wench to still the fire in my loins at this time of night?" he asked his voice as smooth as warm velvet.

Seeing her wavering gaze, he chuckled. And a new surge of desire coursed through him like a river of lava. He bent close and his tongue flicked leisurely across her soft pink lower lip.

Danielle twisted her head aside, but not before he caught the startled reaction in her eyes. With casual indifference, his huge hand took hold of the remnants of her bodice. He rent it all the way down to her navel. His vision blurred with lust at the sight of her silky flesh and his throat convulsed with unconcealed desire. He hesitated, licked his suddenly dry lips.

"Maybe we will do it your way after all, demoiselle," he muttered hoarsely. "As I have said, I have all night." He stripped her gown off as easily as if it were made of paper. "It will be interesting to see how long it will take until your defenses break down and you beg me to possess you," he mocked. Exercising exaggerated indifference, his fingers plucked gently at a nipple until it pebbled into a hard bead. He gauged her reaction through narrowed eyes, an amused smile playing about his generous mouth. Ah, yes, a willing wench would be more fun.

The instant response of her untried body shook Danielle to her toes. The nuns had warned her that her body would betray her some day. Was this what they had tried to tell her? Transfixed she followed Talon's hand as it traveled leisurely from nipple to nipple and then slowly down to her navel. Mesmerized she watched him follow this path with his tongue and gently blew on the wetness left behind. Danielle shivered, mortified that it was not from cold.

Talon grinned down at her, his eyes never leaving her delicate face as his free hand forged into new territory. With all the patience born of endless days at sea, he reached back toward her knees and gently stroked his way upward. Always stopping short of his ultimate goal, always allowing Danielle to regain her breath.

Bewildered, she stared into his teasing eyes. "Please, Viking, let me be," she begged. She knew she had reason to be afraid. This barbarian held a power over her that was frightening as well as intriguing.

Talon's head arched back and he laughed mightily.

"I warned you that you would beg me to take you in the end. I haven't even come close to the end yet, demoiselle."

Incensed by his utter disregard of her plea and his consequent laughter, fury built inside of Danielle. She struggled against his hold, her eyes blazing green fury.

"Is that all you ever do … laugh?" she hissed her frustration. "Surely, God will strike you dead for your misdeed." The rest of her tirade died in her throat as his fingers found their ultimate target.

"Don't you like what I am doing, my little spitfire? You have gone so still, it worries me," he teased. His probing eyes never left her face as he increased his rhythm.

Danielle tried to blank out her mind. God knows she tried, but the sensations were so new, so wondrous that she was sure her whole being would dissolve into a puddle of desire. Screaming for release, she bucked against his stroking fingers with the ferocity of a wild horse, while condemning him to everlasting hell for torturing her in that manner.

"Didn't I tell you that you would beg me to take you?" he whispered into her ear as his tongue traced the outline of it. A strange feeling came over him. It became suddenly imperative that he would give her pleasure before he would take his own. It was something he'd never considered when bedding other women.

"Yes! Yes!" Danielle gasped, "Whatever it is, you have won. Please stop this torture or I will surely die."

Talon released her hands, but he continued his rhythmic stroking of her womanhood. She was wet and hot and he was looking forward to burying himself in her slippery depth. Cursing under his breath, he fumbled with the heavy belt that still held his tunic in place. With any other female it would have been enough to tuck the ends up, but this demoiselle was different. He felt a need to be totally naked with this one, to savor the softness of her skin against his. Alternately cursing the stubborn belt and his misshapen hand, he did not notice that an old nun appeared in the doorway.

The Mother Superior suppressed an outraged gasp when she spied the Viking kneeling between Danielle's slim thighs. She quickly crossed herself and mouthed a silent prayer in hopes that she had not come too late and that her plan would work.

Maybe it was a good omen that he could not untie the belt that held his tunic together. He was a brute all right. Huge, heavily muscled. She cleared her throat to gain his attention. *Bon dieu,* he certainly seemed set in his effort. She cleared her throat a second time, surprised when he suddenly tossed his shaggy mane out of his eyes and glared menacingly at her.

"What is it, old woman? Get out of here and let me be about my business," Talon growled.

Danielle turned her head, shame coloring her face and neck a bright pink. She had never wanted to be dead more than in that instant.

"I was only wondering, if you might not like a small libation, sir?" the old nun asked quietly.

"You can bring me a drink as soon as I am finished here," he answered crossly.

The old nun smiled gently. "I have a special wine that is said to give a man exceptional powers. Would you not have a small glass? The wench can wait."

Danielle gasped that the Mother Superior, a woman who coveted her vow of purity, would betray her charge in such a lurid manner. To her surprise the Viking stood up and bade the nun to fetch the wine.

Glaring down at Danielle, who scrambled to get up from the bed, he commanded, "You stay put. As soon as I have had my wine, we will finish what we have started. I did not realize what a strong thirst I have worked up over the last hour. If it is true that her wine has special powers then you will be as glad as I." He winked at Danielle so she would not miss his meaning.

The Mother Superior hurried down the hallway to her own sparse quarters, praying all the while that the Viking was sufficiently intrigued by the offer of a special wine that he would leave Danielle alone until she returned.

"Please, dear Lord, let me not fail this child as I have failed Sister Celeste," she murmured as she hurried along. "I thought she was having a bad dream when I heard her cries for help, I never expected to find that red haired Viking rutting between her virgin thighs."

The Mother Superior wiped a tired hand across her damp brow. This night was proving almost too much for her. Her mind raced in circles. At least most of her charges were safely tucked away. The Lord willing she could save Danielle's virtue as well. With shaking hands she withdrew a small packet of white powder from among her few possessions and emptied it into a silver goblet, then carefully she added the sweet red wine and stirred it all together.

Talon finally succeeded in loosening the belt of his tunic and started to curse the old nun for dawdling so long. As if on cue the subject of his curses reentered the little room, a serene smile wreathing her wrinkled countenance. Glowering, arm crossed over his bare chest, Talon stood in the middle of the tiny room, naked save for his fur boots. The Mother Superior demurely averted her gaze from his jutting erection as she held out the silver goblet. She refrained from crossing herself. God, what a huge brute. Danielle would never survive his coupling.

"Here, drink this, my son," she coaxed. "It will sustain you through the night."

Danielle was no longer concerned with her own nudity, so casually displayed before strangers. She was furious that the

Mother Superior would not berate this heathen Viking nor even lift a finger to help her. In fact the two of them acted like conspirators and treated her with so little concern as if she were not even present.

Talon drank the whole goblet of dark red wine without pause. It was a bit too sweet for his taste, but it certainly soothed his parched throat. Grinning his appreciation, he was about to hand the chased silver tumbler back to the old nun, when he thought better of it and laid it on the floor next to the bed.

"I'll keep this goblet as a memento, old woman," he announced as if he were doing her a favor. "Now get you gone so I can be about my pleasure."

The Mother Superior's face fell in disappointment, but she turned on her heel and left the room, closing the door softly behind her. She had done what she could; the rest was in the hands of their savior. Hurrying down the hallway, she quietly cracked the door to the room, where she had found Asgard taking his gratification on the screaming nun.

The red haired Viking lay on his back fast asleep, snoring loudly. Sister Celeste lay next to him, her face a blank mask, her unseeing eyes staring at the ceiling. For a moment Mother Superior thought the girl was dead, but then to her relief she saw tears coursing down the young nun's pale cheeks.

Sidling up to the bed on noiseless feet, the old nun clapped her hand firmly but gently across the young woman's mouth. She held her finger to her own lips to command her to silence and then beckoned her to get up and follow her from the room. Once outside she took her hand and dragged her along with her.

"Come on, Sister Celeste," she urged. "You have done no wrong and the Lord will not condemn you. We have urgent business ahead of us before these men wake up and wreak further havoc."

The young nun did not respond but allowed herself to be pulled along. Nor did she resist, when the old Abbess worked a small cross set into the scrolled stone works of the altar. The altar slid aside on well-oiled hinges to expose a steep ladder that led into a pitch-dark cellar.

"Get in and stay there until I come for you," the old nun commanded sternly, glad when Sister Celeste climbed down the ladder in mute obedience.

"If you want to get something done, you always have to do it yourself," the Mother Superior grumbled as she went from cell to cell to make sure that all the nuns were accounted for. Only then dared she breathe a sigh of relief and knelt in thanks before the altar that now held her most precious possessions in its bowels. For herself she held no concern.

When the Abbess finished her prayer of thanks, she crept once more to Danielle's room. All was quiet within. Holding her breath, she opened the door, and slipped soundlessly inside. The Viking lay loudly snoring beside Danielle, one muscular leg flung securely across her, pinning her to the bed with no hope for escape. What to do? What to do? If she made her presence known to her charge, it might create a whole new set of problems. The Mother Superior pondered the situation a moment longer, then fled the room. If she could convince the Viking by morning that he had had his way with the girl, maybe she could persuade him to take his friend and be on their way. Biting her lip, she cut deeply into her palm and squeezed her blood into a shallow dish. Again she crept into Danielle's cell, glad to see that the exhausted girl had dropped into a fitful sleep.

When all was done, she moved to one of the pews and sat down serenely to wait for the sun to herald the next day.

CHAPTER FIVE

Talon woke up as irritable as a bear. His head droned as if a beehive had taken residence inside his skull. He felt drained of all energy, but when he turned and saw the lovely wench sleeping next to him, he grinned in satisfaction. She looked rather pale and exhausted. Scratching his chest, he tried to remember the events of the night before. He shook his shaggy mane to clear the cobwebs from his brain. For the life of him he could not remember taking this woman. Surely, with a maid this lovely and pure, he should be able to remember something?

He sat up and ran both hands through his hair, trying to find the answers to his questions. They were covered with a woolen blanket, he noted. He did not remember that either. His manroot lay limply against his thigh. Curious, he lifted the covers and peeked beneath. Sure enough, there was blood on her thighs and on the sheets, so he had consummated the act, but blast it, why didn't he remember? Annoyed, he stood up, yawning loudly.

Danielle woke with a start. Her eyes flew open. Startled, she stared at the naked barbarian next to the cot.

"Oh, *mon dieu*," she gasped. She had never seen a naked man in broad daylight. The splendor of his finely muscled body sent all kinds of delicious shivers through her own, but shame had a way of quelling her wayward thoughts in a hurry.

She was about to throw back the covers and meet her fate standing up, when she remembered that she, too, was naked as a newborn babe. Tears of vexation welled up in her eyes. She brushed them impatiently away. No, she would not give him the satisfaction of knowing that she was distraught. Instead, she drew the blanket up to her shoulders, but not before she spied the blood between her thighs. Mortified, she blushed several shades of red and dropped her eyes before the speculative gaze of the Viking.

Danielle could not help but worry if the barbarian was planning to leave any time soon or whether she would have to endure his ministrations again before he left. The thought of his large hands roaming intimately across her body brought a flood of unexpected heat coursing through her making her feel ashamed anew.

As if he could read her thoughts, the Viking announced lazily that he was ready to leave. A tiny smile lifted the corners of Danielle's mouth. She was glad that she would not have to suffer him any longer, though his next sentence made her eyes snap wide in alarm.

"Get dressed, demoiselle you are coming with me," he commanded imperiously. "I am not sure how well you satisfied me between the sheets, but I aim to find out later in the day, when I've got my wits and my energy back again." He frowned down at her and cupped his square chin with his hand. His forehead wrinkled in perplexed thought.

"Aye, if you sap a man so thoroughly that he has no strength left to plow you again in the morning, you'll be worth another tumble." He wasn't about to admit that he could not remember anything about last night.

Danielle wanted to protest, but her angry words were forestalled by a gentle knock on the door. Her eyes widened when the Viking reached for his knife rather than his clothes to cover his nudity.

Talon stood to one side of the door and waited for it to open. Knife at the ready, he jumped in front of the startled old nun.

When he saw who it was he lowered the weapon, but he did not discard it. He grinned down at her as if she were an old friend.

"Did you bring me some more of your potent wine, old woman? It seems that it must have worked wonders, for I am sapped of all strength and desire as if I had spent the night with not one but several females."

Something flickered briefly in the old nun's eyes, but was gone as quickly as it had come. She lifted her chin and stared at the huge Viking with determination. Gone was the friendly demeanor of the previous night. "Nay, I did not bring you any more wine. I feel that you have overstayed your hospitality. It is high time that you and your companion leave us in peace."

Talon clapped his hand to his forehead. "I'd forgotten about Asgard. That son of Loki must have found his own pleasure and never gave it a thought whether I had a woman to ease my manly needs. Damme, but where is that misbegotten Viking?"

As if on cue, Asgard entered the room, assessing the scenario with a sweeping glance.

"I see you got the best deal as usual, Talon, my friend," he offered. Glancing at Danielle sitting up in bed, the blanket held tightly to her chest, Asgard grinned in appreciation of her beauty.

"I did not have your good fortune, Talon. I had to dip my manhood inside a scrawny, dried up bird that squawked pitifully all the while I was pumping away at her. This morning she had flown my bed and I am sure she is hiding somewhere." Gesturing at Danielle, he argued, "Your pigeon here looks plump and soft. I wouldn't mind having a quick taste before we leave."

Talon was in the process of shrugging into his tunic. At Asgard's suggestion, his disheveled head came up to impale his friend with an aquamarine gaze of unadulterated contempt.

"Forget it, the demoiselle is mine and mine alone. I have no intention of sharing her with you or anyone else."

Danielle seethed. How dare they compare her to a bird and speak of her once again as if she was a nonentity? She was about to voice her protest, when the old nun signaled her to keep quiet.

"Now look here, Talon, since when do we not share our women? And this one is a foreigner to boot. You know that I would think nothing of your sharing the favors of my own wife, if you but asked."

"There is no problem unless you make one, Asgard. I have decided that this girl is mine and that is final."

Asgard turned angrily away. In the doorway he pivoted around and glared at Talon.

"Okay! Have it your way." And then he grinned. "Well, you had better be quick about it. The sun is rising fast and no one at camp knows where we are."

"They won't leave without us at any rate." Leaning forward Talon pulled on his boots and nonchalantly cross-gartered them when he sprung his second surprise on Asgard.

"The girl is coming with us. I aim to keep her."

"You can't be serious. What about our plans to sail to Paris? Where would you keep her?"

"Why don't you let that be my worry, Asgard?"

"By Loki, I don't want any part of that scheme," Asgard muttered angrily, before another idea popped into his head. "Why not make the old one swear that she keep the girl for you until we come back this way? I am told that these nuns take vows very seriously. If you get her to promise she would not dare to cross you." He stared expectantly at Talon, sure that his suggestion was a good one and would be accepted.

Talon contemplated Asgard's idea a brief moment and then he shook his head in rejection.

"I know the nuns take all vows seriously, but I have a powerful hankering for this female. Nothing less than taking her along will help satisfy my urges."

"Well, suit yourself. You are thinking with your male parts instead your brain, Talon, and I foresee nothing but trouble."

Talon finished adjusting his clothes and straightened up. Glaring at Danielle, he stabbed the air with a long finger.

"Have I not told you to get ready, wench? Either you put on some clothes or I'll take you along stark naked. Pack enough to last you for a while, but not over much." Even as he spoke, doubts pricked his conscience. Asgard was right. The girl did not belong in a boat with twenty virile men. Besides, where would he keep her when they raided the city of Paris? It was only because his friend was so adamantly opposed, why Talon decided to go through with his idea no matter how hare-brained.

Danielle stood up and glared back at her captor. "I have no intention of going with you," she declared angrily, hoping that the tall Viking would not notice her quaking knees.

Talon's hand shot out and it closed cruelly around her slender neck.

"You had best learn quickly that you had better obey my commands or suffer the consequences. You will go with me and you will go as my slave."

"Your slave--?" Danielle whispered, swallowing hard against the terror gathering in her breast.

Holding out one delicate hand she implored, "Please, don't do this to me. You got what you came for and no other man will ever want me for wife. Let me stay here with the good sisters, please--"

Talon watched the girl before him and for the first time in his life he was torn between purpose and pity. She was so beautiful and delicate and he knew that she was likely to die, if he dragged her along to Paris. She would never make the arduous journey back to Scandinavia, yet he had to have her. He wanted her like he had never wanted another woman before her. It hit him then that his attraction to her was not purely sexual.

It was almost like a physical blow when Talon admitted to himself that the girl elicited feelings in him that he hadn't known he possessed. And he didn't even know her name. Too proud to ask her, too shocked over his discovery that he should feel something beyond anger and rejection, Talon turned to the only emotion he was most familiar with ...violence.

With lightning speed he tore the blanket from Danielle's grasp. Again he was amazed at the porcelain beauty of her flesh. His mouth went cotton dry and wryly he noted that his manhood had suddenly regained its potency. Had it not been for the urgency that they get going he would have taken her then and there so powerful was his need to bury himself deep inside her.

"I'll not warn you again," he spoke from between gritted teeth. "Either you put on some clothes or I'll drag you out of here without a stitch on your back."

The Mother Superior stood silently by and watched Danielle and the Viking spar with words. She prayed she would be forgiven for sacrificing one of her lambs to save the rest. Her heart quaked with remorse as she walked to Danielle's trunk to pull a simple dress from it.

"Here, child. Put this on, whilst I rummage for a change to take along with you."

"Oh, Mother Superior, please help me," Danielle implored, tears trembling along the edges of her eyelids.

The old woman shook her head and there was sadness in her eyes. "There is nothing I can do for you, my child. *Le bon dieu* will look after you. Somehow I have a good feeling that all will work out."

Danielle's mouth compressed into a thin line. "Sure everything will work out," she echoed bitterly. "I am nothing but chattel. No, worse, the Viking tells me I am his slave. My destiny is sealed. I wish he'd killed me instead of disgracing me like this."

Slowly, she dragged her dress over her head and smoothed her hair with her hands. The usual sparkle gone from her expressive eyes, she watched as the old nun came up to her and held out a small parcel of clothing to her. The Abbess made the sign of the cross over Danielle.

"God will be with you. Trust Him and His wisdom," she whispered.

"I don't care about your God. He is never there for me when I need Him," Danielle spat hatefully and turned to leave. Behind her she heard the sound of cloths ripping, but she did not care until Talon's cold voice stopped her in mid-stride.

"Not so fast, child," he mocked, partly out of anger that the old nun had not mentioned the girl's name and that he would not allow himself to ask. "Let us not forget that you are going with me as my prisoner, my slave ... not as my guest."

Danielle faced him and spied a length of blanket he held casually within his hand. She blanched, because she knew without being told that he meant to tie her up. Her chin snapped up in a way Talon was beginning to recognize and her green eyes blazed her hatred at him. Holding out her hands in front of her, more so to shame him than in true submission, she invited him to tie them.

Talon chuckled with wry amusement. "This makeshift rope is not meant for your soft little hands, demoiselle." His arm shot out to grab her by the neck and ever so slowly he dragged her to him. "This is meant for that lily-white swanlike neck of yours, child." And without further ado he tied the rag around her neck. Tugging at it he urged her to come along. Behind them, the old nun blanched and collapsed onto the rumpled cot. To this very end she had hoped the Viking would change his mind and leave them be.

Dragged behind like a dog, Danielle could not keep from silently weeping as she attempted to match her steps to the two men in front.

"You should have had your pleasure with the girl and then slit her throat, if you ask me."

"I don't recall asking you, Asgard," replied Talon in a voice that warned his friend to leave well enough alone.

Talon turned back to his prisoner and saw that she was valiantly struggling to keep up and that she had one hand tucked beneath the rag around her neck to keep from choking.

"If you cannot keep up with us, just say so, demoiselle," Talon jeered. "Maybe it would be better for all of us if I took Asgard's advice and cut your throat after all," he conjectured with an evil smile at Danielle. Only he knew his threat for a lie.

"You miscreant," railed Danielle under her breath, her eyes shooting daggers at his back. "Somehow I will make you suffer for this humiliation." And then she remembered that she had threatened Jean-Jacques in a similar fashion and where had that got her?

The first rays of the sun were warming the new day, when the threesome straggled into camp. Danielle thought she had been brought straight to Hell when she caught sight of the motley assortment of men assembled there. Dressed in their animal skin tunics and boots, and armed to the teeth, they seemed more beast than human. Her heart did a funny little skitter of alarm at that thought. From beneath lowered lashes she stole a look around. Some of the creatures were covered in dirt and blood and so hairy that she became convinced that they weren't quite human after all. Involuntarily, she pressed up against Talon's side.

It was the delicate smell of her that drew Talon's attention rather than the movement itself. He glanced at her from the corner of his eye, surprised to see genuine fear in her pale face. And for one instant he saw his warriors as she might see them.

To take the bite from his words, he chortled with feigned glee. "You need not worry about my men, demoiselle. They will not touch you or harm you as long as you are under my protection."

"In other words I am still dependent on your very whim," Danielle replied sarcastically.

Her glib answer angered Talon and he tugged cruelly at the rag rope still tied about her neck. "Never underestimate the power of my protection, girl."

"My name is Danielle, not girl, not demoiselle, but Danielle," she said spitefully. Somehow, she had lost most of her fear. Until she could escape, she would have to adjust to her fate as best as she could. She would not allow herself to think that her life hung in the balance, dependent on the whim of a man who might at any moment decide that he was tired of her and simply slit her throat. A sudden tug on her tether made her stare up at her tormentor.

"Come with me, demoiselle." Talon could not admit just yet that he would rather call her by her given name nor did he understand why he felt the perverse need to torment her. She was especially lovely when her green eyes blazed at him with repressed anger and those soft lips trembled with pent-up frustration. Ah yes, later he would taste them again, those petal soft lips. He allowed himself to hope that her eyes would light up with a different light.

Talon shook himself from his reverie. What in the world was he thinking? She was a slave, by Thor, and nothing more. Besides, females were for the taking and then discarded for the pleasures the next wench could provide.

Talon led Danielle to a small tree and began to untie her bonds. She held her breath and quickly took a nonchalant look about her.

"Don't even think it, slave girl," he growled. "Even if you managed to escape you would not get far. Hold out your hands. I will tie you to this tree to afford you some shade."

She didn't see it coming. She didn't even have time to cry out before she found herself sitting in the sand. He'd knocked her legs out from under her. "You beast," she hissed furious that he could manipulate her in any fashion he pleased.

"You will stay here and think about how you will improve your temper, demoiselle. And while you have all that time to yourself, think about this, too." He leaned close and captured her lips in a rough kiss that shook her to the bone. He rocked back on his heels and grinned insolently at her. "I can tell by the heat in your green eyes that my kiss does not leave you unaffected. So think of all the wondrous things I'll do to your body later on and how you will thank me when I am done." He laughed uproariously as he walked away to leave her sitting, trussed up like a chicken ready for the spit.

Danielle was physically and mentally exhausted. How could she endure much more of this? With wary eyes she began to look around the Viking camp and what she saw made her shudder. These men were true barbarians, pirates without pity or remorse. What was she ever going to do? In desperation she began to compare Talon and Asgard as well as the other leader whose name she did not know with the rest of the men.

Those three seemed to keep to themselves. Having singled them out, she noticed that their tunics were of costlier furs and that they were the only ones who wore hammered silver bands around their upper arms. They stood taller than the rest of the men and her Viking was the tallest of all. With a groan of disgust she wondered when she had come to think of him as "her Viking?" The man was a brute. His muscular build, the breadth of his shoulders and the arrogant tilt of his head all attested to that. It was also the first time she took real note of his gloved left hand. None of the other men wore gauntlets. The more she studied its significance, the more she became convinced that it was some sort of tribal symbol. Shrugging, she settled back against the tree. Nothing would come of her speculation. The only chance she had to regain her freedom would be to hold her temper in check and lull the brute into thinking that he had cowed her sufficiently. Exhausted, she closed her eyes.

"Wake up, demoiselle. Wake up." Talon bent over the sleeping girl and a teasing smile tugged at the corners of his generous mouth. He had been watching her for several minutes and marveled at her unspoiled beauty. He was helplessly enthralled by this girl and it was not a feeling he relished. Until he met Danielle, Talon had always been completely in control of his passions. From the moment he had laid eyes on the little French girl, his whole world had gone topsy-turvy. "By Odin," he swore under his breath, "what possessed me to drag this wench along on this raid?" Even as he questioned the wisdom behind his decision, he vehemently defended his actions in the same breath. It was lust, he decided, pure, unadulterated lust, which befuddled his brain. As soon as he had his fill of her, he would think clearly once again. That solved, he plucked a nearby blade of grass and tickled Danielle's nose with it.

Danielle was not quite ready to wake up just yet. She swiped at the offending tickle with her hand, trying to make it go away. She woke up with a start. Her green eyes snapped open to spit fire and fury at Talon. Her mouth opened, but nothing came out. Instead great tears welled up to course down her cheeks as the memories and the hopelessness of her situation caved in on her.

Talon hunkered down next to her, a silver bowl with fragrant stew in his hands. "Hey ... demoiselle, there is no need to cry. Here eat something, you'll feel better." He was at odds what to do about her. Her tears took him by surprise. He held the bowl out to her again before he realized that her hands were still bound. Grinning, he pulled his knife from his boot and cut through her bonds. "There, now you can eat and then you'll feel better."

"You buffoon," she gritted. "Is that all you can say? Eat something and you'll feel better? How would you feel if you were someone's prisoner?" Angrily she shoved the bowl away, although her stomach growled audibly in protest.

Affronted, Talon's own ire rose. Grabbing the bowl, he shoved it back at her. His eyes turned ice blue to match the coldness of his voice. "Eat!" he commanded. "There is no room for the weak or sick here. In either case, I would be forced to take Asgard's advice and slit your throat. If nothing else it would sure save us all some trouble." He stood up and left her to her own devices.

Thoroughly chastised, she took the bowl and began to wolf down the food, but not without glancing in his direction ever so often and making faces behind his back. It was the only way she had to keep a smidgen of her pride intact. Though he had told her in anger that there was no room for the weak or ill, she knew he spoke the truth. Besides, only if she stayed strong would she have a chance to get away from him

Talon needed time to get his temper under control. He had to, the woman drove him berserk. Whenever he was near her he wanted to kiss her senseless. He was a Viking. Such feelings shouldn't enter his mind. He had to taste her again, maybe that would get her out of his blood. With that resolve he turned back and walked up to her. "I see you took my advice," he jeered. "Now for lesson number two." He slit the bonds on her ankles and pulled her roughly to her feet. "Come with me," he bade curtly and started to walk away, expecting her to follow.

Not used to be spoken to in such fashion, Danielle dug her heels into the sand and stood her ground. Her chin rose up in defiance as she waited for him to realize that she was not going to trail behind him like a sheep.

Talon had gone several steps before he noticed that Danielle was not behind him. Spinning on his heel, he was just in time to see some of his men sniggering in open amusement, while Danielle still stood where he had left her. His hands clenched into fists at his sides and his face turned the color of ripe strawberries. He expelled a mighty breath and marched back to where his reluctant prisoner waited, feigning indifference.

The minute Danielle saw him stalking back, she knew that he was furious, not just angry, but boiling mad. His eyes were frigid pools of blue and a small muscle ticked in the side of his clenched jaw. She dropped her gaze, wishing she had not acted on foolish impulse.

Without so much as a by-your-leave Talon took hold of her arm and then to her utter amazement he turned her over his knee. Too late she realized his intent. She struggled, but Talon pinned her with his superior strength, then whacked her backside with his open palm.

"Tell me, when you have had enough and that you will follow my orders in the future," he gritted out under his breath.

"Never," she grunted as tears gathered in her eyes and fell unheeded to the ground. "Never," she spat and struggled in earnest.

Talon hit harder and his men cheered him on. "Admit that it hurts and that you will obey from now on," he implored.

Danielle's bottom felt as if it was on fire, but still she was too proud to admit defeat. Stubbornly, she shook her head. And her tenacity won her Talon's grudging admiration. Grinning at his men, he called something in his native tongue, then swept her up and threw her over his shoulder. To the cheers of the crew he carried her from the cove.

Danielle was mortified to be hauled off like a bundle of rags, but was so naive that it never dawned on her what Talon might have in mind. He did not stop until he reached the secluded spot he had found while she was sleeping.

Instead of simply putting her on her feet, Talon spanned her waist with his hands and slid her slowly along the length of his hard body. His eyes gazed at her with the blue heat of a summer afternoon sky. She felt soft and light in his grasp, her scent elusive but decidedly feminine in its allure. Despite the simple novice's gown, she stirred his passions, because he knew what delights were hidden beneath. It made him hard with instant desire. He could have taken her without her consent, but another desire flared in him that shocked him to the core. Until this diminutive demoiselle came along Talon had only cared about his own pleasure. By Loki, why would he feel the need to make her want him, too?

He rubbed deliberately against her, watching for her reaction. Danielle's cheeks flamed and a momentary flicker of curiosity showed in her eyes when his shaft poked against her belly. Talon chuckled. By Odin, when he had her this time, he would make sure that he would remember every detail about her afterwards. A small frown flitted across his broad brow as he tried to recall the night before. Why couldn't he remember anything save for the milky white skin and the shape of her breasts? Impatient now to get on with his consummation, he let her slide the rest of the way to the ground. He held her close a moment longer, savoring the warmth of her body against his. Gazing deeply into her eyes, he gently cupped her chin and dipped his head to catch her lips in a tender kiss.

Danielle was helplessly caught up in the sensations that kiss evoked in her. It stunned her. She knew almost nothing of what went on between men and women, but she had not expected any tenderness either. She tried to remember that Talon was her captor, not a suitor with honorable intentions. His gentleness caught her off guard, made her vulnerable. Heat coiled deep inside her and her breasts swelled with a need of their own. She shivered with anticipation, not knowing what to expect.

Talon was quick to gauge her feelings. He deepened his kiss, his tongue playing havoc inside her soft mouth. Danielle leaned into him, weak with the unfamiliar throbbing at the junction of her legs and wishing something would appease it. Beyond rational thinking, she sighed with pleasure when his hand peeled her gown away from her shoulders. She barely noticed or cared that he bunched her gown around her waist. Of their own her hands buried themselves in his hair urging him downward to suckle and lave her breasts, while her pelvis danced against his swollen manhood in frenzied invitation. Shame had long been replaced by need. A need Talon knew how to stoke with expert knowledge.

He lowered her to the mossy ground. Never breaking his kiss he divested himself of his tunic and pulled her willing body against his heated flesh.

"Talon," Danielle whimpered, her passions fully aroused. Her head twisted from side to side as she fought the tides of desire. "Please Talon," she begged.

Talon smiled down at her, pleased that she had called him by name, that she wanted him as much as he wanted her. He pulled her gown slowly downward, exposing her flat belly and the soft nest of curls to her womanhood, her shapely legs. She was even lovelier than he remembered.

Danielle frantically dug her nails in his back, loving the feel of his body gliding across hers. She writhed wildly beneath him without knowing what it was she so craved.

Talon chuckled, "I see I was not the only one who did not get his fill last night," he muttered against her throat as his fingers found her, evoking a sob of desire from her. "Hold on little wildcat," his voice gentled. "Open your flower to me, so I can taste of your sweetness."

Danielle barely heard his words, but she stiffened when his hands spread her legs. As he kneeled between her, she suddenly regained some of her senses and with feeble hands she tried to stop him.

"No! No, don't do that," she cried in alarm as a frisson of fear skittered along her spine.

Too late. Talon was beyond reason. The tip of his manhood was already sheathed in the moist heat of her. Holding her slender hips he tried to slide the rest of his length inside her. Cursing, he realized that she was extremely tight. Why then hadn't he remembered at least that much? Lust made his member swell even more. He could barely contain himself, especially since Danielle thrashed wildly beneath him, trying hard to dislodge him.

Talon stopped when he saw her tear-filled eyes. Feelings of tenderness surged through him. Feelings that were unfamiliar and unexpected. He bent forward to kiss the lids of her eyes, crooning to her that everything would be all right. "Hold on, sweeting," he encouraged her as he raised her hips high with sure hands. It would be rough going, but he was confident her warm dampness would aid them both.

Danielle screamed a choked scream of pain and surprise. Her eyes opened in shock and she stared accusingly up at Talon, gaining little satisfaction from the disbelief reflected in his gaze.

"By Odin," he grumbled under his breath before anger suffused his face like a thundercloud. "You can thank that wily old nun back at the Abbey for that," he gritted through clenched teeth, feeling his manhood soften. "She fooled us both into thinking that I rend your maidenhead last night. Now I understand it all. She drugged the wine to dupe me, then poured fake blood across us both."

Danielle was stunned by his remark. The pain did not matter so much anymore, the loss of her virginity was inevitable she realized. At last she felt no longer forsaken. The old Abbess had not abandoned her after all. The Abbess had tried to save her. Danielle's lips curved into a wistful smile.

Talon misread her smile as a sign of acquiescence. "The worst is over," he crooned. "From here on in I promise you nothing but pleasure." Lifting himself off her, he began to kiss her in a lingering fashion, teasing her with a series of slow plunges and withdrawals until she squirmed for release. Talon made love to her slowly, patiently waiting until he knew she had reached her climax. She was so sweet, so tight and passionate it took a supreme effort on his part to pull out before his seed exploded.

Puzzled, she looked up at him and he grinned. "I have no intention of getting you with child." My firstborn will not be born a bastard, he thought privately. His future with Danielle could be nothing more than that of master and slave. Any children from such a union would be readily taken into the clan, but Talon did not want that for his own. As if in answer his gloved hand throbbed within its confines, reminding him of his struggles as a youth. No, Talon wanted to be there for his son. A Viking's life was survival of the fittest. He would never forget how his father had shunned him after the smithy accident. He'd been a lad of ten, eager to please, so much in need to be loved. That's why it'd hurt doubly when his sire dubbed him Talon. So Talon set out to prove he was as much man and more than the next warrior, and still his father refused to acknowledge him. In defiance he adopted the hateful sobriquet of Talon as his battle cry.

Danielle was thoroughly confused. What did the Viking mean about not getting her with child? She still was not certain how it would come about at any rate.

Talon did not leave her much time to think about it, however. Gracefully, like a huge cat, he rolled to his feet and stretched out his good hand to her. "Come swim with me, princess. The water is fine and I will show you what I mean by fine." He cocked one golden eyebrow and grinned wolfishly down at her. He was glad Danielle's presence prevented him from experiencing the usual melancholy he felt when he reminisced about that fateful day.

Danielle followed him hesitantly to the edge of the river. As a child she had romped in the nearby stream at Honfleur-sur-mer, but she had never learned to swim.

Talon waded into the shallows and then dove cleanly into the water, only to surface again much farther out, looking for all the world like a sleek, golden god rising from the depth.

He flashed her a white-toothed grin and waved his hand. "Come on in, princess. I promise you will love it."

Danielle's heart skipped a beat at the sight of him. This was all wrong. He was her enemy, her captor. She barely even knew his name. She should not feel anything but hatred for him. It was sinful to cavort about in the altogether. Trying to sort those feelings, she waded only a short distance into the river pointedly ignored him as she sifted wet sand through her fingers.

Suddenly, Talon's head emerged from the water barely two feet away. Danielle shrieked with surprise and scrambled to get away. Talon was faster, his reach longer than she expected. With lightning speed his arm shot out, his hand grabbed a slender ankle and yanked hard on it. Danielle screamed, this time out of sheer terror. The last thing she heard before she fell face first into the river was a sarcastic chuckle. She was still choking on water and river mud, when Talon pulled her up against the length of his slick hard body.

Glaring fiercely into her flashing green eyes, he growled, "Remember that when I call you, you should come running to me." There was an edge to his voice and even without so many words it reminded her that she was nothing more to him than his slave.

Danielle flinched at his cruel words. She stiffened in his arms and lowered her lashes in an effort to hide her pain from him.

Talon held her away and stared thoughtfully down at her. What had made the wench turn into a stick? Dismissing her pain for a female mood, he wrapped his arms tightly about her to bring her once more into intimate contact with his quickly stirring body.

Danielle could feel him harden against the softness of her stomach and she decided to stay aloof to his overtures. Her chin set at a stubborn angle, she squirmed against him, her hands pushing firmly against his muscled chest.

"It's hard to get, you want to play, my little vixen?" Talon murmured as his mouth swooped down on hers and captured it in a teasing kiss that took Danielle's breath away. Before she could protest, his gloved hand splayed across her bottom holding her tightly in place, while the other traced circular patterns around her puckered nipples. All the while Talon continued to kiss her in leisurely fashion.

He sensed the change in Danielle as soon as her body sagged against him. She pressed herself against his turgid staff, small moans of pleasure escaping into his mouth. Talon deepened his kiss and casually allowed his hand to stray past her stomach to the junction of her legs. He grunted with satisfaction, when he found the core of her.

Talon said nothing, did not prepare her for what was to come. He simply lifted her legs around his waist and without preamble he pressed his swollen member inside her.

Danielle was not ready for this invasion, innocent that she was, and a small cry of pain mingled with surprise escaped her lips. She arched away from him, trying to get away. Her efforts were futile and served only to arouse Talon more wildly than he had ever imagined in his life. He stroked into her with untamed lust, murmuring unintelligible endearments in the ancient Viking tongue.

He spiraled toward ecstasy on silver wings. He was never more sure that he was close to death, past caring that he would not die in battle and would not see Valhalla. He screamed his wonder to the heavens as he spilled his seed into Danielle's womb. When he opened his eyes to marvel at the most awe inspiring experience he had ever had, he saw that Danielle had followed him to rapture as well.

Danielle was completely exhausted, too tired to care whether she drowned or not. She felt sated and she wondered what exactly had happened. She had so wanted to deny Talon his pleasure. In doing so she had experienced a sensation so devastatingly beautiful that she had prayed it would never end, while she feared she could not endure it another minute. It had come about when Talon yelled his release. Danielle did not know that the heat, which had spread inside her, had been his seed. All she knew was that it had been the most wondrous feeling she'd ever experienced.

Neither spoke, but they stood there in the river holding onto each other, aware that something special had passed between them. Talon was loath to acknowledge it and Danielle too uninformed to understand it.

Finally, Talon lifted her into his arms and carried her back to shore. Gently, he laid her down, then stretched out next to her, pulling her into the curve of his large body. They still did not say anything, but Talon tenderly kissed her temple before he dropped off to sleep.

He woke as the sun was setting in the West with Danielle's naked body snuggled against his seeking warmth against the encroaching chill. He gathered her closer, then raised himself on an elbow to look his fill of this small stranger who had managed to turn his world upside down.

She was beautiful to look at. Her hair held a special fascination for Talon. He snatched a lock and reverently rubbed it between thumb and forefinger. Aye, it resembled midnight silk just as he'd imagined. Her lashes formed delicate fans across high cheekbones that held just a touch of pink. His avid gaze came to rest on her mouth. It reminded him of plump wild strawberries in summer and without thought he bent and to place a soft kiss on them.

Danielle awoke with a start, her eyes snapped open to fasten immediately on the teasing lips above her. Peevishly, she rubbed her hands along her arms. "I am cold," she grumbled.

Talon leered down at her. His large hand caressed her bare middle and stroked toward her back. "I can remedy that," he growled playfully as he captured her hand. He guided it to his manhood, which sprang to life the minute she came in contact with it.

He laughed, a deep rumble that shook his massive chest. Wagging his finger, he teased, "Judging by the color of your face you already feel warmer than you did just a moment ago."

Danielle blushed furiously. This Viking was despicable. All he cared about was her body. . And that thought did indeed warm her throughout as she remembered their earlier coupling. Against her will her gaze became heated and Talon did not miss the telltale passion in their depths.

"Ah, wench," he groaned as he rolled over her to capture her lips in a bruising kiss. "I don't know what it is you do to me. I cannot get my fill of you." He stopped short of telling her about the uninvited, unwanted and unfamiliar feelings she evoked in him. Impatiently, he pushed these thoughts to the recesses of his mind. Maybe some other day he would sort them out.

He took her quickly, but he made sure she would find pleasure in their union. There was regret in his voice when he told her they would have to get back to camp.

Danielle dressed in silence, her thoughts a nervous jumble. What was to become of her, once the Viking decided that he had enough of her? Would he kill her, turn her over to his men or simply abandon her? Oh please, Mother of God, let him kill me before he gives me to his men, she prayed as she buttoned the last of her buttons.

Talon watched her obliquely and wondered what was going through her mind. He felt her withdrawing into her own world and it angered him. To shake her out of her apathy, he jeered crudely, "Let's go. I am sure the men are anxiously waiting to see if you can still walk." It gave him a perverse satisfaction when Danielle blushed with mortification.

CHAPTER SIX

Ragnor met them as they strolled into camp. "Where have you been?" he demanded, but his embittered sidelong glance at Danielle was more eloquent than words.

"Why ask, if we both know you have the answer to that question already?" Talon bit out, his shoulders squaring in an effort to gain control of his annoyance at his long-time friend. "Why are you so concerned over my whereabouts? We are not leaving until nightfall."

Ragnor backed off a little. It would not do to rile Talon. Friends or no, Talon was the best as well as the most fearless fighter among them and Ragnor had tasted the bite of his battleaxe more than once. Pasting a lopsided smile on his rugged features, he held out his calloused hands in entreaty. "Let's not fight amongst ourselves, but since there is still time before we break camp, I would like to sample the wench myself."

Ragnor reached for Danielle, whose face turned ashen as she saw her worst fears become reality. She need not have worried. As soon as Ragnor's arm clamped about Danielle's, Talon stepped in front of her, angry blue eyes flashing at his friend.

"Take your hands off her," he snapped coldly through clenched teeth. "She is mine and I aim to have her by myself."

Ragnor stared at Talon for a long hard moment as if he'd gone daft. A silent battle of wills ensued until Ragnor grudgingly released Danielle's arm. His eyes narrowed to slits of undisguised hostility. His broad back rigid, he returned to his men. A deafening hush had fallen over the camp. The exchange had not gone unnoticed. Only when Ragnor issued terse orders to tend to their chores, did a measure of normalcy return.

Danielle smiled tremulously up at Talon, glad that this cross had passed her by. Her heart had soared when he had come to her defense, but her hopes were quickly dashed when she noticed the savage expression on his handsome visage.

"Don't get your hopes up, wench," he sneered. "I can yet change my mind and share you with the whole crew."

Talon did not like himself for frightening the girl in this way, but neither did he have any intentions to encourage her affections for him. He would have to remind himself that she was merely a slave. A beautiful slave, his thoughts teased him, beautiful and nothing like any other woman he'd ever met. Disgusted with himself for letting his mind wander, he caught hold of her hand and dragged her back to the tree. There he forced her to her knees, then tied the hated rope once more about her slender neck. Without sparing her a glance or a word, he turned his back and left.

Danielle curled into a tight little ball and allowed her misery to wash over her. She felt numb, past tears. Exhaustion took its toll and she dozed fitfully until the sun started to dip low on the horizon. The encroaching chill in the air made her shiver and shook her out of her lethargy. Rubbing her arms, she looked around. With troubled eyes she watched the men mill about and stow their gear into the two boats. Both crafts were already part way in the river. A sliver of hope raced through her. Maybe they would be so engrossed in their tasks that they would forget her. She closed her eyes and prayed hard that she might be delivered. Somehow she would find a way to free herself and get back home.

Danielle did not hear Talon's approach. The sound of his steps swallowed up in the sand and the noise of the crews getting ready to leave. She gasped when his hand fell heavily on her slim shoulder, her gaze snapping upward to his uncompromising countenance.

"Praying to your god, princess?" he chuckled nastily. "He'll not come to your rescue. Get your bundle and follow me."

Mutely, she pointed to the rope about her neck. Talon was tempted to cut through the noose. No, he had no choice but to preserve the master slave correlation, despite the fondness he felt for the girl. With the slash of his knife he cut her loose from the tree and took the rope into hand, tugging her toward the riverbank as if she were an animal. Mortified, she had but two choices: follow or be strangled if she resisted.

Danielle did not dare lift her eyes as Talon boosted her over the gunwales. None of the warriors came to her aid, but let her scramble painfully across on her own. She sensed that by tacit consent she had become a nonentity. So be it, she thought angrily, and lifted her chin to that stubborn angle that Talon already knew quite well.

Talon pushed her none too gently toward the stern of the ship and promptly tied her to an iron ring set into the bulwark. Had she looked up at that moment she would have seen the regret in

Talon's blue gaze

Instead Danielle's eyes roamed over the haphazardly stowed silverware, carpets and foodstuffs. She wondered briefly where they came from, not realizing that they were part of the loot taken during the attack of nearby Rouen.

Before she could think further, the ship rocked into motion, shaking Danielle down to the roots of her being. She had never been in a seagoing vessel and the unexpected swaying scared her nearly senseless. She did not realize that she had screamed, but like a vengeful ogre, Talon loomed suddenly over her and shook her until her teeth rattled.

"Hush, you addle-brained female," he commanded gruffly. "What in Loki's name has gotten into you?"

Danielle was almost beside herself with fear. Without warning her stomach began to heave and her eyes rolled back in her head. Talon recognized her symptoms in time to cut her loose, then held her over the gunwales so she could empty her stomach into the waters below. He carefully concealed his sympathy for her, though his large hands were gentle as he held her over the side. When he was sure she was done, he dragged her back to her place among the stolen loot.

Danielle was glad when Talon did not tie her to the wall again. She knew that her life depended on him and if she wanted to live she would have to keep quiet. The easy sway of the vessel finally lulled her into an exhausted sleep.

Danielle could have sworn she'd only just gone to sleep, when the ship ground ashore. She had no idea where they were and no one told her. In fact, it appeared as if the warriors had forgotten her presence as they disembarked without so much as a backward glance. A sliver of hope chased through her.

Ignoring her wildly beating heart, she crept to the bow of the ship and peeked over the gunwale. Night had fallen some time ago and she had to squint to make out the clusters of men huddling on shore. They spoke in whispers and it appeared as if they were eating cold rations, since they had not lit any fires. Danielle's mouth watered, but she had no time to waste.

Quickly, she scurried to the opposite side of the boat. Nothing but wide-open spaces. A tiny smirk lifted one corner of her mouth. She could be gone before anyone would ever take notice. Without a moment's hesitation she lifted her skirt and swung her leg across the gunwale. "Oh please, dear God, let me escape," she prayed silently.

Freedom was inches away. Her heart beat in wild anticipation, when suddenly a large hand entwined itself in her midnight tresses and pulled her nonchalantly back into the ship. A tortured wail tore from her lips. The hateful hand slowly forced her head.

"Can't I leave you for even a few minutes?" Talon scowled, so close his warm breath feathered across her cheek almost like a caress. "I left you unfettered, because I felt sorry for you. And you would thank me for my generosity by running away and making a fool of me."

Danielle winced as his huge hand twisted in her hair. Tears sprang up in her eyes, making them luminous like two large emeralds. With trembling lips she tried to explain her need for escape, unaware that Talon had stopped listening. He was staring intently at her quivering mouth.

His hand relaxed its grip and slid to the base of her head. Cradling it in his palm, he bent and captured her lips with his own. It was a tender kiss, full of wanting and giving.

His tenderness took Danielle off guard. Leaning into him she offered her mouth more fully, opening beneath his gentle assault to allow his tongue access to her own and the sweet warmth within. She felt his arm tighten about her and Danielle reveled in the security his embrace afforded her. She wanted to stay there forever.

They were both lost to the splendor of the moment, before Talon sensed that they were no longer alone. As he pulled away in guilty embarrassment Danielle glimpsed the unguarded regret in his aquamarine gaze, but she dismissed it as a figment of her imagination. The Viking only liked to toy with her emotions.

Talon was loath to break their contact completely. He allowed his hand to linger on her upper arm as he spun around to check who the intruder might be.

Asgard stood near the gunwale, disdain obvious in his eyes. Jerking his thumb in the general direction of the camp behind him, he explained gruffly, "We need to get going, Talon. Leif has the charcoal ready. They are waiting for you." As soon as he had given Talon his message, Asgard disappeared.

"Where are you going?" Danielle asked hesitantly, her voice tinged with fear.

Talon was tempted to say that it was none of her business. Shrugging, he decided that it would hurt nothing to tell her.

"Asgard and I are going into Paris to explore the lay of the land. We'll be back before nightfall." He grimaced. "Alas, you have proven that I cannot trust to leave you alone. It's your own fault that I am forced to tie you to a tree again."

Danielle swallowed hard. The prospect of Talon gone and her tied to a tree terrorized her. "What if a wild animal comes? What will I do then?" she asked unsteadily.

Talon laughed and cupped her chin in his hand. "The only wild animal that might take a bite out of you is me," he teased and kissed the tip of her nose. Then in the attempt to set her mind at ease, he added, "Don't worry, the warriors will all stay in camp until Asgard and I return. Nothing is going to happen to you." He knew that she wanted assurance that no other man would touch her. He wasn't about to tell her that he had staked his claim and that none of the men would dare to approach her. That would be an admission that she mattered. By Loki, she could not matter.

He helped her scale the gunwale, and easily set her to the ground. The words of thanks died on her lips when she glimpsed his face. The mask of indifference was in place once again and his forehead was marred by a frown. Gone was the tenderness as he half dragged her to a large bush. Danielle quaked at the sight of the length of hemp rope, but even if Talon noticed, he gave no indication of it. He snatched both her hands and tied them together and then to the bush.

"Don't try to escape," he growled, "I will beat you, if you try."

Danielle's heart sank. Why did the Viking play havoc with her emotions? One moment she was so sure that he cared for her in a small way, but the next he showed nothing but hatred. Her heart constricted. Why then did she feel abandoned, more so than she did when she realized that her own brother never meant for her to leave the nunnery again? Nothing made sense anymore, but she'd rather die than give Talon the satisfaction to see her distress. She lifted her chin high and stared in the opposite direction, ignoring her tormentor with that quiet hauteur that had unwittingly gained her the name princess from him.

Talon saw her misery, but he was helpless to do anything about it. His duty to his men must come first and they had to prepare for the raid on Paris. Squaring his broad shoulders, he strode to where Asgard and Leif were squatting in the sand. Asgard was already partially transformed with the help of the charcoal. He grinned up at Talon, who wrinkled his nose in distaste.

"You look as if you'd fallen into a heap of ashes," he commented sourly.

"Well, just wait til you had your turn with Leif's artwork. I feel about as good as I look. How else can we blend in with the townspeople unless we camouflage our hair?"

"It's not actually so bad to have dark hair," Talon mused as the silken midnight tresses of a certain wench teased his mind's eye. "What bothers me are the outlandish clothes we must wear. By Odin, they cover a man's most vital organs like a glove. I don't know if I can stand to be bound up that way." He frowned as he looked with distaste at the assortment of clothing Leif had chosen from the pile of loot.

Danielle sat steeped in her misery, drawing circles into the sand with her slipper and following her movements with listless eyes. Suddenly within the perimeter of her vision a pair of men's leather boots appeared. Her gaze shot upward, full of hope and expectation, only to drop to the ground again when she saw that it was Talon.

"What do you think, wench? Do I pass for one of your countrymen?" Talon drawled lazily. He had seen the hope that had transformed her delicate features to even greater beauty, and he had seen it fade as quickly when she realized it was he standing before her.

Danielle shrugged with Gallic indifference. She was not about to tell him that he easily resembled a French nobleman, albeit one who was in dire need of a good wash. Nor did she admit to herself that for a moment she wished he could be her countryman instead of her captor. "I well know why you are angry, princess. You have no one to blame but yourself. You should not have tried to jump ship as soon as I turned my back." His voice hardened. "And never forget, you are mine and I aim to keep you." He spun on his booted heel and left.

Spitefully, Danielle stuck her tongue out at his back. "I hope they skewer your arrogant hide to the portals of the city gates," she muttered, though deep in her heart she knew she did not mean it.

Talon heard her antagonistic retort, but kept on walking. And not for the first time he wondered what had possessed him to take her from the nunnery, when he knew even then that his impulsive decision could cause nothing but hardship.

It was as if Asgard read his mind. "Tell me, have you regretted your decision to take the wench with you, Talon?" he asked shrewdly. "She seems rather ill-tempered with a vinegary tongue to boot. Have you considered how she will be received at Herjolfstad? I can't imagine that Arwynna will be too pleased to have her as a rival."

Talon slowed his steps and his hand shot out to bury itself in Asgard's jerkin. His handsome face resembled a thundercloud about to burst. "Have you ever considered that you prattle on and on like an old woman, Asgard? And have you ever thought that I don't care to hear your rhetoric? In fact, if you so much as mention that wench back there one more time, I think I'll strip your worthless hide off your back."

Talon released Asgard as abruptly as he had snatched him. He did not want to think about Arwynna nor Herjolfstad. Too much was yet at stake. He shook his massive head and a cloud of charcoal dust enveloped him for his trouble and he promptly sneezed.

Asgard guffawed in glee, their disagreement forgotten. "May Loki take these stupid disguises. I don't know why we couldn't just sail up the Seine right into Paris and sack it like we do all the other cities. Sometimes I despair of Ragnor's logic."

"He wants to make sure we won't be outmatched by the soldiers of their King Charles, the Bald. Since their great King Charlemagne died, there has been nothing but uproar over who should rule. The whole region has been split up into three parts and King Charles, the Bald has his hands full trying to keep what little was allotted to him. It should be easy pickings from what I have heard."

"My point exactly. If things in Paris are as bad as we hear, then we might just as well sail into the heart of the city and take what we please."

Asgard shrugged and kept on walking. Talon matched his long strides easily to those of his friend's. "Let's humor Ragnor this time, but when we go on our next raid, let's go it alone."

Asgard threw a sidelong glance at his friend, a crafty look in his eyes. He nodded. "I've long disliked to tag alongside the *Seadragon*. A single boat can land more readily undetected than two."

"Aye, my sentiment exactly. It's a deal then?'

"It's a deal."

The remainder of the journey the two men seldom exchanged more than a grunt, afraid to be discovered for the intruders they were.

CHAPTER SEVEN

Asgard and Talon walked unchallenged through the city gates of Paris and wandered nonchalantly through the streets. Once in a while they would feel a questioning glance thrown their way, but no one actually stopped them to ask their business.

"I feel conspicuous around the French," whispered Asgard. "They are not a very tall people, are they?"

Talon chuckled. "You should have realized that when we tried on some of the clothing we plundered from Rouen. It took a while before we found something that fit us, remember? And I am still afraid to breathe deeply for fear that I will split a seam somewhere."

Pretending indifference, the two men listened avidly to the passers-by and people at the market place. Within an hour's time they had found out what they had come for.

In the meantime Danielle fretted under the covert stares of the remaining warriors. She felt like the main course at a banquet for the starving. Trying to be casual about it, she twisted around to inspect the location of her tether. Despite Talon's dire threat of a beating she was not about to give in to fear. She would escape if the opportunity arose.

"I could cut you loose, wench, in return for a quick taste of your charms," a lecherous voice rasped close to her.

Danielle spun abruptly toward the sound of the man's voice. Her heart skipped a beat when she came face to face with the most barbaric looking creature she had ever seen. The stink of sweat and blood about him made her nostrils flare with revulsion.

Fighting down the nausea that threatened to envelop her, she decided to stare him down with hauteur. A scant moment later she wished she hadn't. Where there should have been a right eye, there was but an empty socket. Danielle swallowed convulsively, her shocked gaze riveting unbidden on the rest of his twisted features. His nose was flattened, probably broken numerous times she'd wager, and hung at a bizarre angle over the reddish mustache that flowed into a wild beard. He was hideously scarred and the whole was emphasized by the tangle of wispy reddish hair that covered his head.

He snickered. "I see that I'm not to your liking like the fair Talon, but I can be your pass to freedom. My male appendage is no different from his, it's never suffered any scars from war."

Danielle whimpered with fright and watched in morbid fascination as the brute stood over her, running his thumb with careful malice across the blade of a long wicked looking knife.

"Get away from the wench, Ghor! Talon has claimed her for himself and made it clear that he does not intend to share her." Ragnor had come up behind the brutish creature and though he only heard part of the conversation, it was enough for him to feel it necessary to put a stop to it.

"I dinna do anything," whined Ghor, his solitary eye glaring a mute warning at Danielle. "The wench lured me over to her with sweet promises, if I would cut her loose."

"Tell it to Talon, it's none of my concern. I gave my word to look after her until he returned, that's all."

Shaken to the core, Danielle breathed a ragged sigh of relief. She dared not dwell on what might have happened if Ragnor had not come to her rescue or if Talon had not asked him to look after her. She reclined weakly against the rough bark of the tree as she tried to still her trembling limbs.

It was close to the noon hour before Talon and Asgard returned. As soon as they entered the camp they walked off with Ragnor and hunkered down to report their findings, but not before Talon spared an ever so casual glance in Danielle's direction.

"It looks good, Ragnor. We should not have any more trouble than we had in Rouen. According to our information there are about twenty soldiers left in the city to guard the castle and Charles the Bald has reportedly gone West to help his brother Lothair. There is no one to give orders."

"We'll sail toward dawn then. Once we beach our craft, we will swarm the city and demand our due."

"Done and done!"

Asgard and Talon stood and made to leave about their own affairs, when Ragnor stayed Talon by holding on to his arm.

"There was one small incident, Talon. While you were gone the wench tried to entice Ghor to cut her loose in return for her favors."

Talon's face hardened and his eyes narrowed to mere slits. "Did you ask the wench, if Ghor spoke the truth?"

"She is your responsibility, Talon. I knew that she would be naught but trouble the moment you brought her with you. Besides, she is nothing but a slave, while Ghor is one of us and a fine Viking warrior."

Talon nodded tersely. He kept his fury well in check except for the small muscle that leapt visibly beneath his two days growth of stubble.

"Aye, you are right about Ghor being a fine warrior, but that does not mean he can't be a lying one."

"Your mind is clouded, because your manhood is clamoring beneath your tunic, my friend. You of all people should know that women are a fickle lot and will quickly warm the bed of the man who promises the most to her."

Talon winced at the oblique reminder of Arwynna's betrayal. He had been ready to wed with her, but at the last moment she had chosen his older brother Thorson. It had been a doubly bitter pill to swallow for Talon. He had not only lost his bride to his brother, but was reminded at the same time that Thorson would inherit all the lands and livestock once their sire passed on. Holgar Herjolfson was not expected to see another winter.

Talon ran his good hand agitatedly through his thick mane, then stared in surprise when it came away smeared with soot. He cursed roundly trying to let off some of the anger that had built up in him. Ragnor was right women were a fickle lot. Not enough time had passed to forget Arwynna's betrayal. It still tore at his gut like a vitriolic potion. What made it worse was that she had pursued him on a hunting trip after she'd chosen Thorson over him. She had offered herself like a trollop. He vividly recalled the scene within his tortured mind.

"Ah, Talon," she had sighed. "Your brother is not half the man in bed that you are. Pleasure me, my body is on fire for you."

Talon had been tempted to take her up on her offer, especially when she opened her tunic and bared her supple breasts to him, taking them into her hands and holding them up like two luscious fruits. Aye, he had been tempted, but only for a moment.

"You chose your bed, Arwynna, now lie in it," he had told her. "I will not have it known that I would stoop so low as to plow my brother's wife." Staring at her malevolently, he could not resist one parting shot at her. "You know as well as I that there are more maids who clamor to share my bed than I can handle."

Arwynna had cocked her head to one side and slowly closed the front of her tunic. Her eyes had been two pools of icy blue, steeped in hatred. "Some day you'll come to regret that you have turned my offer aside," she spit at him, then spun on her heel and fled.

Aye, women were a fickle lot and Talon would not lose his heart to any of them ever again. He would take from them, but he would give nothing in return. And with his mood so low and black he marched purposefully toward Danielle. Forgotten was the length of green ribbon he had purloined from one of the vendors at the market, all he could think of was that she had been ready to play him false with another man.

Danielle looked up at the sound of his footsteps. She had been dozing off and on in an attempt to make the time pass faster. Talon stared down at her and promptly mistook her guarded look for an admission of guilt, although that look had changed immediately to one of glad welcome.

Danielle was overjoyed to see Talon, though one glimpse at his forbidding visage and the words to tell him so died on her eager lips. Uneasily, she shifted on the sand, waiting for what was to come.

Talon squatted before her, his face a hairbreadth away from hers. She half expected him to kiss her until the frown marring his brow quickly wiped away that illusion. "I hear you missed me," he said silkily, lulling Danielle into believing that all was well after all. One dark golden brow shot up in mocking question.

Danielle took a deep breath, one that made her lush breasts heave enticingly toward Talon. The gesture momentarily reminded him of that other time in place when a pair of breasts had been thrust at him to make him forget a wrong. Before he found time to formulate a sarcastic remark, Danielle's temper surfaced.

Her small chin lifted several inches higher as she sniffed in disdain, "I don't recall having said that I missed you, Viking." Oh, and there was no doubt in her mind that she would irk him even more. No, she would not give him the satisfaction of knowing.

Talon did not move but skewered her with a frigid gaze. "I did not think that you had, wench. As I hear you tried to hawk your favors in my absence."

Danielle gasped in alarm. Her bound hands flew toward her throat, only to be caught up short, dismally reminding her that she was a prisoner. Tears of disappointment welled up in her eyes and she made no attempt to stem them.

"Is that what they have told you?" she whispered in

unbelieving misery. She paused, her bound hands twisting abjectly in her lap. "If that is what they have told you and you choose to believe them, then so be it." She dropped her head as the tears rolled down in earnest and great big sobs tore from her throat. "I ... I asked for none of this." She held out her bound hands in accusation. "You stole me from the nuns and you took my maidenhead in cursory fashion as if it were your due. You never asked how I felt about it all and you never noticed my pain. You are a brute, a beast, a barbarian. You are no different from those other men." She blurted her innermost feelings without much thought or care. She had nothing more to lose. "Worse," she hiccuped, "you believe your fellow Vikings that I would offer my favors as if I were a common trollop."

Talon hunkered before her, stunned that she would talk to him without regard of the consequences. Where he had been ready to pronounce her guilty just moments ago, he was now thoroughly confused about what he should believe. He shifted uneasily on his haunches.

"Then let me hear your version of the circumstance," he invited bewildered.

Danielle looked toward the river and her mouth drew together in a tantalizing moué. "I don't care to tell it anymore," she sniffed.

Talon reached out and his hand cupped her saucy chin. He gently forced her to turn her head to meet his scrutiny. "I will have your version now, wench, or I swear I'll crush your dainty bones with my hands," he threatened.

"Ah yes, sir Viking. That surely should solve the problem." she mocked him, her eyes big as saucers.

Like dew-kissed moss her eyes, thought Talon, as his grip fell away from her face. He wanted to draw her to his chest, hold her close and kiss away those salty tears. Indeed, he wanted to hear her say that Ghor had lied. Hear her say it of her own free will, although by now it was clear to him that Ghor had indeed lied.

Frustrated Talon stood and left her weeping. With angry strides he left the camp and headed toward the river. When he was certain that he was well out of view of the men, he chose a large boulder and with a ragged sigh slid down against it.

Darkly, he scanned the broad expanse of water, wondering for the umpteenth time what had happened to him in those last couple of days. Never in his life had he been so out of control. He, who led men into battle and went on daring raids. He, who slew wolves with his bare hands and wrestled bears. Why in Loki's name could he not simply send this girl on her way?

His hands reached automatically for the flat stones next to him and with practiced ease he skipped them across the smooth surface of the river. Somehow this childhood game seemed to soothe his jumbled nerves, but it could not erase Danielle completely from his mind.

He saw her emerald eyes in every leaf and bit of moss. He even imagined he could smell the delicate scent of her on the breeze. He grunted in despair, because he acknowledged to himself that unless and until he grew tired of her, he had no intention of letting her go.

Reluctantly, he pulled himself to his feet. His stomach grumbled in protest and with a start he remembered that Danielle had not had anything to eat all day. His mouth twisted with grim satisfaction. It was one way he could remind her that she was his slave. He would not force her to beg for food, but he wanted her to obey him and acknowledge him as her master.

The warriors had made small fires and fish and fowl was roasting everywhere, the mouth-watering smells hanging heavily in the still air. Talon chanced a look toward Danielle. She was curled into a small, dejected ball beneath her bush and a tiny frisson of guilt stole through his heart. Without asking he tore a large haunch of roast rabbit from the nearest spit and carried it to her.

Danielle's stomach ached with hunger. Why had she felt compelled to anger Talon? None of the other Vikings cared whether she lived or died. They either stared her down with a malevolence the likes she had never encountered in all of her young life or they ogled her as if she were a tender morsel. Steadfastly, she screwed her eyes shut. Maybe she would just go to sleep and never wake up again.

Suddenly the aroma of roasted rabbit tantalized her tortured brain. Against her will, Danielle's eyes flew open. An involuntary moan sprang from her parched lips and her pink tongue crept out to lick across the bottom half. Her gaze riveted hungrily on the chunk of meat dangling casually in front of her and her throat worked convulsively against the rush of saliva in her mouth.

Talon's heart lurched in his broad chest. What had possessed him to reduce her to this hardship? Even as he searched his soul, he knew he'd do it all over again. He couldn't let her go, not until he'd slaked his lust for her. —Liar, his conscience screamed at him. Liar, you care he for her in more than just a physical way. ---Angry with himself for allowing his thoughts to run wild, he gruffly shoved the meat at her. "Here, take it. I know you must be famished."

Mutely, she held out her bound hands and Talon winced at the sight of the red welts that had formed around the edges of her tether.

"If you would promise me that you would not run away, I would leave you free," he said softly without looking up.

"How can you ask that of me, Viking, when all I have to look forward to is more abuse and deprivation?" she replied caustically. But she accepted the roast rabbit and bit greedily into the juicy flesh, savoring the taste as it appeased the ache in her empty belly.

Talon watched in silence as she ripped the meat from the bone with her small white teeth. He pondered how he could answer her pitiable question. On this raid there was no time for amenities, and once they returned to his homeland, he doubted she would fare much better.

Talon was so lost in thought about their homecoming that Danielle had to ask twice whether she might have a drink of water.

His head snapped up upon her second try.

"What was it you said, wench?"

"I wonder if I might have a drink, Viking."

"My name is Talon and I would that you address me that way."

"My name is Danielle, but all you are wont to do is call me wench and princess and all sorts of demeaning titles," she retorted mulishly. "And now you probably will punish me and not give me any water because I dared to mention your own shortcomings."

Talon bit back a laugh. She never stopped to amaze him. Despite being dependent upon his good will, she would not back down even if it meant that she might have to suffer his wrath. It fired his blood that she would dare to defy him so openly and he could feel himself harden. In an attempt to regain his control, he abruptly got to his feet. Staring down at her, he gritted, "I'll get your drink, but it will be wine rather than water. I want you pliable after I had my meal," he added in way of explanation why she would have to drink wine.

Danielle felt her blood rush through her body in hot

anticipating waves. She did not want her body to react to the Vikings words. In spite of it all a small knot formed at the junction of her legs and began to throb in a disturbing fashion. Fearing that Talon might discover her discomfort Danielle attacked the roasted rabbit with a vengeance, and heaved a ragged sigh of relief, when she saw that his back was already turned.

Talon came back moments later, a haunch of meat in one of his huge hands and a large goblet in the other. He grinned, white-toothed and amicable. "I thought I'd spend some time with you and we could share this wine together."

"There is no need for you to spend any time with me, Viking, but I'll gladly share the wine with you, since I have no other means of soothing my parched throat."

Talon chuckled. "I guess you have reason to be cross with me, princess, but I promise I will make it up to you later." Leaning closer to her, he whispered huskily, "Later I will teach you to ride like you have never before, my sweet."

Danielle tossed her tousled mane. "I know how to ride, Viking, there is nothing you can teach me there."

Talon chuckled and his shoulders shook with mirth. "Ah, so you are familiar with the rhythm? So much the better."

Danielle thought Talon strange indeed, but she held her tongue. She would have liked to know where he was going to get the horses, but she was in no mood to make idle conversation.

When he led her away from camp some time later, Danielle felt a tiny prickle of apprehension course through her veins. Anything was better than enduring the constant looks of animosity, so she allowed him to lead her along the edge of the river until they were out of earshot of the warriors.

"Where are the horses you spoke of, Viking?" she finally asked boldly, tired of watching her step along the uneven shores of the river Seine.

Talon turned her into his chest, splaying his hand across her buttocks to bring her in closer contact with his engorged manroot. He smiled down at her. "I thought you might like to ride a stallion, my sweet," he whispered hoarsely into her ear. "I will lie back and let you set the pace, as long as we will gallop together toward the splendors of the heavens."

Danielle squirmed to get free of his disturbing embrace to voice her protest, but his hand was already beneath her skirts and probing gently among the triangle of curls. Danielle's eyes widened with surprise when he quickly found his mark without fail.

Just before his own lips captured hers in a searing kiss, he groaned, "You are so ready for this stallion ...so sweet...so hot, I wish we could go on forever."

They set sail in the middle of the night. Danielle was too sleepy to care and was scarcely aware that Talon carried her aboard his ship.

The *Raider* and the *Seadragon* sliced in silent menace through the tranquil waters of the river Seine, their solitary sails catching the gentle evening breeze. Tension ran high among the warriors as they anticipated the battle at Paris in the early morning hours. As usual Talon had given orders that there should be no conversation. Seasoned warrior that he was, he knew that their imposed silence would enhance their thirst for a good fight. Before they had left their encampment he had reminded them that Valhalla and glory were never far away.

CHAPTER EIGHT

Before the break of dawn the *Raider* and the *Seadragon* pushed away from shore for the last leg of their journey to Paris. An undercurrent of excitement drove the men to unprecedented speed, since Paris was touted as a rich prize.

The two ships glided silently down the River Seine and sailed undetected right into the heart of the city of Paris. At Talon's signal, the boats were docked and the warriors disembarked with lightning speed, snatching their shields as they nimbly jumped over the gunwales to dry land. Quick expert hands anchored the two crafts, while the rest of the crews milled about, anxious to be off.

Danielle awoke from the thump of wood against embankment. In her heart she knew that they had reached their destination. She had no idea what to expect and knew no one would tell her anything. Feigning sleep, she watched their hasty disembarkation through hooded eyes. Let them forget about me, she prayed.

Talon was the last man to jump overboard. As soon as he disappeared over the gunwale, she briefly closed her eyes in silent thanks, a slow smile tugging at the corners of her lovely mouth.

"Still sleeping, princess?" The deep mocking voice above her left no doubt to its owner. Talon stood over his captive, long legs spread in an easy stance, his brawny arms crossed over his broad chest, he waited for her to respond.

Danielle gasped. Her eyes flew open, forgotten was her deception. "I thought you had gone!" she answered, unable to keep her disappointment from showing through.

"I can tell from the tone of your voice that you were truly mourning my departure," he mocked sarcastically. "Truth to be told, you did a creditable job of pretending, princess." He chuckled without humor. "But you are never far from my thoughts, my sweet. The delights of your delectable little body seems to have a way of intruding into my consciousness at the most unexpected moments. They keep me heedful to the fact that despite your willingness to pleasure my body, I cannot trust you out of my sight."

"How dare you presume that I am a willing participant to your depraved ways?" she hissed.

Talon's handsome visage creased into a genuine smile, lighting his eyes with a devilish twinkle. "Remind me when next you are lying in my arms how unwilling you are, my little firebrand ... Just tell me how wrong I am to suspect that you would jump ship as soon as I had turned my back on you." He hunkered down and brought his face within inches of hers, challenging her to deny his accusation.

Danielle's gaze slid from his. Anguish constricted her heart. She turned her head away from him, unwilling to reveal the extent of her distress.

Talon reached out and captured her chin in his large hand. With gentle pressure he forced her to face him. Heavy telltale droplets clung to the tips of her sooty lashes, just as he'd suspected. Whatever he had been about to say, escaped his mind. Instead, he leaned forward and kissed her softly on the lips. His own heart was heavy in his chest. God he should let her go, but damn if he could.

"I thought you might have flight in mind," he mused aloud, "and to think I almost left without tying you up."

Danielle's head dropped to her chest and mutely she held out her hands for him to tether. Talon angrily gnashed his teeth, blaming Danielle for making him do this to her. Impatient to be off, he cursed roundly when he tied the rope too tightly and had to do it over again.

"Woman, you'll be my undoing, yet!" he grumbled as he pounced to his feet with animal grace. Without another word or even a backward glance he vaulted over the side of his ship and was gone.

"Good riddance!" called Danielle after him, spite lacing her angry remark. She stared with hateful eyes at the tether that bound her to the wall of the ship. Then it dawned on her that Talon would be gone some time. If only she could loosen her bonds she might make good on her escape yet. With a vengeance born of desperation, she began to gnaw at the rope, totally absorbed in her quest to gain her freedom. She squirmed and railed for several long minutes, until she realized that the rope was not only too thick to gnaw through, but that she succeeded only in making the knots tauter than before. Disheartened, she crumpled to the floor, tears now flowing in earnest.

Her own misery was quickly forgotten when she became aware of the first din of battle. Curious, she rose and crept forward. Since she was tethered to the portside wall of the ship, she had an unimpeded view of the ensuing battle.

Danielle's eyes grew round with horror at sight of the gruesome spectacle before her. The citizens of Paris were sadly ineffectual against the brutal onslaught of the Vikings. The puny forces of King Charles, the Bald were no match. The feral cries of the Viking horde punctuated the ghastly scene at regular intervals. Clapping her hands over her ears, Danielle turned away and curled into a fetal position. She didn't know how much time had passed before she realized that the noise had stopped.

Danielle raised herself up once more to peek cautiously over the gunwale. Mercifully, smoke hung heavily in the air and obscured her view, but she could hear women screaming for mercy.

Danielle pressed her fist against her mouth to stifle her own screams of outrage of what was being done to her helpless countrymen. With dull eyes she searched for Talon's tall figure. Was he joining in the rape? Could man so tender and caring be bloodthirsty and without compunction at another time? He would not force a woman to his pleasure. Sweetly, her body responded with an answer of its own. When he had taken her, she had been his prisoner, but he had not forced her. He had coerced her, coaxed her with his hands and tongue until she was beyond reason. It had not been right, but it could not have been totally wrong, since her body was eager for his touch by the time he'd impaled her. Shame flooded her face. She would burn in hell, because lust had made her a traitor to her country and her virtue.

Hours later Talon found her hugging her blanket to her for comfort, her face streaked with dirt and tears. Though his heart gave a guilty lurch, he steadfastly turned away. She was there. That was all that mattered. Later, he would try to make amends. His first duty was to his men.

"Get this plunder stowed as quickly as you can. I want to be off and breathe clean salt air," he bellowed as his crew scurried to oblige. Talon noted with quiet satisfaction that his pile of loot was much larger and costlier than Ragnor's. His warriors had done him proud.

The *Raider* settled low in the water once the booty was stowed. It would be rough rowing until they would reach the open sea and the wind could catch their sail. The shields were fastened to the gunwales, more crucial than ever, since the waves of the North Sea would surely splash over the boat's hull.

Once they were underway, the purloined food was distributed among the hungry warriors. Talon chose an apple, some bread and cheese along with a goblet of wine and carried them to Danielle.

"Here," he said gruffly as he held the food out to her. "Eat! It will be hours before we stop and take stock of what we have and need before we set sail for home port."

Danielle lifted her head but a fraction, too miserable to care. "You stink of blood and sweat, Viking," she accused hatefully. "It turns my stomach. I don't think I can swallow."

He squatted next to her, a sneer on his handsome visage. "I am sorry that I offend your tender feelings, princess," he scoffed, "but raiding is what a Viking does best. Our country is poor and we have but pittance, so we feel that it is our given right to even the odds. The only way we can do that is by fighting for our share."

Danielle speared him with an angry glare. "Have you ever thought you might simply trade off, Viking?"

He snorted disparagingly, "Trade off with what? There is naught to trade in my country."

Her chin shot up. "Sometimes we are blind to the treasures we have, simply because we are used to them and do not see them with the eyes others see them."

Talon grinned, his generous mouth revealing his even white teeth. "Ah, my little vixen, it warms my heart to know that your delectable curves yield a brain as well. But trust me, there is naught to be bartered within my country." His own chin thrust forward in a mulish attitude. His blue eyes shifted about as he battled with his inner self whether he was going to confide in Danielle that he was a second son with no hope for an inheritance. Finally he said, "My only chance for riches and a life of my own lies in the opportunity of waging war against those who have plenty and will not miss its loss."

Danielle was about to tell him of the error of his ways, but he sliced the air with his hand commanding her to silence as he continued his tale.

"You see, it is our custom that the oldest son will inherit all, regardless of how many other siblings will go without or how much there might be to share. I happen to be the second son of Holgar Herjolfson and, therefore, I am entitled to nothing, except that which I can provide through my strength and battle skills." He paused and stared thoughtfully down at Danielle, willing her with his gaze to understand and agree with him. He did not mention that he'd been forced to prove his mettle in more ways than any other warrior, since his hand was disfigured in the bargain.

"Our customs are no different than yours, Viking, yet we do not go about and raid our neighbors to gain their riches."

"Ho, wench! I did not say that we raid our neighbors, only those people who have no Viking blood in their veins."

Danielle snorted rudely, "Yes, but at the rate you Vikings force yourself upon the women, your blood will flow soon enough in many a bastard abroad." Aghast over her own audacity, Danielle's eyes widened. She clapped her slender hand across her mouth, afraid of the punishment over her impudent remark.

"Not mine," stated Talon hotly. "I take no foreign wench. I have as many as my heart desires back in my own country ... " and then he faltered and stared at Danielle in abject embarrassment. He saw himself in his mind's eye when he had pulled his manhood from her hot silken sheath and had grandly proclaimed that he would not get her with child. That image was immediately replaced by the memory of the river encounter. He had not pulled out, but spilled his seed within her. Guilt rushed through him, and he stood abruptly, his blue gaze dulled with the sudden misery that assailed him. Wordlessly, he left her side, leaving her to stare bewildered after him as he went to lean against the bow.

"What is troubling you?" Asgard asked solicitously. "I see you have had words with the wench again. Did she prick your manly pride?" Asgard chuckled in glee, hoping to get under Talon's skin.

Talon regarded his best friend with a baleful glare. " 'Tis none of your business, Asgard, and I wish you would leave me alone. I have some things to ponder on."

Asgard sniggered. "Yes, I can imagine," he suggested lewdly. "It must be tough to have a female slave so close at hand and no opportunity to topple her for a quick plowing."

Talon turned on his friend, his fist closing angrily about a handful of Asgard's tunic. "Is that all you can think about? Didn't I see you take your pleasure on a wench back there in Paris? Have you ever stopped to think how many of your little bastards might be born after each raid?"

"So that is the way the wind blows? The wench accused you of having planted a bastard in her, is that it?"

Talon's face suffused with fury. "No, she did not accuse me of getting her with child and besides it would be far too early to tell." Now that the seeds of doubt had been sowed by Asgard's baiting question, they gnawed at Talon's gut.

"Nor would it matter. Our clan will accept your get into its fold without great obligation to yourself. You could provide for the whelp and never need acknowledge his existence."

"I know, Asgard, I know, but it has always troubled me to see small children cast about as so much chaff with no one to call their sire. I have always taken great pains not to beget a child on any of the maids that freely come to my bed."

Asgard scratched his head thoughtfully. "You have a good point, Talon. I don't think that I have ever carelessly sired a child myself. Your rhetoric makes great sense."

"I saw you take a woman today and you paid no heed. So what about her?"

"She has no need to worry. I slit her throat."

Asgard walked away from Talon, wondering what had gotten into his childhood friend. Had he gone soft, no longer able to stomach the harshness of the Viking life? Asgard shook his massive head in denial. No, Talon would come to his senses as soon as they reached their homeland again. If not, then someone would have to see to the French witch who seemed to manipulate his friend's belief in their cause.

Asgard was not the only one who sent hateful glances in Danielle's direction. As she calmly munched her apple, she had the disquieting feeling that someone was watching her. Thinking it might be Talon she raised her head, only to find him still standing near the bow with his back to her. Disquieted, she let her gaze drift idly about, until it locked with the venomous stare of one single bloodshot eye.

Ghor did not even blink when Danielle caught him staring at her, nor did he look away. Danielle's heart skipped several beats at the enmity she glimpsed in his scrutiny. *Mon dieu* I am done for if he ever finds me alone, she thought fearfully.

Just before they reached the mouth of the Seine River where it empties into the North Sea, the Viking ships made one last stop. With practiced efficiency they stowed their plunder evenly beneath the lashed floorboards. Shields were checked one last time to see if they were tied securely to the gunwales. Each man was responsible for his own tholepin, which held his oar. Then and only then did they make camp for one last meal until they would reach the shores of their homeland.

After the fires were banked, Talon stood and addressed the assembly in their Norse tongue. "Tomorrow we will brave the cold waters of the North Sea and we will sail without stop to Hedeby. We have done ourselves proud. Our people will cheer us for our brave deeds and the magnitude of our plunder. When winter falls, there will be praises sung about us around the hearth fires."

The warriors cheered Talon and clapped each other on their broad backs in glee.

"Let's not forget that there are many months yet to raid and plunder, Talon," roared Eric from his perch beneath a tree.

Talon grinned. "Ah yes, there are many more months left, but never have we come away with as much silver as we have this trip. The great all-knowing Odin has indeed blessed us and we shall not soon forget."

"Praise be to Odin!" the men echoed into the still night raising their arms toward the sky in imitation of their leader. Some banter followed Talon's speech, but then the men settled down to sleep. The camp fell silent, except for loud snores and restless shifting, but Talon continued to be wide awake, his body clamoring for the softness of Danielle's. He had settled her close to his own furs earlier in the evening, as much for security as for the convenience of having her near.

Hands linked behind his head, he listened intently until he was sure everyone slept. Stealthily, he inched closer to Danielle until his front made contact with her rounded bottom. He waited for some response, disappointed when none came. His hand slid furtively under her skirt and unerringly found its way between her thighs. He smiled into the darkness as he flipped his tunic out of the way and gently probed among the silken curls until his manrod found her entrance. He grew harder as he imagined her shock when she'd feel him suddenly inside her.

Danielle awoke with a start. The solid male length seeking entrance elicited nothing but horrendous fear. She squirmed and would have screamed, had not a hard hand settled solidly upon her tender mouth and prevented her from making a sound. Only when she recognized the deep voice whispering into her ear did her heart stop slamming against her chest.

Talon was intent on having her and never for a moment considered how she might feel to be taken without warning. "Sssh! Hold still, you little wildcat," he hissed. "You'll break my manhood in two if you don't stop thrashing about like that. Besides, you don't want to wake the whole camp. I wouldn't have tried it this way if I had known you would resist me so, but give us a chance."

Danielle was furious. She didn't want to give in, but her body went slick with desire as he slid inside her. She wanted to scream her pleasure, but Talon cautioned her to be quiet. The imposed silence was as much agony as it added to her delight. Whispering endearments he stroked her with ever increasing speed. Danielle's breast swelled in need to be touched. She struggled to turn, wanted him to penetrate her fully and Talon obliged. His hand covered her mound and pressed gently against it. The sensation he evoked was so mind boggling that Danielle exploded into a myriad of toe curling spasms. Limp, she was barely aware when Talon found his own release. Breathing heavily, he rolled away from her.

She thought him asleep, when he suddenly raised himself on one elbow to nuzzle her ear. His arm drew her into the curve of his massive body and easily held her there. "I'm sorry if I frightened you. It will be a long time before we find a bit of privacy to come together again."

Still angry, she hissed, "Is that all you ever think about, Viking? There are more things to life than pleasuring your body."

Talon chuckled. "So you admit that you find pleasure when I come inside you?"

"I never said that," she muttered, shuddering as his roaming hand made a liar out her.

He played her emotions like a finely tuned instrument until she squirmed with desire. Turning her to face him, he asked hoarsely, "Can you deny that you crave my touch as much as I need yours?" So help him, but he could not get enough of her. His shaft throbbed to bursting. Still, he needed to hear her say that she wanted him. Searching her face, he waited.

Danielle stared up at him, stunned by the heat in his intent gaze. She wanted to disagree, wanted to hear him say he loved her. Her traitorous body clamored to have him fill her, though she knew he was only driven by lust. Slowly, she nodded. "You win again, Viking," she sighed as he slipped inside her.

He rode her hard driven by inner demons he couldn't conquer, elated when she matched his strokes with equal fervor. It took all his self-control not to roar his triumph when he spilled his seed inside her once again.

Why did he feel such a need to brand her as his? And he knew that this last coupling had been nothing short of trying to make her forever his. How did she manage to evoke such strange longings in him?

Thoughtfully, he studied her sleeping features. Even by the dim light of the moon he could see that she glowed from the aftermath of their lovemaking. His features softened as he continued to watch. Making sure she would not awaken, he wrapped his body protectively around hers, then covered them both with his fur.

Not since his childhood accident had he felt so utterly content. For the first time in many years his crippled hand twitched inside the tight leather gauntlet, a sure sign that he was suffering from inner turmoil. He'd allowed the wench to get under his skin. He who had learned to steel himself against feeling anything at all to prove he was as much a man as one who had two good hands. It was mind-boggling. He should push her away. Instead he drew her closer.

Danielle snuggled into the curve of Talon's big body, feeling secure in his embrace, and unaware how desperately the hulking

Viking needed her to keep his imaginary devils at bay.

CHAPTER NINE.

"You have two choices," Talon told her as the two Viking ships prepared to glide into the swells of the North Sea. "You can promise to give me no trouble and I leave you free to move about, or I will tie you up."

Danielle didn't have to think about that. Where would she go? A watery grave was not one of her choices to be sure. Little could she guess that her newfound freedom would not last long? The shores of France had barely disappeared from the horizon, when the winds picked up and whipped the waves to enormous heights. Powerless the *Raider* bobbed like a nutshell from once crest to the next. The warriors fought hard to keep her upright, working the oars in frantic rhythm

Huddling against the wall in the bow, feeling helpless and abandoned, and being tossed mercilessly about Danielle watched in mute horror. *Mon dieu*, the sea tossed these sixty-five feet crafts about like toys. Moments later the first wave closed over them like a wall of water and left her soaked to the skin, filling her mouth and eyes with burning brine.

Talon appeared at her side almost immediately holding a length of rope. His face seemed hewn from granite, his eyes were cold and appraising. He mouthed something to her, but the roar of the wind snatched the words before Danielle could understand them.

Mesmerized, she stared as he held out the hated rope and her mind went blank with terror. Fear lent her strength. She fought him, lashing out at his face and hands, kicking toward his groin and legs. No way was he going to tie her to the bow.

Determined, Talon held her down, no longer caring if he hurt her or not. "Hold still!" he roared furiously into her ear. "If I don't tie you to the ship the next wave might carry you overboard."

Shivering she went limp. Nodding her understanding, her eyes wide with apprehension she watched him tie her by the waist to the ring in the wall.

Hunkering next to her, he handed her his knife. "Keep it near you. In case we overturn, you can cut yourself loose. Hang on to anything that will float and I will come to you as soon as I can."

In the next moment he was gone, back to helping guide the ship.

Danielle was stunned that he would trust her with his knife and that he promised to come to her if the need arose. Her breasts heaving with exhaustion, she cast a look of disbelief at his back. That Viking toyed with her feelings like the wind toyed with their boat.

The raging storm gave her little time to dwell on that thought, because no sooner than Talon left her side another wave crashed over the bow, filling Danielle's heart with renewed panic.

The gale lasted through the night and into the next morning. By that time Danielle hung limply in her harness, too weak to care. One bleary glance at the crew told her that they had not fared any better. To a man they were soaked with seawater, and where it had dried it left a salty ring behind. Her dress was stiff with it around the bodice and her skirts were too heavy to lift. She did not care. Dazed, she closed her eyes. She told herself she would rest just a moment and then cut loose from her bonds. Instead she fell into an exhausted slumber, shuddering against the cold that seemed to seep into her very bones.

Much later she awoke and found her clothes, except for her chemise, gone. Instead she was covered with a dry woolen blanket and she wondered in awe where such a treasure might have come from. The boat swayed gently across limpid waves, the night's storm gone and the sun shining brightly on the horizon. Bushed from their night's battle with the sea most of the crew was basking in its warmth and to her chagrin she noticed that many had shed their clothes. Embarrassed she averted her gaze.

Talon appeared at her side a few moments later holding out an apple to her. He smiled hugely. "You look peaked, princess, but I am proud that you proved to be so little trouble."

Danielle made a moué and raised a critical eyebrow, spearing him with a frank gaze. "I had little choice in the matter as I recall. I was trussed like a chicken ready for the spit," she replied saucily. Somehow the feeling of being safe made her almost giddy.

"If I had not tied you to the wall, you might have been washed overboard. Many a strapping warrior has lost his life to the sea that way. The waves are stronger than they appear and they suck you with them if you don't take the proper precautions."

"I know that now," nodded Danielle solemnly. "I have never been to sea and there is much I don't know it seems." She stared up at him and saw the ugly red scratches that marred his cheeks. She winced visibly. "I am sorry I fought you, Talon. I was terrified beyond reason."

"Aye, and it turned you into a veritable tigress. I can't say that I blame you."

"Talon! Come over here and take a look!" Asgard called. He pointed southward where a small dark shape was looming against the morning sky. "Do you think that's the *Seadragon?*"

Talon squinted against the glare and wagged his head back and forth. "Could be, but we cannot take the chance to wait and let her catch up with us. If it is an enemy, we might not be able to outrun her, since we are loaded with plunder and sit low in the water. Ragnor will understand if we do not wait up. We'll go looking for him after we've unloaded our cargo."

By late afternoon the *Raider* reached Hedeby. The moment the people on shore recognized the ship they dropped what they were doing and came running to greet the men. Talon quickly related the tale of their horrid crossing and his fear for the welfare of the *Seadragon.* Those who had only come to gawk sprang into action and helped them unload.

Talon carried Danielle ashore. "I'll be back shortly," he told her curtly, then turned and headed back to the *Raider.* Waiting to be told what to do next, Danielle sat on the ground. Still weak from her ordeal she watched with weary eyes as treasure after treasure was piled on shore. And a rocky shore it was. Desolate without vegetation to soften its appearance.

Shock robbed her of speech a short while later, when the *Raider's* crew jumped back into the boat and headed out to sea. What was she to do now? Pulling her blanket closer about her she cast a look around. Most of the onlookers were leaving and none bothered to ask if she needed anything. Danielle pushed out her lower lip in resignation. Talon's words came back to haunt her. "You are nothing but a slave, never forget that."

Apprehension wrapped itself around her like icy tentacles. She had no idea where she was or when Talon would come back. If he did not return, how was she to go on? Despair gripped her heart. She would have never thought that her life could go from bad to worse. Raising her chin in defiance she decided she wasn't going to sit there and die. Somehow she'd find her way home. Resolutely, she stood up and on shaky legs she walked to the nearest house, gripping her blanket like a shield.

The house was a single story of carefully cut and stacked sod with but one window and a door. She knocked, though her expectations were at an all time low.

A tall, work-worn woman with wispy blond hair opened the door and stared curiously at Danielle and then beyond her toward the sea. She spoke in the Norse tongue, the sound of it guttural and harsh to Danielle's ears. Interpreting her words for a rebuff, Danielle started to turn away fresh tears stinging behind her lids. Her knees threatened to buckle when a hand patted her shoulder. Shyly, she lifted her gaze. The woman's face had softened, and muttering something, she stepped aside and waved for Danielle to enter. Gruffly, she pointed to a chair and made motions for Danielle to sit down.

Wearily, Danielle did, as she was bid, glad to be indoors where it was warm. With dull eyes she looked around. There was precious little furniture. She assumed that the tiered planks against one wall were beds. They were neatly covered with a variety of blankets and furs. Plunder, Danielle guessed bitterly. There were two hide covered chairs on either side of the fireplace, one of which she occupied at the moment. A long, crudely built table with benches on either side dominated the cramped room. Considering the simplicity of the interior it seemed incongruous to find a finely woven tapestry hanging over the mantle. She was about to dismiss it as more plunder before she realized that it bore the same motif as the long skirt her hostess was wearing. Shame washed through her that she'd become so judgmental.

The woman had gone back to her task of stirring a large kettle over the open fire of the hearth. The smells that permeated the air teased Danielle's nostrils. As if on cue her stomach promptly let out a loud rumble of protest. Even if she had dared, she would not have known how to convey that she was starving. Though the woman did not let on that she heard Danielle's stomach rumble, she ladled some of the savory stew into a wooden bowl and handed it to her unexpected guest.

Danielle shyly smiled her thanks and waited politely to be given a spoon. She colored to the roots of her hair when it dawned on her that she was expected to eat with her fingers. Hungrily, she dipped her hand into the warm meal and ate with relish, then lifted the bowl to her lips and drank the broth.

A satisfied grin lifted the corners of the woman's mouth as she watched Danielle eat. Only then did she dish up food for herself and four small children who seemed to appear out of nowhere when she called. Danielle noted that none of them spoke while they were eating and that they too ate with their hands.

She was still hungry after she had finished her portion, but she refused a second helping, conscious that the children needed it more than she.

When she was shown to one of the planks in the corner, Danielle complied, not knowing what else to do. Gratefully, she tugged the extra blankets around her and fell promptly into a dreamless sleep.

"Wake up, princess." Danielle heard a voice from far away. She only snuggled deeper into her blanket, hoping whoever it was would go away ... But her wish was not coming true. A large hand gently patted her cheek. "Princess, you need to get up, we have to go."

Danielle reluctantly opened her eyes and stared sleepily at Talon hulking above her. A small tremor of relief went through her at the sight of him. He had come back. Then consciousness returned and with it fury swept through her with gale force. She pushed herself up on one elbow and eyed the warrior with an angry glare.

"Save your breath, I warn you," he commanded coldly. "We are in *my* country now. Remember here you are nothing but a slave. If you should raise your voice, I would be obliged to lift my hand against you and I am not in the habit of striking helpless women."

Danielle's eyes turned a stormy green and her breast heaved with repressed fury. Her lovely mouth compressed into a thin line of disapproval. She rose from her cot and without uttering a single word she followed his imposing figure until they had almost reached the door.

"This woman has been very kind to me," she said quietly, her eyes to the floor, "I wish I could repay her because she does not seem to have much to spare."

Talon's step faltered. Touched that Danielle would think of others while she herself was really in no better position, he turned to her and murmured, "It's been taken care of, princess, whilst you were still sleeping." It didn't escape Danielle that he uttered the word princess without the usual hint of sarcasm.

Once outside, Danielle immediately spied the *Raider* anchored at dockside. The shields of her crew still attached to her gunwales, while the *Seadragon* was moored close by and stripped of her own. It was a sign that they were done for the day. The *Raider* was lying low in the water again, the cargo they had disgorged earlier in their haste to go to the *Seadragon's* aid apparently loaded back in her bowels.

"Are we going somewhere, yet?" she asked curiously.

Talon chuckled, "Aye, you inquisitive wench. We are going to Herjolfstad, my home. It is but a short trip up the coast."

After Danielle was settled in her now familiar spot beneath the curve of the bow, Talon paid her no heed for the remainder of the voyage until they were within sight of Herjolfstad.

"Come up here, wench, I want you to see your new home from the advantage of the sea."

Danielle made her way on shaky legs to where Talon was standing. Gripping her upper arm to steady her, he pointed into the distance and there was a quiet pride in his deep voice.

"It's a craggy coast to be sure. It's wild country and cold, but it has a beauty of its own, you will find. And right now is the time of the midnight sun. It will not go down for three months."

Danielle stared back at him. "How will you know when to sleep?"

"You'll know," he chuckled, his massive chest rising and falling rhythmically with his mirth.

A small crowd of people quickly gathered as they docked. Waving and grinning Talon jumped nimbly ashore with Asgard and Leif right behind him, while Danielle was told to stay aboard until Talon would come for her. She watched as one by one the men gathered their gear until no one remained but her.

So she had been told to stay put, but that didn't mean she couldn't chance a look toward shore. Her eyes were drawn immediately to Talon, who seemed to be in deep conversation with a man not quite his height, but with the same features and coloring. With a proprietary attitude she was not aware of Danielle thought that the other man paled in comparison to Talon's magnificent physique.

A tall, strikingly beautiful woman caught Danielle's attention a moment later. Although she stood closer to the other man, there could be no mistaking the yearning in her gaze each time she lifted her eyes to Talon, not even from a distance. A tiny stab of jealousy pricked at Danielle's heart, when Talon's words came back to her that he had no lack of women to warm his bed at home.

Of a sudden Talon spun on his heel and marched purposefully back to the ship, his mouth compressed into a thin line, his chin tilted to a stubborn angle. Danielle saw a small muscle clenching and unclenching in his jaw, a clear sign that something had not gone to his liking.

Talon vaulted over the side of his ship, landing easily on his feet. He fixed her with a stormy glare. "Stay put until the cargo is unloaded," he bit out, then jumped back overboard again.

Danielle huddled deep in the shadows of the bow, feeling lost and dejected as she watched the warriors unload cargo all around her. No one paid her any attention or looked ever in her direction.

She had almost given up hope that Talon would ever come for her, when he leaped into the now empty ship to hunker down in front of her. "I have very little time to make long-winded explanations right now. Just listen. Things have changed. My sire died in the days I was gone. It was expected. My brother Thorson is now the rightful leader of the clan, but I don't care to live under his rule. We have never seen eye to eye. Unfortunately, I am forced to accept his hospitality for this night before we move on. You will have to stay in the slave quarters." He smiled encouragingly when he noticed the apprehension in her pale face. "It's not as bad as it sounds. In fact, once you see my stronghold, you might prefer the slave quarters to its Spartan surroundings." He chuckled, but there was no gaiety in the sound.

Talon offered his hand and pulled her up. He chucked a long finger under her quivering chin to tip it up. "It'll be all right, Danielle, you'll see," he consoled, and then his lips slashed across hers in a tender kiss that conveyed his inner turmoil better than words.

"Remember, we are now master and slave. If I call you, you come running and do my bidding without so much as an objection." He settled both of his huge hands on her slim shoulders and shook her gently. "Is that understood, princess?"

Danielle stared up at him, her eyes enormous in her pale face and she nodded numbly. Her mind was spinning with confusion. All along he'd made it abundantly clear that she was never more than a slave, so why the sudden emphasis?

"Don't gainsay any of my orders," he commanded, but there was a pleading tone in his otherwise stern voice. "As long as we are here, always walk three paces behind me."

Danielle meekly followed Talon and never looked up as she mulled over the strange rules he had set before her. She almost collided with his broad back when he stopped before a longhouse of sturdy wood. She gasped and reached out a trembling hand to steady herself, but quickly recoiled at the squelching look Talon threw her.

The longhouse was built low and had but few windows and these were covered with stretched animal hides. The woman Danielle had seen from the ship stood just outside the door and favored Talon with a brilliant smile of welcome.

"I have missed you sorely, brother-in-law," she said in a sensual voice that left no doubt to her meaning. Her voluptuous body swayed gracefully to underscore her words.

"Let it be, Arwynna," entreated Talon huskily. "You are my brother's wife now, so be content. You are mistress of his home and his people and wasn't that what you wanted all along?" They spoke as if Danielle weren't present, but since they spoke in the English tongue she was a painful witness to their conversation.

Arwynna waved a tired hand. "I didn't know what price there would be to pay, Talon." She lowered her voice. "My offer still stands. Your brother is too engrossed in counting his coin and being chief to his clan than being a husband and tend to my needs. Meet me at the foot of the hills tomorrow at dawn. I'll be waiting." Without waiting for an answer, she turned on her heel and went inside.

Talon stood for long moments staring after her. Danielle could not see his face, but she didn't fail to notice the weary slump of his broad shoulders. Curiosity gnawed on her insides. She would have liked to know more, but Talon forestalled her near blunder with a warning look. "Follow me," he bit out brusquely and led the way toward a low hut in back of the longhouse.

He opened the door and motioned Danielle inside. "You will stay here with the rest of the women for the night. They will help you find your way around. I will come for you in the morning." Without another word he turned on his heel and strode away.

Danielle entered the small hut of sod blocks. Like all the other buildings it had a thatched roof and a sturdy wooden door. Danielle wondered briefly at the purpose of such a stout door, since the settlement was surrounded with a double ringed palisade of thick tree trunks that looked impenetrable to her.

It took her a moment to accustom her eyes to the gloom within the room. There were no windows here she noted, but a few slivers of sunshine still managed to creep through around the doorframe. The corners of her lovely mouth drooped in dismay.

There would be no comfort here. She recognized the long planks against the wall now as beds. She counted twelve narrow places. Ten of them were occupied, judging by the various bulks that huddled under a variety of meager covers. All of the women were sleeping, except one.

"My name is Marla," she said quietly as she approached. She swept the length of Danielle's slender body with an appraising gaze. "The others are sleeping, since it is night." She waved a work-roughened hand toward the door and shrugged tired shoulders in defeat. "I can't get used to sleeping while the sun is shining. Maybe for that reason alone we should be grateful for this windowless hovel. At least this bit of gloom helps us close our weary eyes, when we are allowed to seek our pallets." Her voice was tinged with bitterness and hopelessness. Danielle shivered delicately as it occurred to her that she might resemble this poor wretch before long.

"I am Danielle," she whispered, afraid to wake any of the others. "Are you a slave, too, Marla?"

The other woman laughed harshly. "I can tell that you have not gotten used to the idea, yet. The Norse people have no use for any other type of worker. You see, slaves have no say in anything and get no pay. If one of us dies, they just go out and capture someone to replace us," she remarked wryly. She stabbed the air with a dirty finger. "I can vouch that you never get accustomed to being a slave. You are treated less kindly than the animals and you do their bidding in anything they please. I am just glad Thorson never took a liking to me. I would hate to be forced to pleasure him in bed."

"But he is wed to Arwynna, is he not?"

"Aye, and they deserve each other. One is as cold and calculating as the other. Why they married I'll never know." She shook her head as if trying to fathom their reason. "I know that he takes more pleasure in bedding a young slave of a mere fourteen summers than he does his wife, and Arwynna will bed anyone who is not afraid of Thorson's wrath," Marla sneered.

Danielle shivered again. She did not want to hear anymore. Somehow Marla 's dire words made her uncomfortable. Nor did she want to think about whether Talon would accept Arwynna's invitation to meet him at dawn. "Are you English, Marla?" she asked in way of changing the subject.

"Aye, and I wish I were back at the miserable fishing village whence I came from. At least it was home and though we rarely had enough to eat, I was my own woman. I was promised to marry, but then the Vikings came and snatched me ...You sound different, Danielle, you speak my language almost without a trace of an accent, but there is a lilt at the end of your words."

"I am French. My mother was English by birth and she taught me her language." She paused and dropped her eyes at Marla 's bright inquisitive gaze. "I, too, was taken by force. My brother had delivered me to the nuns for safekeeping while he went on a trip. Some safekeeping! It did not matter to the Viking. He abducted me without so much as a by-your-leave."

Marla cocked her head to the side as an idea formed in her fertile mind, "Do you think your brother might come and ransom you? These Vikings will do anything for money. It is their whole purpose in life, I think. All they crave is money."

Danielle shook her head. "I don't think that Jean-Jacques will come after me. How would he know where to look?"

"Ah, you have a point there, Danielle." The other woman sighed heavily, "It was a nice thought while it lasted." Thumbing toward the corner behind her, she said, "You might as well choose a bunk and lay your head down. They come soon enough to awaken us again."

Marla handed Danielle a thin blanket to add to the other she was clutching and went back to her own pallet. Moments later loud snoring proclaimed that she had finally found that elusive slumber.

Danielle lay awake for a long time, pondering what was in store for her. She had learned that whenever a small ray of hope sprang up in her breast, Talon's voice would mock her and remind her that she was nothing more than his slave.

CHAPTER TEN

A sudden change of light woke Danielle. Blinking against the bright sun pouring through the open door, her gaze collided with Talon's cool appraising eyes. She gaped as she took stock of the rest of him. Dressed in a soft woolen tunic that clung to his muscled torso like a second skin it stopped short at mid-thigh. A finely braided leather belt cinched the garment to his lean waist, and a heavy fur lined cape, held together with two elegantly wrought clasps of gold and silver, was thrown casually across broad shoulders. His arms were bare, their bulging biceps straining against the heavy arm circlets he always wore. Leggings of the same material as the tunic were tucked tightly into his cross-gartered fur boots. Except for the fur boots and arm circlets he did not resemble the barbarian she had come to know. Why under different circumstances, she would have a hard time believing that he was less gently born than she.

The mockery in his deep voice cut her fantasy short. "Did you sleep well, princess?" he taunted. "I am ready to leave. You had best hurry if you don't want to be left behind. We have a long way to ride."

"Ride, did you say?"

"Yes, ride. My stronghold lies a day and a half's ride northwest of here. Traveling slows once we get into the foothills."

Danielle threw her blanket aside and stood up, and then sucked in her breath in view of her state of undress. Too proud to snatch the blanket back up, she faced him unflinchingly. "I don't know what you did with my clothes, Viking. And I can't ride in my shift," she noted acidly as she pointed to the thin cotton garment. *Let him deal with being called Viking, if he insists on calling me princess*, she thought primly.

Talon inhaled sharply and his eyes flashed with sudden heat as his gaze followed her direction. Thanks to an errant shaft of pale sun Danielle might as well have stood there naked. Backlighting the flimsy material of her undergarment it outlined every luscious curve of her body. The vision shook Talon to the tips of his boots and intense desire coursed through him. He nodded dreamily. "Aye, I had better cover you up or I might not make it out of here." Muttering to himself, he turned and was gone.

A few minutes later Marla appeared with a woolen tunic and matching leggings, but not near as fine as Talon's. She also carried a small pair of fur boots in her hands. "Your master sent these to you. Said to make sure you wear them, since you are going into the foothills and the winds up there are fiercely cold."

Marla leaned closer to Danielle, dropping her voice to a mere whisper. "If you ask me, you are better off with Talon than you would be here. He may look gruff, but he is fair they say." She pressed the garments into Danielle's hand and hurried to the door. "I had better be gone. They expect a day's work from you or you don't eat. Good luck, dearie!"

Danielle hurriedly pulled the heavy tunic over her head and

tucked the leggings into the fur boots in the manner she had observed from Talon. The boots were a bit large, but at least they were warm. Despite the constant sun, Danielle was beginning to feel cold, unsure if it was from the weather itself or the uncertainty of what the future held for her that robbed her of warmth.

Talon was waiting for her. Sitting atop an enormous black stallion, which pranced impatiently, challenging his master with his constant sidestepping, he swept Danielle with an appraising stare. Appreciatively he noted that the tunic he had sent afforded him a tantalizing glimpse of long, shapely legs. She was an appealing baggage he decided, one he would have to guard well or be in danger of losing. The thought stung him and his thick golden brows drew together, giving him a forbidding countenance.

Danielle turned questioning eyes up to Talon. By the look of his dour expression, she could tell that he was displeased about something. Something inside her rebelled and she decided she would just steer clear of him Unfortunately, that did not solve her dilemma about what was expected of her next.

"Your horse is tied behind the wagon with the extra mounts," he called to her as if he could read her thoughts. "It's the little gelding. His name is Sundevil. He is quite docile and you won't have much trouble riding him."

"I know how to ride, thank you very much," she replied tartly, forgetting that she was supposed to play the obedient slave.

Talon chuckled, his good mood somewhat restored by her saucy answer. "Yes, I seem to recall you riding that stallion near Paris and a creditable job you did," he answered with a devilish grin. "I also recall that it left you quite sore," he growled so low that only Danielle would hear him.

Embarrassed she lowered her eyes. A deep blush crept from the top of her head to the base of her slender throat, where a tiny pulse began to beat erratically as she recalled that exact moment. How dare that rake refer to their lovemaking in such a crude manner? What if anyone caught on to his meaning? Feeling quite warm beneath his mocking gaze, Danielle rushed toward the shaggy horse and nimbly climbed into the saddle. She dared not glance at Asgard or Leif, who were avidly watching from atop their mounts.

Talon galloped ahead as the wagons followed at a lumbering pace, each guided by a male slave. Asgard and Leif brought up the rear, while Danielle rode somewhere between the wagon and the two Vikings.

"Good riddance," she muttered after Talon's broad back, then let her eyes roam over the foreign countryside. To her left the sea lapped against ancient rock, adding to a thick layer of salt each time she retreated. Steep mountains, covered in dense forest rose to her right, and nestled between these mountains she glimpsed lush green meadows. Reveling in the clean, crisp, salty air Danielle took a deep breath and closed her eyes. Ah, she could almost believe that she was back at Honfleur-sur-mer.

Talon rode up and broke into her reverie. Grinning down at Danielle, he ran a gentling hand along the horse's massive neck and boasted, "Lucifer was restless after my absence. He won't let anyone ride him but me. Normally he is as mild-mannered as a lamb and listens to my mere command...."

"Yes, gentle as a lamb. That was quite obvious when we left your brother's homestead," jeered Danielle.

Talon's mouth tightened at her gibe and he leaned down to her. "I will teach you yet to keep a civil tongue in your head. 'Tis said that you should not judge a book by its cover and it surely holds true with you. Outside you are pleasing to the eye, but inside you are all tart and vinegary." He wheeled his mount and angrily rode ahead again.

Danielle grimaced. "I guess it's all right as long as you make fun of others, but lo when someone dares say something about you," she grumbled after him. It never failed to surprise her that Talon's feelings were so easily ruffled. Instead of dwelling on it for long, she simply let her eyes rove and continued to enjoy the beauty that unfolded before her.

Apparently, Talon did not bear her a grudge, because he slowed his horse almost immediately and allowed Danielle to catch up with him.

"How do you like our Norseland?" he asked casually.

"It is beautiful and sometimes even breathtaking. So different from home and considering the time of year, I find it quite cool."

"Aye, your country is rather warm and our fur boots and tunics seemed out of place at times." He leaned closer. Grinning down at her, he winked broadly. "That is why we don't wear anything underneath. The cooling breezes tend to keep us comfortable enough that way."

Danielle shot him an offended glare. Highly amused he threw his head back in mirth and laughed uproariously.

Asgard raised a questioning brow at Leif, who threw up his hands in droll disgust. "Looks as if Talon and the wench found something funny to share."

Leif shrugged. "With those two you can never tell what they'll do next. One moment they fight like two roosters and the next they coo like doves."

Asgard chuckled. "I've heard tell that people in love do such things. Do you think they are more fond of one another than they both know?"

"Could be, but if that is the way of lovers, give Odin that I never fall in love. Aside from that, it would go hard on them if it were true. The wench is but a slave and Thorson would not permit her to be anything more to his brother."

"I don't think that Talon would let his brother or anyone else stop him if he sets his mind on having her, do you? In fact, if Thorson objects, you can bet that Talon will do exactly the opposite."

Leif nodded his agreement. "You're right. Talon can be pigheaded unless the honor of the clan is at stake."

As if he sensed that his two friends were talking about him, Talon turned in his saddle and gave them a casual salute. Then he checked the position of the sun.

"We will make camp for the noon meal soon," he confided to Danielle.

She smiled up at him. "I am as hungry as a bear, master," she teased. "You sure don't feed your slaves regularly, do you?"

Talon stared at her. "When was the last time you ate, wench?"

Danielle blushed. "I didn't mean to complain," she muttered.

"Well, tell me anyhow," Talon prodded.

"I had a bowl of stew at the home of the woman with the children."

"You mean that is all you had to eat yesterday? Why didn't you tell me?" Talon spouted angrily.

Danielle lifted her chin a notch. "I wasn't sure just how to broach the subject. You told me to walk three paces behind you and act the slave. When was I supposed to ask?"

"Would you jump into the sea yonder, if I told you to?" he retorted in exasperation.

Danielle only dropped her gaze and did not answer. To her amazement a strip of pungent dried meat appeared under her nose. She looked questioningly up at Talon.

"What is this?"

"Never mind what it is called, just eat it, wench," he growled. "And never go about hungry again or I will teach you the hard way not to withhold anything from me."

Despite the spicy smell, the dried meat was quite tasty and Danielle gnawed at it with relish. When they finally stopped for the noon meal, she was still hungry but at least her stomach did not ache from it.

"We'll make *Dragon's Lair* by this time tomorrow," announced Talon as they rode on. "Good thing, too, since there will be much work that needs to be done before we can put our heads down for the night."

"Would you tell me a little about the place where you are taking me?" Danielle asked hopefully.

Talon regarded her long and hard. "There is not another dwelling for days on end once we get there," he said brusquely. "You won't be able to escape, if you have that in mind. Dragon's Lair sits on a plateau of natural rock in a valley surrounded by tall mountains and you can only reach it via a narrow path. It's a fortress in every way, since the walls of the plateau fall away steeply on three sides, perfect against intruders. The living space of my stronghold is carved directly into the sheer mountainside. Dense growth of trees and brush take away some of its starkness. There is also a clear stream nearby that attracts plenty of game."

"But why is it called Dragon's Lair?"

"Oh that?" Talon leaned casually forward in his saddle, visibly relaxed. "Legend has it that once there lived a mighty dragon in that valley. He was perfectly content to stay there and live in peace. He would look down from the plateau and watch for intruders, chasing them away with his fiery breath and mighty roar. However, one day, while the dragon was sleeping Loki, the spirit of evil and mischief, came to the valley. When he saw that the dragon was asleep … " Talon peeked out of the corner of his eye at Danielle. The rapt expression on her face pleased him immensely.

" … Anyway, Loki could not pass up the opportunity to tease the dragon. He changed himself into a large wasp and began to torment the dragon. The more the dragon roared, the more it encouraged Loki to sting the poor beast. It amused Loki to see the dragon thrash about, too big and clumsy to crush the wasp. In the end the dragon went mad with the pain. In desperation he jumped down from the plateau, swishing his tail against the attack of the wasp, and in doing so he swept the valley clean of all trees and brush. Still Loki would not let him rest, but kept on stinging and buzzing about, until the poor dragon, driven by agony, jumped into the sea and drowned."

"I feel sad for the dragon. Is it true then that there are no trees or bushes in that valley?"

"Yes, there is not a single tree, only grass. In the springtime the meadow is dotted with small red flowers. They are called dragon's blood. It's said they are the droplets of blood the dragon spilled when he fought against the evil Loki."

"Do you have any more legends to tell?" Danielle asked, her eyes bright and eager.

"Aye, I will tell them to you in good time. Right now we must look toward making camp. The midnight sun is deceptive, despite its constant rays, you still need rest and so do the horses."

They bedded down on the barren ground, each wrapped securely into large blankets fashioned out of wolf skins. Asgard took the first shift to stand watch.

CHAPTER ELEVEN

Danielle was quite cross when Talon told her it was time to get up. She had slept only fitfully, keenly aware of each change of watch. "I cannot understand why you find it necessary to post sentries in this barren land, when you can see for miles on end and the sun never goes down," she remarked tartly.

"The wolves still eat, despite the sun, and the occasional bear might find its way to our camp as well," Talon told her curtly. He left her then and rode ahead. Danielle did not mind, because she was in no mood for friendly conversation.

By midday they rode into the valley Talon had so aptly described in his tale. With a whoop he spurred Lucifer and galloped ahead, clearly ecstatic to be home.

Danielle pulled her palomino up short, stunned by the beauty before her. The plateau with its sheer cliff walls loomed at the far end of the valley against the backdrop of a majestic mountain covered in dense greenery. Talon had not exaggerated. The valley itself was one of lush abundance. If it were not for the muted roar of the sea in the distance behind them, the serenity would have been complete. Awed, Danielle simply stared, feeling rather insignificant amid such natural splendor.

Talon wheeled Lucifer around the moment he realized that Danielle had not followed him. Bringing the stallion to a halt next to her, a delighted grin split his handsome visage as he swept his arm in an all-encompassing arch. "It's not much, it's untamed and will need a lot of work, but it's all mine. Paid for with the monies I have earned through my fighting skills," he boasted proudly.

Danielle would have liked to ask if that meant that he would lay down his sword and work the land, but she did not dare. Besides, Asgard and Leif had ridden up and she sensed a subtle tension in the three men. Their eyes alight with mischief the three friends briefly joined hands across their horses' backs and lined up in a single row. Moments later their feral war whoops echoed off the mountains as they rode at breakneck speed toward the plateau.

Danielle watched Talon race ahead of the two men and a warm feeling of pride washed over her. All three seemed one with their mounts, muscles bunching and stretching as they leaned low over the necks of the mighty beasts, but Talon still stood out among them. Aye, he was taller and he had the arrogant air of the conqueror about him.

Her sense of pride did not carry her long. She felt left out. Dejectedly, she held her horse to a light canter as she followed the rocky path the three friends had just taken, while the wagons with the provisions rumbled slowly behind her. She felt sorry for herself and with good reason. As usual Talon was thinking of no one but himself.

"Why the long face, princess?"

Danielle gasped. Too caught up in self-pity, she had not heard Talon ride up. Guiltily, she tried to smile, but didn't quite succeed. Telltale tears had gathered in the corners of her eyes and she swiped at them with an impatient hand.

"I am tired, *master*," she pouted. "Tired of being left behind and taken for granted," she added spitefully.

"I came back for you, didn't I?"

"Yes, you did."

"I'll always come back for you," he promised huskily.

"Aye, until the day when you tire of me and leave me behind for good," she hissed.

Talon's mouth hardened at her accusation. "You play me false, wench. I may not be the man to answer to your every beck and call, but I hold my promises sacred. And it is up to you whether I ever tire of you." Angered he rode slightly ahead of her, his exuberant mood wiped away. He had come back for her, because he had wanted to share his pleasure with her, his joy of being in his own stronghold. Why did he even bother?

Danielle angrily tossed her head. Why did she feel the need to test his patience? If she wanted to gain her freedom, she would have to quit acting the shrew. One thing was sure, however, she had not been brought up to be a slave and no man would ever own her.

At the arched stone entrance, Talon checked Lucifer and waited for Danielle to catch up. Together they rode into the enclosure where Asgard and Leif had already dismounted. The two friends grinned engagingly at Talon and Danielle.

"We have already checked the inside of the main house and there are no wild animals in residence, but a lot of dust has accumulated. Nothing that can't be set right by evening," Asgard reported.

"We'll have to wait for the wagons before we can set the slaves to work. The leather buckets for water are loaded on those wagons as well. Guess we have naught to do but to unsaddle the horses and rub them down."

Danielle slid off her mount and left it standing in the middle of the grounds, intent on having her own look around.

Talon's cold voice stopped her in mid-stride. "Where do you think of going, wench? In uncivilized country such as this your horse is your greatest asset toward survival. You take care of your beast before you take care of yourself."

Danielle opened her mouth to protest and tell him that such was stable boys work, but she caught herself in the last moment. Some day she would tell him of her home and the luxury she was used to, but this was not the time. Clenching her small hands into fists at her sides, she told him primly that she didn't know how.

"How come you ride a horse so well and yet you do not know how to take care of one?" Talon asked suspiciously.

"I guess I never had one of my own," she lied.

"All right then, this time I will do it for you, but I want you to stand next to me so you'll learn for yourself."

The wagons rumbled through the stone portal a short time later and the two male slaves began to unload them at Talon's instructions.

"Take a leather bucket and get water, wench," he commanded imperiously. "While we unload you can rid the place of cobwebs and dust."

Danielle stared at Talon with horrified eyes. How was she to rid a place of cobwebs? She had never done any menial work in her life. Even in the cloister the nuns had done all the cleaning, though she had helped out in the garden. Not wanting to anger him any further, she grabbed up a bucket and lugged it in the direction he pointed out to her.

Gamely, Danielle dipped the heavy bucket into the well. She almost lost it, when she tried to pull it back up. Her near mishap upset her so that she was tempted to leave the bucket behind and tell Talon to send one of the men, but her pride would not let her. She would bring water and if it killed her.

Talon saw her coming, straining at the strap of the bucket and he went to help her. Sputtering, he pointed at the bucket, which was filled less than half way.

"Is that all the water you brought back, wench?"

"It is all the water I could carry, Viking," she snapped.

"Well, those nuns surely taught you poorly," he huffed as he emptied the water across the rocky floor and handed her a brush broom to sweep it clean.

Danielle accepted the broom with trepidation, her eyes like two green shards of glass. "What do you want me to do with this?" she asked coldly.

Talon's blue gaze rested on her one incredulous moment. "It's called a broom and you use it to brush the water and dirt off the floor," he explained with exaggerated patience. "Am I right when I presume that you cannot cook either?" he questioned silkily a moment later.

Danielle shook her head in denial. "No, I never learned. There was no need."

"Bah! Next you will tell me that you had servants doing it all for you." Talon turned on his heel and left her standing. Under his surly direction, the male slaves set to cleaning the house as best they could. Once the cleaning was done, Danielle took over by setting the furniture and bedding right.

Somewhat mollified, Talon walked up to her and caught her in a rough embrace. He smiled wolfishly down at her. "I guess all things work out for the best. Maybe it is just as well that you do not do housework or cooking. Instead you will have more energy to keep my bed warm," he growled into her ear. "I have sorely missed your pliant little body, my sweet."

She pushed against him with both palms, "I have not missed you nor your mauling, Viking," she told him primly, though even that mere contact made her go hot all over. No way was she going to let on that she wished he could work his magic on her without delay.

Although Talon would have dearly liked to prove her wrong, there was no time for dallying. If they were to have fresh meat for their evening meal, the men would have to hunt for it. Armed with bows and arrows the three friends set out on foot.

Unsure what to do next, Danielle walked about the stronghold and climbed on top of the roughly laid walls. The view that unfolded before her was even more breathtaking from up there. It was a picture straight out of a fairy tale book. The meadow spread wide as far as the eye could see and it seemed to end at the edge of the sea. Danielle held her breath when she saw a small red deer daintily pick its way along the edge of the meadow. She could see smaller game scurry through the waist high grass, but she did not know what kind they were. Life could be good here, but never as a slave.

Homesickness swamped her. Honfleur-sur-mer. Oh, God, would she ever see it again? Had Jean-Jacques gone back to the nuns for her and found her gone? Did they miss her? Maybe Marla was right and her brother was even now on his way to ransom her. Her emotions fluctuated like the tides of the sea, until she thought she could bear no more and turned her back to the beautiful vista.

The three men came back in high spirits. They had shot a small deer and a brace of hares. Danielle was spared the gutting, since they had done so in the forest already.

Talon fixed her with a baleful stare. "Well, wench, I surely don't know what I will do with you. You are no good at keeping a man's house clean and you cannot even fill his belly with warm food."

Asgard and Leif kept prudently out of Talon's musings. Danielle bit her lip, horrified that he should act so crudely. And then to her horror Talon laughed loudly as he clapped Leif on the back. "Well, at least she is good at keeping a man's bed warm," he guffawed. The two men joined in the laughter, making Danielle feel even worse than before. Mortified, she jumped to her feet and fled to the privacy of the bedroom.

Talon followed her shortly, slightly contrite. He hunkered on the edge of the bed and stroked her heaving back as he listened to her bitter sobbing. "I did not mean to hurt you, Danielle. I don't know why I said the things I did."

Danielle ignored his attempts at apologizing and cried even harder. It did not even make one whit of difference that he had called by name.

Talon leaned closer, ready to make further amends. Instead, her scent kindled his desire. Without conscious intent his hands began to roam in ever widening circles, kneading tender flesh in sensuous rhythm. He felt himself go warm and hard, wishing more than anything that Danielle would be eager for his touch. He smiled wryly to himself. He had come to console *her*, but this wisp of a girl had a hold on him like no other woman before her.

Try as she might, Danielle felt hard pressed to keep herself aloof of Talon's sensuous roaming hands. His warm breath tickled the nape of her neck and sent shivers of delight along her spine. Danielle forgot her misery and smiled into the wolf pelts, but vowed she wouldn't give in too easily. Let him work for his pleasure.

The subtle shift in her demeanor did not escape Talon. So why did she not turn over to allow him full access to her body? Sliding closer he made sure she would be aware of his arousal. Still no response. Willing himself to stay patient, he bent over her and rained tiny kisses across her cheek, dipping his tongue against the side of her throat and working his hands underneath her breast to tease and pluck.

Danielle tried hard to deny him though she wanted him more than ever. Sighing in resignation she finally turned to her side, and the moment she did Talon dragged her into his arms. He kissed her with deliberate slowness, while his hands busily roamed over her body, trying to find a way of undressing her.

"You shameless wench," he muttered huskily. "I am becoming wise to your little games. You are enjoying my futile attempts to disrobe you, aren't you?" He tickled her ribs, thinking it would hurry her surrender. Instead Danielle burst into a fit of the giggles and curled into a tight little ball to escape his teasing.

"Enough," Talon gritted from between tightly clamped teeth. "I've waited as long as I can." His blue eyes flashing, he dipped his massive hand into the neck of her tunic. The sound of tearing fabric was deafening.

"Ah!" he sighed appreciatively. "You are a sight for sore eyes. It's been too long since I had a chance to feast on the perfection of your body. Let loose already of that rag, I want to see all of you and then I want to bury myself inside of you."

"You beast," she gritted, holding the ragged edges of the torn tunic together, glaring green daggers at him. "You just ruined the only decent garment I have. What am I to wear, answer me?"

Talon chuckled. "Well, if you have nothing to wear, I guess you will just have to stay in my bed. And did I ever tell you that my manroot responds to your sharp tongue and flashing eyes as if it had been dosed with an aphrodisiac?"

Danielle's scathing retort died on her lips as his mouth swooped down on hers and captured them in a breathtaking kiss. Casually, he swung his muscled leg across her slim hips, holding her prisoner against his hard length, while he played further havoc with her senses. After long minutes, Talon stopped and stared deeply into her mossy green eyes, now glazed with passion. "Tell me," he asked quietly, "is the prospect of spending time with me in bed really all that bad?"

Danielle threaded her fingers through his white-gold mane, an impish smile curving her kiss-swollen lips. "No, it isn't, Talon. What I want to know is if you are paying me back by deliberately making me wait and suffer?"

Talon chuckle dissolved into a groan of delight as Danielle's hand closed around him. "Now who is meeting out punishment?" he rasped. "I suggest you release me and use both hands to hold on. I promise you that you are in for the ride of your life."

Wide-eyed Danielle swallowed in anticipation, watching as he ever so slowly eased into her wet hot woman's place. Then her eyes closed on their own volition as they rode wildly into a sunset of their own making.

CHAPTER TWELVE

Days ran into weeks, but Danielle never grew bored. Talon took her hunting with him and showed her how to fish. She'd accepted the fact that this was her life now. In fact, she felt quite at home in the wilderness. And since Talon had sent Leif back to Herjolfstad to buy two slave women from his brother, she felt no longer isolated.

One day when she and Talon were fishing in the stream, she remarked idly. "I have always wondered why you sent Leif to buy the two slave women for you?"

Talon quirked a bronzed brow at her. "You have to ask, my sweet? I sent Leif, because I knew he would choose wisely. Women who could do the work, but who were comely enough to entertain him and Asgard during the night."

Danielle sputtered. "Why, that's horrid. Those poor women have no choice," she fumed.

Talon shook his head and laughed. "Nay, I think not. They know they are better off at Dragon's Lair than in Herjolfstad. Some night I will let you listen at the door to their brazen banter and invitations to the men."

Danielle tossed her head, setting her midnight tresses to swirl about her shapely head like a silken curtain. "Bah," she chided, "you men seem all alike. And heaven forbid that you might admit that your thoughts are forever underneath a maiden's skirt. But no, it is the brazen wenches fault for turning your heads in that direction." Huffing with indignation, she made a show of concentrating on the fish that darted past in the shallow stream.

Talon chuckled aloud at her resentment. "Why," he teased, "I had no idea how clearly you view the situation." He sidled closer and his arm snaked around her narrow waist. "You tempt me sorely, sweet," he whispered hoarsely. "You have no idea how beautiful you are, when your eyes sparkle like green jewels and your mouth puckers as if in invitation of a kiss." He turned her into his embrace and captured her lips with his own, searing them with the heat of his passion.

Danielle's loins tightened with desire. Dampness pooled between her legs and she waited for Talon to lift her off the ground and slide into her right there by the stream's edge. Instead he set her abruptly down. Small spasms continued to erupt deep inside her as she waited for him to consummate what he'd started. Surely by now he'd learned what his kisses did to her? Disappointment rushed through her. Since when was he satisfied with just a kiss? Curious she watched him from beneath lowered lashes. He was staring moodily into the distance. What had set him off this time? She did not have long to wonder about it.

Without sparing her a glance, Talon sighed and clicked his tongue in distress. "I hate to leave this idyllic place, even though it is only for a short space of time," he mused aloud.

Danielle held her breath and stood transfixed, trying to understand what Talon was telling her. She waited, but he did not elaborate. Had she misunderstood him? Surely he wouldn't think of leaving Dragon's Lair. He loved it here far too much to think about leaving. Still she needed to know.

"What do you mean by leaving?" she ventured cautiously, unaware that her voice betrayed her anxiety.

Talon paused a moment, giving her a long, hard look. "You sound as if you might miss me if I were gone."

"Nay, not miss you," she denied vehemently and tossed her head for good measure, "I am just curious. I thought you were content here. However, thinking on it, it seems you are forever honing your battle skills. I guess the bully in you might not like this peacefulness."

Talon latched on the word bully and hung on to it like a terrier to a bone. "Bully? Bully, I am, you say?" he thundered in exasperation. "Have I not been a model of consideration of late? Did I not bring extra wenches to help with the work?"

Danielle giggled. He looked so comical in his self-righteous indignation. "Aye," she admitted, "you have been all that, but your moods turn with the wind." She clapped her hand over her mouth wishing the words could be unsaid.

Talon stood quite still, allowing her scathing words to sink in. He saw the fear in the depths of her green orbs, knew that she was unaware how she unwittingly displayed all her emotions through those two bright mirrors into her inner being. It shamed him that she should view him this way, because he knew that she was helpless against this superior power and his wrath. He made a mental note to treat her more gently, and then he grinned wryly down at her.

"Ah, Danielle, you never fail to amaze me." He shook his head and allowed his aquamarine gaze to linger upon her. "But whatever you accuse me of is far from reality. 'Tis true, I am content here. I have even given it some thought to make a living from fair trade, but you see, Asgard and Leif are warriors like myself and they have a hankering to go raiding again."

"Why can't they go on a raid by themselves?" Danielle asked sharply.

Talon drew himself up to his imposing height. "The *Raider* is mine and as her captain I am the one who will sail her and no other. Besides, it wouldn't hurt to replenish my coffers. You can never have enough coin in this world."

"I guess Marla was right when she said that you Vikings treasured money above all else," she sniffed.

"I wouldn't say that, sweet," he declared huskily as he reached for one of her midnight tresses and toyed with the silky length, achingly aware of the soft swell of her breast beneath his casual touch. "Raiding is in my blood and I like the thrill of an honest fight."

Danielle bit her tongue instead of telling him what she thought of the Viking idea of honest fighting.

"Aren't you afraid that some day you will be maimed or killed on one of your forays?" she asked quietly.

Talon shook his head with such conviction that she could only gape. "Nay, I am protected by the mighty Odin," he boasted. "See these arm circlets? They are inscribed with the sacred runes and the runes will keep me from harm." He pointed at his dagger and toward his sword. "All my weapons have runes on them, as do Asgard's and Leif's." He smiled at her benevolently, as if she were a child who was too young to understand the mystery of life.

"Are you telling me that all Vikings are immune then against harm and death?" she questioned sarcastically, her eyes darting to his disfigured hand.

Talon broad chest puffed with pride. "Nay, not all. Sometimes Odin favors one of us to die in battle and we go to Valhalla. There you march with other heroes doing glorious battle forever more."

"What of the wives these heroes leave behind and the innocent children?" Danielle fixed him with a heated glare.

"Danielle you test my patience. I know you cannot understand the profundity of our Viking logic, but trust me we look forward to die in glory and go to Valhalla. Let it go at that. I do not aim to waste my time trying to make you understand. It's men's doings...."

"Aye, men's doings," mimicked Danielle quite exasperated that he should find dying on a battlefield so palatable. She turned from him then, not wanting him to see how upset his news made her.

Talon saw the surreptitious shake of her slender shoulders and he spun her around and pulled her against his solid chest. He gently kissed the top of her head and stroked the length of her back with his large hand.

"Why are you spilling tears, Danielle? Is it because I might get killed or because I will leave you behind?"

"Leave me behind?" she screeched. "Why would you leave me behind? You thought nothing of dragging me through the countryside after you stole me from the good sisters. Why of the sudden would you want to leave me behind?"

Talon stared at her in utter amazement. "Woman!" he roared. "It's not the Viking way or that of any other warriors to take their women along. What would you do whilst we are fighting? What if someone crept aboard and stole you from me?"

"You never thought about it back then," she stated primly.

"Nay, and I did not care for you as much either."

Hope leapt into Danielle's teary gaze. Did he have some feelings for her after all? Could she hope that he was ready to return the love she felt for him? She attempted to look into his eyes to discern the truth, but he stubbornly stared at a point far above and beyond her head.

"When are you planning to leave then?" she wanted to know.

"Asgard and Leif will ride to Herjolfstad on the morrow and begin to provision the *Raider*. I plan to leave three days hence."

Danielle was devastated by his announcement. Shaken, she limply dropped her spear to her side, no longer intent on impaling any fish.

"What will I do in your absence?" she whispered dejectedly.

"I won't be gone so long that you will miss me overmuch. Our forays rarely last more than a few days, since we do not roam far afield. Your native land has proven quite lucrative to us and we plan to go back there." He paused and stared at her pale face, cheering up visibly as an idea hit him. "Is there something I can bring back for you?" he asked in the hope that it would revive her spirit.

It was on Danielle's tongue to ask him to bring her back some gowns, but she quickly dismissed the idea as utterly frivolous. Even a riding habit would be out of place in this wilderness. Alas, it would be nice to feel like a lady again and dress accordingly. No sooner than she thought that the hateful phrase that she was nothing but a slave mocked her mind. A slave had no reason to dress like a lady.

If Talon truly cared for her, then there was no gift she would want more than to be free, unless he would but say one word of love. Tell her that she was the only one he wanted. If he made her his wife, she could be happy in this lonesome, rugged country. She shrugged mentally. Wishful thinking would bring her nothing and she would certainly not enlighten him to her deepest feelings. Moments later the idea struck her that this might be the one opportunity for her to escape. Somewhere there had to be someone who would carry her back to Honfleur-sur-mer on the promise alone that he would be rewarded once they reached their destination.

"Judging by your lengthy silence, it must be something very dear to your heart or something difficult to obtain, my sweet. Tell me anyhow what it is and I will try my best to bring it to you," Talon coaxed.

Danielle raised her eyes guiltily to his. "What did you just ask me?"

"Where is your mind, wench?" Talon fumed. "Here I am trying to please you once again and you don't even favor me with your full attention."

Danielle dropped her gaze before his fury. "I'm sorry, Talon, I was just thinking back. I really don't have any particular wish. If you bring me something, I'll be happy, if you can't, don't let it bother you."

"Humph! Isn't that just like a woman? If you but told me, it would make life a great deal easier for me."

"And what will make life easier for me?" Danielle snapped back.

"I treat you well enough, considering you are my slave. Your work here is not hard and don't deny that you derive as much pleasure from our romps in bed as I do," he growled, thoroughly vexed with her. Gathering his spear and the leather bucket with their catch, Talon stomped off, not caring whether Danielle followed or not.

CHAPTER THIRTEEN

After they had waved Asgard and Leif on their way, Danielle noticed that Talon moved about restlessly. Nothing seemed to please him. Indeed, that night he turned over on his side without even an overture at making love to her. Miffed, she rolled away from him and fell into a troubled sleep.

The following two days were sheer hell for Danielle. She watched him quietly as he sharpened his war ax with near vengeance. Resolutely, she walked up to him, locking her hands behind her back for strength. "Why don't you ride to Herjolfstad and check if Asgard and Leif are getting the crew ready? I am sure you'd feel better if you could see for yourself."

Talon stopped the stone wheel, disbelief robbing him momentarily of speech. Then his expression changed to one of sheer pleasure. "By Odin, but you are right!" he whooped with glee. "What do those two milksops know about outfitting a ship for a raid? The sooner I go, the sooner I'll return."

He hurried from the smithy, leaving Danielle to stare after him. Within a short time he emerged from their home, dressed in his wolf hide tunic and armed to the teeth with a broad sword hanging from his lean waist and a wicked-edged knife protruding from his boot. Grinning, he spread his long arms wide and beckoned Danielle within their circle.

"You are a wonderful wench," he murmured as he tightened his embrace and leaned down to kiss her passionately. His kiss deepened and Danielle felt him growing hard against her belly. Her own body responded hotly. Her pelvis did its own little dance of invitation against his throbbing manhood. She was vaguely aware that Talon dropped his bundle and war ax. Without breaking their kiss or saying a word, he swept her into his arms and carried her to their bed. Feverishly, he unfastened his tunic, irrationally remembering that other time when he could not master the ties on his garment. All the while his gaze hotly devoured Danielle, who worked just as intently on ridding herself of her clothing. Their sighs mingled as Talon dropped to the bed beside her.

"I could not go without tasting your sweet body one more time, princess," he murmured. "The thought of returning to you will surely see me through the fiercest battle."

Danielle barely heard his words as she gave herself up to the ecstasy of the moment.

Long after Talon had kissed her goodbye, Danielle lay on their bed and basked in the afterglow of their lovemaking. As her body cooled, her mind quickly turned to other thoughts. She would miss Talon's hard demanding body dominating hers. She would miss his kisses and the tender moments they had shared, but Danielle wanted her freedom more. She could never hope to be any man's wife after having been a captive, but she could not live as Talon's slave either.

Since the day Talon announced his departure Danielle had

forged a plan. She knew it was too risky to go south and to Herjolfstad, so she decided she would go north and take her chances. Somewhere there had to be other Viking settlements. If luck were with her, she would find someone, who'd be willing to help her to return to Honfleur-sur-mer.

She put her scruples aside and saddled Sundevil. Methodically, she raided the larder and gathered a fair amount of food and supplies. She would not starve, she vowed. For good measure, she stole a hammered gold goblet. It would come in handy as payment toward her escape.

Myra and Eloise, the two slaves Talon had bought to supplement his household workers, watched Danielle with awed eyes.

"What are ye aiming to do, lovey?" asked Myra finally, when she was no longer able to keep her curiosity at bay.

Danielle fixed the maid with a baleful glare. "What does it look like I am doing? I am leaving. I am not going to be any man's slave ever."

The two women exchanged glances. "He really don't treat ye like a slave, you know. We have to do as he tells us, but he never gives ye any orders." They simultaneously rolled their eyes. "Besides, you'll never find a finer figure than his to pleasure your body," they giggled, shivering at the thought of how it would feel to have Talon making love to them.

"You twits! No wonder you are nothing but slaves," Danielle chided them bitterly. "There is more to life than being ravished by a man. What if you get with child, what then? Will you not mind if your babe is then nothing but a slave either?"

Myra was thoroughly incensed by Danielle's superior attitude. "The Vikings treat their bastard offspring quite well, I'll have you know. They are treated as part of the community, never as slaves."

"Aye, never as slaves, but never quite as good as the children born to their chosen wives. Or do you deny that?"

Myra dropped her gaze before Danielle's wrath. "You are right," she agreed. Then catching her second wind, she turned on Danielle again with redoubled fury. "But even if I bear a bastard, the child will have a better life in this wild land than it would back home, even if it were born on the right side of the blanket," she spat venomously at Danielle. Feeling they had the last word in this confrontation, the two women turned to leave, but Myra could not refrain from adding one more threat.

"You know you'll not get far," she predicted. "Our master will follow you and bring you back at the end of a neck chain. And I'll be here to tell you I told you so," she added full of spiteful glee.

Danielle felt contrite after the two women left. She should have been more charitable toward them. They had resigned themselves to their lot in life and seemed content enough. Who was she to tell them what was right in life and what was wrong? Sighing, she finished her meager packing and mounted Sundevil.

Once she left Dragon's Lair and the familiar valley behind, Danielle began to have doubts about her rash decision. What if other Vikings thought her fair prey? They hardly would treat her as well as Talon had. And who was to say that another clan would jump on the opportunity to take her back to Honfleur-sur-mer on promises alone? Shaking her head against her inner argument, she urged the gelding to a canter, always keeping the sea within view. Freedom always came at a price and she was willing to pay whatever it would cost.

Talon had warned her that once the summer months were past, the nights would come suddenly and prove quite dark, especially if you had become used to the midnight sun. Of course, Danielle forgot those warnings in the month gone by and was ill equipped when it became darker of sudden and then pitch black soon after.

She was forced to slow the gelding to a walk and frantically searched for a safe place to spend the night. She was armed with a dagger, but now that she was alone, she realized what little use a dagger would be if a wolf or a bear decided to make her their evening meal.

A sigh of relief escaped her lovely mouth, when she discovered an overhanging boulder a short time later. It would at least afford her and Sundevil some shelter for the night. Valiantly, she struggled to light a fire, but it was no use. Blinking back tears, she admitted that Talon had spoiled her by taking care of all the small details in their every day life.

Her small chin shot up in defiance. No, she would not give in. She would simply have to do without a fire and huddle in her wolf pelt until sun-up. Hobbling the horse so it would not run off in case something might spook it, she gnawed on a piece of dried meat and stared moodily into the yawning void before her.

Come morning Danielle was stiff with cold and her muscles ached from the cramped position she had fallen asleep in. Crossly, she climbed once more on Sundevil and headed further

North.

By the second day, Danielle wished she had never had this hare-brained idea in the first place. She was exhausted from lack of sleep and constant cold. She was sorely tempted to turn around and accept her lot as a slave, but as the word slave penetrated to her tired mind, she recaptured her fighting spirit and rode on with renewed purpose.

Finally, at the dawning of the third day, she spied a palisade, much like the one at Herjolfstad and her heart soared with joy. Plying her heels to the gelding's flanks she rode with near breakneck speed toward the beckoning gates.

As Danielle rode through the gates of the settlement, all movement seemed to come to an abrupt halt. The people of the tiny community regarded her with something akin to awe. Her heart beat an unsteady tattoo in her breast as she allowed her gaze to wander over their bright heads. With grim satisfaction she noticed their threadbare garb and the poor repair of their dwellings and she knew that she had lucked out and come to the right place. If anybody was sorely in need of extra coin, it was these people. Her smug contentment quickly faded when she realized of a sudden that she would have to play her cards with great care or end up a hostage. Swallowing against the feeling of rising panic, she lifted her chin and gritted her teeth.

Danielle allowed the corners of her lovely mouth to lift with a hesitant smile as she greeted the villagers in their native tongue. She counted herself lucky that she had learned enough to make herself understood. Talon had been of little help, jealously guarding her from any exposure to their language, but Asgard and Leif had no such qualms and had taken great pleasure to teach her.

An old man stepped forward and reached for Sundevil's ornate bridle. "What brings you to our village, mistress?" he asked her suspiciously.

Danielle stayed atop her horse and favored the man with a direct stare. His hand on Sundevil's bridle did nothing to soothe her fears, but she tossed her head imperceptibly and decided she had better brazen it out. "I am looking for passage to the coast of France!" she stated clearly. Pointing toward the fjord to the West, she added smugly, "If that is your ship, I would like to hire it to take me back."

The old man regarded the stranger with a puzzled frown. Surely, the wench was dressed too finely for a slave and the mount was adorned with ornate leather and silver harness as only the freemen would have ...unless the wench stole the beast ... but nay, she would not have made it this far, if that were the case.

"Why is it you are traveling alone, mistress? Have you no husband or slaves to protect you?" he asked slyly.

Danielle gulped. She had not thought of being asked the most obvious. Quickly, she improvised and crossed her fingers behind her back hoping the old man might swallow her tale.

"Oh yes, I have a husband, but he is on a raid right now and I had word that my father is gravely ill. Time is running short. I need to go and tend to him."

The old man inclined his head to one side and regarded her solemnly. What the lass said could surely be true and prove her a decent woman who put her sire's welfare above her own. Somehow it pleased him to hear that she cared for the old one and his manner toward her softened just a trace.

"That still does not explain why you are traveling on your own, mistress," he pointed out politely, yet firmly.

"Ah, you see," Danielle lied baldly, "it would have slowed my progress severely." She held out the chased gold goblet to him. "This is yours as proof of my integrity. Once you get me home, I'll pay you whatever coin we will bargain for!" she wheedled.

The old man scratched his head. "I've never bargained with a woman, but if the price is to my liking, I might consider your contract." He pulled on Sundevil's bridle. "Come along then, mistress. We will go to my home and talk more of your plans and payment."

Ever courteous, the old man assisted Danielle from her horse and waved toward his lowly hut. One look at the shabby dwelling made it clear to Danielle that these people could not afford the same luxuries as Talon. Somehow that served to raise the hair on her nape in discomfiture.

"My name is Sweyn, mistress, what be yours?"

"I am Danielle Herjolfson," she lied resolutely.

The old man sucked in his breath and laying his head to the side, he inquired cautiously, "Be you mate to Thorson then, mistress?"

Danielle shook her head, weary of all his questions and impatient to get on with the business at hand. "Nay, I am mate to his brother Talon," she declared.

"Aye," Sweyn nodded sagely. "I know of him. He is a fierce warrior that one, I hear tell. He would not take kindly to being played for a fool." He stared pointedly at Danielle, waiting to see if she would give any sign of duplicity.

But Danielle was no longer the timid maid she was the day she was forced to leave Honfleur-sur-mer. She had come of age when Talon kidnapped her and she had hardened when he told her that she was nothing but a slave. The Danielle who faced Sweyn was self-possessed and knew what she wanted, nor would she stop at anything to get it. She fixed Sweyn with a bold stare and drew herself up to her full height.

"No one is playing Talon for a fool. I simply have need to go to my sire's home and there is no time to lose. So let us sit down and barter for my passage."

Sweyn backed down reluctantly. The woman seemed to be honest and he could always use the extra coin. His village did not have the necessary warriors to raid at will and so their existence was but a meager one. He envied Talon his prowess and his success, so if his mate would set him on a merry chase, then he did not get any better than he deserved.

Sweyn motioned Danielle into his hut and she had to bow to enter for the door was low. Inside the single room the rank odor of decaying fish was overpowering. Involuntarily, she wrinkled her nose in dismay. Her stomach revolted against the fetid stench. It took all her mettle to keep from disgracing herself.

An old woman, raw-boned and stooped from age and hard work left the hut at a nod from Sweyn, leaving him and Danielle alone to bargain.

"I am sure that my husband will come after my horse as soon as he gets word from our slaves, so will you keep him as well as a tab for his care?"

Sweyn nodded his assent, marveling at the cool calculating beauty before him. No wonder Talon wed the wench, though it was said that he had spurned many a maid worthy of him and his riches.

"So tell me, mistress, where is it you wish for me to take you?"

"Have you heard of Le Havre, Sweyn? It is at the mouth of the river Seine. From there a few leagues to the Southwest lies my home Honfleur-sur-mer."

Sweyn nodded, silently calculating how much he should ask for his troubles, surprised that the legendary Talon had shackled himself to a Frankish wench. "I've heard tell of it, mistress. With good weather, we should land on your shores within two days. The Shewolf is ready to sail whenever you want to. I will not take more than a dozen men and can have her provisioned within the day, if you wish." He turned his hand palms upward. "Our needs are simple, but what of yours, mistress?"

The prospect of getting home and without a great deal of fuss made Danielle reckless. She smiled hugely at Sweyn. "I can survive a few days of hardship and I am a fair voyager," she boasted.

"It is done then, mistress. I suggest you avail yourself of a pallet and rest until we have provisioned the Shewolf. I will come for you when we are ready."

Danielle was only too glad to lay her weary head upon a pallet, but she would have much rather done so in the fresh air. However, she was not about to insult her host by suggesting such, afraid he might back out of their agreement.

Despite her aversion to the stench in the small hut, Danielle fell into a deep sleep. When a rough hand on her shoulder shook her awake, it was much too soon for her liking.

"We are ready to sail, mistress!" Sweyn told her gleefully. He was glad to have a cause to sail the sea and bring something more than fish home these days.

Danielle stretched her legs and tried to rub the sleep from her eyes. Suddenly, she was assailed with second thoughts. What if Jean-Jacques refused to pay her passage? What if Talon came after her? She shrugged her misgivings off as Sweyn urged her to come along. She would cross those bridges when she came to them.

It had been quite some time since Danielle had been aboard a Viking war ship. She had forgotten how small they were. A length of barely sixty feet and a width of fifteen was all that held the angry seas at bay. And the Shewolf carried no armored shields to give her that added protection against the swells.

She noted that Sweyn had been heedful of her comfort and that he had fashioned a pallet for her in the bow. Gingerly, she made her way to it and took a seat. As she wrapped her wolf pelt about her against the growing chill, she craned her neck for one last look the coastline. Within moments the Shewolf glided into the open sea and Danielle fought to keep her balance as the small ship bobbed ominously across the waves.

In the days to come she would focus on the hideous carved wolves' heads that adorned the bow and stern of the small craft, just as Talon's was outfitted with a pair of dragonheads. She missed him sorely, but she would not allow herself to dwell on it.

She insisted that she would rather be without him than be his slave.

CHAPTER FOURTEEN

Three days to the day after they left Sweyn's village, the Shewolf made land just beyond the cliffs that comprised Honfleur-sur-mer's Northern border. Danielle looked upon her homeland with some trepidation unsure of the welcome she might receive. No, this was her home ... she squared her shoulders, jutting her chin out at the angle Talon had come to love ... Jean-Jacques be damned. She had a dowry and he couldn't deny her the right to live in the manor.

"Follow me, Sweyn, but leave your men behind, lest someone get the wrong idea and thinks they are going to be attacked," Danielle said, pasting a fake smile on her lips to take away the sting of her declaration.

Stubbornly, Sweyn shook his grizzled mane. "I cannot do that, mistress. I am a man of war and as such I never go without someone who will protect my back. If you are plagued by the thought that we would give the wrong impression, then I shall take but half the men with me. Let's not forget that you have promised us some fowl and staples along with the coin we bartered. I will need the men to help carry it back to the Shewolf."

Danielle saw the wisdom of that, but it did not ease her mind when she looked upon the motley crew of Vikings. Their mode of dress was enough to scare the heartiest of men out of a year's growth. She chuckled suddenly when it hit her that her own get-up fared hardly any better.

"Well, then let's get started. Honfleur-sur-mer lies just beyond that hill!" She pointed westward.

Jean-Jacques lounged against the window of the study and stared moodily into his ever-present glass of wine. As he lifted the goblet to his lips, he caught a movement out of the corner of his eye. He choked on the draught, spewing it over his white stock and the sleeve of his morning coat.

"Emile!" he roared from the top of his lungs. "Get over here and help me bar the main portal. That stinking band of Vikings is back again, just when I thought them well on their way."

Jean-Jacques set the silver goblet down with more vigor than he meant to, leaving a crack in the ecru marble top of the small side table. Then, with a speed no one would have guessed he possessed, he ran for the foyer to bolt the double doors. With equal alacrity he took two stairs at a time and headed for his chamber to retrieve his sword. He would not stand meekly by this time and watch these barbarians loot his home of valuables. They left him with little enough as it was. Luckily, Honfleur-sur-mer was built out of granite and refused to catch fire. Unfortunately, some of the furniture had suffered and Jean-Jacques would not so quickly forgive that.

Danielle walked ahead of the small group, her heart in her throat. Somehow Honfleur-sur-mer looked more imposing than it ever had before. It rose formidably into the sky with its dual stories of gray stone and lead-paned windows.

She frowned. Something was amiss, but she could not put a finger to it what it might be. And then it dawned on her. Dark fingers of soot marked several windows. She gasped. Honfleur-sur-mer had been on fire!

With an anguished moan, she broke into a run toward the house, not caring if her Viking crew could keep up with her or not. When she reached the front portal, she was aghast that it was bolted shut. Never in all her life could she remember of the heavy double doors ever being locked. She balled her hands into angry fists and pounded upon the door with all the fury she had pent-up inside her, ever since she had been forced to leave her beloved home. It was like the latest slap in her face.

"Open up, Jean-Jacques!" she screeched heatedly, angered beyond all reason that she was shut out. "Open up this instance!" she insisted, sure that her brother had locked her out on purpose.

"*Monsieur*! That is a lady calling for you?" Emile ventured at his master.

Jean-Jacques had gone pale at the first sound of Danielle's voice. His hands gripped the nearest table for support.

"Mon dieu, how could that bitch have survived and come back here?" he muttered under his breath. Aloud her said, "Let's not be too hasty, Emile. Those barbarians are treacherous. Make sure it is indeed a woman before you let her in." He was simply playing for time, unable to admit that it was truly Danielle come home.

Danielle tried to peer through the window next to the big doors, when Emile's sallow face appeared between the drapes that had survived the torching.

"Emile!" she cried happily, glad to see a familiar face after all this time. "It is I, Danielle, let me in."

"What would you have me do, *monsieur*?"

Jean-Jacques waved his hand, his mouth turned down at the corners. "What else but let the lady in," he muttered sarcastically.

As soon as the bars were thrown back from the door, Danielle ran inside, stopping short at sight of Jean-Jacques. Hands on her hips, she asked coldly, "Why did you make me wait so long outside? You knew it was me, don't deny it!" Her flashing green eyes darted past her brother and scanned the familiar hall. Shock colored her voice. "We were raided," she stated the obvious. Her eyes wide, she stepped further into the hall, craning her head around and around, forgetting in her misery that the six Vikings were close on her heels, forgetting that she meant to berate Jean-Jacques for his boorish behavior.

"When did all this happen?" she whispered tearfully.

"Ha! The brutes have only left two days past," Jean-Jacques complained with a bitter edge to his voice. "We are lucky we were left with our lives and a few possessions, since the lout in charge was only interested in gold and silver. They tried to burn us down. Luckily, granite does not burn and there was not enough furniture to bother with."

Danielle's heart gave a funny lurch as she imagined that Talon might have been to her home and raided it two days earlier. She desperately wanted to know that it wasn't so. At the same time she became painfully aware that she needed to take care of Sweyn and his men. She certainly did not want to bring about more trouble.

Danielle bade Sweyn wait a moment, while she had a private conversation with her brother. Sweyn told his men sit on the ground, while he remained standing, his hand on his sword. Jean-Jacques threw a baleful glare at the Viking band and gingerly grabbed Danielle's elbow.

Disdainfully, Jean-Jacques sniffed the air. "You stink, sister mine! And pray tell what do you think you are doing by bringing these barbarians into our home?"

Danielle threw him a quelling glare. "I can well imagine that I stink after a gruesome voyage across the sea and these men, barbarians that they might be, brought me home. I promised them pay for their troubles and a few chickens and some staples to boot."

Jean-Jacques guffawed as if she had just told him the best joke he had ever heard. "Pray tell where am I to get the coin to pay for your passage? And why should I give them some of our fowl?"

Danielle drew herself up, her hands fisted at her slender sides. "I know we have the coin to pay and I know where they are kept! Nor will you succeed to cow me into subservience again. I had to suffer loneliness and despair at the cloister and had you come for me, when you had promised, I would not have been abducted by the Vikings." She could not bring herself to put the sole blame on Talon, although it was undeniably his doing alone.

Jean-Jacques drew back, surprised at the sudden fury Danielle unleashed upon him. There was a new hardness about his sister, a self-assurance that brooked no nonsense. He wisely backed off.

"'How much ransom are they asking?" Jean-Jacques inquired.

"They are not asking ransom, you foppish fool! They brought me back upon my own request. I bargained with the old man for my passage and if you knew the hardships of crossing the sea, you would not quibble about the price." Angered at his indifferent attitude, Danielle advanced upon Jean-Jacques and buried her hand in the folds of her brother's morning coat. "Pay him you fool!" she hissed, "or I cannot guarantee the consequences. You and I can squabble later, but let these men be on their way!"

Hesitantly, Jean-Jacques went back to the library, leaving Danielle behind to assure the Vikings that their pay was forthcoming. His hands shook with repressed fury. He had counted on the coins as his own once the nuns wrote that Vikings had abducted Danielle.

"Damn it all!" he muttered, "Leave it up to my dear sister to come away unscathed. Everywhere I went the Vikings raped the women and slit their throats. But not Danielle, oh no, she even finds a way of sweet-talking these barbarians to bring her home. Damn her!"

Jean-Jacques was glad that his sire had hidden his money in several different places about the manor. He pressed his stubby fingers against the center of one of the delicate wooden roses that adorned the mantel of the fireplace in an elegant garland pattern. A slim panel slid aside, then up and out of the way. Behind it lay a deep hollow that held silver and gold coins as well as several velvet boxes containing precious jewelry. Jean-Jacques reached for the coins, counted the exact amount and then hastened to slide the panel back in place again.

He sneered as he handed the coins to Danielle. "Here, settle your bargain and send them on their way. Their stench offends me as does their presence in my home."

Danielle counted the coins into Sweyn's hand. In the Norse tongue she thanked him for bringing her and promised to send Emile outside to settle the rest of their bargain.

"Emile!" she called with undisputed authority. "Please see to it that these men get the fowl and sacks of meal that I have promised. Just have one of the stable boys help you bring it to the front steps."

"Goodbye, Sweyn! May Odin watch over you on your voyage home."

Sweyn nodded his thanks, but as he turned to leave, he pinned her with a shrewd look. His voice was ever so soft, when he asked, "How does your sire fare, mistress?"

Danielle was taken aback for a fraction of a heartbeat, but then she smiled brightly at Sweyn, "He is in good hands, Sweyn!" Which was no lie.

Once the Vikings had left the hall, Danielle turned to see Jean-Jacques stare at her with malevolent eyes. "Save the color of your hair, you resemble those barbarians more than you might give yourself credit for. You even speak their harsh tongue."

Danielle tossed her dark tresses and advanced upon her brother. "How dare you of all people find fault with me or my appearance. You left me to my own devices. You had no intention of ever bringing me back from the nuns, did you?" she accused.

"How very astute of you, dear sister. Unfortunately, you did find your way back. Now I will be forced to devise another plan of getting you out of this manor."

"You will have a hard time doing that, dear brother. I'm no longer that shrinking little girl you dragged from these halls. I know how to defend myself and I am not above cutting your black heart from your bloated body," she spat. To prove her point, she lifted the dagger she carried at her side. "I know how to use this," she threatened, "and I will if I have to."

Danielle turned on her heel, leaving Jean-Jacques gaping after her. Summoning Emile, she softened her voice. "Please, see to it that I have a hot bath brought to my chambers."

Once inside her girlhood room, Danielle found that she was shaking like a leaf. Why had she come back? She had known all along that she would meet with resistance from Jean-Jacques. His change of personality had begun with the death of their father. Though she had denied it at the time, she could no longer ignore it. He did not jest when he spoke of ridding himself of her. Something changed him, made him almost desperate. She had to find out the why of it.

Jean-Jacques flung himself into the wing chair behind the ornate desk in the study. In his hand he held the ever-present goblet, but in his heart he plotted murder. He would not stand for the bitch to come back and ruin all his plans. He wanted everything, including her dowry. He had it within his grasp before that loutish Viking came and stole great quantities of the family silver. Jean-Jacques chuckled without humor. The barbarian had not gotten everything though. It had been worth it to grovel at the Viking's booted feet, because in the end he had believed that there was nothing more than those few coins, the goblets, and silverware. Maybe he could make Danielle believe as much.

CHAPTER FIFTEEN

Talon was in high spirits. The raids had gone as planned. The costly plunder they brought back would see them well through the winter. He was impatient to be reunited with Danielle. During the lonely nights, when they camped along the rivers, the vixen with the bright green eyes had haunted his dreams. Privately, he admitted that he wanted no other but her. Yet, he was unwilling to speak any words that would bind him to her. He shrugged. What choice did she have but stay with him? He smiled, smug with the knowledge that she was his for the keeping.

When the Raider dropped anchor at Herjolfstad, Talon's impatience knew no bounds. He urged his men to work faster and labored like a man possessed. Once the plunder was stored and the Raider anchored properly, Talon saddled Lucifer. With but a brief "I'll see you at Dragon's Lair," to Asgard and Leif, he leaned low over his horse's neck and rode out of the city. He stopped only long enough to rest the stallion and drink from a small rivulet that flowed in icy consistency down the mountain.

Talon's aquamarine eyes lit with pleasure, when he spied Dragon's Lair in the distance. His heart soared at the prospect that he would soon hold Danielle in his arms again. He had brought her a gift. Though she had never told him exactly what she wanted, he was sure that she would be delighted with the velvet gown of a color that would be a near match with her beautiful eyes.

Lucifer sensed his master's urgency and stretched his tired muscles to capacity in the quest to eat up the distance before them.

The stronghold seemed quiet as Talon approached it from the narrow path. He was troubled by the fact that Danielle had not met him on Sundevil as she had been wont to do of late, when he had returned from a day's hunt. Where was the wench? His gaze quickly searched the compound for any sign of the woman of his desire as he rode through the narrow portal.

Myra and Eloise came out of the main house and stood uncertainly gaping at their master.

Talon rode closer and peered down at the two slaves whose eyes slid away under his scrutiny. "Where is Danielle?" he asked silkily, careful to keep his mounting fury under control.The two women exchanged nervous looks, but then Myra stepped boldly forward. "She's gone, master!" Upon seeing his handsome visage cloud over with rage, she hastened to explain their innocence. "We tried to stop her. We told her you would go after her and bring her back in a neck chain," she added spitefully.

Talon sat motionless atop Lucifer, stunned by the girl's revelation. The light had gone out of his eyes and his heart beat painfully in his chest. She had left him. He found that hard to believe, but knowing Danielle, he could not discount the truth of it. Swallowing against the bile that rose in his throat he asked with deceptive calm. "When did she leave?"

"She left the very day you left, master!" whined Myra. And then it dawned on her that this might be the opportunity to better her own lot. She sidled up to Lucifer and ran her hand along Talon's bare thigh. Her brown eyes were hot with wanting as she lifted her gaze to Talon's. "I can make you forget all about her, master," she purred. "I know tricks to make you writhe with untold pleasure, master. I promise you won't miss her, if you let me warm your bed."

Talon stared at Myra as if she were a poisonous snake. Slapping her hand away from his thigh, he hissed, "Don't ever touch me unless I give you permission." Guiding Lucifer toward the stables, he vaulted from the saddle before the stallion came to a stop. He wanted no part of any other woman. He wanted Danielle.

Absentmindedly, he rubbed Lucifer down, his mind running in endless circles. He fed the horse and then he went to his quarters. Even as he entered the room, he knew that Danielle was gone. It was empty of her meager belongings and only a hint of her scent lingered in the air. Talon threw himself across his bed and pounded the furs with angry fists.

"Damn her! Damn her!" he screamed hoarsely into the wolf pelts and then realized that her scent clung to the bedding as well. It was at once tantalizing, as it was painful. He could not stand it. Her absence gnawed at his insides with a vengeance. How dare she leave him? How could she betray him like that? Angered, he flung himself from the bed and went to the storeroom. There he grabbed a small keg of ale. What he needed was a good draught to drown his misery. .

"May Loki be saddled with all women!" he toasted the empty room.

Myra and Eloise listened outside his door in somber silence. "Maybe we should not have told him right away that Danielle was gone."

"And what else would you have said, when he asked about her, Myra? The man is daft about her whether he admits it or not."

"We'll see just how daft he is. Just give him a chance to simmer down a bit. I'll show him how a real woman can make a man feel."

Eloise sneered at the other girl. "He won't let you near him, Myra. Forget it. And what about Asgard? What will you do about him?"

"Well, Talon can always send for another woman to satisfy that one. I for one would like to have the privileges the high and mighty Danielle enjoyed along with the master's prowess in bed … Asgard is well endowed, but I bet he can't compare to Talon."

Eloise gasped. "You are a wicked one, you are Myra! But I am willing to take you up. I bet you my comb that Talon won't allow you into his bed much less afford you the same privileges as he did Danielle. You had to be blind not to notice that she was special to him."

"We'll see, Eloise, we'll see."

Asgard and Leif arrived the next day. Talon's hasty departure from Herjolfstad had been the butt of their jokes during their ride toward Dragon's Lair. As they rode through the stone portal, Asgard grinned lewdly at Leif.

"Looks to me as if Talon is still rutting between the wench's legs to make up for all the time he missed," he chuckled.

Leif nodded in agreement, but his brow wrinkled in concern a moment later. "It is odd that no one seems about, don't you think? Eloise and Myra are not working at any tasks and the men are not to be seen anywhere either. Don't you find that strange?"

Asgard twisted around in his saddle and scanned the courtyard. "Aye, maybe they took their master's example and are somewhere in the stables rutting amongst themselves. On the other hand, what if someone has intruded on Dragon's Lair?"

The two friends rode cautiously toward the stables, dismounted, daggers and war axes in hand. They listened. All was quiet within.

"Ho, is anyone about? Asgard challenged, the hair on his nape rising with misgivings. The two male slaves hurried from the stables, sleep still clouding their eyes.

Asgard threw his reins at the first man. "What is going on here?" he demanded gruffly. "Why are you asleep at this time of day? Is something amiss?"

The slave bowed his head to avoid Asgard's inquisitive gaze. "We weren't asleep," he argued vehemently. "We were mending harness, we were."

Asgard snorted his disbelief. "Where are the women?"

"Don't know. Haven't seen much of them, since yesterday."

Asgard and Leif exchanged questioning glances, knowing the slaves would not tell them anything for fear of reprisal. Worried, they hurried into the main house. All was ominously quiet. Further alarmed, the two men yelled for Talon to make himself known.

Talon opened the door to his room, looking haggard with a day's growth of beard, unsteady on his feet. Under his eyes were deep hollows. His usual hearty tan had a sickly tinge to it.

Asgard gaped at his friend in unabashed astonishment. He stepped nearer, peering suspiciously into his face.

"What happened to you? You look sick." His question was filled with concern.

Talon battled to focus his sight on his friend, but his blood-shot eyes would not quite obey his befuddled brain's command. He tried a lopsided grin to lessen his plight, only to fail miserably.

"Had a few draughts of ale, Asgard," he stumbled across his

words and nearly lost his balance in the bargain, when he tried to emphasize his explanation with a wave of his hand.

"I'd say you had a few too many, my friend," countered Asgard and quickly closed the space between them. He was just in time to catch Talon before he fell.

"You are too drunk to even stand, Talon!" he rebuked his friend. "In Loki's name, what in hell is going on here? Why are you drinking yourself into oblivion?"

"Get her out of my mind ... I will ... just another little drink ... she'll be gone forever...." babbled Talon as Asgard lowered him to his bed.

Asgard was fast loosing patience. He grasped Talon's shoulders and shook him roughly. "What in the name of Odin are you trying to say?"

"Danielle is gone ... gone ... won't be back," Talon groaned.

"Where has she gone to?" Asgard asked perplexed. He shrugged broad shoulders as he exchanged a puzzled look with Leif.

Talon rolled on his stomach and turned his head toward the wall. "Don't know. Don't care. Women are all the same. Deceiving, lying bitches. Make you believe they care for you and then poof! they run out on you. Gone without a hint or a word."

"Are you saying that Danielle has escaped?"

Talon nodded mutely without turning his head.

Asgard sat on the edge of the bed. "Do you know where she has gone?"

"No! And I don't care," was the muffled answer.

Leif entered the conversation for the first time. "If you don't care, why then are you drinking yourself senseless?"

Talon did not answer, but rolled over to fix Leif with a baleful glare. Leif only shrugged, nettled that Talon, the great warrior, would allow himself to turn into a maudlin drunkard because some wench had run off.

"So you don't know how long ago she left?" Asgard muttered impatiently. "For all we know she could be dead by now or at the very least in the hands of another Viking tribe."

Talon jerked up from his prone position, then sank back just as quickly, holding his head in both hands. "By Thor, my head thunders as if he'd used it instead of his hammer!" he moaned. "She ran away the day I left for Herjolfstad," he finally roared, suddenly in full command of his senses again.

Asgard left and bellowed for Myra. The maid came running from the direction of the stream, where she and Eloise were idling the day away. Breathless she skidded to a halt before Asgard and stared up at him with wanton eyes. Sliding her hands suggestively along her ribcage and pushing her breasts invitingly in his direction, she purred, "I have missed you sorely, master Asgard. Is there something special you want of me?" She allowed the question to hang in the air.

Asgard licked his lips, feeling himself going hard and hot at the sight of her. Momentarily forgetting his reason for calling her, he reached out to cup a plump breast. His eyes devoured her hungrily, but then he remembered why he had called her and dropped his hand as if he had burned it.

He saw the disappointment in her face and grinned. "Don't worry wench. You are a sight for a starving man's eyes. I promise I'll plow you so hard and fast that you'll scream for mercy ... just as soon as I can tell Talon where Danielle has gone."

Myra wrinkled her nose in distaste. "Oh, that one. She left the day her master left. Saddled Sundevil and set off, saying she wasn't going to be no slave to no man ever. I told her he'd come after her and bring her back on a neck chain." There was malice in her voice and Asgard frowned.

"I never knew you to be such a bloodthirsty wench, Myra. Do you happen to know which way she went?"

"Me and Eloise watched her from the ramparts and it looked like she was heading North."

"Good! Is there anything else you might remember?"

Myra shook her head and boldly reached for Asgard's crotch. "I'll be waiting for you to keep your promises, master. Should I go to your pallet already?"

"Greedy wench!" Asgard laughed. "I have no idea what Talon will do, but until I find out, you might as well go about your own duties. I'll find you." He fondled her breast in farewell before he hurried back to report to Talon.

"If she left the day you did and has not found shelter or stumbled upon another village, you might as well give up on her, Talon. Our Norse country is not forgiving. She has few skills to survive on her own and aside from marauding tribes there are wolves and bear." Asgard shook his mane regretfully. "I don't think you would find her alive if you cared to search for her."

Talon sat on the edge of his bed, still bleary-eyed and very much subdued. He wagged his massive head. "I can't understand why she would run off. I was good to her. She had everything a wench might want. I even bought those two women out yonder, so they could ease her lot. What more could she have wanted?"

"Myra made mention that Danielle said she would be no slave to any man. Didn't you say she once told you she was high-born?"

"Ah yes, but what does have to do with anything? I was good to her. I never beat her and I allowed her to go with me wherever I went."

"Who knows what women think. I have it on good authority that you treated her well, better than any other man would have, and this is the thanks you get."

Talon was already off on another tangent. "I want the wench back!" he railed, his brows coming together in an angry scowl. "She took Sundevil, you say?"

"So Myra said. I am surprised the horse has not come back ... If something happened to the wench, wouldn't you think Sundevil would return to you?"

"Unless something happened and the gelding was lost as well," Talon expanded on the idea.

"It is up to you if you want to follow her. Leif and I will go with you, naturally."

Talon stood up, still a little wobbly, but quite alert now that he had made his mind up to track Danielle. Crossly, he called for a cup of hot mead and once he had swallowed the brew, he felt better.

"Let's not waste time, Asgard. There are several hours of daylight left yet and we might as well get going."

Asgard frowned. He had envisioned spending the night between Myra's soft thighs, not on hard ground, taking turns at standing watch.

Adrenaline rushed through him in anticipation of the search. His buzzing head completely forgotten, Talon raced about like a man possessed, yelling orders, while piling supplies to take along. With a weary eye to the sky, he finally announced that it was time to leave.

His reluctant friends mounted their horses and followed Talon out of Dragon's Lair. Talon saw no need to waste time on tracking. Now that he thought it over rationally, the wench had to have gone North. She would have traveled through Herjolfstad, had she taken a Southern route. She was too shrewd to risk that.

It rankled his ego that she would rather forfeit her life than spend it with him. Was being a slave so appalling to her that she would rather die? Talon's thoughts chased each other as he rode grimly along the winding, rocky path that followed the delineation of the sea.

"We'll make camp as soon as the sun sets," he called over his shoulder. "Then we will be well rested by early morn. By midday tomorrow we'll begin to track."

Asgard shifted uneasily in his saddle. "Do you really think you will find a trace of her having passed this way, Talon? It's been a week."

Talon grunted sourly. "She is but a wench. She will be careless about leaving signs."

Before noon the next day, Talon had found the place Danielle used to shelter for the first night. "These horse droppings are not so old yet and the horse was grain fed, you see. Once in the open she would have to let him graze to survive. There are no other signs of additional mounts. And who else but a fool would ride through this wilderness by themselves?" he asked sarcastically, though deep inside him there ignited a new spark of hope that he would find her alive.

He would tan her hide, he thought savagely, as Lucifer's hooves devoured mile after mile.

When the Viking village came into view, Talon knew almost with a certainty that he would find Danielle there. He spurred Lucifer, leaving Asgard and Leif way behind.

"No need to race our horses to that settlement, Leif. If she is there, Talon might like a private moment."

Leif snickered, "I sure would not like to be in that wench's boots, because I have a feeling that Talon will tan her hide so thoroughly that she might have to ride back on her belly. She certainly has him tied into knots."

"I don't remember ever having seen Talon act like this over any wench. I can't say that I blame him. I myself would gladly give a king's ransom to spend one night between her lissome thighs. She stirs a man's blood and those green eyes of hers bespeak a rare passion. Aye, I can easily see what's gotten into Talon, now that I truly think about it."

"Why, Asgard, I've never heard you wax so poetically. Why you might turn into a good storyteller yet in your old age," Leif teased and received a nasty blow to the upper arm for his trouble.

The two men rode into the village in time to see Talon walking in the company of an old, white-haired man toward what appeared to be the main house.

Sweyn smiled at Talon. "I have heard much about you, Talon Herjolfson. It does an old man good to be able to lay eyes on such a renowned warrior." He raised his hands palm upward in abject lament. "Your wife mate told me that you were away on yet another raid. I envy you your youth and strength. I am too old to forage afar and there are not enough young men in the village to lend a strong arm." He inclined his head, "I hope your journey proved successful."

"Did you say my wife mate told you I was on a raid?" Sweyn totally missed Talon's sarcastic tone of voice when he repeated the words wife mate.

"Aye! And a beauty she is." He punched Talon playfully in the ribs. "I am surprised that you took so many days to retrieve her mount. She asked me to keep him for you and that you would pay me for his fodder."

Talon was seething inside, but he kept his temperament in careful check. The minx had just about thought of everything. Just where was she? He glanced surreptitiously about the compound in hopes to glimpse her from afar. What manner of games are they playing here with me, he thought bitterly.

Talon entered Sweyn's hut and was assailed by the fetid fishy smell of it. His eyes took in the poor furnishings, but he never betrayed his inner feelings. It occurred to him, however, that he was indeed lucky to be as well off as he was. Gingerly, he sat down on one of the low stools by the hearth, bracing one elbow on his knee, while he waited for Sweyn to continue his chitchat.

"So have you word from your wife mate how things are faring with her sire?" Sweyn asked innocently. "I was so pleased to see one so young be so concerned about the old ones."

Talon choked down his surprise at the old man's words. What was he prattling about Danielle's sire? Feverishly, he racked his brain in an effort to recall, whether she had told him that her sire had passed on some time before she had been sent to the nuns. He brightened visibly, when it came to him that she had.

Leaning toward Sweyn, he stared into the rheumy eyes of the old man. "What exactly did she tell you of her sire?" he asked with deceptive calm, his own aquamarine gaze carefully shaded by thick golden lashes, lowered just enough to hide his true feelings.

"Well, she told me she could not wait for your return, that her sire was in dire need of her care and would I take her to him. She promised me good coin, once I delivered her safely." Gleefully, Sweyn slapped his knee and cackled in remembered mirth. "And pay up she did, despite that uppity fop, who tried to bar her from her own home." He clapped Talon's shoulder with admiration. "A rare beauty you've got there, Talon Herjolfson, and a smart one as well. Never complained once during the crossing."

Talon swallowed hard against the fury that built inside him. The wench had outfoxed him, had made a fool of him and somehow he had better find a way to extract himself from this situation with some of his pride still intact.

Talon stood up and scratched his chest beneath his woolen tunic and then he stifled a fake yawn.

"When did you say she came to your for help, Sweyn. You see, she must have received word right after I left and she must have been quite desperate to go looking for help."

"Aye! Now that I think of it, she was quite anxious to get going. My crew and I just returned but two days ago."

Sweyn sensed that there was something amiss with Talon, since the man seemed preoccupied with some inner thoughts he was not about to share. He wanted no problems from the mighty warrior and in retrospect he wondered if he had done the proper thing by taking the man's wife mate back to her own kin. He shrugged inwardly. If truth be told he had done it for the coin. He was a poor man and as he had told Talon, no longer capable of making his living by the sword. He stared silently at Talon, waiting for that one to take up the conversation again.

"So you say you took her to her kin and went with her to receive your pay?"

Sweyn nodded eagerly, glad that the huge man was not angry over his actions. "By Odin, I did! And a big house of stone it was. Has windows such as I have rarely seen. We approached it from the river Seine, but it abuts on the North Sea."

Talon took careful note of Sweyn's description. He knew that he had not enough to go on by a long shot.

"Did I hear you mention this was on the East of the river Seine?"

"Oh, it lay on the West side and it was but a few leagues after we entered the mouth of the Seine."

Talon scratched his head. It sounded almost like the manor he had raided. The owner certainly had been a fop and a coward on top of it. Talon sneered as he recalled how that man had cringed in a corner and begged for them to leave him alone. He shook his head in derision. No, Danielle would not have kin so yellow bellied. She was made of sturdy stuff. She never would have given by meekly. His chest puffed with remembered quarrels. She always stood her ground against him, although he would not let her forget that she was but a slave and he the master.

"I wonder if my men have arrived yet? My stallion craved a faster ride than their mounts and so I rode ahead," he lied. No need to let Sweyn in on the fact that he had hoped to find Danielle present.

When Sweyn and Talon strode outside, Asgard and Leif were dismounted and leaned idly against their lathered horses. Their brows shot up in unasked questions and Talon glared at them in mute warning. Waving a large hand in Sweyn's direction, he forced himself to speak with calm indifference.

"Sweyn here tells me that my..." he almost choked on the words and his square jaw jutted in silent challenge, "Sweyn told me that my wife mate hired him to take her back to her kin. You see, her sire had fallen ill and needed her care."

Asgard lowered his gaze and found much to admire about the toes of his boots, while Leif was taken with a sudden fit of coughing that forced him to bury his face in his horse's mane. It took both men a great deal of time before they faced Talon with bland expressions that were a credit to their acting abilities.

"You say your, ah, wife mate hired Sweyn here to take her to her kin, Talon?" Asgard asked in feigned concern. "And did he say when she is planning to return?"

Talon seized upon the small straw that Asgard unwittingly threw his way.

"Did she tell you to return for her at a specific time, Sweyn?"

Sweyn turned a puzzled frown toward Talon and shrugged in clear confusion. "The mistress gave me no instructions to come back for her. I thought you would collect her in good time yourself, Talon Herjolfson. I served only as a means to get her there, since time seemed precious and you were on your raid." Sweyn did not like the way this conversation was going. He did not want to become embroiled in a domestic quarrel. He did the only thing, which came to mind.

"Let me go and get the lady's mount for you. You will see that we kept our word to care for the animal. I don't even expect coin for his care, since your wife mate has paid me handsomely already." Sweyn grinned up at Talon, pleased with himself, then quickly disappeared in the direction of the stables. And not a minute too soon as far as Asgard and Leif were concerned.

They grinned snidely at Talon and then guffawed as they clapped each other on the back. "Gee! Will wonders never cease?" Tears of mirth ran down the men's cheeks as they twisted about in unrestrained glee. "The wife mate surely played you for a fool, didn't she?"

Talon stepped threateningly closer to his two friends and glowered at them. "Stop your silly blathering. I had quite enough strain upon my temperament already. If I had the wench before me I would slit her throat for playing me for the buffoon." He beat his chest with both fists. His generous lips pulled back in anger from the even line of white teeth. "I am a warrior, a man of honor and feared by my enemies," he ground out from between gritted teeth. "I will not stand for this insult."

Asgard chuckled. He knew that Talon could beat him in a fair fight, but that he would not attack him here or now. He was simply furious as any man would if he he'd been duped by a mere female. Emboldened by this reasoning, Asgard decided to speak his mind.

"Admit already that she got the better of you, Talon. She is a fetching baggage and one with brains to boot. She holds you by the short hairs ... always has ... even from the very beginning. Either that or you are going soft in your old age, my friend. You had every opportunity to slit her throat, but you never did. It's up to you to come to terms with that."

Sweyn opportunely interrupted Asgard's discourse by bringing Sundevil around. The Palomino snorted his greeting as he recognized Talon. He was saddled, and shirred with the best braided leather reins his stable had to offer, Talon noted grimly, as he ran an appraising hand across the gelding's flanks. He grudgingly admitted to himself that there was more to Danielle than a pretty pair of legs and a supple body to warm his bed. As Sweyn handed him Sundevil's reins, Talon pressed several coins into the old man's hand.

"You did a creditable job of keeping the gelding and I thank you. If I have ever use of your services again, I'll let you know."

"Won't you stay for a small repast or a cup of brew?" Sweyn offered, though he hoped these men would ride away as fast as they had come. He had sensed the underlying tension among the three as he had walked toward them with the gelding and he would just as soon not have to deal with any trouble from them.

Talon shook his head. "Thank you, Sweyn, but we had best be on our way." Already his mind was on the voyage he was planning.

CHAPTER SIXTEEN

Talon rode Lucifer hard as they left the compound, occupied by a variety of thoughts. Damn Danielle. He was not sure whether he was more relieved that the wench was safe than he was angry that she had escaped. One thing he knew with a certainty. He wanted her back. She was his and he aimed to keep her.

Asgard and Leif slowly caught up with Talon once he reined Lucifer in to an easy canter. Talon knew they would not indulge his pride, they would demand to know the whole story. He needed their help, since he aimed to go after Danielle. Nothing and no one would stop him.

The two friends saw the inner battle Talon fought with himself and despite his anticipation of their ridicule they did not snigger when he asked them to help him.

"I am not sure why I want to go after the wench, when it is so obvious that she wanted to get away from me," he mused aloud. "I am not even sure if I can find her according to the sketchy description Sweyn gave me, but I intend to give it my best."

"Why didn't you ask Sweyn straight out to come along?" asked Leif, ever the practical one among them.

Talon favored his friend with a sour look. "Never! I can't let that Viking in on my troubles after he praised my battle prowess as well as my good judgment in choosing such a beauty." He spit onto the path as if he could rid himself of the bitter taste that thought left behind.

"How many grand manors can there be along the Seine?" he scoffed. "And Sweyn mentioned that it was only a couple of leagues from the mouth of the river and to the West of it. I promise I make it worth your time. While we search for the wench, we simply raid the manors we come across until we find her. How does that sound to you?"

"It is as good a plan as I'd expect a befuddled mind to come up with," Asgard replied with a straight face and laughing eyes.

Talon wheeled Lucifer around and rode up to his friend. "When we make camp for the night, I claim the right to challenge you to a fist fight," he snarled.

Asgard grinned at him, but could not keep from mocking him further. "What if your handsome face is marred by my fists? How do you think the fair Danielle will like that, I pray?"

"Just wait and see whose visage will be scarred after this night. It's time I showed you who is in charge here," Talon threatened, although his voice betrayed a hint of elation. He relished the thought of the forthcoming tussle. There was a great deal of pent-up frustration inside him.

Talon barely took time to hobble Lucifer and see to his needs, once they made camp for the night before he challenged Asgard to the promised fist fight. Not to be outdone, Asgard tossed Leif the reins of his mount so as not to waste time. The two men quickly stripped their tunics and stood but clad in leggings and cross-gartered boots, both spoiling for that fight.

Talon threw the first punch, but Asgard was quick to fend it off with his forearm, only to jab at Talon's prominent jaw. It was a game they were both proficient at and one they enjoyed to the fullest. Only this particular round of fisticuffs had turned into a serious challenge.

"When I am through with you, I want to see you groveling at my feet, you babbling cur." Talon growled as he punched Asgard squarely in the ribs.

Asgard reciprocated with a punch to Talon's cheek that left an instant bruise behind. Dancing out of Talon's long reach, he grinned his appreciation of the damage he had inflicted. "Had enough yet?" he taunted.

Talon charged him with murder in his blue eyes. "Only when I see you bite the dust, traitor," he grunted and caught Asgard with a vicious uppercut to the chin.

Asgard staggered under the brutal onslaught and went down on one knee. Talon saw his advantage and closed in quickly.

"Enough, you fighting cocks!" shouted Leif, "You both had a good shot at the other and I say that is enough. If you plan to sail once we get back to Dragon's Lair then you better stop right now." He stood with legs braced apart, his fists balled at his lean hips. "As it is, you both got your pound of flesh and by the morrow you each will have the bruises to prove it. I say let it be and let's all get some rest."

Talon was not about to give up so readily, but Asgard held up a fending hand. "He's right, you know. We need our wits about us. Any time we sail the seas, we need all the strength we can muster should a storm catch us unawares." He stuck out his hand and Talon grasped it warmly. Grinning sheepishly, he wagged his head. "Leif is right as usual, but it was a good fight, wasn't it?"

"Aye, it was good fight, but now I could eat yonder horse." Asgard chuckled. Talon joined in after only a moment's hesitation, and soon the three friends were roaring with inane laughter, the tension that haunted them the past days broken.

"I could easily eat a horse myself and I didn't even misuse my energy like you two fighting roosters. Thanks to the both of you it is too dark to hunt. We'll have to do with the dried meat and provisions we brought." Leif chided the two as if they were but small boys. They drew straws for the first watch. It fell to Leif. Talon and Asgard wrapped themselves into their wolf' pelts and went to sleep as their fire slowly turned to embers.

A pale sun was still struggling to scale the horizon when Talon saddled Lucifer. He'd drawn the last watch and was raring to go. The black stallion snorted his impatience, sensing his master's urgency.

Asgard and Leif grumbled at the early hour, but nimbly jumped to their feet and soon the small party was on its way back to Dragon's Lair. Little was said along the route. They stopped only long enough to relieve themselves and let the horses graze and drink. They ate as they traveled.

When they arrived back at Talon's stronghold, their exhaustion was evident. Myra and Eloise, their faces full of curiosity, were on hand to greet the weary men.

"You did not find your slave, master?" Myra asked, feigning disappointment

Talon glared balefully at the curious woman. "No, we did not find her," he huffed and left her standing.

Myra was hardly cowed by his brusque manner. She didn't care one iota about the haughty chit, in fact she had hoped they would either bring her back at the end of a chain or find her dead along the way. It would serve that arrogant bitch right. Well, if the master refused to satisfy her curiosity, there were other ways to find out what she wanted to know. With a smug little smile, she sidled up to Asgard and with a furtive glance to check if no one was looking she groped his crotch.

Asgard jumped in surprise, but his manhood responded

instantly to her questing touch. He grinned hotly into her wanton eyes.

"I see you missed me as sorely as I have missed you, wench!" he noted huskily." Turning her toward the stables, he gave her a light shove. "Go find us a likely bale of hay and be ready for a good plowing. I am in sore need of loosing myself inside your man-pleasing warmth."

Myra giggled coyly and with a lewd wink at Asgard, she hurried into the dimness of the stables. Asgard followed quickly behind and without preamble his hands worked roughly on her clothing. Myra stayed his feverish movement and asked crossly if he meant but to use her for his own pleasure.

"I am in no mood to play your games, wench. Now spread your legs and let me enter," he growled. "You are the one who wakened my rod with your lewd fondling and now it wants to be appeased. When I have slaked its ravenous hunger and had a bit of rest, I might feel inclined to go a little slower the second time, but do not push me too far. You are mine to do with as I please and it pleases me just now to plow you hard and fast."

Myra dared not protest. Asgard was a moody one and she knew it. He could be tender one moment and barbaric the next. She let him have his way, but it was a bitter draught to swallow. When Asgard rolled away from her with a grunt of satisfaction, he playfully slapped her bare rump. "You've been a good girl, Myra," he chuckled, "Next time don't tease a man who's gone without the warmth of a wench too long."

Myra remembered that she had meant to ask him about Danielle's fate, but she no longer cared to know. Straightening her clothes, she made to leave, but Asgard's long arm snaked out and pulled her back. "Not so fast, my pigeon. I am but getting my second wind and I promise to pleasure you this time as well." Mollified, Myra sank back to the hay.

It was not long after Asgard had availed himself of Myra a second time that Talon's voice rang in the courtyard and he seemed in none too good a mood. Asgard rose reluctantly and walked outside, slowly adjusting his clothing as he did so.

Talon favored him with a sneer. "I should have known that I could find you between Myra's thighs. I hope you have taken the sharp edge off your sexual appetite, because I aim to ride for Herjolfstad early on the morrow."

Asgard chuckled. "If you are feeling frisky yourself, the wench is yours to do with as you please. It certainly might help to put you in a better mood. You have done nothing but snap at us, since you found that Danielle had flown the coop."

Talon was about to answer Asgard with another cutting remark, when he thought better of it and choked his anger down. He would need Asgard's help and they had been friends far too long than to let anything get in the way. Suddenly, Asgard's suggestion seemed like a good idea. He grinned hugely at his friend and headed for the stables.

Myra was busy adjusting her tunic and was running her fingers through the tangle of her mousy brown hair. She was startled to see Talon approach with a purposeful gleam in his blue eyes. A small shiver of anticipation coursed through her body and she subconsciously cupped her breasts in brazen invitation.

"Is there naught you are looking for, master?" she asked with faked innocence as she batted short spiky lashes at him.

Talon studied the offered fare and was inwardly shocked that his body did not immediately respond to Myra's temptation. Perplexed, he took another step closer and dipped his hand into the neck of her tunic to capture one of the ripe globes. He almost recoiled, because the flesh was neither as soft nor the breast as firm as he remembered Danielle's to be. He shook himself inwardly. He would have Myra, if for no other reason than to prove that Danielle meant little to nothing to him.

Talon closed the space between them and brought his lips down on Myra's in a half-hearted kiss. Myra did not notice. She stretched to her toes and leaned her supple curves against the hard length of him, grinding her rounded hips against the soft bulge of his manhood. Her arms circled his neck and she plied her mouth arduously upon his offered lips, her tongue teasing and seeking in an effort to increase his interest.

Talon tried hard to concentrate on the wench. The smell of her recent coupling with Asgard stung his nostrils. Try as he might, his manhood would not react to the girl's eager ministrations. With an exasperated grunt he pushed Myra away.

"It is no use, girl, I guess I am simply too fatigued or preoccupied to make use of your body." He shook his head and turned to leave.

Myra's fingers plucked on his sleeve. Her head tilted coquettishly to one side, she fixed him with hungry eyes. "I can come to your chambers after you have rested!" she offered hopefully.

Talon shook his head again. "Nay, I do need my rest, since we are leaving before sun-up. I'll do my wenching once I reach Herjolfstad."

Myra's face contorted into an ugly grimace and she stuck out her tongue once Talon turned his back. So, the virile Viking was not so manly after all, she thought spitefully. She could hardly wait for the chance to tell Eloise that the mighty Talon, Viking warrior and master of Dragon's Lair, couldn't even raise his manhood to impale a willing wench. Smugly, she tossed her limp tresses and flounced out of the stables.

As the day wore on, Talon grew progressively morose. He went to his chamber and lay down on the wide bed. Longingly, he buried his nose in the furs and breathed the faint scent that was Danielle's very own.

"Witch," he muttered. "You have bedeviled me so that I cannot bed another wench. You vex me sorely, Danielle," he complained bitterly into the emptiness of the room, "and when I find you, you will pay dearly for causing me so much pain."

Talon decided not get up to take his evening meal with Asgard and Leif. He pleaded fatigue and general malaise.

"Talon has gone soft. I almost wish he wouldn't find the French witch. She has him wound around her finger and he doesn't even see through her ploy."

"Which ploy is that, Asgard? I am not sure I follow your train of thought."

"Why ... I," stuttered Asgard, "I don't rightly know myself what she is after, but I can tell you one thing for certain. The wench is not content to be a slave, even though Talon has given her more freedom than slaves are usually allotted. Why, he asks little more than that she pleasure him in bed."

"Did Talon not tell us once that she is a high-born lady? Would that not be cause enough for her not to be doing slave chores? If not for Talon, she might be wed to a Frenchman of her own kind and live a life of luxury."

"What has gotten into you, Leif? If I didn't know any better, I could think that you have eyes for the wench yourself."

Leif shrugged eloquently, "Can you blame a man for casting his sights toward one so lovely as her? Her eyes are the color of Spring moss and her hair is like a silken curtain of midnight sky."

Asgard stared at his friend. "By Odin, you are smitten by her." He leaned closer and lowered his voice. "I give you one piece of advice my friend. If you value your friendship with Talon and even more, if you value your life, don't ever tell him in so many words how you behold Danielle or he will surely castrate you!"

Leif glared at Asgard. "I remember your having said much the same about Danielle," he snarled. "You know as well as I that there is no harm in looking at her. She has never so much as given us reason to believe that she harbors any interest in either of us."

Asgard sprang from his seat and buried his hammy fist in Leif's tunic front. "You silly cur! Curb that loose tongue of yours or I'll cut it from its moorings. You prattle like an old woman. Right from the beginning Talon has made no bones about it that he did not mean to share this particular woman, despite the fact that we are wont to share our females, even if we are wed to them. The French woman knows that, too, and I have my suspicions that she played that knowledge to her advantage. She meant to gain Talon's complete favor, because her main concern was her freedom. Had Talon treated her like the slave she is, he would have tethered her to his bed in his absence to make sure that she would still be there when he returned."

"Aye, if he had done that, I could just imagine her joy upon his return. She would probably bury her eating dagger in his heart when he was sleeping, not that I would blame her. What has all that rhetoric to do with the fact that she has never glanced your way?"

Asgard snorted derisively. "I see that she has turned your head indeed. Your mind has gone soft. As to your question, it has everything to do with what I was talking about. She refused to play up to me, because she planned to trick Talon and trick him she did. Now, the poor besotted fool is going to do his damnedest to get her back. And for what, I ask? Why won't he look for a willing wench? Before he met the French woman he had plenty of women warm his bed. Surely, there was one among them which could capture his fancy."

"Danielle was more than a romp between the sheets for him, Asgard!" Leif shouted angrily. "She was saucy and she was bright. She could speak two tongues and was mature beyond her years. Remember how well she duped Sweyn! She even learned enough of our tongue to command the old Viking to take her many leagues across the sea to an unknown destination." He leaned across the table, holding onto the sides with white-knuckled fury and jutted his chin forward at a belligerent angle.

Not to be outdone, Asgard jumped to his feet and brought his own visage within inches of that of his friend. "Which brings me to the fact that I think the woman is a witch!" he roared. "There is no other wench who knows as much as she. By Loki ... there are few men who know as much," he admitted in wonder. And as if that admission had taken all the fight out of him, he frowned at nothing in particular and plopped heavily back on his seat.

Talon burst from his room, his previous problems forgotten, he appraised his two friends with an anxious stare. "What's eating you two?" he questioned with rancor. "Can't a man stew in peace and quiet? Your shouting would wake the dead. Pray tell why are you at odds with each other?"

Leif pointed an accusing finger at Asgard, while Asgard glowered at Leif. "It's his fault!" they shouted in unison.

Talon's generous mouth lifted in a lopsided grin. "You sound like two spoiled brats." He approached the table and grabbed a chair. With studied nonchalance he straddled it and glanced from one friend to the other. "Let's have it and don't hold back. Somehow I have this strange feeling that I am at the bottom of your disagreement and we best lay our problems on the table before we embark on a long sea voyage." He shook his head. "We can't have differences dividing us, when our very lives depend on trusting each other once we reach the open sea ... Who wants to go first?"

Leif stared with unconcealed enmity at Asgard. Waving a dismissing hand, he hissed, "Why not let him go first. All he does is shout me down anyway."

Talon could see that he had his work cut out for him. He chuckled, though there was no cheer in the sound. "I can't believe we are grown men with the same goals and beliefs in life." Again he shook his head, sending his flaxen mane flying with the vehemence of it. He pulled a coin from the pouch at his waist and tossed it into the air. "Call it Asgard." Asgard chose the face of the coin and won.

"Okay, you start and Leif and I will listen without interruption. Then it will be Leif's turn and you will allow him the same courtesy." He pierced them with a quelling stare. "Agreed?"

Asgard was momentarily silent, trying to collect his thoughts. He seemed to have found a sudden affinity for the shape of his hands as he studied them with great care. His eyes did not meet Talon's questioning gaze. "I feel that you should abandon your quest to find the French wench," he blurted. "She is no good and will only come between us. I contend that she is not happy with being a slave and that she will continue to make trouble once you succeed in bringing her back. You would be better served to find a Viking maid to warm your bed." He lifted his eyes to Talon and there was a defiant gleam in their depths.

"And what are your feelings about this matter, Leif?" Talon asked calmly as if Asgard's angry words had no effect upon him.

"I actually agree with Asgard, though there are some differences of opinion about the wench. I don't think she is a bad influence, but I do agree that she would not be happy with being a slave. She is no simple woman like Myra or Eloise. There is an iron will beneath her satin skin."

Talon raised a golden brow. "Ho! Hold on my friend. How would you know of her satin skin, I pray?" He half lifted off his seat and his jaw jutted out in acute irritation. He gripped the table with his huge fists to keep himself from connecting them to Leif's jaw, but the agitated way in which his chest rose and fell, left little doubt to his true feelings.

Leif held up his hands and grinned engagingly, "You are too touchy about the wench, Talon. I only surmised by the looks of her."

Talon sat down heavily and there was a telltale tick beneath his eye that bespoke of his aggravation being barely held in check.

"I see you two have made yourself my judge and jury and my guardians to boot." He leaned forward and rested both elbows on the table. "Well, let me tell you something. I do as I please!" he roared at them and then leaned back again, breathing deeply and his eyes took on a faraway look. "I don't know myself how I feel about this wench. I am seething inside that she had the gall to leave whilst I was away. Even you have to admit that she is a clever wench, considering what lengths she went through to escape." He buried his massive head in his hands and spoke through the screen of his fingers. "I guess I want to confront her. Show her that she can't run from me. Show her--" Talon faltered and let the sentence die away. "I guess I want to prove to myself that I don't need her," he finished quietly, all the fight gone from his voice.

Asgard and Leif stared at each other and then back at Talon. They shrugged. What more was there to say? Of course there was always hope that Talon would find a suitable substitute and truly purge her from his mind. Asgard and Leif stood up, raising their tankards of ale.

"To a successful raid! Praise be Odin and that He watches over us! Valhalla and glory!" they roared into the still night.

The morning had long dawned before any of the three men was able to leave his bed. Talon and Asgard actually looked worse than they felt, since the bruises from their fight two days prior showed vividly against the pallor of their visages.

CHAPTER SEVENTEEN

Danielle awoke to sunshine refracting through the multi-colored panes of her windows. Sleepily, without opening her eyes, she reached across the bed and was surprised when her hand came away empty. Talon must have gone already she thought with acute disappointment. It puzzled her that he should rise without their usual morning romp. Her body clamored for his touch ... and then she sat up in abrupt comprehension. She was no longer at Dragon's Lair, but at home at Honfleur-sur-mer.

Danielle hugged herself happily for a brief moment. "Home," she sighed. Home again at last and nobody will ever take me away again, she promised herself with conviction. She climbed from her bed and went to the window, throwing it open to the crisp late summer morning. The breeze carried a whiff of salt air with it and Danielle was assailed by a sudden sharp pang of loss. Tossing her ebony mane in defiance she turned away from the window, no longer interested in the scenery below or the tangy morning breeze. She stopped in front of the precious silvered looking glass and stared critically at her own countenance. Making a face at herself, she stripped off her lawn nightdress and postured naked before the mirror.

Languidly, she ran her slender hands along her lean ribs and then allowed them to move upward to cup her breasts. Unbidden thoughts and sensations ran through her as soon as her fingers closed about the tender globes. Her mind conjured the image of Talon doing the very same thing to her, evoking strange urges and throbbing deep within her secret being. She gasped as the coil of passion in her loins became almost unbearable in its intensity. Her hand flew to the spot trying to quell with its touch this disturbing pulsation. She swallowed hard against the surging desire and wished that Talon could be here to soothe her ache.

Her mind seized upon that thought and her body responded

with breath robbing sensations. Automatically, her hand stroked into the hot wet dampness in imitation of Talon's caresses, as her knees threatened to buckle beneath her.

The door to her chamber suddenly flew open without any prior warning. Jean-Jacques stopped short with one hand still on the door handle. A lascivious chuckle burst from his fleshy lips.

Danielle froze in mid-movement, her hand stilled amid her dark curls. A telltale crimson colored her throat up to the very edge of her hairline.

"I see that you enjoyed your sojourn to the land of the barbarians," he sneered in obvious delight at her predicament. He deliberately closed the door behind him and advanced slowly toward his sister. He leered at her, his hungry gaze never leaving her delectable curves.

"I never knew what treasures you kept hidden beneath your fashionable gowns." His hand crept to his crotch and Danielle's eyes were inexorably drawn to the growing bulge at the junction of his legs. She swallowed her fear and snatched up her lawn gown to cover her nudity.

Jean-Jacques advanced within a foot of her and chuckled. "We could help each other, *ma petite*," he cajoled. "Since you are breached it will make little difference who follows the initial path. I am sure I could pleasure you better than your former lover. Or has it been several lovers, *ma chérie*?" He waved his pale hand in unconcerned dismissal, "No matter. It is obvious that you crave a man's attention and I will be happy to provide it. How about it, *ma chouchou*?"

Jean-Jacques diverted his attention from Danielle as his finger sought the ties of his breeches. It was enough time for Danielle to break free of his almost hypnotic gaze and she reached for the dagger Talon had given her and held it menacingly in front of her.

"How dare you enter my chambers without so much as a knock?" she hissed aghast. "Get out this instant, and don't ever get the notion that you might touch me. Not even if you were the last man on earth. You are too vile for words."

Jean-Jacques' eyes flew to hers and he saw the determination in them. He backed off a step when he caught sight of the wicked dagger in her hand. His raised his hands in surrender as he chuckled without humor. "I will not touch you unless you want me to, dear sister. But let me warn you, once you have tasted the attentions of a man, you will crave them forever." He chuckled again and his shoulders shook with glee. "You must have really enjoyed this ravishment of your person."

"Get out, you beast," she snarled, "Get out or I'll slit your gullet from your throat to your crotch and while I am at it, I will divest you of that puny appendage you call your manhood."

Jean-Jacques tilted his head and sneered, "So you have become a connoisseur of male attributes, little sister, *n'est çe pas*? Well, let me tell you, you little slut, my cock crows just as loud as the next man's and it is a goodly size." He raised himself to his full height and turned to leave.

He stopped at the door and spoke over his shoulder. "Just remember I'll be here, should you need me. I'll forgive for the time being that you insulted my endowments." He closed the door with great care behind him.

Danielle sank to her knees, holding her night shift before her and cried bitter tears. She had been stupid to leave Dragon's Lair. She should have known that her welcome here at Honfleur-sur-mer would be less than cordial. Jean-Jacques had shown her his true colors the day he took her to the nuns. She raised her hand to her forehead and sighed miserably. No, she could not have borne to stay on as a slave. She wanted more from life. She wanted a home and security. She wanted children. Above all she wanted someone to love her and hold her dear.

Danielle cried again at the thought of wanting to be loved. Talon certainly had not loved her. He has lusted after her. He had treated her well most of the time, but that was not enough to look forward to for the rest of ones life.

Danielle stood up, but this time she studiously avoided the looking glass. Listlessly, she pulled a shift over her head, surprised that her bosom was wont to overflow its confines. The gown she chose proved to be a problem as well as she strained to tie the tiny velvet bows at her waist. Fully dressed, she dared to take another glimpse of herself in the mirror. Her complexion was a deep golden hue with rosy highlights, lost was the aristocratic pallor she once favored. She frowned. Considering the hardships she had been through these past three months and the many meals she had missed, she should have lost weight instead of gaining it.

Danielle turned from the looking glass and pulled the cord, which rang a bell down in the servants' quarters. Moments later there was a timid knock on her door. It reminded Danielle how Jean-Jacques had made free with the knowledge that her door was not locked. She would definitely have to do something about that omission.

"Come in!" she called

Lisette, the chambermaid who had served the D'Arçenau family these past three decades, entered with a ready smile upon her pale lips. She curtsied.

"Welcome home, *mademoiselle*." Dropping her gaze, she added shyly, "Emile and I have been wondering when you might return. *Monsieur* was always vague when asked. After a while we simply did not inquire anymore, since it used to agitate him so. We are so glad you are back, *mademoiselle*!"

Danielle held out her arms and enfolded the older woman in a warm hug. "Thank you, Lisette! It feels good that someone is glad of my return."

"Ah, *mademoiselle*." There was genuine regret in Lisette's voice. "It's just not the same as it was when the old Marquis was alive." She was about to elaborate, but then caught herself and shut her mouth with a firm snap and a shake of her head.

Danielle patted the old woman's shoulder in shared grief. "I know. I miss my father sorely. Since his death there had been a bewildering change in my brother. Why is he so agitated all of the time? Father's death left him a wealthy man. Jean-Jacques now owns all of the estate except for one small tract of land set aside for me as my dowry. What more could he want and why does he act so miserly toward me?"

Lisette murmured, barely audible, "Some men don't ever have enough, no matter how much they have. You are in his way, *petite*. Take great care when you walk about by yourself. I would not put anything past your brother's deviousness." She crossed herself and asked God's mercy for her shortcomings.

"Thank you for your warning, Lisette. I had a taste of Jean-Jacques's deviousness when he forced me to go to the cloister. Nor does it come as a surprise that he finds me a hindrance. I just don't understand why. And don't worry, my friend, I am no longer that silly little girl I once was. I found an inner strength that will see me through the toughest of times." She snatched her dagger. "And this will give my newfound strength the needed enforcement."

Lisette nodded her approval. "You should always carry it with you, *chérie*. Times are so uncertain and not just inside the manor house. Did you know that Vikings raided us? Rumors run rampant that now that they have found our shores and so little resistance, they are coming in droves and care not where they raid and pillage."

It was as if a dam had broken inside Lisette and she shook her finger in admonition. "Do take care, *petite*. Why ... just a few days ago this hulking brute of a man walked into the manor without so much as a by your leave. He brought with him a horde of the most churlish barbarians I have ever laid eyes on."

Danielle hung avidly on every word Lisette uttered without the other woman being aware of her captive audience or just how interested Danielle truly was. Her heart beat a rapid tattoo in her chest. Judging by the description she was almost certain that this hulking brute had been none other than Talon. How could there be any other man so awe inspiring as he? So savage, so beautiful, so virile, so ...

"Pardon me, what did you say, Lisette?" she interrupted her own daydreams.

"He held your brother at the tip of his wicked sword and laughed while *monsieur* cowered at his feet. The Viking had a beautiful set of white teeth, *mademoiselle*, ah and he sported big, big muscles on his arms and legs." Lisette shivered delicately, "If it was me and I was younger, oh lala, I would not mind to have a man like that ravish me." She giggled like a young girl at her own jest.

"You say he was very big and had good teeth? What else captured your eyes, Lisette?" prodded the curious Danielle.

"He was enormous." Lisette puffed herself up in poor imitation of the man she tried to describe. His legs were like the trunks of a tree and on the arms he had large bands of silver with funny little marks. He seemed invincible, *mademoiselle*."

Danielle laughed delightedly at the older woman's remarks. "You sure did not miss much about his physique, Lisette ... They did not call him by name per chance, did they?"

Lisette stopped in her recount of the incident and stared curiously at Danielle. "Why do you ask, *mademoiselle*?" There was suspicion in her voice now and she no longer seemed willing to divulge any more information.

Danielle feigned indifference. "Oh, nothing in particular. I was just wondering what kind of a name a brute like that would have. Nothing so mundane as Jean-Jacques, I wager."

Lisette shrugged. "I do not remember, *mademoiselle*." Busying her hand with picking up Danielle's discarded night shift, she asked over her shoulder. "What is it you needed of me, *mademoiselle*, when you rang?"

Danielle plucked at the front of her gown. "I seems like I've gained some weight in my absence. Would you please ask one of the maids to alter it for me?" She waved a languid hand toward her wardrobe. "Nothing fits properly anymore. You could say I grew up in more ways than one." She frowned and took another look at herself in the mirror. "The strange thing is that I never thought I had eaten that much, since the food rarely was to my liking. Oh, well--" she allowed the sentence to hang in the air, pivoting on a dainty foot to face Lisette.

Danielle reached out toward the older woman in sudden concern. "Lisette, you have gone extremely pale." She pressed the servant down into one of the chairs nearby. "Can I get you something? Is there something with your stomach?" She shook the mute woman as panic rose in her breast. "Talk to me, Lisette, you are scaring me."

Lisette fanned herself with a limp hand. She stared at Danielle as if she was seeing a ghost. "It is not my place, *mademoiselle*--" she croaked. "I cannot tell you--" She gasped for air and Danielle ran to throw the window wide to allow more fresh air to enter the room. Then she ran back to Lisette and knelt by the older woman grasping her hand, trying to chafe some life into her.

"Lisette, you are like family to me," she entreated. "You can tell me anything, anything at all."

Lisette's eyes flooded with tears and she tried valiantly to blink them away. "I know you were kidnapped by the Vikings, *chérie*. It is no secret, that. I dare not say it aloud, but I know I must, since you do not seem to have the slightest clue." She peered closer at her charge. "They did … did they do the things to you …?" she whispered barely audible to Danielle.

Danielle rocked back on her heels and now it was her turn to go pale and faint. She gripped Lisette's hand in a death grip, making the older woman wince in pain. "What are you trying to tell me, Lisette?" she croaked.

"Unless I miss my guess, *chérie*, then this manor will see a bastard born within its walls by the turn of the New Year," she breathed.

Danielle's hand flew to her stomach. "You are mistaken, Lisette!" she cried, "You are wrong. My belly is as flat as it was when I left for the monastery."

"Are you sure then that no man spilled his seed inside you, *chérie*?"

Danielle shook her head miserably, not sure of the answer. Talon had boasted that he would not get her with child. She had taken him by his word. Had he lied to her? Damn that Viking and his empty promises.

"*Chérie*, there are ways to rid yourself of the unwanted brat, if you remember when your last woman's ails came upon you."

The answer hovered readily on Danielle's lips, but she could not get herself to utter them aloud. If she were uncertain about the babe's sire or if she truly did not want it, she would not hesitate to take Lisette's offer, she knew. Since there was no doubt that this babe was definitely Talon's get, she would birth it, and the consequences be damned. She would have something to love for her very own, since no man would have her for wife. After all it seemed it was common knowledge that she'd been kidnapped. She would never see Talon again as surely as she knew that he did not love her. So this child would be a wondrous reminder of what could have been, if he had loved her in return.

"I don't recall, Lisette," she lied. "Times were so uncertain and I was jostled about from one place to the next until I lost all count of days and months."

"We still could try, though it would be more dangerous, *petite*," Lisette persisted.

Danielle shook her head. "Nay, I do not like to take chances. What if we don't succeed and the babe is born with a defect?"

Lisette's eyes turned hard and cold. "We'd kill it," she stated matter-of-factly. " 'Tis done each day in the village when they don't have enough to feed a new mouth and where the man insists on his husbandly rights, no matter what." She mimed as if she would spit upon the floor in revulsion. "Bah! Men think nothing of burdening a woman with a babe. It makes them proud as a rooster, but when the babe comes into this world and there is not enough food to go around, they blame it on the woman. So, many of the women help each other with potions and daring feats with knitting needles."

"Stop it, Lisette! Stop it! I do not care to hear any more," screamed Danielle and clapped her hands over her ears.

"I am sorry, *mademoiselle*, but that is the way of life for those who cannot afford that extra mouth. I was but trying to help you."

"I know," wailed Danielle. "I know." She sank to her knees, crying bitterly that she had to suffer yet another blow to her pride.

Lisette knelt down beside her and stroked her hair. "Hush, *petite*," she crooned, "Hush. We will make it all right. When the time comes Lisette will find a couple who will raise the babe."

Through a curtain of tears, Danielle stared up at Lisette. "I am not going to give my babe to some strangers," she sniffed.

"*Chérie*, you do not seem to understand the stigma that goes with having a little one outside of matrimony. It will go hard on the babe as well." Again she stroked Danielle's hair, drawing her close to her meager bosom. "If I were younger I would claim the child as mine, but alas this bony frame could not profess the ability to bear a babe at this point of my life." She sighed.

Danielle stared with reddened eyes at Lisette. "That is very kind of you to offer, but I believe I can fend for myself. Until then, will you help me keep my condition a secret from the household and especially from Jean-Jacques?"

"Oh, *petite*, you do not have to worry. It will be our secret, though I must warn you that the time will come when you can no longer hide it from anyone. In the meantime I will alter your clothes myself. I will bring you breakfast every morning and make sure that you do not give yourself away with the morning sickness." Lisette chuckled at Danielle's skeptical look. "Oh, I see you do not know what I am talking about. Just so you know, do not be alarmed if your stomach revolts when you get up some morning. It is common and it passes soon enough, but it is a sure give-away that you are with child, *petite*."

Danielle clung to Lisette as she tried to absorb all this overwhelming news. The older woman waited patiently until Danielle's sobs subsided. Then with a last gentle pat she disengaged herself and stood up.

"*Petite*, let me see to your gowns, while you go and face the world. Go downstairs and eat some breakfast." She patted Danielle's flat stomach and smiled, "Just remember, you are eating for two now."

When Lisette had gone, Danielle moved back to the window and inhaled the cleansing ocean breeze. "Viking," she whispered to the wind, "if I had you near me I would split your thick head with your own war ax. How could you lead me to believe that I had nothing to fear from our pairing?"

Danielle leaned wearily against the window frame and stared unseeingly into the gardens below. "Oh Talon, I can't help but speculate what you would do, if you knew I carried your child beneath my breast," she wondered aloud. "Would you send us both away or would I stay your slave and our child would be absorbed into the Viking population with the rest of the bastards born to your slaves?" She never even considered any other possibilities, thinking them too far-fetched to contemplate.

Resolutely, she turned from the window and the view beyond. She would take one day at a time. With Lisette she had a loyal ally. Without warning her mood changed to one of rebellion and she hastened to her wardrobe in search of her riding habit. There were more ways to skin a cat than one, she thought grimly.

Half an hour later Danielle was mounted on a spirited mare from the well-stocked stable. She had passed over her own docile mount Minette, telling the groom upon his questioning gaze that she was in the mood for a livelier ride.

Danielle took unprecedented chances as she rode the young mare across the open fields. She breathed in the cooling winds from the North Sea and marveled at the feeling of complete and utter freedom, forgetting for a time her troubles.

CHAPTER EIGHTEEN

As the three friends rode for Herjolfstad, little of their personal feelings had changed. Asgard and Leif still resented Talon's idea of searching for Danielle. Though Talon had in the meanwhile succeeded to make the two men believe that they were going on raids rather than search solely for Danielle. For the first leg of their journey they rode in companionable silence, each caught up in their own thoughts.

"Have you considered that our regular crew will still be reeling from our recent raiding success?" Asgard asked idly as they neared the compound of Hejolfstad. "Most of them will have settled in for the winter and won't be willing to chase after more plunder."

Talon nodded sourly, "I have taken that under consideration. We will simply have to do with what's available to us. Are we not agreed that the three of us are the mainstay of any raid we undertake?"

Asgard nodded his agreement, "Aye, 'tis true. Still, I wonder if we can find enough bodies to man the boat."

"We'll be raiding small settlements, not such towns like Rouen and Paris. Just how many people will oppose us in such places?" Talon countered. Then he chuckled with genuine glee, "Remember that fop at Honfleur-sur-mer? I have a good mind to pay him a second visit if for no other reason than to see him grovel at my feet again. Somehow, I have the feeling that he would scrape up more coins if we but pressed him hard enough. Even while we were there, I had a strange inkling that he was toying with us." Talon's brows drew together. "Indeed, I think we should go back. But this time let's burn that granite mansion down about his aristocratic ears."

Asgard and Leif laughed aloud, their heads thrown back in total enjoyment. "Let's do that," they shouted. "I can just see his pinched visage if we show up at his doorstep again."

Leif slapped his thigh, "Oh, this is going to be fun. Maybe this raid will prove to be a good idea after all. I'll miss the fierce fighting we had in Paris, but a coward such as that French pig is worth the trip."

They continued in that vein for quite some time, relishing the thought of seeing the Frenchman quiver and beg. They rode on until it became too dark to ride and they made a meager camp. By mid-morning next day they arrived in Herjolfstad.

Thorson was riding up from a morning's hunt, feeling benevolent, because he had taken a young slave girl along and taken his pleasure on her tender body. He was still savoring the thought of her tearful pleas for mercy as he drove himself into her fragile body. The stupid twit did not realize that her pleas were just the fuel for his jaded tastes.

As he swung down from his mount, he heard the rhythmic clop of several horses behind him. Curious, he turned to check who might be riding in. He frowned when he recognized his younger brother at the head of the small group.

"What brings you to town this morn, brother?" he greeted Talon suspiciously.

Talon favored Thorson with a flippant grin. "Those of us who are footloose and fancy free, can spend their time at anything they please, brother mine," he taunted.

Remembering his romp with the young slave, Thorson replied with equal arrogance. "And those of us who are landed, can do as they please as well ... even more so," he added in order to goad Talon into loosing his temper, "because our living is assured."

Talon's hands tightened on Lucifer's reins and the small muscle beneath his eye twitched at Thorson's taunt. "Aye, brother, I am well aware of how much land you own, but I am satisfied with Dragon's Lair, since I earned it with my own two hands." With deceptive casualness he leaned over Lucifer's neck and spoke softly, "You will grow soft and fat, Thorson, because your hunger for an honest fight will soon disappear altogether. I, on the other hand, can enjoy my days of raiding and the chance to die in battle to go on to Valhalla and eternal glory."

Thorson's mouth tightened in envy and his blue eyes, so different from Talon's, narrowed with repressed fury. "So, you are telling me then, that you are off once more to raid?" he ground out, his teeth audibly grinding together.

Talon laughed low in his throat. "Aye, brother dear, care to join us?"

Thorson was stung by the taunting invitation. He sneered, "Nay, Talon, I have my hands full where I am. At least *I* have two able ones. However, I will buy a trinket here and there from you when you return ... *if you return.*" He turned on his booted heel and entered his house without an invitation that the three men join him.

"That was a low blow," remarked Leif, chagrined that Thorson would mention his brother's crippled hand. "Still, you got the better of him, Talon. But now that he is angered by your taunts, where do you propose we lay our heads for the night?"

Talon grunted. He pointed toward the harbor. "Pray tell, what is wrong with spending our night aboard the Raider? One night more or less should not matter."

"Let's stable the horses then and make sure that they are taken care of whilst we are gone."

"Won't Thorson mind if we use his stables?"

"Has my brother ever minded to earn the extra coin?" asked Talon sarcastically.

The following day, the three friends went about in earnest to find a fitting crew. One of the first to apply was Ghor. Talon experienced a fleeting moment of reluctance as he remembered the brief encounter between the man and Danielle. Just as quickly he set his qualms aside. They'd be lucky to fill the Raider with half a crew much less a full complement of warriors.

They went from house to house to recruit their men and by the third day they had a scant fifteen men aside from themselves.

"It will do for this trip," Talon conceded. "We'll keep to our original plan to plunder only single dwellings that look lucrative.

No need to tell the men that. Once they see the amount of spoils there are to be had and how easy it is to come by, they will not grumble."

The Raider slipped its moorings early next morning amid the usual farewell waves from the small crowd of curious onlookers. Arwynna was among them she waved as enthusiastically as the rest of the women. Only she knew that she had propositioned Talon once again only the night before.

Arwynna cornered Talon, while he was seeing to Lucifer. With all the wiles known to her she tried to persuade him to sink with her to the hay, but Talon had pushed her away from him.

"I do not care to tell you again, Arwynna," he had hissed angrily. "You chose my brother over me, because you are a greedy wench. Your loyalty belongs to a man's purse and mine was not filled heavily enough for your tastes. I will not bed my brother's wife, no matter how little regard I bear him."

Arwynna ran her hands longingly along his lean ribs and crushed herself against his reluctant body.

"What harm would it do, Talon? Even if you should get me with child, Thorson would never know, since the babe would resemble him as much as it would resemble you."

"The difference, my dearest sister-in-law, is, that I would know. I could not live with that knowledge. If I create a babe, then I want to claim it as my own, not hanker after one who is claimed by the woman's unwitting husband."

Arwynna favored him with a cold glare. "So do tell, how do you spend your long lonely nights in that hovel you call a stronghold?" she hissed bitterly. "Do you still have your black-haired slave or have you ridden her to death yet?" There was a strange longing in Arwynna's statement, but Talon did not catch the hitch in her voice.

"Why should it matter to you, Arwynna? Always remember, you had a choice and you chose the purse rather than the man." Talon finished his task by then and took up his bundle to leave.

"I'll be here waiting for you, Talon," she called after his retreating back. "Some day you will come back to me. I am a patient woman."

And so Arwynna had come to the docks under the pretense that she cared for all the warriors, when in reality she had only eyes for Talon's majestic figure standing tall in the bow of the Raider, looking only ahead, but never back.

CHAPTER NINETEEN

Jean-Jacques stood near the window of the study. It was thrown open to catch the fresh breeze from the sea. Several weeks had gone by since Danielle had returned out of nowhere. He was still at odds how to rid himself of the chit again, but even more important, how to rid himself of her forever. He sneered as he recalled how sadly the nuns had failed him.

The aged Marquis, the one who had been eager to marry Danielle without her dowry, had died of the very pox she had accused him of having. It meant Jean-Jacques would have to travel further afield from Honfleur-sur-mer, if he hoped to find another old man who would take a young girl in wedlock, despite the fact that she was no longer a virgin.

The thought of Danielle not being a virgin any longer, initiated strange stirrings in Jean-Jacques' loins. He felt himself harden. Who was to deny him, if he forced her to his will? She was a beautiful woman, she promised to be a fiery romp between the sheets. And Jean-Jacques disclaimed all wrongdoing by pointing out to himself that the girl was but his half sister. Besides, the filthy Vikings had already ruined her. Surely they had taken turns upon her delectable body.

Jean-Jacques throat convulsed as his mind's eye drew him a vivid picture of Danielle's body writhing beneath the burly form of a Viking warrior. Ah, and Jean-Jacques had just enough insight to see it all in life-like images. Had he not seen Danielle's ripe young body? Had Honfleur-sur-mer not been invaded by some brutish Vikings? Put the two together and *voilà* you have the perfect scenario.

Jean-Jacques sighed in bliss, only to see the object of his desire gallop by at breakneck speed. "*Merde*!" he cursed, as he felt his meager manhood deflate as quickly has it had surged into life. "Ah, what I will not do to you, *ma petite soeur*," he mused. "All I have to do is bide my time."

Danielle rode out every day, since Lisette opened her eyes to her condition. Riding was the only relief she found from her constant thoughts of Talon and what might have been. She grimaced. At first she had ridden in hopes to lose the babe, before she admitted that Talon had planted it deep in her belly. It was not likely to slip out, because she bounced up and down across the countryside.

Danielle bit her lip in vexation. She would not be able to keep Jean-Jacques in the dark much longer. The morning sickness assailed her only now and again and thankfully only when she rose too quickly from her bed. Not that it mattered. He would never surprise her again with an unannounced intrusion into her chambers, since Danielle had taken precautions and installed a lock on her door. But her belly was growing with astonishing speed and she had all she could do to walk erect and keep its roundness hidden.

Danielle made her way carefully down the sweeping staircase that commanded the foyer of Honfleur-sur-mer. She had draped a shawl loosely across her shoulders in an attempt to hide her advancing pregnancy just a while longer from her brother's ever scrutinizing gaze. She was almost across the marble floor, when something caught beneath her slipper and she lost her balance.

A frightened scream tore from Danielle's lips as she fought to keep from falling. The shawl flew away and she landed heavily on her back. She struggled valiantly to gain her feet, painfully aware that her protruding belly was clearly outlined by the clinging folds of her gown.

Jean-Jacques was just in time to see her hands reach toward the telling roundness. He stopped in stunned surprise, no longer caring for Danielle's immediate health or welfare, but drawn to this new discovery that his sister was evidently with child.

Jean-Jacques kneeled beside the quivering girl and extended a questing hand to her belly. His salacious smirk was more telling than any words he might have uttered and Danielle's instincts for self-preservation sprang to life in full force. She slapped his hand away with a force born of desperation.

"Keep your filthy paws to yourself, brother mine," she snarled and her fury lent her the strength to sit up on her own. Her green eyes shot daggers at him. "So you now know the obvious," she sneered. "I am with child."

Jean-Jacques cackled as if Danielle had told him the greatest joke he had ever heard. "Ah, tell me *chèrie*, is it the fruit of one lover or several?" He was enjoying his coarse jest and tittered once more.

Danielle raised her hand to slap his sallow face, but Jean-Jacques was quick to move out of her reach. "I will not dignify your foul question with an answer," she shot bravely back at him, though her heart was breaking that he had found her out so soon.

Jean-Jacques rocked back on his heels. "I thought you smarter than that, Danielle," he mocked, enjoying the misery that was evident on her flushed face. "Why did you not rid yourself of the little bastard?" He cocked his head to one side and his pale eyes narrowed as something seemed to dawn in him. He stroked his chin in mock contemplation. "Ah yes," he sighed theatrically, "I see it now more clearly. You took up riding because you thought it would rid you of your unwanted burden." He laughed spitefully and slapped his knee to emphasize his glee. His narrow chest was still heaving from the exertion of his laughter, when he jumped to his feet and looked disdainfully down at her. "I've heard of stupid village woman who thought that rolling a boulder up a hill would rid them of their get, but it will only make them stronger to bear their husbands seed again and again. Who would have thought you would try something as dumb as that?" he chortled in high good humor. Then without the slightest attempt to help her, he left Danielle sitting in the middle of the hallway.

Lisette had come running at Danielle's scream, but she dared not to come forward without being bidden. She rushed toward Danielle once Jean-Jacques left. Concern written on her wrinkled face, she got down on her knees and hugged Danielle's slender frame. "*Ma petite*, are you all right?" Her voice held all the tenderness and caring Danielle was in need of at that moment.

Danielle made a face and bit back tears that threatened to well up. Ruefully, she rubbed her posterior and nodded her head. "I think so. Apart from my hind end I don't think I sustained any damage."

"No matter, you will go up to your room and rest in bed. I will personally bring you a tray."

"Lisette, I am not an invalid simply because I slipped and fell," Danielle insisted with an air that brooked no argument. "I much rather stay and face Jean-Jacques while I am still smarting from physical pain. I will not allow that braying jackass to get the upper hand."

Danielle walked into the dining room with her head held high and her gaze immediately sought out Jean-Jacques. He was seated at the end of the long rosewood table, the place allotted to the master of the manor, already delving his spoon into a bowl of soup. A spotless napkin of finest damask was tucked crudely into the top of his linen shirt.

Danielle noted with no small stab of pain that the heirloom candelabra were missing and that in their stead pair of wooden candlesticks stood near Jean-Jacques elbows. She knew she would not need to ask their whereabouts. With all certainty they would either grace the table of some Viking or had been melted down for their value.

Jean-Jacques made a great show of ignoring her and ladled the soup with insouciant pleasure into his mouth. Danielle stood but a moment before she realized that he would not accord her the common courtesy of seating her at the table. Tossing her head, she simply drew back a chair and seated herself.

Emile was quick to bring her a bowl of the clear soup and place a napkin on her lap. Danielle smiled her thanks at him and began to eat her own soup with the same serenity as her brother. When she was done, she glanced up to see him staring speculatively at her. His face seemed contorted with fury, though she could not be sure in the dim light of the room.

Jean-Jacques put a quick end to her reflection by voicing his sentiment. His hands braced upon the table, he leaned forward and pierced her with a venomous glare. "I have come to the conclusion that it is no longer feasible to keep you under this roof," he spat. Plopping back against his chair, he steepled his fingers and pretended to be absorbed in deep thought. Waving his hand languidly in her direction, he conjectured, "Seeing that you are breeding without the benefit of matrimony, I do not deem it proper that you flaunt your condition before the decent folk of this region."

Danielle gaped at him and leaned forward to make sure that she had heard correctly. Then she laughed in outright amusement. "Pray tell, who is to notice, brother mine? The farmers and trade people come to the back door to barter their wares and then who else is there?"

" 'Tis enough, you brazen slut. You should have had the decency to let them slit your throat after they were finished with you," he roared.

Danielle nodded solemnly, "Aye, and to be sure you would be the first to forfeit your life after you were forced to forfeit your innocence," she replied with sarcasm dripping from her rosy mouth. "I, sir, had no choice in the matter. I was kept fettered like a hound and I tried several times to escape my captors. Until I came back to Honfleur-sur-mer I had not the slightest notion that I would have to pay yet another price for being ravished."

Danielle stood up to emphasize her ensuing words. "You will not succeed in getting rid of me this time, Jean-Jacques. This innocent babe inside my womb will be born within these walls. Do not try and thwart my intentions or the consequences of your actions will be dire," she gritted and raised her clenched fist.

Jean-Jacques smiled at her with benevolent amusement. "Why do you rail at me with empty threats? You know as well as I that there is no one in this household to tell me nay. Who was there the last time when I spirited you away to the nuns?" he taunted, "Who would deny me the right this time? They will all agree that a soiled dove like yourself needs to be among the pure of heart to salvage her sullied soul. Indeed, it would be a blessing for the little bastard to be born inside the hallowed walls of a cloister. The good sisters could pass the babe off as a foundling and some day in the far off future you might even return to Honfleur-sur-mer."

"I see you have it all figured out, Jean-Jacques, except that you are forgetting that I am no longer a cringing child. I have learned to fend for myself and vermin like you does not faze me anymore. I beg you to try one of your foul deeds upon me and see how quickly I will snuff out your attempt."

"I can bide my time, *chèrie*. You will not be so quick on your feet in the months ahead." He flipped his hand palm upward. "You must admit yourself that tonight was but a small taste of what is to come where your agility is concerned?"

Danielle exhaled audibly, her agitation at his threat apparent. "It was but something on the marble floor, some careless servant spilled something and I slipped upon it."

Jean-Jacques snickered. "Yes, *ma chèrie*, but you floundered about like a stranded whale. The more your belly grows before you, the more apt you will be to fall." He sliced his hand through the air. " 'Tis nothing but an observation, one I heed you bear in mind."

Danielle crumpled her napkin and threw it on the table. Pushing back her chair, she turned to leave. "I seem to have lost my appetite after all," she declared, then forced herself to walk slowly from the dining room.

Danielle admitted that her brother was right. She could not keep her vigilance up forever, but she would not allow him to banish her from Honfleur-sur-mer ever again. Somehow she would have to come up with a solution or a bribe to make him change his mind. Discouraged, she climbed the broad staircase to her chamber and locked it securely behind her. With savage fury she flung the shawl on her bed. She would no longer need its concealment now that Jean-Jacques was aware of her condition. But she would ride, she swore, and she would work as usual and not coddle herself. After all, if the Viking women could do it, so could she. Somehow these quiet resolutions afforded her a small bit of comfort and she pulled off her dress and made ready for bed.

By the light of her candle Danielle read in a slim book of poetry her sire had given her many years ago. She still took delight and solace from the verses even now, but tonight her mind was inclined to wander and she stared out at the waxing moon.

Against her will her thoughts went to Talon and she sighed into the night. She missed him sorely, but she knew that by now he would have replaced her with another slave. Her hand crept to the bulging mound where his child grew, and she wondered if the babe would have its sire's coloring or look more like her? What difference? she thought bitterly. You'll be a bastard no matter who you favor. She snorted into the gloom of her chamber. "Aye, Talon, when this babe makes its entrance into this world, I will remember your noble words that you had no intention to get me with child. What a dunce I was to believe your empty promises."

Angrily, she climbed from her bed. "I should have eaten more," she grumbled as she pulled her shawl around her shoulders against the chilly night air. "I guess I will have to raid the larder or never go to sleep this night."

Danielle padded on bare feet down the stairs and had her mind set toward the kitchen, when something caught her attention out of the corner of her eye. Curiously, she drew nearer the open study door, where Jean-Jacques walked about, holding a well handled parchment that seemed to have great importance to him. Danielle flattened herself against the wall in the hallway and watched her brother with growing interest.

Jean-Jacques seemed totally absorbed in trying to find a place to hide the paper. Danielle was sure that was his intention, because he folded the document and tried to stuff it inside the secret niche of the fireplace mantel. He cursed softly, when the thing would not fit.

Danielle held her breath, lest he might discover her presence. Jean-Jacques wandered about the room, dissatisfied with each new discovery, until he finally settled upon a mounted stag's head. He climbed on a chair and pulled away the frame upon which it was mounted from the wall. Danielle frowned. Something was amiss here. Why would her brother want to hide a document? The servants could not read, so that left ...Danielle gasped out loud... and then her eyes widened. *Mon Dieu*, Jean-Jacques had heard her. Pulling her shawl tighter about her shoulders, she ran for the kitchens, her heart beating a steady tattoo. She had a chance. Her eyes were used to the dark, while her brother would take a few seconds to adjust to it.

Taking deep breaths, she forced herself to stay calm. She could hear the slap of his leather soles on the tiled floor. Acting unconcerned, she foraged through the larder, but her heart still beat like a drum.

Jean-Jacques' pale gaze raked over her as he entered the kitchen. She seemed composed enough and she certainly didn't breathe labored. Bracing a hand against the doorframe his eyes narrowed in suspicion. "Did you just spy on me in the study?" he grated through clenched teeth. Danielle lifted innocent green eyes in his direction and managed to look quite naive in the process. She stopped in her quest of tearing some bread from a loaf and opened her mouth in piqued rebuttal.

"Are you accusing me of spying, dear brother?" she demanded and her chin took on that stubborn angle. "If so, I would like to know what I would find interesting enough about you to waste my time with it?"

Jean-Jacques threw her another murderous glance and without another word he spun on his heel and left the kitchen. Danielle let out a relieved whoosh of air and valiantly choked back the laughter that bubbled in the back of her throat. What she wouldn't give if she could have captured Jean-Jacques' misery on canvas. Of course, they said that where there was smoke there was usually a fire. As she sat on a nearby bench and leisurely chewed her bread and nibbled some cheese she had found as well, she began to wonder what Jean-Jacques might be hiding. Now that her curiosity was aroused, she decided that it would be wise to find the document and see what it said. Jean-Jacques acted so out of sorts that it stood to reason that it contained something important. Maybe it could aid her in securing her place at Honfleur-sur-mer and therewith her future. She surely would not marry simply to give her unborn babe a name. No other man measured up to Talon and he was out of the question, since she would never see him again. Besides, he only wanted her as a slave.

That settled Danielle climbed the stairs to her chamber. In passing the study, she noted that Jean-Jacques had prudently closed the door, but she could hear him muttering to himself and pacing about.

Danielle awoke to brilliant sunshine and threw open her window to let in the fresh sea breeze. It was quite early yet and barely anyone stirred below. Suddenly, her ears pricked at the sound of a horse's hooves. Her eyes lit up with a devilish light and her mouth curved upward, when she saw Jean-Jacques riding away from the manor on his Dapple Gray.

Danielle wasted no time to don her gown. She literally flew down the stairs. Quietly, she let herself into the study and made straight for the stag's head, dragging a wing chair beneath it, so she could reach its frame. Carefully, she lifted the ornament a scant few inches from the wall and felt with her hand underneath it. There was nothing.

Disappointed, she stepped from the chair and put it back in its place, allowing her gaze to scan the room in slow speculation. Would Jean-Jacques hide his document in the study or would he take it to his own chambers? Shrugging, she decided to keep looking, at least until she exhausted her options. With great care she rummaged through the drawers of the wide ornately carved mahogany desk, putting everything back just as she had found it. Finally, she plopped into the wing chair and made a moue of disgust. She would never find the document at this rate.

Use your head, Danielle, she told herself. Where would you put a paper you wanted to keep from someone? Idly, her eyes wandered about the room until they lit upon an old rarely used pewter candelabrum. It stood forlornly in a corner, something not used, but still too valuable to be thrown out. She jumped up and went to peer into its depth, and there it was ... the document.

With long fingers she reached inside and pulled on its edges when the sound of approaching horse's hooves caught her attention. Now what? She replaced the candelabrum as if it had burned her fingers and ran from the room and up the stairs. Panting, she pulled off her gown and tugged the night shift back over her head. With a gamin smirk she climbed back under the covers and congratulated herself that she was fast becoming a consummate actress. Reclining against the pillows, she rang for Lisette to bring her breakfast.

Below she heard Jean-Jacques imperious shout for Emile. There was a clatter and then all was quiet. A few minutes later Lisette knocked on the door and brought a tray of freshly baked bread with butter and wild honey and a small jug of milk to Danielle. Tidying the room, the old servant waited patiently for Danielle to finish eating, so she could help her dress and get ready for the day.

Danielle did not break with her established routine of riding over the estate grounds, but she was impatient to get another chance to see what that mysterious document would hold. Despite her denial the night before, Danielle knew that her brother had not believed her. Of all things, Jean-Jacques was certainly no fool. He would be watching her from now on. She would have to be extra careful.

It was three days and an accident later before Danielle had another chance to check on the candelabrum. It happened shortly after the stable boy brought Danielle's mount around. The horse seemed skittish right from the beginning, but Danielle thought little of it. She was a good equestrian, but the minute her weight came down on the saddle, the horse screamed in agony and pawed wildly at the air. Danielle was unprepared and allowed her reins to slip from her fingers. The animal knew immediately that there was no longer any guidance. The mare pranced and bucked until Danielle slipped from the saddle and landed ignominiously on the hard ground. The stable boy rushed quickly to her side and was barely in time to pull her to safety or she would have been crushed beneath the hooves of the panicked horse. The noise brought everyone running, everyone except Jean-Jacques. As it was Danielle ended up with a sprained ankle and was carried into the study by a solicitous Emile.

"Ah, *ma petite*," crooned Lisette as she bathed Danielle's foot in cold water. "You poor, poor mite. I guess you will have to stay here for a day or two before you can climb the stairs again."

Lisette's suggestion was like music to Danielle's ears. She groaned pitiably. "Ah, Lisette, I guess you are right. I won't be able to walk on this ankle for several days, I vow."

Jean-Jacques strode into the study at that moment and he scrutinized Danielle's ankle with cold detachment. "What is this I hear?" he asked, "You are to spend a few days in my study?" He shook his head. "I don't think so, my dear sister. A man needs his privacy and I claim this room as my own." He waved his pale hand with studied arrogance and pivoted on his foot. "We shall get a couple of the servants to carry you to your chambers."

Danielle's heart sank, as her hopes for another look at the hidden document seemed to disappear before her eyes. She sniffed loudly. "I guess you are so cold-hearted that you would not even allow me a few hours of respite so that I might catch my breath?" she whined.

Jean-Jacques snorted in disgust. "Oh, all right. Since you seem to be incapacitated, I guess there is no harm in letting you rest here for an hour or so."

Danielle hid her triumphant smile behind a lacy handkerchief. Feigning exhaustion she closed her eyes. Her ploy worked as she hoped it would, because shortly thereafter everyone left the room. She held her breath and waited a few minutes longer. A groan of genuine pain escaped her lips as she forced herself to stand up, but her need to know the contents of the hidden document won out over the desire to sit back down.

She hobbled to the old candelabrum and reached for the document. Trembling with fear of discovery she unrolled the parchment. Danielle immediately recognized the spidery handwriting as that of her father's. Her eyes literally flew across the tightly written lines, and then she gasped. No wonder, Jean-Jacques wanted her out of the way. He was but her half brother. Feverishly, she read on.

Her father had made no provisions to support her brother's grandiose lifestyle after his death. According to the will Jean-Jacques was no more than the caretaker of the estate until such time as Danielle might have children, who in turn would inherit Honfleur-sur-mer upon their majority. Danielle gaped at this unexpected piece of news. What had prompted her father to cut Jean-Jacques so completely out of the inheritance? A sliver of pity sliced through her heart. It was after all not Jean-Jacques' fault that he had been born on the wrong side of the blanket. No, she could not let pity stand in her way. Jean-Jacques certainly hadn't shown her any. How fortunate that she found the parchment. Now she had some premise for bargaining.

She carefully replaced the document and hobbled back to her chair. She would have to think the matter carefully through before she confronted Jean-Jacques.

CHAPTER TWENTY

The Raider glided soundlessly to shore near the outskirts of Le Havre. "We'll only raid the manor homes that dot these shores," Talon explained to the anxious men. "There is more valuable plunder to be had in these old houses than you can find in a day's time in one of their bigger towns. They have no high walls to keep us out and they have precious few servants who can stave off our assault." He chuckled wickedly. "It should prove as easy as taking the treasures from the English monasteries."

The crew did not care where their spoils would come from. If their chief told them they had easy pickings, then they would have to believe him and follow his orders. They had taken an oath to that effect and were pledged to do obey without question for the duration of the voyage.

Talon continued, "I want all the residents brought before me first, so I can decide what we will do with them. We will torch only those places, which give us a great deal of trouble. The less time we spend burning their homes, the more time we have to raid."

His logic was met with roaring cheers. Ghor alone wondered why Talon was changing from his usual strategy of plundering, raping and then slitting the victims throats. Ghor loved to rape and pillage, but most of all the rape, since his victims were helpless against his attacks and he would not have to answer to anyone for his cruel methods. Aye, Ghor thought, a raid was the only way he could get his fill of women. He harbored a silent rage, blaming his looks rather than his brutality why none of the maids in the Norseland would have him, not even the slaves.

Ghor hid an evil grin beneath his unkempt beard. Despite it all, his rod dipped regularly into the soft heat of a female. None ever lived to tell about it, because he'd become adept at staging accidents. He was a master of duplicity and managed to be far away when the unfortunate soul was found dead. So how was he supposed to corner a female and take his grisly pleasure upon her, if they had to herd all the inhabitants together for Talon to decide?

Talon scrutinized his crew in order to fathom their reaction and he noticed that Ghor was not meeting his gaze. The short hairs on his neck rose as he watched the man ply his thumb lovingly across the wicked edge of his long knife. Now why he should feel wary about this man, who had proven time and again that he was a worthy warrior? Disgusted with his thoughts, Talon turned abruptly away. "Let's go," he growled as he gave the signal to disembark and advance toward the manor house atop the nearby hill.

As Talon had promised the mansion presented little resistance and the occupants were quickly rounded up. Those few who managed to flee were not hunted down. Talon dismissed the frightened people with a casual wave of the hand. Some of his warriors took his gesture as a sign that they could make free with the womenfolk and several separated the younger maids and took them aside for their carnal urges. The rest of the servants cowered together and averted their eyes as the men fell upon their hapless victims, laughing cruelly when a girl screamed in pain and fear.

Talon, Asgard and Leif along with those who had no desire for a turn upon the maids, ransacked the house. In their quest for riches nobody paid any attention to Ghor and his absence from the line of anxious males until there were no more valuables to be found.

Talon wondered where Ghor might have made off to, when the subject of his thoughts strolled leisurely from around the side of the house. A satisfied smirk upon his ugly features he adjusted his tunic. Talon frowned, but thought no more about it as he selected the lord of the manor and dragged the shaking man inside.

"I will grant you your miserable life, if you show us where you are hiding your coin, old man," he cajoled silkily and idly juggled his knife in his large hand. With a gurgling chuckle he turned to Asgard and spoke in the Norse tongue. "It would not do us much good to kill the old goat. This way we can come back and plunder again." The three friends guffawed, while the old Lord shivered and his watery eyes never left their hulking figures.

Talon advanced threateningly upon the man and grabbed the stock of his white shirt in one huge fist. Slowly, he hauled the old man's face within inches of his own visage and snarled again his order for him to show them where he kept his coin.

The old Lord was quavering and unable to understand the huge barbarian, but when the point of the knife nicked the wrinkled folds of his neck, he knew he would have to part with some of his hidden cash. His eyes fairly rolled to the back of his head as he feebly tried to loosen Talon's grip.

At last Talon understood the poor soul's intent and abruptly he let him go. On shaky legs, the old man tottered toward the fireplace and pressed a hidden latch. The Vikings shoved the hapless man aside as they reached with greedy hands inside the hollow, hooting with satisfaction when they came away with several pouches of silver coins. Taking advantage of their preoccupation the old Lord fled the room.

"Let him go," advised Talon. "He showed us where we might look in future and for that alone he earned the right to live." With the delight of a small child he searched for the tiny catch and practiced opening and closing the hidden panel until even Asgard and Leif lost their patience with him. The money was divided between the three friends before they joined the mayhem outside once more.

"Make haste, men," Talon urged. "The plunder needs to be loaded. Gather enough fowl and smoked meats for our evening meal." As he surveyed the pile of plunder, a wry smile lifted the corner of his mouth. Indeed the raiding of a single manor had proven more bountiful than the sacking of some small townships. Aye, his warriors would come to like these easy pickings.

Talon decided that it would further his cause if he allowed his men a night of revelry. His heart was not in the raiding as it should have been, but that needed to remain his secret. When his gaze had skimmed across the frightened faces of the people herded together by his warriors, he'd walked away in disappointment. One special pair of green eyes and a certain tousled mane of midnight hair had been missing.

At camp Talon's mood finally mellowed after several rounds of stolen ale and he began to enjoy the merrymaking as much as the rest of the crew. Asgard took advantage of Talon's drunken state and challenged him to a contest of arm wrestling. The rest of the warriors quickly formed a circle and urged the two brawlers on. Bets were made on the outcome and among raucous hooting and hollering they were shoved toward the middle of the circle, where they met standing toe to toe. Someone drew a crude line between the two and according to the rules the first man to push the other across that line would be declared the winner. Asgard grinned impishly at Talon as he held out his right hand for his friend to grasp.

Talon fixed Asgard with a drunken stare. He found it hard to concentrate on the simple task of standing on his feet, much less focus on the contest ahead. Nonetheless, he gamely extended his right hand and clasped Asgard's. The rule dictated that they both kept their left arms behind their backs.

"Come on Talon, don't let that milksop budge you from your place," a hoarse voice shouted near Talon's ear. "I've bet my whole day's take on your victory."

Talon was momentarily distracted and Asgard pressed his advantage, coming dangerously close to making Talon lose his balance. But Talon was not their leader by chance. He was a fighter and victory was like a healing balm to him. He grunted, the sinews of his massive neck bulged with the effort, until he'd dragged Asgard inch by strenuous inch across the line.

There were loud cheers and those who had bet on him, came to clap him on the back. He was handed another tankard of ale and he downed it with gusto, laughing with glee as he spied Asgard's sour expression.

"You should know that I always win at arm wrestling, Asgard," he declared drunkenly and raised his cup in a silent toast.

Asgard grinned at Talon and nodded, "Aye, I should know by now, but I had hoped you'd be too far into your ale." The men guffawed at that and since this had been so much fun, others challenged each other for a game of arm wrestling as well.

The merrymaking did not stop until most of them lay in an ale-induced stupor wherever they fell. Morning dawned without anyone caring to head out for another raid. The crew groused about the brightness of the sun to the noise of the gently flowing Seine River.

It was well past noon before any of the warriors had the desire to eat something. Talon lifted blood shot eyes to survey his men and decided that they were all in the same sorry shape, besides the day was too far gone to bother with and this was no ordinary raiding voyage. If it were not for finding Danielle, he would be whiling his time away at Dragon's lair right now.

"We will seek our pallets early this night," he warned later on. "Tomorrow we will rise before sunup and raid the next manor we come upon."

Danielle was plain out bored. She had been forced to stay off her injured ankle for nearly three days. Today she would to ride out, pain or not. She requested one of the more docile mares, well aware of her shortcomings.

It was a beautiful day. There was already a hint of autumn in the air, although summer was not yet over officially. Danielle smiled hugely as she cantered about the countryside. God, it was good to be home. She sniffed the air, delighting in the fact it carried the smell of the sea.

As she topped a low rise, she reined in the mare and looked longingly out toward the North Sea. Despite her rapt delight in the scenery, she caught a furtive movement out of the corner of her eye. Curious, she turned in her saddle, forgetting about her injured ankle. Searing pain shot through her and she jerked roughly on the reins as a result. The poor mare taken off guard promptly bucked.

"Easy, my pretty," Danielle crooned as she flattened herself against her mount to keep from being tossed to the ground. "Easy, I am sorry I startled you," she apologized. Carefully, she straightened in the saddle, patting the mare's sleek neck to further calm the animal. "That was close," she mumbled distractedly, when an angry whizzing sound passed by her ear.

A dull thud froze Danielle in her saddle. Numbly, she stared at the quivering arrow embedded deeply in the trunk of a nearby tree. It took her a full minute before it dawned on her that this arrow had been meant for her. There was no game on this part of the estate. Not waiting to see who might have tried to kill her, she spurred the mare on in a zigzag path, hoping her erratic movement would thwart further attacks.

Knowing her life was at stake, Danielle dared not look back to see if yet another arrow would come her way. Instead she raced for a nearby copse to wait and see. Her heart thumping, she watched anxiously from behind the cover of gnarled old birch trees, but her assailant had apparently fled. Finally, after she deemed she had waited long enough, Danielle guided the mare through the stand of trees and exited at the opposite end.

She didn't want to admit it, but Jean-Jacques was the only person who could possibly harbor her any ill will. He was the only one to gain anything if she were dead. What better way than by accident? Who would gainsay her brother if Danielle were killed?

Danielle groaned aloud. This was it. She should not have waited this long to confront Jean-Jacques with her knowledge about the hidden document. Of course, he would be furious that she'd spied on him, but that could not be helped. She raised her chin in mulish stubbornness and rode on. She would suggest that Jean-Jacques call their sire's solicitor at once to set things straight between them. What could be simpler? She laughed delightedly as she congratulated herself on this wonderful solution.

A smile on her rosy lips, her cheeks pink from the brisk ride, Danielle strode purposefully into the study where Jean-Jacques was imbibing his first glass of wine for the morning. A trace of her ready smile faded when she spied the inevitable goblet in his hand.

"*Bonjour*, Jean-Jacques," she called out to him, but even to her own ears her voice sounded stiff and phony. She cleared her throat in an attempt to recapture her former joviality. "I see you are having a morning libation," she said, mainly to make conversation and for lack of having anything else to say.

Jean-Jacques' thin lips twisted into an insolent smile. "And what is it to you, dear sister?"

Danielle shrugged. "Personally, I don't care one whit if you drink or not. I did not come here to quibble with you about your drinking." Her green eyes snapped their displeasure as she advanced a little further into the room.

Jean-Jacques waved a languid hand. "Then get to the point, Danielle."

Danielle faltered. How was she to broach the subject of her close encounter this morning without making it sound like an outright accusation? How was she to broach the subject of the discovered document?

"Well, cat got your tongue, girl?"

Danielle took a deep breath and glared at her half brother. She would not allow him to get under her skin. Not today, not ever again, she vowed bitterly. She would have this out with him and come to a mutual understanding.

She tossed her silky mane and caught her lower lip between her small teeth. "No, the cat did not get my tongue, but I am at an impasse about how to begin what I have come to say to you."

"I can't remember that something as trivial as that ever stopped you," he taunted.

"Jean-Jacques ... I ...was it you who tried to shoot me this morning?" she blurted out, ashamed that she was not able to keep her emotions in check, ashamed to accuse her brother of something for which she had no proof.

Jean-Jacques stared idly into the bottom of his now empty glass and then at her. "Why would you think me capable of doing such a thing, sister?" he asked with deceptive calm.

Danielle sat down on the edge of a nearby chair, because suddenly her legs refused to hold her. She twisted her hands in quiet agitation. Staring at his sallow face, she plunged on. "Because I know about our sire's will," she admitted.

Jean-Jacques stood motionless for several moments. Pushing away from the mantel, he advanced upon her. He lifted his arm to backhand it across her face as fury got the better of him. Only at the last second he remembered her threat that if he ever hit her again, she would see him dead and he dropped his hand to his side.

"You conniving bitch," he snarled. "So it was you after all that night when I confronted you in the kitchen? My," he said admiringly and stepped back to get a better look at her, "what a consummate actress you are. You could not have learned that from the nuns. My guess is that you got good at it when the Vikings took their turns on you."

Danielle jumped to her feet, livid. "You are disgusting, Jean-Jacques," she screamed. "I had not meant to spy on you, but the door to the study was open. You walked about so furtively that you aroused my curiosity." She held both hands in front of her in entreaty. "Look, it doesn't need to change anything. I came here today to tell you that there is plenty for the two of us and how much could one small babe require?"

He sneered and looked pointedly at her stomach. "Ah yes, the little bastard of questionable parentage. I knew he would enter into this conversation sometime."

"Leave the babe out of it for a moment and listen to me. There is no need for us to fight. The manor is big and we don't even have to meet if we don't want to. Papa left enough money to see us comfortably through the rest of our lives."

"Not anymore there is," Jean-Jacques gritted. "The Vikings got a large portion of our coin when they raided Honfleur-sur-mer. Then you had the stupidity to bring more of the savages and pay them voluntarily. And on top of that I am to support their heathen offspring, too?" His hand slashed angrily through the air to emphasize his point.

Danielle stamped her foot, then rose in agitation to prowl the study. "Honfleur-sur-mer can survive without the benefit of coin. We have land and we can convert our harvest into money and even without money we would never starve." Driven by her fury, she laid a dainty hand against his chest and gave it a light shove. "And from this day forward, do not call that babe within me a bastard ever again. Just remember that your own birthright is questionable."

Danielle was tempted to tell him her true reasons for returning to Honfleur-sur-mer, but she would not give him more fodder for his malicious tongue. Instead she repeated her earlier request.

"Look, Jean-Jacques, let's be reasonable. Let us decide on a fair deal so we can both live in peace. As I said, we don't even have to see each other. This house is plenty big enough for both of us."

Jean-Jacques poured another glass of wine and waved it in her direction. "You are a persistent baggage, I give you that. Apparently, you don't see that I need not make any bargains with you? You are a mere female. Apart from you no one knows that I am not the legitimate heir to Honfleur-sur-mer. Our sire saw to it during his lifetime that I was accepted as such. What twist of fate or quirk of mind made him concoct this unjust will can never be answered. I won't stand for being stripped of my rightful inheritance. So you see, once I rid myself of you I am home free." He leaned close, suddenly sure of his victory. "I tell you what. I will give you until the end of this month to make up your mind if you would rather die by accident, " he laughed cruelly at his malicious jest, "or whether you will voluntarily go back to the nuns and birth your brat in their midst. I am sure in time you will see that you have no other choices but the ones I offer." He leered at her and wagged his eyebrows. "Of course, once a slut always a slut. As soon as you have rid yourself of that little bastard, you can come crawling back to me and play my whore in return for your keep."

Danielle's face lost all color and she sat abruptly down on the chair again. "Our father must have recognized you for the cad you truly are or he would have never cut you from his will. You think you have it all figured out, don't you?" Straightening, she fixed him with narrowed eyes. "Well, Jean-Jacques, let me put it to you as clearly as I can. I was never a whore to anyone. I am no longer a virgin, true. But the man who took my maidenhead came to care for me and treated me well. I just could not stay on, because ... ah, well what would you know of honor? ... So hear me well. I will not back down and I won't be driven off again. Honfleur-sur-mer is my home and I aim to stay here. Two can play at the game you suggest. Guard your back, Jean-Jacques, because I feel much like an animal trapped with no way out. An animal trapped with no way out will fight for its life to the death."

Once she'd issued her deadly warning, she jumped to her feet and ran from the study. She vowed she would not bend to her brother's will. The battle lines were drawn and from now on she would simply resume to wear the dagger Talon had given her.

Damn Talon. Why had he broken his promise and gotten her with child? If only he hadn't taken such delight in pricking her with his barbs about her being his slave. She would have stayed willingly. She would have served him with a happy heart if he given her but one sign that he loved her without reservation and amenable to treat her as an equal.

Danielle ran all the way to her room. Throwing herself across the bed, she allowed the tears to flow. Even after the last tears were shed and her sorrow subsided to an occasional hiccup, Danielle still wasn't feeling any better. Her heart ached at the thought that her life had taken such a dreadful turn. In a fit of self-pity, she decided she could not face another confrontation. Sniffing, she climbed under the covers and pulled the bell cord, summoning Lisette.

"I don't feel like getting up for supper, Lisette. Please have someone bring me a tray later on."

"*Ma petite*, it is not good for one in your delicate condition to brood in bed," the old servant scolded gently.

Danielle turned angry green eyes on the older woman. "Bah, who cares about me or my condition? My brother would rather see me dead and the man who got me into this predicament only wants me for a slave." And with that statement, Danielle burst into a new fit of uncontrollable weeping.

Lisette crooned and patted her sobbing mistress, but was at a loss for words. What solace could she give to Danielle when she knew that everything said was true?

CHAPTER TWENTY-ONE

Talon and his crew were not exactly pleased with the plunder they gained from their raid early that next morning. The manor had looked imposing enough from the distance, but when they closed in, they saw that the building was dilapidated. Only a handful of old servants remained, their master having died some time ago. Too old to make a run for it, they stood mutely by as the Vikings took what they thought their fair share.

Amid the grumbling of the men, Talon decided that it would be prudent to sail further down river and look for another more likely place. As they glided around a bend of the Seine, Talon recognized the area as one he had raided not too long ago, so it might not be worth their while to visit this manor again.

A devilish glint lit his aquamarine eyes when he waved for Asgard to come join him at the bow. He pointed toward the manor in the distance. "What you say? Is this the same manor we raided no more than a few weeks past? I doubt there is much to be had, but to see the look on that cringing fop's face would be worth a raid." He chuckled and the muscles of his broad chest rippled with tremors of suppressed mirth.

Asgard responded with a roar of amusement. "I say let's do it, Talon. I would be willing to forego any booty just to see that milksop blubber in fear."

"Somehow, I have the feeling that we might not have to forego our share of any loot," mused Talon, almost to himself. "I can't help but remember how the lord at Guilfleur showed us the secret panel inside the scrollwork of his mantel. It makes me wonder if our weakling lord might not have a similar hiding place?"

Asgard grinned appreciatively at Talon. "You have a wonderfully devious mind, my friend. Let's ask Leif what his thoughts are on the matter."

The idea of a few hours of diversion appealed to Leif as well as the crew. The Raider was quickly beached and secured with eager hands. The warriors scaled the gunwales with more exuberance than usual, their war cries more spine tingling than ever.

Danielle sat atop Cinnabar, her favorite gelding, adjusting the folds of her riding skirt, when a rough hand suddenly encircled her dainty ankle. For the briefest of moments she was too shocked to react to such brazen conduct. Slowly, with all the disdain she felt deep within her, Danielle turned her head, ready to scold her assailant with a scathing reprimand.

The words died on her lips as she stared straight into a face distorted by undisguised hatred and depravity. Her mouth worked soundlessly as her one-eyed attacker tightened his grip on her foot. He tugged harder, hoping to unseat her from her horse.

"I guess I'll get me finally a piece of that high-born, too good for the likes of me," he croaked hoarsely as his broad lips flattened into a lopsided grin to reveal the blackened stumps of teeth which Danielle remembered all too well.

Danielle would not have thought it possible that she could remember those reviled features with such clarity. Her heart plummeted to the pit of her stomach. Revolted that he still had his filthy hand on her ankle, Danielle lifted her riding crop. That was as far as she got.

With an evil chuckle that sounded like a death knell in her ears, Ghor snatched the crop out of her grasp. Snarling, he broke it easily in two and threw it into some nearby bushes.

"You'll not hit me with that thing," he hissed, his grip tightening painfully now. "I'll give you a choice, though. You can dismount of your own accord or I'll drag you from your mount." He edged closer, malicious glee in his watery blue eye. "I'll have you right here in those bushes over yonder, Missy. My rod is hard as iron for you. It'll make you squeal like you never have before or ever will again."

Danielle knew those were no empty threats and his last words struck terror in her heart. He meant to kill her once he had raped her. "Let go of me, Ghor," she pleaded quietly.

He shook his tangled mane and snickered softly to himself. "I've waited a long time for this chance." Lightning fast his hands shot upward, gripped her cruelly about the waist and dragged her from the gelding. Cinnabar gave a startled whinny and galloped a short distance away, then stopped and began to crop some tender grass nearby.

The impact of her fall knocked the breath out of Danielle and Ghor took advantage and quickly straddled her prone form. Knowing that her very life depended on whether she could hold him off long enough until help arrived, she twisted in a desperate quest to get free.

Ghor sneered at her puny attempt. "Fight all you want," he grunted, spittle dripping from his mouth, "I rarely have me a beauty like you or one with so much fire."

Small mewling sounds of sheer terror erupted from Danielle's throat as she fought to get away from Ghor. "Let go of me," she demanded again, knowing there was no reasoning with this crazed creature. Oh. God, she was doomed. If she let herself go limp, she'd be done for, but the more she fought him, the more aroused her became. Bile rose in her throat as he groped under her skirt. Resolutely she clamped her legs together, though it proved a short-lived victory, because he easily wedged his knee between her thighs forcing them apart.

Twisting her head back and forth, Danielle felt her strength waning rapidly. She no longer believed that she would get help from the manor. She imagined that the rest of the Vikings were ransacking the house. They surely would hold the servants at bay. As for Jean-Jacques she had no delusions about his feelings. He did not care whether she lived or died. But Danielle did not want to die. Suddenly, she realized just how many reasons she had for wanting to live. With the last bit of her energy she screamed, amazing herself for whose help she pleaded.

"Talon! Talon! Help me!" Though once she called his name, Danielle had only a split second to wonder, if Talon was among the attackers or whether he'd even cared if he were, before Ghor's hand cut off her air supply and she lost consciousness.

Talon had cornered Jean-Jacques inside his study. As once before Jean-Jacques cowered at his feet, shivering like a wet mongrel and pleading pitifully to spare his life.

Talon's broadsword was leveled at Jean-Jacques convulsing throat and he chuckled with humorless glee. "Ah, my friend, it warms my heart that you are as cowardly as ever." His voice oozed contempt. "I see you are armed this time and I wonder if you might like to fight for your honor?" Talon turned and winked broadly at his friends.

The blood drained from Jean-Jacques' already sallow features and he shook his head vehemently. With a speed that surprised even Talon, the man unbuckled his sword and threw it at Talon's feet. "Here." There was a small trickle of spittle at the corner of his slack lips. "Here, you take it. I don't want to fight you," he babbled, then clambered to his knees and tried to scoot away from his tormentors.

"No so fast," Talon chided. Ah, this was more fun than raiding. Chuckling, he deftly wielded his sword in a half arch, and catching the tails of Jean-Jacques' morning coat with its tip, he skewered him to the floor.

"What more do you want?" Jean-Jacques sobbed. "I already gave you all my coin and you took anything else you deemed of value. Look around. If there is aught else you might want, you can have it," he screeched, naked terror shining in the depth of his pale, protruding eyes.

Talon shook his head in feigned pity as he slowly advanced on the kneeling man. His icy aquamarine gaze pierced Jean-Jacques cringing form as he casually withdrew his sword from the floorboards and held it loosely in his hand.

"Ah you slimy, little worm, who boasts himself a man. We know that your kind hides their coin in different places, and cleverly so," he goaded. "I will give you to the count of a hand to show us your secret cache or I will cut off one finger at a time until you have satisfied our curiosity."

Jean-Jacques sobbed loudly and his nose began to drip as huge tears coursed down his ashen cheeks. He spread his hand palms upward and hunched his thin shoulders in outright defeat. "You have taken all I had to give when you were here last," he lied. "I--" He got no further as a bloodcurdling scream rent the air.

Talon went rigid. That voice! Had he found her at last? His heart skittered as soon as he recognized it as Danielle's, but the sound of agony it carried froze the blood in his veins. Shoving Jean-Jacques out of the way Talon and his two friends raced for the back of the house.

His eyes turned to icy shards when he spied Danielle's lifeless form sprawled beneath Ghor. The warrior was so intent on ripping the clothing from her body that he was oblivious to anything else around him. He never heard Talon calling to him.

"Get your filthy paws off her, Ghor!" Talon roared with the frustration of an injured wolf. He launched himself at Ghor, knocking him off Danielle. His lips were a white line of fury as his huge fists pounded Ghor's ugly visage. Ghor crazed with unrequited lust lashed out at Talon with equal viciousness.

Asgard and Leif, who were only a step behind Talon, quickly lifted Danielle out of the way. They were not sure if the girl was still breathing. Her fate was in the hands of the great Odin. Their immediate worry was for Talon. It was no secret that Ghor was a skillful warrior, one without scruples or qualms.

The two fighters rolled about the hard packed earth, grunting with the effort to gain the upper hand, exchanging merciless blows. Their labored breathing was the only sound to be heard as Asgard and Leif stood helplessly by, bound by an unwritten rule that prevented them from interfering in a battle of honor.

Suddenly, there was the glint of steel in the early morning sun. Ghor had managed to free his long bladed knife. For him this fight had reached the point of no return. His mind was made up that he would fight to the finish. No one would dare deny him his right to the girl once he'd won. And Ghor had no doubts that he would be victorious. Lust and hatred spurred him to greater strength and Talon was hard pressed to dodge Ghor's thrusts with the knife.

Luckily, Talon was younger, more agile, his crippled hand never held him back. Besides, he had the use of two good eyes against Ghor's solitary one. Or so he thought until Ghor reached for a handful of dirt and threw it into Talon's face. Momentarily blinded, Talon released his hold on Ghor to wipe his burning eyes. Ghor quickly took advantage of the situation and drove his wicked blade home.

Talon grunted as a searing pain exploded in his side. He froze to stare in confusion at the ever-widening stain that soaked his tunic. Still in a state of shock he watched numbly as Ghor pulled the knife free and quickly feigned a move to cut Talon again.

"Watch yourself, Talon." Asgard was beside himself. His fists clenched and unclenched at his sides, because he was unable to come to Talon's defense. Unless Ghor managed to stab Talon again, he would not dare to interfere. This ceased to be a fair fight when Ghor chose to throw sand. Asgard was tempted to toss Talon his own dagger, but his faith in his friend's superior strength stopped him from doing so.

Talon shook his flaxen mane to shake the stupor from his brain. He knew that he was no longer fighting against the breach of his authority. This was a battle of life and death. Deep in Ghor's eyes he recognized a crazed flicker, a flaw he should have acknowledged long before. He of all men should be aware of how difficult it was to live in a world where survival belonged to the fittest. He could identify with Ghor how deeply it cut to be shunned for a flaw that was none your own making. Ghor had lost his appeal to his battle scars, not much different than Talon whose hand was disfigured during that freak accident so long ago in his father's smithy. Fighting off the ghosts of the past and the weakness from the loss of blood Talon did as he'd done so many years ago, he roused himself and fought back. He ignored the searing pain in his side and lunged at Ghor, taking him to the ground once more.

"In a moment you'll join the bevy of strumpets that I dispatched during my lifetime," Ghor wheezed as he struggled to shove Talon from his chest. "I will have the black-haired witch as soon as I finish you, you arrogant bastard. Always better than the rest of us, aren't you?" he taunted. "Well, we'll see about that. You never fought a real man, have you? Came by your position because your sire is the legendary Holgar Herjolfson."

Stung by those words that reminded him of Thorson's taunts,

he gritted, "You know that I had to fight for the honor to be the leader of the Raider. I had to earn my ship through the skill of my fighting arm. I earned my stronghold in the same manner."

Ghor took advantage of Talon's momentary lapse of concentration and rolled him over in the dirt. The warrior stared down at his warlord with renewed hatred. "I don't care, Talon," he cackled diabolically. "Yonder wench is spreading her milky thighs for me already," he sniggered with a wrench of his head in Danielle's direction.

Talon followed Ghor's one-eyed gaze and saw Danielle sprawled motionless in the grass. A sick feeling lodged itself deep in his gut. It was not helped much by Ghor's subsequent words.

"I doubt you could enjoy the wench's favors anyway, even though you have such tender feelings for her," he tittered with unrestrained delight. Then he leered down at Talon, whose face was slowly turning a sickly shade of puce as Ghor's meaty hands tightened around his throat. "Because I am quite certain the wench is dead, Talon ... and you will join her shortly."

A red fog of fury clouded Talon's eyes. It leant him a strength he did not know he had left. With a mighty heave he lifted his muscular frame off the hard ground and curved his powerful hips in a sudden twist to the opposite direction. Ghor lost the death grip on his throat, and though it was raw, Talon let loose of a mighty war cry that sounded more beast than man.

Ghor floundered. It was the break Talon had been hoping for. His brawny arms pushed hard against Ghor's torso and his thickly muscled leg pinned the man's hips to the ground. He flipped Ghor with a painful grunt, not paying any heed to the bleeding gash in his aching side. It was but a small victory, because Ghor still held the long-bladed knife in his powerful hand and was as determined as ever to plunge it into Talon's heart.

"You can win this fight, Talon," roared Asgard as doubts began to assail him about his friend's stamina.

"Come on, Talon," encouraged Leif. "You are the champion arm wrestler."

Talon barely heard his friends' supportive shouts. There was no time to dwell on anything but the knowledge that this was his last chance. His strength waned ever more with each spurt of his life's blood flowing from his side. He clamped his legs tightly around Ghor's enormous bulk and squeezed for leverage. Then he concentrated with his whole being on the arm with the deadly knife. Slowly, he pressed the wicked blade downward. It seemed to stay in a state of suspense above the broad expanse of Ghor's chest. Suddenly Ghor's resistance shattered, and by sheer dint of Talon's downward push, the knife plunged deep into his ribs.

Ghor's eyes widened in surprise and he was about to say something more, but only reddish foam bubbled from his lips. With a last sigh his head lolled to the side and he was dead.

Talon rolled off the man's corpse and sprawled exhausted in the blood soaked grass, uncaring whether he lived or died himself. In fact, he willingly entrusted himself to the less than tender care of his two friends. And Asgard and Leif did not disappoint him. After seeing to his wound they carried him upstairs and laid a still unconscious Danielle next to him.

TWENTY-TWO

Danielle savored the feel of the soft feather mattress beneath her, but she was not quite ready to open her eyes just yet. She felt sore all over and her throat was raw. It hurt to swallow. And then it all came back to her ...Ghor! What had become of the brute? Had he managed to brutalize her? Mercy, where was she or was she dead? And then she did open her eyes, because she wanted to know for sure.

Danielle frowned and shifted her weight to a more comfortable position, only to come in contact with a hard expanse of warm flesh. She gasped and jerked her head in that direction. Her gaze changed to a soft mossy green.

There beside her, as naked as the day he was born, lay Talon fast asleep. Danielle rose on one elbow to feast her eyes on his beloved form. The crude bandage that covered his muscular torso gave her a start. He'd been hurt. Her hand reached for him, aching to touch and comfort. She snatched it back as if she'd been burned. No, it wouldn't do. Oh God, she loved him, but he could never know, since he did not love her in return. Longingly, her gave traveled the length of his magnificent body, trying to consign every contour to memory. She grimaced in disappointment when her view was cut short just below his lean waist by the artful drape of the sheet that covered him. Still, she went hot with wanting.

Fully awake now, Danielle became aware of the stench of unwashed flesh. She wrinkled her nose as she took an experimental sniff of the air. Talon's bandage was dirty and blood soaked, and now that she had time consider it, so was Talon. The man was in dire need of a bath. Forgetting her own aches, Danielle threw back her covers, noting with disgust that whoever had put her into bed had not bothered to take her filth encrusted gown off either. Huffing her indignation, she swung her legs over the side of the bed, but a large hand buried itself in the folds of her dress and held her back.

Danielle's heart skipped a beat. She wanted nothing more than to turn into his embrace, bury her face against his broad chest, listen to the beat of his pulse and feel safe if only for a brief moment. Instead she jerked ready to do battle only to encounter Talon's amused aquamarine gaze.

"Why you ...you rogue," she blurted. "You have been awake all along, haven't you?"

Talon chuckled, but it quickly turned into a painful cough and he grabbed his injured side. "Yes," he admitted, unable to keep the mirth from lighting his eyes. He'd been watching her through half closed eyes. His first impulse had been to haul her close and kiss her senseless and then bury himself deep inside her heat. By Thor, he'd missed her more than he'd believed possible, but he could not let on that he cared for her.

"You should know by now that a warrior cannot allow himself to sleep in oblivion while in enemy territory," his voice hoarse with pent-up emotion.

"Indeed. You dare to consider this enemy territory, when it is you who came to invade, terrorize, steal, rape ...ugh," she slapped at his hand. "Let go of me, you brute. I want to go and see just how much damage you have done this time."

Talon raised himself on one elbow, grunted with the pain it caused, and quirked an inquisitive golden brow. "How do you know I have come before?"

"I have been told," she answered imperiously and tossed her head for good measure. "Now let me go." Her eyes shot daggers at him. She was frustrated, torn between the joy of seeing him and knowing he'd only come to plunder. For a time she had hoped Talon would come for her. Damn him, but this wasn't the way she had envisioned it.

Talon smiled lazily at her. "Why do you want to get away, my sweet? Does my proximity bother you too much? Or are you embarrassed that I caught you staring?" Instead of letting go of her gown, he gave it a firm tug and dragged Danielle down on the bed again. His lips were only inches away and quite took Danielle's breath. Idly, sure of his purpose, he allowed his index finger to stroke ever so softly across the exposed swell of her breasts, and then he dipped his hand nonchalantly into the bodice to tease an already erect nipple, his aquamarine gaze all the while intent upon her rapturous face.

He chuckled deep in his throat when he gauged her reaction and saw the answering light in the depth of her eyes, which had gone almost black with desire. "Why don't you admit that you have missed me, princess?"

"Quit calling me names," she hissed, shamed that her body reacted to readily to his touch and that deep inside her desire coiled as tightly as the Gordian knot. Digging her hand into the feather mattress, Danielle fought valiantly for control of her senses. Her gaze gave lie to her next sentences to Talon's the great amusement.

"I am not bothered by your proximity at all, you pompous jackass. I am but bothered by the dreadful stink of you. In fact, I don't like myself much at this moment. And apart from all that your bandage needs changing." She jutted her chin in the obstinate way Talon loved about her. "Let me call my maid Lisette and ask her to have bath water brought up." With a sidelong glare she added, "If that is all right with the conquering forces?"

"Does that mean that once I am cleaned and you are bathed and perfumed, you will come and join me back here in bed?" he teased, knowing full well that this would nettle her and her answer would be an emphatic denial. His aquamarine eyes were luminous with desire and he waggled his brows to add a touch of humor lest he would betray his true feelings to her.

"Whether you bathe or not is none of my affair, Viking. I'll not come back to this bed as long as you are in it, I promise."

"Why, you little spitfire," he teased. "In that case I had better take advantage of you right this minute." He released his grip on her and lunged toward her. The moment he did it he realized that it was a mistake. For once Danielle had been faster than he, and all he encountered was but the warmed indentation of her body. Talon groaned with real pain and clutched his injured side. He grimaced and gritted his teeth, too proud to admit his suffering.

Danielle was halfway to the door, but the sound of his agony stopped her in her tracks. Her eyes grew concerned when she noticed the bright red stain that began to soak the dirty bandage anew. Contrite, she hurried back to the bed and knelt next to him.

"Talon," she pleaded, "let's call a truce for just a moment. Your wound needs tending and I have someone who is good at that." She bit her lip, loath to voice her next question, but aware that there was no way around it. "You don't think your men have harmed Lisette?" she whispered.

"Is this Lisette young and comely?"

Danielle giggled as the humor of it struck her. She shook her head and choked on her mirth. "More like wrinkly and sagging," she tittered.

"Well then there you have it. Unless you had no other females on the estate, I would think that she would have escaped my men's notice."

Danielle sobered and her face bespoke her revulsion at his remark. "Don't you Vikings have anything else in mind but rape and pillage?" she asked pointedly.

"It is a hard life to sail the seas and fight for your livelihood. The warriors feel they deserve a break from their hardships and the soft bodies of females let them forget for a short time that their own lives may end just around the next corner."

"Hmph! Do you even believe your own assumption or are you just inventing this to soften my heart toward your savage practices?"

Talon shrugged. "Well, I do see it that way at times, though I have not craved the gentle ministrations of any female save one for a long time." He let his sentence die away on a portent of intimation and leered at her expectantly.

Danielle blushed as his meaning came through to her loud and clear. She stood abruptly and turned from him to hide her confusion. "Well, let's see if Lisette has managed to escape your Viking warriors tender mercies," she threw sarcastically over her shoulder and pulled the ornate cord by her bed.

Talon watched her hungrily, liking what he saw. "Your idle life becomes you, princess. You have rounded out nicely since you have returned home."

Danielle had a biting retort upon her tongue, but choked it back as soon as it arose. She would not tell him that she was carrying his child. Better he did not know. It would be easier to persuade him to return to his native country alone. She had no intention to spend the rest of her life in a stark stronghold that offered few creature comforts. Nor had she any desire to fend for herself, whenever Talon and his warriors would sail away for yet another raid. It was no place to raise a child either or God forbid birth one.

"So I have," she answered instead. "You see I need not beg for my food here nor do any of the servants at Honfleur-sur-mer."

Talon looked around. "So that is what you call this place? It suits you, princess. And despite your dislike for that name, it suits you, too."

There was a timid knock on the door and a shaking Lisette entered. Her rheumy eyes went wide with shock at sight of the nude Talon in Danielle's bed.

"Oh my, *ma petite*," she gasped. "Has this brute hurt you?"

Danielle rushed to the older woman and embraced her tenderly. "No, Lisette, somehow he ended up in my bed. I still don't know the details, but as you can see for yourself, he's hurt and bleeding. I want you to bring your medicines. Can you get to them, since I am sure whether his men are still about."

Lisette made a face and rolled her eyes heavenward. "Oh yes, Miss, they are still here, but thank the good Lord most of them are too intoxicated with *monsieur's* wine to bother the maids." She wrung her hands in dismay. "Are you sure you are all right, *petite*?"

"Yes, Lisette. Just go and get your medicines." In an aside she whispered, "The sooner we can get this brute out of the house, the sooner they will all leave us alone."

When Lisette had gone, Danielle seated herself in a chair that faced the bed. "Just how did you manage to get into my chambers and my bed?" she asked icily.

Talon lifted his hands palm upward and shook his tousled mane. "Beats me. When I first came to after my fight with Ghor, I was laying next to you. Only after I assured myself that I had not died and gone to Valhalla did I allow myself to fall back to sleep."

Danielle slipped to the edge of the chair. "You fought with Ghor?" she questioned breathlessly. She tried to recall what had happened after Ghor's cruel hands had gripped her throat, but for the life of her she could not.

Talon grinned wolfishly at her. "Yes, I killed the bastard. He meant to ease his lust upon you and I could not allow that. You are mine, Danielle." There was a powerful essence within those three words that made Danielle shiver. Talon's smile softened and he repeated himself. "You are mine, Danielle, now more than ever. I saved your life, and therefore, your life belongs to me."

Danielle sat up ramrod straight. "Surely, you jest. Nobody belongs to anybody and that is all there is to it."

Talon shook his head. "You are wrong, princess. You are mine. My slave for the rest of your life." He paused and regarded her thoughtfully, "Why do you think I came to Honfleur-sur-mer? I was here but a scant two weeks ago. I knew there was little else to be had, but I hoped that you would be here ... I want you, Danielle. Forever."

"But you can't have me," she cried and tears of frustration rolled down her suddenly pale cheeks. "I belong here. This is my home. This is where I am mistress and I don't intend to trade my position to become your slave." She stood and paced the room, her hands working agitatedly at the folds of her torn gown. "I will not come with you, you hear? Never! Never! Never!"

Talon slowly reclined against the soft pillows and regarded her in silence. "We'll see," he whispered inaudibly, "We'll see."

Lisette entered the room as Danielle cried out her last bitter never and Lisette turned questioning eyes to her mistress. "*Ma petite*. Don't let this brute upset you in your delicate...."

Danielle cut the old woman off effectively with a decisive slice of her hand. "Never mind, Lisette, just do your work. When you have finished, see that a bath is brought up. I reek of the filth that Viking there brought into my home and I aim to scrub it off me," she accused with venom.

Lisette tugged at Talon's bandage with none too gentle fingers. Vexed at her behavior and unable to follow their rapid French, Talon snatched her hand and held it fast in his enormous paw. His eyes were like blue steel as he stared angrily at her. "Watch how you treat my wounds, you old witch," he cautioned. "A wild cat would be gentler than you are."

Lisette's stilled in mid-air. Though she had not understood his words, his meaning was clear and she continued her ministrations a bit more gingerly. She never favored Talon with so much as a look or word. Once she was finished she directed her advice toward Danielle.

"Tell this barbarian that he will have to move carefully for a few days so the wound will heal properly. Not that it will make

any difference since his hide is full of ugly scars already." She
sniffed in disdain as she gathered her medicines. "Will there be
anything else, *mademoiselle*? I have given directions for a bath
and it will be up shortly. Will you need assistance?"

Danielle shook her head, but she pointed to a large
embroidered screen. "Please make sure to put this screen in place
to shield the tub from prying eyes, Lisette," she directed.

Lisette did as she was asked and then left the room, still shaken
by the advents in the house.

Talon lay exhausted against the pillows, his mind racing as he
tried to contrive a way to persuade Danielle to come away with
him without force. He loved the minx, but he was not about to
tell her. He was a Viking warrior and had to retain the upper
hand. Once she confessed that she had tender feelings for him,
he would allow his own to be known to her, but not before.

Danielle sat silently in her chair, contemplating her situation.
Talon had made no bones about it that he meant to take her back
with him. She would rather die than go back to the loneliness
and degradation her life at Dragon's Lair would be reduced to.
Never. He did not love her and she'd rather cut her tongue out
than let him know that she loved him.

Two burly men brought the warm water and left. Danielle
disappeared behind the shielding screen and hurriedly disrobed.
She added essence of roses and whipped the water into a foamy
lather. Quickly she stepped into the steaming tub and Talon
could hear her exhale in satisfaction as she lowered herself into
the soothing bath.

It was at great cost to his comfort that Talon rose from the bed.
Draping the sheet about his lean middle, he tiptoed toward the
hindering screen. His mind played tantalizing games with him
and his manhood clamored beneath the linen shroud, despite the
constant pain in his side.

Unabashed, he stuck his head around the corner in time to
watch her lift a slender leg from the steamy water. Ever so
casually, she ran a soapy rag along its length. Talon licked his
lips and swallowed convulsively. His manhood no longer just
clamored but throbbed and raised the sheet suggestively before
him. The luscious tops of her milky white breasts were barely
visible above the foam, but the memory of how they fitted into
his palms, the taste of them, made him forget what few scruples
he had harbored moments earlier.

He stepped around the side of the tub, grinning impishly down at her. "Is that offer still open that I would bathe with you?"

Danielle squeaked in alarm at his sudden appearance and crossed her arms protectively over her bosom. Her eyes flashed green venom. "Get away, you brute," she sputtered. "How dare you intrude on my private bath? I never said you could share mine, but that you should have one yourself," she corrected him acidly.

Talon shrugged and dropped the sheet, one hand already on the rim of the narrow tub. His gaze followed hers. When he lifted his eyes again, there was a wealth of emotion in their depths. "I see that I still hold some appeal for you despite your constant denial to the contrary." Gingerly, he stepped into the warm soapy water and was mildly surprised that Danielle did not get up to flee.

Danielle dared not budge for fear he would notice the bulge of her once flat belly. After all, it had not taken Jean-Jacques long to recognize it for what it was. Anger at being trapped so unfairly lent her strength.

"Well, Viking, if you want a bath so badly, maybe you should have it all to yourself. Just hand me the linen behind you, so I can step out."

Talon grimaced and shook his tousled mane. "Only if you promise to help me bathe, my sweet. You see, I am quite helpless, since I should not get these bandages wet." He leered drolly at her, making her giggle despite her fury. "While you are at it, you might ease the ache in my mighty rod as well," he suggested with feigned austerity as he pointed to his erection.

Danielle slapped the soapy cloth she had used at his impudent manhood and Talon yelped in mock distress. "Why wench, would you hurt your own source of pleasure?" he asked innocently.

"Bah," Danielle scoffed. "I've little choice in whether it brings pleasure or not. You take what you want, when you want it, with hardly a care for me."

"You wound me sorely, Danielle. Haven't I heard you moan beneath me that I should ride you harder and faster, that I should penetrate deeper and never stop?"

Danielle blushed to the roots of her hair and dared not meet his questing eyes. She was saved from an answer, when loud knocks at the door interrupted their ribald banter.

"Hand me that linen now, Viking," she demanded. "Don't make me suffer any more humiliations than I have had to suffer already."

Talon reluctantly handed her the length of cloth and she wrapped it carefully about herself without affording him much but a hasty glimpse of her entire form.

Danielle went to the door just as it was thrown open and Asgard and Leif strode in without so much as a by your leave. They ignored her except to ask where Talon might be.

"I am here, you sons of she-wolves," Talon grunted. "You couldn't have chosen a worse time to interrupt."

Asgard stepped around the screen, then snorted in derision. "Some Viking warlord you are, malingering in a tub full of scented water, playing games with a wench, while your men chomp at the bit to go raiding. What do you want us to tell them?"

Talon grinned up at his friends, wordlessly acknowledging their assessment of the situation. Faking a grimace he groaned, "My injured side gives me much pain. I don't think I would be of use to any of you, since it affects my fighting arm."

"Bah, it'd be the first time you would let a small injury stop you from a raid, Talon. If anything I would wager that it is another part of your anatomy that pains you," Leif scoffed. "You can't expect us to loll about this place for much longer. The younger wenches are fair worn and the wine cellars won't still our thirsts much longer either."

Talon chuckled at the candid admission of the younger man. "Somehow I have the feeling that the wenches would be glad for a small respite." He scratched at the bandage covering his bare chest and stared balefully at his two friends. For the first time in his life Talon was torn between his loyalty to his men and his love for a woman. He had hoped that Danielle had missed him and would welcome him with open arms. He wanted her back, but this time he wanted her back of her own volition. He rubbed a tired hand across his eyes. "Give me two days and then come back for me," he finally said. "Take the men down river and let them raid to their hearts content. You lead them in my stead, Asgard."

The two friends hesitated, exchanging worried looks. "We could stay over another day, if that should gain you strength. The warriors are not opposed to resting for another day." Asgard pulled a chair closer, leaned toward Talon and changed the subject. "We have thrown Ghor's carcass to the fishes. He is better off among them than he would be planted in the earth of a foreign land. He was a good warrior until his lust robbed him of his sanity."

"Aye, he was good warrior until then and you did the right thing to commit him to the sea. I still say that it would be better for the men, if you took them down river and let them raid another manor or two."

"Aye, Talon," Asgard's eyes gleamed with anticipation. "I'll treat the Raider as if she were my own." At the door, he turned and grinned. "Should we bring you a pretty bauble or would you rather have a comely wench?" In answer Talon threw the soapy rag at him, but Asgard nimbly dodged the wet missile.

CHAPTER TWENTY-THREE

As soon as Asgard and Leif left, Danielle came charging around the screen like a maddened bull. "I heard what you said," she accused. "Go with them and keep on raiding. 'Tis the Viking thing, isn't it? The sooner you are out of my sight, the sooner I can forget all about you," she hissed, two pink spots high on her cheeks a telltale sign of her aggravated state.

Talon threw her a wounded look. "Ah, and here I thought you would only be too glad to have me with you for a meager two days." He opened his arms to signal defeat. "Well, wench, at least have pity on me for this day and help me wash off the stink that my fight with Ghor left behind. Although I find it appealing when you wrinkle your little nose just so, I do not care to be the cause of it," he teased, suppressing his mirth.

Danielle tightened the linen cloth about her, not realizing that it was damp enough to cling in all the right places and would leave little to Talon's already vivid imagination. His eyes widened for a fraction of a second. He went completely still, but Danielle was far too incensed to notice. The discovery that Danielle was carrying his child, and he had no doubt about the parentage, evoked a multitude of emotions within him. He carefully hid them behind hooded lids.

"Oh, you beast," railed Danielle. "You rub me sorely in all the wrong places." The moment the words were out she bit her lips, wished she could make them unsaid. Talon would surely twist them to his liking.

Talon did indeed not disappoint her. He leered drolly at her. "I could rub you in all the right places, wench, if only you would give me leave to do so," he offered.

Danielle huffed and spun angrily away. "Just give me a moment to change into a gown and I'll help you wash your miserable carcass," she snapped.

"Don't bother with the gown, my sweet. I like you just the way you are. I could feast my starved senses upon your lush form while you take care of my needs."

"Indeed," sneered Danielle as she stepped around the privacy screen. Her heart beat a crazy tattoo in celebration of having succeeded to dupe him about her condition. She hurriedly pulled on an old gown in case she would get it wet, then twisted her hair into a casual knot atop her head with becoming little tendrils drifting down over her ears and nape.

She stepped around the divider once more, a no-nonsense expression on her flushed face. "All right, Viking, let's be about the business of making you less offensive," she quipped and snatched up the washrag like a battle flag.

With much care she avoided wetting Talon's bandage, but the touch of her soft hands along his flesh drove him near to distraction. He gritted his teeth as desire coursed through him with such intensity that it left him almost limp. Danielle was oblivious to his discomfort. She prattled on about his wound and how it would need great care lest it would infect.

When she was done with his massive chest and the powerful arms with their heavy silver bands, she casually dried him with a cloth and handed him the rag to do the rest.

"Surely, you don't expect me to wash the rest of you?" she challenged in disgust, when he raised a golden brow in mute question. "There is nothing so wrong with you that you can't finish your own ablutions."

Talon craved her touch on the rest of his body despite the discomfort it brought with it. He thought quickly of a ruse to lure her into doing his bidding.

"It's not as if you were unfamiliar with my body, Danielle," he wheedled. "It should leave you quite unaffected considering that you have no special feelings for me. It's only that I am afraid I might wet the bandages and that old harridan Lisette won't like to redo them quite so soon." He stared at her with a bland expression, hoping his little speech would trick Danielle to fall for his ploy.

"All right then, but you will have to stand up and you have do stand quite still, if you want me to wash the rest of you."

Talon almost jumped from the water with glee, but caught himself in the last moment and heaved his massive frame from the tub with feigned difficulty.

Danielle swallowed hard at the gorgeous sight of him. His bronzed skin slick with damp, inviting to the touch. The muscles of his chest rippled with every small move and his manhood stood proudly before him. Engorged with desire it rose from its nest of thick golden curls, its size underscored by the length of Talon's long, powerful legs. Danielle stood mesmerized, staring at that part of him, unable to keep sweet memories at bay. She shook with wanting, her knees suddenly too weak to hold her up. Averting her eyes, she slumped to the ground, studiously soaping the already soapy rag.

Talon stood as still as a statue, secretly enjoying her obvious discomfort. He could wait until she made the first move and then injury be damned he would have her. He would never admit it aloud, but she had haunted him even before Dragon's Lair had been out of his sight, when he had left on that fateful raid. Had he known she would escape ...well, he hadn't so it was a moot point to ponder.

With a determination born of desperation Danielle pulled herself up by the rim of the tub and leisurely washed along Talon's flat stomach. Time and again she dipped the rag into the tepid water and washed and rinsed, carefully avoiding his raised manhood.

Talon was almost beside himself with hot hunger. "Can't you hurry a little, Danielle?" he asked through gritted teeth.

When Danielle raised her eyes to him, they were dark green with blatant longing. "Aye, I'll hurry," she replied hoarsely, but her trembling hand would not follow her inner command to wash across the cause of her intense desire.

Quite vexed, Talon snatched the rag from her slack hand and finished washing himself. "There," he growled. "I am done. Will you hand me something to dry myself, wench?"

Danielle nodded mutely and handed him the same linen she had used earlier. Talon accepted it with ill grace and then he could no longer deny himself. With something akin a howl, he drew her to his hard naked length and captured her mouth in a rough kiss.

On a small sob, Danielle melted into his steely arms. Her body clamored for his without shame. She reveled in the feel of him through the thin material of her gown and pressed closer without thought. Talons mouth did not leave her lips as he held her close. Lifting her, he bore her to the bed and gently pressed her into the feather mattress, the pain in his side no longer a factor.

He broke his kiss only to gaze lovingly into her eyes. "I've missed you, wench," he admitted hoarsely, as his fingers nimbly undid the tiny buttons of her bodice. And then for a long time there was no more conversation. He took infinite care to make love to her in the most tender fashion he was capable of. Together they reached heights beyond any of their fantasies and the emotions they experienced left them lying breathless in each other's arms afterwards.

As their bodies cooled so did Danielle's ardor. Wordlessly, she disengaged herself from Talon's embrace, not willing to let him see the tears in her eyes. There had been no words of love, no terms of endearment, no vow of any kind. I missed you wench was not enough for a lasting relationship. Without the knowledge that there would be more between them than carnal passion, she was not about to let him glimpse the true state of her own heart either.

It angered Talon when Danielle turned away so abruptly. He had made tender love to her, paced himself with disregard to his own rampant passion. Had made sure that she had reached her own glory before he followed her to join in ecstasy. What more could the wench want? He missed her warmth, there was a hollow feeling inside him such as he had never known before.

Talon slid close to Danielle's shaking body and enfolded her into his hard embrace. "Did I hurt you, my sweet?" he murmured against her hair.

Danielle shook her head in denial. He had been as tender as she could have asked for, but why did the lummox not realize what truly ailed her? Why could he not bring himself to tell her he loved her, if indeed he did?

"If I did not hurt you, then why is it that you are crying?"

Danielle shrugged her shoulders in obstinate silence.

"Bah, I am sick of your little games, Danielle," he roared in frustration. "Whenever you are ready to tell me your problem, I am here and ready to listen." He rolled away from her and curled into a tight ball, perplexed as well as hurt.

Danielle waited until his breathing took on a regular rhythm before she crept from bed. Quietly she left the room and headed downstairs. As luck would have she encountered Jean-Jacques, who was dressed and on his way out. Once she would have inquired where he was going out of concern for his welfare, but those times were forever gone.

Jean-Jacques stopped in his tracks when he spied her descending the staircase. His features still bore the telltale marks of the harrowing ordeal he endured. His eyes were sunken deeply into their sockets with deep dark circles underneath them, making his sallow skin even more sickly pale than usual. Whatever humiliation he had suffered at the hands of the jeering Vikings, it had not dulled the edge of his sharp tongue. He leered lewdly at Danielle, then made a big show of studying his nails while he drawled lazily, "The servants have informed me that most of our unwanted visitors have left, save one. As I hear he is enamored by your obvious charms, dear sister. Have you serviced him well this morning?"

"You swine," Danielle spat with all the contempt she could muster, though her face turned crimson as his barb struck home.

Jean-Jacques snickered at her evident mortification. He leaned close and sniffed the air about her. "I see you don't deny my claim, dear sister. And even if you did, you have the smell of a well drilled slut about you."

Danielle was shaken by his crude behavior. She wanted to hurt him back. "You swine," she repeated. "At least I am pleasured by a man. God only knows where you find yours. And where were you when I was attacked and nearly killed?" she spat venomously.

"Why you filthy Viking whore, how dare you insult me in that manner. Look to your own deliverance. I would not sully my hands to help you." He slapped his riding gloves into the palm of his hand, then spun on his heels to leave her standing in the hall.

Thoroughly angered by her brother's crude remarks, Danielle padded toward the kitchens. Despite her fury, she was still hungry, in fact it seemed she never filled up anymore.

Emile, Lisette and several of the maids were busily trying to set the place back in order. The Viking raiders had left half eaten food on counters and tables and spilled wine and ale in careless abandon.

Danielle sniffed and wrinkled her nose. "Savages," she muttered under her breath as she picked a broken plate off the floor.

"Can I get you anything, *mademoiselle*?" Lisette asked solicitously.

"No, I'll manage on my own. You have enough on your hands if this kitchen is ever set to rights again. Hopefully, they'll leave as soon as they pick up Talon."

Lisette clucked her tongue, choosing her words very carefully. It had not escaped her during her brief encounter with Talon that the Viking had a tender spot for Danielle. "The one upstairs...is he--?" she meant to ask, if Talon was the leader, but one look at Danielle's blushing face told her more than she would have been willing to divulge.

Lisette blushed herself and rolled her eyes back in her head. "Oh," she said in way of understanding.

Mortified, Danielle grabbed a chunk of bread and some cheese and fled from the kitchen. She was chewing the last of her meal when she entered her chamber. Talon was still in bed, reclining against the pillows, his hands laced behind his head. There was a pensive mood about him.

As Danielle shut the door behind her, Talon sat up. He regarded her with intensity. "I smell the sea through yonder window." He jerked his head in that direction, but his gaze never left her. "Would you show me this Honfleur-sur-mer which you call your home?"

His request took Danielle completely off guard. What was happening with this savage Viking? Was there actually hope that he could adjust to gentler ways? She noted that he had shaved and that his normally unruly mane had been combed into a semblance of style. Danielle rubbed her hands against her sides and swallowed hard. "If you can sit a horse despite your wound, we could take a ride to the cliffs. It's not far, but the view of the North Sea is breathtaking from up there."

"I can sit a horse." Talon jumped nimbly from the bed without paying any heed to his nudity. With a wry grin he grabbed up his bloodied wolf skin tunic and held it up for Danielle's inspection. "We should have washed this in the river," he explained in way of an apology. "I just hope it won't spook your mount."

Danielle took a long look at the offensive garment. "Since we have no way of knowing, we should not take a chance." She walked to the bell pull and rang.

Lisette appeared in short order and entered upon Danielle's curt bidding. At her strangled gasp, two pairs of eyes cut in her direction. Poor Lisette's eyes threatened to pop out of her head as she stared speechless at Talon, who stood there quite casually in the altogether.

Talon followed the older woman's gaze as did Danielle and for a moment there was a strained silence in the room. Shrugging, Talon held the wolf's skin in front of his loins and chuckled as he watched Lisette struggle to regain her composure.

Danielle on the other hand was quite beyond embarrassment. "Lisette, please go to my sire's chambers and select a pair of breeches and a shirt which might fit this Viking," she asked matter-of-fact. "I have promised to take him for a tour of the estate."

Lisette fled from the room muttering something about the downfall of the world. She returned posthaste with a pair of serviceable woolen breeches and a simple linen shirt with only a hint of lace at the throat and the cuffs.

"It will fit him snug, seeing as how large he is," Lisette said to Danielle as she handed Talon the clothing.

"Take the fur tunic with you and see that Emile cleans it, Lisette. Tell him a good dunking in a soapy solution should do the trick."

For some unfathomable reason Talon disappeared behind the screen to dress and Danielle was unprepared for the sight he presented short minutes later. She gasped when he stepped out. He looked every inch the country squire. Her sire's breeches fit him like a second skin, molding themselves to his massive muscular thighs, clinging to slender hips and a lean waist. The shirt, once loose and bulky on her sire, fit snugly across his broad shoulders, the sleeves barely meeting his wrists. He wore it open at the neck, exposing a goodly expanse of bronzed chest. And Danielle's gaze involuntarily fastened on the impressive bulge at the junction of his thighs.

"You ...you ...you look as fine as any Frenchman I have ever laid eyes on," she stammered.

Talon swept her a bow that would have been acceptable at any cultured gathering. It evoked the oddest feeling of pride inside her. She smiled at him with genuine pleasure and Talon's heart did a sudden flip.

"So, let's get on with our little jaunt around your estate," he proposed, deliberately breaking the enchanted mood that threatened his very existence.

Flustered, Danielle hurried out of the room with Talon close at her heels. She had Cinnabar saddled for him and she took the little mare Minette.

"This is a fine horse, you have," Talon commented as he patted

Cinnabar's sleek neck. He sniffed the air and his aquamarine eyes changed to a softer hue when he detected the distinct smell of the sea upon the gentle breeze. "Show me the North Sea first," he pleaded.

Danielle spurred the little mare as Talon followed on Cinnabar. At the bottom of the hill, she stopped, but before she had the chance to dismount, Talon was by her side to lift her from the saddle. He held her close to his solid form and stared deeply into her eyes. Slowly, he lowered her along the hard length of him, savoring her softness through the layers of their clothing. There was a question on his tongue, one that had plagued him for a while, but he could not bring himself to ask it.

They were both short of breath when they broke apart, but each was unwilling to give the other the upper hand. Danielle forged ahead and Talon climbed easily after her. Neither remembered his injury. Once on the top of the granite plateau, the dazzling vista of the North Sea unfolded before their gazes.

Talon stood slightly apart from Danielle, his face to the sea and there was a dreamy look about him as he stood so. He breathed deeply, as if he could not get enough of the clean salt tinged air. Danielle threw him a sideways glance and as usual she was awed by the sheer power and male beauty this man exuded and the effect his maleness had on her.

"Do you come here often?" Talon asked huskily without taking his eyes from the roiling waves.

"Mostly I come here whenever I am troubled and need to be alone," she confessed, thinking back to the time she had come to this plateau with the thought of ending it all.

"Have you come here lately?"

Danielle was loath to share her problems with Talon. She had made up her mind that she was strong enough to carry her own burdens. She needed no man to fend for her. She pursed her mouth in a most becoming manner Talon noted out of the corner of his eye. "Aye, it is a grand place to pass the time," she answered evasively. "You can sit here for hours and stare at the sea and it is never the same. The sound of the waves crashing against the granite cliffs below is right soothing."

"Has life been good for you, since you have returned to Honfleur-sur-mer?"

Danielle did not know how to reply to that. She had hoped to find Jean-Jacques more amenable to her return. Had hoped he would take her up on calling a truce and live in harmony. None of it had happened. Jean-Jacques was still as unconcerned about her welfare as he had been when he had taken her to the nuns. No, she certainly couldn't say that life had been good, but to her it was preferable to the loneliness of Dragon's Lair. And even if Jean-Jacques continued to be a problem, Danielle was sure she could handle him.

"You haven't told me yea or nay, princess. What is it then? Are you content here or not?"

Her green eyes flashed their anger at Talon. "I am happy enough, thank you. I will also be quite busy replenishing our larder and the wine cellar for the coming winter, no thanks to you," she snapped.

Talon chuckled. The wench never ceased to surprise him. She didn't give an inch and by the same token she asked for nothing. And he loved it when she was angry. She was a beauty at any rate, but when she was upset, her eyes flashed with green fire and two bright pink spots would appear on her cheekbones, while her mouth, ah yes, her mouth. ...She would run the tip of her tongue ever so sensually, yet quite without design, across the lower lip, and it always succeeded to make his heart skip several beats and play funny games with his breathing...

"Why you should know by now that we Vikings have no scruples to take what we want or need." He wagged a long finger in her direction. "At least we took no lives and left your manor standing."

Danielle snorted rudely and made an exaggerated curtsy. "My thanks, kind sir, for little favors."

They stood in silence then for many long moments, each caught up in their thoughts. Talon was furious with himself. Why did he always end up making her angry? He wanted to win her favor. Yearned to have her tell him that she loved him, but instead he found ever-new ways to rile her temper.

A harsh gust of wind blew in off the sea. Caught by surprise, Danielle was hard put to keep her balance. She leaned into the wind, her arms flailing out from her sides as she fought from being drawn closer to the cliff edge. In one long stride Talon was behind her, his strong arms encircled her slender form, dragging her against his solid chest. Only his mouth betrayed his inner tension. He was no fool. If anyone knew the havoc strong gusts could play, it was Talon.

It felt good to be enfolded in his powerful embrace. Danielle relaxed against his solid chest, a soft sigh escaping her lovely mouth. In the process of wriggling against him, an enticing gap was created at the top of her bodice. It presented Talon with a tempting few of her breasts, one that made his mouth go dry with desire.

He decided that the time for a confrontation had come. Still standing behind her, he rubbed his cheek against hers, eliciting something like a contented purr from her lips. The smell of roses tickled his nose. Together with her very own woman's scent it played further havoc with his senses. Ever so slowly Talon slid his large hands along the length of her body until they covered the small mound of her belly. He casually laced his fingers together, holding it tenderly within their warm hollow.

He felt Danielle stiffen against him. He waited for her to say something, not realizing her shock that her secret had been discovered robbed Danielle momentarily of rational thought.

Talon rubbed his cheek against hers once more, just a little harder than before. His breath was warm in her ear, his voice deceptively tender. His hands had begun a rhythmic circular stroking over her small bulge. "When were you going to tell me about this, Danielle?" he asked silkily, beneath the tenderness unmistakable menace.

"What ...tell you about what?" Danielle stammered trying to hide her agitation.

He propelled her around so she was forced to face him. One long lean finger pushed her chin upward. "Why have you kept this a secret?" He would not put it into words. Let her explain. He could be stubborn to a fault. Just so he'd leave no doubt about what he was speaking about, he cupped her belly with a possessive hand.

"It's none of your affair," she said with equal stubbornness.

Talon bent closer to her, his eyes flashing their anger into hers. "It is my affair, since I know that this babe is of my making," he thundered, his aquamarine eyes stormy.

Danielle lost some of her bravado, no longer sure that she had the upper hand. "When did you find out?" she whispered.

Talon allowed a small smile to lift the corners of his generous mouth. "I had an inkling when I first glimpsed the fullness of your lovely bosom, my sweet," he teased and leisurely caressed the object of his admiration with a tentative finger. "But you left me no longer in doubt, when you appeared around the screen wearing nothing but that damp linen. It outlined every delectable curve of you and emphasized that wondrous place that holds my son." His smile widened and his eyes were shining with love. He bent and kissed her tenderly. "Ah, Danielle, you make me the proudest man on earth. Just wait till I tell Asgard and Leif." He crowed like a proud rooster, lifted her high into the air and spun her in ever tightening circles.

Danielle squealed with fright, since they were still dangerously close to the edge of the cliffs. "Put me down, you lummox," she screamed. Talon only regained his senses when he recognized the sheer panic in her voice.

"I'm sorry, my sweet. I got carried away with happiness."

"Well, save it," she remarked snidely, determined to take the wind out of his sails. She could not lose the advantage at any cost. "How would you know that the babe I carry is yours? He could be any man's."

Talon saw through her ploy and was not daunted for a moment. He dragged her close to his unyielding body and fixed her with a piercing stare. "Then tell me who the sire of this babe might be," he demanded.

Danielle's eyes cut away from his, because she did not know how to carry her lie any further.

Talon shook her slightly within his embrace. "Tell me who the sire is. I want to know for sure. Is it that fop back at the mansion perhaps?" Talon knew that no other man could have fathered the babe, but he had a perverse need to hear it from her lips and he held her away so he could see her eyes. He also wanted to know the exact relationship between Danielle and the lord of Honfleur-sur- mer.

Danielle's laugh was brittle and she shook her head in denial. "If you are talking about my half-brother Jean-Jacques when you are speaking about that fop, then you will know the answer yourself." She dropped her gaze and involuntarily it fell on her belly. Her eyes snapped up at Talon. "Why did you get me with child? You promised that you would not. You said no slave would ever bear your babe. So why did you burden me with it then?"

Talon tried to pull her back against his body, but Danielle wrenched free. Shivering with emotion she wrapped her arms around herself. "I will not stand for it that my child will be usurped into your community, a nonentity. I will not have him grow up with people pointing their fingers at him and saying "That little bastard over there is Talon's get from his French whore. No, Talon, I will not stand for that. This babe is mine and mine alone." Her last words were full of anguish as she turned and ran down the slope, leaving Talon standing dumbfounded and speechless.

Danielle was atop the little mare before Talon reached Cinnabar and she galloped down the hill at breakneck speed.

"Come back here, wench," Talon bellowed after her. "Come back here or I swear I'll tan your bottom."

Danielle was beyond hearing his threats. Tears streamed down her pale cheeks and the pain of feeling betrayed made it hard for her to take a deep breath. She dug her heels in the horse's flanks, not caring where she went or whether it was safe.

Talon whipped his hand across Cinnabar's hindquarters and dug his heels into his flanks. "By Odin, I'll never understand the female species," he swore under his breath. "She did not even give me time to tell her that I will claim the babe legally, damn her."

Danielle twisted in her saddle to see if Talon was following her, and as she did so, the mare stumbled and lost her footing, bringing them both down in a headlong crash. Danielle reacted instinctively when she felt the mare stumble. She flung herself from the saddle and curled into a tight ball before she hit the ground.

Talon saw the mare lose her footing and a mournful scream tore from his chest. He never stopped Cinnabar, but leapt from the gelding as soon as he came abreast of Danielle's still form on the ground.

He went down on both knees and there were tears in his eyes as he gazed down on the only woman he had ever loved in his life. His large hands felt tenderly about her head, feeling for the bump he was sure to find there. "Ah, Danielle," he sighed. "Why did you run from me? Don't you know that you are the only woman I have ever loved? Don't you know what this babe means to me? He'll be my firstborn son." He whispered all the sweet things that were in his soul, but Danielle did not hear any of them.

Frantic with fear, Talon bent and listened for her heartbeat. It was so faint that he was not sure that he heard it right. And then there was a thundering sound near him and when he looked up he gazed straight into the pale cold eyes of Jean-Jacques.

Jean-Jacques had been out riding and he had seen the Viking chasing after Danielle. When he had seen his sister fall, his first thought was the hope that she would perish from it. Curious he rode up to the couple, but by the time he got there Talon had already brushed away his tears and his gaze was equally as cold as that of Jean-Jacques.

"Is the bitch dead?" Jean-Jacques asked avidly, his greed overcoming caution. His heart filled with dread the moment he met the glowering aquamarine glare directed at him. He held up his gloved hand as if to deflect a blow and sneered, "You are welcome to the bitch, but you might as well know that some Viking already planted his brat inside her. Do with her as you please, it makes me no never mind."

Talon rose slowly from Danielle's side and advanced menacingly toward Jean-Jacques. "You mewling coward. You are not fit to hold a candle for this courageous woman," he snarled and his eyes flashed his contempt. "You best pray to your god that she survives, because if something happens to her, I will not spare your mansion and I won't spare your miserable life ...Now get! I can't bear the sight of you."

Jean-Jacques jerked his mount's reins and galloped off toward the mansion. He would not stick around to see if Danielle lived or died. He planned on being miles away by the time Talon brought her back home.

CHAPTER TWENTY-FOUR

When Talon carried Danielle's limp form into the house, he called loudly for Lisette. The old woman came running, but when she spied Danielle in Talon's arms, she shrieked her dismay.

"Cease your caterwauling, old hag. Your mistress needs your help not your sympathy."

His curt command shook Lisette out of her shock and she quickly led the way upstairs. "I will be back in a moment, *monsieur*. Do not let her sleep. Talk to her and make her answer you. I will return shortly with my medicines."

Talon nodded, then seated himself on the edge of the bed. With a gentleness he hadn't known he possessed, he shook Danielle and begged her to reply.

"You have to answer me, Danielle. I am here, princess. I--" he wanted to say I love you, but the words refused to cross his lips. At least he managed to make Danielle mumble with annoyance when he persisted in shaking her arms.

He grinned down at her, when she grumbled something about wanting to be left alone. "That's my obedient wench," he baited her. "I always like for my slaves to listen to what I have to tell them." He bit his lip in torment a moment later, when he realized that he had said the wrong thing. It seemed she had tuned him out and was heading back into oblivion.

Talon shook her again, urgently, fear clearly coming through in his voice. "Danielle, don't shut me out. Danielle, wake up," he entreated.

Lisette walked into the room without knocking. She carried a basin of cool water and a tray of medicinal herbs. She heard Talon's last words and grimaced in disgust. "If that is the best you can do, Viking, then you might as well let her slip away."

Talon glowered at the diminutive servant and rose from the bed. "What more can I tell her, you troublesome old bag of bones?" he thundered.

Lisette raised herself to her full height, which left her still two heads shorter than Talon and she braced her fists into her waist. "Why you thick-pated, strutting rooster," she yelled back, her fear of him totally forgotten in her concern for Danielle. "Have you ever heard of saying I love you to someone?" She cocked her head at him and watched his reaction closely.

"You may call me a meddlesome or anything else that might come to your dense mind," she jeered, "but you can't call me a fool." She pointed her work-worn finger at him and shook it for effect. "I saw it in her eyes and I see it in yours. And I am certain that you are the sire to the babe she carries beneath her heart. Oh, don't deny it. The truth is as plain as the nose on your handsome features."

Lisette's anger was working itself into a near frenzy as she advanced upon him like an irate bantam hen. "You don't know what a treasure you have in this girl. I could have rid her of that unwelcome burden, but she would not have any part of it. Loves you too much she does." Lisette bobbed her head up and down to emphasize her words.

"Why, you old witch. You are lucky she did not seek your miserable services or I--"

"You what? You had no notion that you had got her with your babe before you came here, did you? And she knew you didn't know, because she found out only after she was here for a while."

Talon stood still and let Lisette's words sink in. His gaze strayed to the bed, where Danielle laid all too quietly, her slender form dwarfed by the sheer size of the four-poster. Then he looked back at Lisette, entreaty in his eyes.

"Please go to her and help her," he begged softly, all Viking bluff and audacity gone from his voice.

Lisette denied herself a satisfied grin. Instead she nodded gruffly. "Aye, but I need your help as well."

"Anything at all, Lisette," he promised eagerly.

She ordered him about like a small boy and bade him sit on the edge of the bed. "And whilst I wipe her brow, you talk sweet words of love to her," she commanded as her old heart soared with pleasure that Danielle might yet find the love she deserved.

Talon held Danielle's small hand tenderly in his own and suddenly he did not find it difficult anymore to tell her that he loved her, but he told her in his own native tongue so Lisette was not privy to everything he wanted to say to her. He stayed with her and did not budge from her side throughout the night, nodding off ever so often whenever exhaustion overtook him.

Danielle awoke during the night and stared in amazement at Talon. She had a terrible headache and very little recollection of anything else. What was that Viking doing there, sitting asleep on the edge of her bed? Too tired to care, she rolled over and went back to sleep.

Lisette found the two, partially entwined and fast asleep. She chuckled and the raspy sound woke Talon. He stared glumly at the old servant before he remembered why she had come. Quickly, he shifted his gaze to Danielle and was relieved to see her bosom rise and fall in even intervals.

Lisette came clucking to the bed. "That babe will be a lusty one, once he is born. It is his second tumble from a horse and still he clings inside his mother's womb," she marveled. She grinned lewdly at Talon, then murmured for his ears alone, "You planted him well I gather," then cackled when Talon's chest began to heave in silent mirth as he accepted her compliment and pride filled his heart.

Lisette left them shortly, promising Talon to come back later with some breakfast. Awake now and his thoughts twirling about his mind, Talon stretched more comfortably on the bed and curved his huge body around Danielle's slighter form. Gently, so as not to waken her, his hand stole to the mound that held his babe, cradling it within his large palm. He smiled to himself as visions unfolded before him of a small shape with curly black hair much like his mother's and blue eyes like his own. He vowed to keep him safe, to love him even if he was less than perfect. His misshapen hand clenched beneath its protective glove, but Talon barely noticed.

Danielle woke to the warmth of Talon's body against her back and the sheltering cradle of his hand on her stomach. She smiled into her pillow and savored the moment. Maybe the hulking Viking really did care.

Conditioned through a lifetime of vigil, Talon was instantly aware that Danielle was awake. He was tempted to pull back his hand and give her the impression that he didn't care, when Lisette's admonition came back to him. The time had come to declare his feelings. Slowly and ever so tenderly, he rolled her over so he could look into her eyes. He smiled wryly, because suddenly he felt as shy as a young boy. The words of love were there on his tongue, but they refused to be spoken. Playing for time, he stroked her hair and ran his index finger across her cheekbone, then along the delicate column of her throat. He licked his lips and almost succumbed to the desire to kiss her and forget about pretty speeches, but he knew it would not do.

"Danielle," he whispered softly and lifted his gaze to hers. "Danielle, I care deeply for you. I want you to be my life mate." He was extremely proud that he had said his piece. Yet, the joyous reaction he anticipated seemed a long time in coming.

Talon's declaration of love took a while before it penetrated to the recesses of Danielle's brain. It came as a shock to her that he would admit for caring for her deeply, but she grappled with the notion of the meaning of lifemate. She swallowed hard and threw him a cautious look.

"What do you mean by wanting me for your life mate?" she asked coldly.

"Why just that," Talon answered crossly. "What more do you want?"

"Actually, I want nothing from you," she snapped at him. "Go your own way and leave me to mine."

Talon rose on his elbow and glared down at her. His patience was at an end. "You'll be my wife-mate whether you like it or not," he thundered. "This babe will not be born a bastard. I was well aware that I would get you with child sooner or later. In fact, I hoped that my seed would take. When I returned from my last raid I intended you to wife, but oh no, you had to spoil it by running away." His nose was only inches from her face, but far enough away for him to see her green eyes grow soft and luminous. He backed off, astonished at her quick change of mood.

"You never cease to puzzle me, Danielle," he muttered.

Danielle scooted backwards to gain some distance between them. "It's good of you that you want to claim the babe as your own, but I don't care. I will not go back with you to Dragon's Lair and you can't make me," she stated firmly and was glad that she was laying abed. Her whole body was quivering from her audacity to defy Talon.

Talon sat bolt upright and Danielle swallowed her desire the display of sinew and muscle and velvet smooth skin evoked in her. "What do you mean you are not going back to Dragon's Lair?"

"Just that. I am not going and you can't make me. It's lonely up there and you are gone a lot. It's no place for a woman with a small child. We will be better off here, while you can go on chasing your own dreams and raid to your heart's content." She raised her chin in defiance, daring him to contradict her.

"You have servants and if you like I can get you more. But you are coming with me to Dragon's Lair, because that is my son's legacy. It is your duty to raise him in the Viking manner. You'll want for nothing, because I have big plans to improve upon my stronghold and before you know it there will be more brothers for him. He won't be lonely."

"Well, you have your plans and I have mine," she retorted and slipped hastily from the bed. She realized immediately that it had been a bad decision. The room spun crazily before her eyes.

Talon saw her waver and bounded across the bed in time to catch her before she fell. "I think you had better stay in bed, wench," he ordered gruffly and pressed her back down.

Lisette knocked on the door at that precise moment and whisked in all smiles and happy disposition. She was carrying a tray with hot bread, butter, honey and milk. "Here is a little--" she chirped, but the rest of the sentence died on her lips. Her eyes grew round with dismay. "My, you two look as if you had a dose of vinegar and here I thought that everything would be sunshine and roses."

Talon pointed angrily at Danielle. "She is a stubborn wench, who will not listen to reason," he complained.

Danielle lay in bed holding her head with both hands and

grimaced. "He wants to dictate my life to me and I won't have any part of it." Childishly, she stuck her tongue out at him.

Lisette clucked like a mother hen and set the tray near the bed. "*Petite*, it is the man's right to dictate to his wife where he wants her to live."

Talon chest puffed out in righteous indignation. "You see, even Lisette sees it my way."

"Well the two of you can go together then, for I will not go back to Dragon's Lair and that is final."

Lisette rubbed her hands on her apron and stared beseechingly at Talon. "You know, Viking, they say that patience is a virtue. A woman in Danielle's delicate condition is often cross and hard to deal with. Give her a little time to get used to the idea."

Danielle shot up from her pillow. "I will not get used to the idea no matter how much time he gives me," she screeched.

"Well, *petite*, let's just drop the subject and you have a little something to eat and then we'll see further."

The aroma of the freshly baked bread was making Danielle's mouth water and she decided that food was definitely a priority. Without offering Talon anything, she reached for a crusty roll and bit hungrily into it.

"Let her be a while, Viking, and broach the subject again later." Lisette suggested quietly on her way out.

For the rest of the day, Talon played the exemplary suitor. He regaled Danielle with legends of his homeland and made her laugh by painting vivid pictures of people from his past, but it was never far from his mind that he would have to convince Danielle to come along of her own volition.

They were sitting beneath one of the old oak trees that dotted the estate, when Talon decided to ask Danielle once more to return with him to Dragon's Lair.

"You could give it one more try at least, Danielle," he offered.

"And then what? What if I still feel the same, say in two months from now? Will you let me come home?"

Talon avoided her intent gaze, because he knew that the answer could be clearly seen in his eyes. He chewed on a blade of grass and stared thoughtfully into space.

"I think you will come to love Dragon's Lair, Danielle."

"Nay, Talon, I have tried to live there and I do not like it. So let's quit beating a dead horse. My mind is made up and that is final."

Talon nodded his head in assent. Not that trusted him, when he gave in so easily to her demands. Yet, true to his word, he did not say another word about his homeland. Instead he resumed his role as avid swain, surprising Danielle with his knowledge of manners and repertoire of amusing anecdotes.

She was smiling at him over the rim of her goblet. "Ah, Talon," she sighed. "If only we could agree on everything in life as well as we agree this evening."

He cocked a golden eyebrow at her and wagged his finger. "Weren't you the one who was so adamant about not speaking of things that cannot be?" he admonished jovially.

"But that's just it, Talon," she cried. "We could be happy at Honfleur-sur-mer. You could learn the business of raising cattle. They do it in your country. And I would no longer have to worry whether you come home from one battle to the next."

He sliced his hand through the air in angry disagreement. "Enough already! I am a Viking and I enjoy to do battle. I cannot change my opinion any more than you want to change yours."

Much later, in the privacy of Danielle's chamber, after the candle had been doused, they turned to each other in a frenzy of need. There was little tenderness as each sought to still the hunger for the other deep within. And afterwards they lay spent side by side, gasping for breath.

"I don't think I will ever get enough of you," whispered Talon and his hands began a renewed search across the soft plains and valleys of Danielle's body.

"Nor I of you," admitted Danielle as she adjusted her position to allow Talon better access. And when he felt she was ready for him again, he made love to her ever so slowly that second time, until both felt that they would die from pleasure. Afterwards they slept in each other arms.

When Danielle woke, Talon had already left the room. She reluctantly got out of bed, the knowledge that Talon would be leaving uppermost in her thoughts. She would miss him sorely, but she would never let him know that. Her place was at Honfleur-sur-mer.

Danielle dressed and was coming down the wide staircase, when Asgard walked into the hall. He was garbed in his battle tunic of wolf skins and fur boots with cross garters. He looked disheveled, but there was a satisfied gleam in his light eyes as he smiled up at Danielle.

"Good morning, Danielle," he greeted her cheerfully, much too cheerful to suit her. "Do you know where Talon is?" he questioned.

Danielle sighed and forced herself to return his greeting. "I don't know where Talon is. He quit the bed before I woke," she admitted.

"Here I am," Talon called as he strode into the hall, a confident air about him. He was dressed in his wolf skin tunic just like Asgard. Danielle's eyes widened briefly in shock. Seeing him attired in her sire's clothes for the last two days had lulled her into a false sense of security. Seeing him garbed in his battle dress brought her sharply back to the reality that Talon was a Viking. A warrior of the sea, who enjoyed doing battle and who did not allow scruples to deter him from his goal. And yet, her heart beat a steady tattoo of longing within her breast.

Talon was wind blown from a ride aboard Cinnabar and there was a ruddy glow about his handsome face. He grinned in welcome to Asgard, exposing a flash of white teeth. Holding out a hand in friendship he advanced into the foyer, studiously avoiding eye contact with Danielle.

"How did it go, Asgard and where is Leif?"

Asgard grinned, pleased. "It went well. The plantation down river was ready for our assault and they put up a good fight. But in the end they had to surrender. We did not lose any of our warriors. Two of the men were slightly wounded." He pointed over his shoulder. "Leif is coming up shortly. He is seeing to the Raider." He cocked his head and there was a speculative frown on his affable visage. "Are you ready to sail?" His eyes cut questioningly toward Danielle.

Talon's face went rigid for a brief moment, but then he allowed himself the merest of smiles. "Aye, I am ready to sail, Asgard. Go on ahead and allow me a few minutes of privacy. I'll follow you shortly."

Asgard waved to Danielle and trotted from the hall. Tension hung heavily between Talon and Danielle when he turned to face her. His handsome visage was devoid of all emotion and none of his inner turmoil showed in his clear blue eyes. He spread his massive arms. "Kiss me goodbye then, Danielle. It is time for me to leave."

Danielle's face lost all its color and her mouth trembled in silent agony. Talon was leaving her and his words sounded final. She would never see him again. She moved into the circle of his embrace and offered her lips up for his kiss, closing her eyes, so he could not see the pain in them.

Talon cupped her head and tilted it for better access, while his crippled hand pressed her against his lean, hard form. His lips captured hers in a leisurely kiss that gradually deepened as passion flared inside him and spread to Danielle's quivering body. Talon could feel her response and he smiled against her parted mouth that clung hungrily to his own.

"Are you still so sure that you want to stay behind, my love?" he whispered.

Danielle mewled like a newborn kitten and tears gathered in her soft green eyes as she stared up at Talon, whose emotions were once more well hidden behind a stern visage. Miserably, she nodded her head and her legs shook almost uncontrollably with desire to render her gesture fraught with dishonesty.

Talon simply bent his head and began to kiss her with renewed vigor, undulating his slim hips against her belly to make sure that she was aware of his quickly arousing state. It was too much for Danielle. With a ragged sigh, her legs refused to hold her any longer and she sagged in Talon's embrace. He chuckled deep in his chest and bent to lift her into his arms. Never breaking his devastating kiss, he strode from the hall without a backward glance. Danielle was vaguely aware that they were in the gardens of Honfleur-sur-mer and that Talon was carrying her toward the river. Only when he lifted her into Asgard's waiting arms, did she struggle to get free and voiced her angry protest.

Her green eyes flashing daggers at Talon, she struggled in Asgard's tight grasp, raining curses and insults down on Talon's unsympathetic head. "You tricked me," she screeched. "You betrayed my trust in you." Turning on Asgard, she screamed, "Let go of me, you witless savage."

Asgard only grasped her more firmly and fixed her with a cold glare. "I am not as patient as my warlord, wench," he gritted out from behind clenched teeth, and to confirm his threat, he twisted her arms upward in a painful angle.

"Tell him to let me go, you beast," Danielle sobbed.

Talon did not favor her with a reply, but vaulted nimbly aboard the Raider and gave orders to set sail. Asgard took Danielle to the bow of the ship and dropped her none to gently to a pile of furs. With the efficiency born of long experience, he bound her hands and feet and for good measure he tied the rope to one of the rings set in the wooden side of the ship.

"There that should hold you until you have cooled off," he said in grim satisfaction.

"You beast," Danielle hissed at him.

Asgard leaned closer to her. "Wench, I warn you. I have permission to see to your safety one way or the other. If you do not keep quiet, I promise I will stuff a rag into that foul little mouth of yours."

Talon stood at the helm of the ship and looked out to sea. His heart was heavy with regret. He would have preferred that Danielle would have come of her own volition, but she had left him no choice. She carried his son and he meant to claim the babe as his own by asking his brother to unite them in wedlock. As leader of their clan Thorson had the power to do so, but he also had the power to deny their union. It was something that Talon dreaded and did not want to face. He was determined to have Danielle for his own, but until he was assured of Thorson's approval, he did not want to boost her expectations.

Talon had not meant to abduct her and have Asgard truss her like a chicken, nor did he have a choice but to give her the cold shoulder before the crew in order to assert his authority.

Danielle was inwardly seething, but she kept her peace, afraid that Asgard would make good on his threat to gag her. Miserably, she glanced about and suddenly came to the conclusion that Talon and his friends must have planned to abduct her. The furs under her and around her attested to the fact that they had been carefully placed there, and she noted that there was a crude drape, which could be used to shield her from prying eyes. All that only served to fuel her anger as she struggled to gain some balance to sit up.

As soon as the Raider entered the North Sea, Talon called Asgard over and asked him to handle the ship. With a wry grin he pointed in Danielle's direction. "I will go and see if the green-eyed spitfire is ready to listen to some reason. Before I go I want to thank you and Leif for aiding me in my effort."

Asgard chuckled and clapped Talon on the shoulder. "That is what friends are for. It may not be the custom in Danielle's country that a groom abducts his bride-to-be, but maybe you can tell her that we do it all the time. How else would lovers bridge the gap between two warring clans? Go to her and Odin be with you, but don't be too surprised when the lady in question is not ready yet for your explanations."

Danielle saw that Talon was coming her way and in a huff she turned her head to the wall. The sudden changing of light in her small space told her that Talon had pulled the drapery in place to protect them from prying eyes. Stubbornly, she avoided looking in his direction.

Talon squatted next to her trussed form and he frowned. "If you promise you won't do anything rash, I will untie your bonds." he spoke quietly.

Danielle twisted around and fixed Talon with a venomous glare. "What do you expect me to be do? Jump into the sea? Well, think again. You are not worth killing myself over and somehow I will escape you again, unless you aim to keep me tied like an animal for the rest of my days."

Talon hunkered next to her and there was real misery in his eyes. "Danielle, listen to me. You gave me no choice and you betrayed yourself when your bones turned to melted honey at my touch. I know you have feelings for me, even if they are but carnal, but they are as undeniable as the setting of the sun."

"How long do you think carnal lust will serve to keep us together, Viking?"

Talon's generous mouth lifted at the corners in a tender smile. "I have great hopes that it will keep us together for a lifetime," he whispered.

Danielle sagged against the mound of furs and her mouth formed a startled O. Talon edged closer and began to untie her bonds, making sure that his hands grazed her body at its most erogenous places. He silently rejoiced when her breath came fast and shallow and her eyes turned luminous with desire. Once she was untied, Talon's ministrations were more binding than any rope or chain. She did not fight him when his fingers sought her, but eased her legs apart, quivering in hopes to have him come inside her. And Talon obliged her jubilantly, taking her quickly, but not without tenderness.

He adjusted her clothing and his own and grinned down at her by way of apology. "It's the only way on this ship, my love. We do not have the leisure of enjoying the feel of our naked bodies against each other, but soon we will be home and I will make it all up to you," he promised. He kissed her nose in a teasing gesture and stroked her damp curls. "I love you, Danielle," he whispered and then chuckled as her eyes grew big and round in amazement.

"Why didn't you tell me so sooner?" she asked breathlessly.

"But I did," he protested. "I told you how much you meant to me and how I loved you when we were back at Honfleur-sur-mer as Lisette is my witness."

"I don't recall Lisette hearing you tell me that you loved me any more than I recall that myself," she countered in evident annoyance.

Talon chuckled, suddenly feeling young and carefree. "Well, maybe you were just a little bit groggy," he admitted and was forced to dodge a playful swipe. He kissed her softly and then he stood up, adjusting the fur tunic a bit more. "I have to get back to the helm, my love. You rest and make sure that our babe stays secure inside you."

Their eyes locked briefly and the love in their depths was undeniable.

Talon swaggered back to Asgard. There was a huge smile on his handsome visage.

"Looking at you I would say that you had more than a good talk," Asgard commented with a lopsided grin. "You make a man want something more permanent when he sees your satisfied mug."

"Aye, it is nice to know that a certain wench cares for you and that she carries your son beneath her heart."

Asgard slapped Talon resoundingly on the back. "Well you wily fox, you. I've been wondering when the fruit of your labors would begin to show some results." The two men guffawed in shared glee, drawing a curious Leif to their side.

"Our warlord here just told me that the wench over yonder is breeding," he divulged expansively to Leif.

"It's about time, Talon. You have been riding her long enough."

Talon sobered and his gaze lit briefly on each of the men. "I aim to make her my wife, when we get to Herjolfstad. I have not told her yet, because I am not sure how Thorson will react to the news that I aim to wed a foreign female."

Asgard and Leif exchanged worried glances. "What will you do, if he denies your request? He is the head of our clan now and he may have a particular girl already in mind for you."

Talon's broad hand sliced impatiently through the air. "I care not if he does have a girl picked out for me." His eyes clouded with bitter memories. "There was a time when I thought my heart would break from the pain, when he wed Arwynna. As long as I can remember he always coveted whatever was mine. Though I guess if Arwynna had truly loved me, she would have chosen me, even though I had little to offer. Now I understand that Odin in his infinite wisdom was but paving my way toward Danielle."

"We'll stand with you, if Thorson decides against you," Asgard vowed heatedly, speaking for both himself and Leif.

Talon nodded his thanks and wordlessly the three friends joined hands to seal the agreement.

CHAPTER TWENTY-FIVE

Two days after their pact the Raider dropped anchor in Herjolfstad. Talon quickly paid off the crew and then the three friends unloaded the rest of the plunder. The goods that were to be sold were stored nearby as usual, while the items that were to make the trip to Dragon's Lair were loaded into a wagon. And then the time was upon Talon to face his brother Thorson with the news of Danielle.

Still dressed in the same gown she wore when she left Honfleur-sur-mer, Danielle trudged beside Talon toward his brother's house. Talon had thoughtfully provided her with a fur-lined cloak. It was nearing the fall season and the sea breeze off the ocean was bitterly cold and cut to the very bone.

"You will no longer walk behind me, Danielle," Talon informed her firmly after he set her to the ground. "We will petition my brother to make our union lawful. Once that is done I will pronounce the babe you are carrying my legitimate heir." He grasped her hand into his huge one and squeezed it encouragingly.

Danielle's stared up at him. Why hadn't he told her this before? And why couldn't he add a simple I love you? Men!

Arwynna answered the door and the hateful glare directed at Danielle left no doubt about her feelings. Leaning negligently against the doorframe, she smiled at Talon. "Welcome back. Was your raid successful, brother-in-law?" And before Talon could answer, she thumbed toward Danielle. "Why do you allow a slave girl to walk by your side by and how dare she wear such fine clothing?" she snapped.

Talon's golden eyebrows snapped together, but he kept a tight reign on his temper. "Danielle is no longer my slave, Arwynna. I have come to ask Thorson to give us his leave to wed."

Arwynna paled at Talon's cool explanation. "You cannot mean to wed the foreign slut," she hissed venomously.

"I beg you keep a civil tongue in your head when speaking of the woman I have chosen to be my mate." Aquamarine eyes flashed with disapproval.

"What is this, I hear?" Thorson asked from behind Arwynna and stepped outside. "You want to claim the foreign wench to be your life-mate? I am not sure that I can give you leave to do that," he added casually, enjoying the color rise in his brother's face.

"Whether you like it or not, Danielle is carrying my babe and I aim to give the child a legal claim," Talon ground out, his square jaw clenching in anger. He swept Danielle's cloak aside and cupped her growing belly with his hand. "I want to claim this babe as my first born."

"What drivel," Thorson asserted, "You who had a different wench warming your bed every night before you went on that foray that netted you this foreign slut."

"You have no reason to insult Danielle's character. She had no say in her fate." Talon would have dearly told his brother that Danielle was of gentle birth and by far a better mate than Arwynna, but his honor would not let him. Instead he pointed to his brother and there was scorn in his voice. "If there are children in this village which bear our family resemblance, I can truly claim that they are not of my making. I took great care not to spill my seed into any of the wenches who came freely to my bed. Unlike you, who is indiscriminate about age and who cares not if the slaves have to suffer your carnal appetite. There is no telling how many of your get grow up amongst our people without claim to a sire."

Thorson advanced upon Talon, his fists balled at his sides and he glared hatefully at the younger man. "Watch your tongue, little brother. There is no shame in venting your lust upon slaves. It is but my feudal right and if a child is born from that union, it is not my fault."

Talon carefully curbed his tongue. Instead of throwing his brother's conjecture back at him, he turned his hands palm up.

"I asked for nothing more than your approval to claim Danielle as my mate. I did not come for censure or to give any. I'd like your decision."

Thorson still smarted from Talon truthful observations and he took some time to answer. His eyes cold, he inclined his head and nodded. "If you want to wed the wench, so be it, but get her out of my sight. It galls me to see you throw yourself at a foreign bitch, simply because she claims to carry your child."

Talon refused to be baited further. He had secured what he had come for. He inclined his head toward his brother and Arwynna. "May the great Odin look kindly upon you," he bade and turned to go.

"That's it then," she asked incredulous. "You state that you want me for your wife and all your brother does is give his permission?"

Talon nodded, "Yes, my love, that's the way it's done. It is a binding commitment, so don't worry about anything else."

Danielle was still trying to digest this strange custom of wedlock when she spied Asgard and Leif waiting outside the stables. Her eyes widened with pleasure when she recognized Sundevil, saddled and ready to go next to the stamping Lucifer.

"How did you ever find Sundevil?" she asked in wonder.

For the first time since they had landed Talon's face broke into a genuine smile. "When I found you had flown the coop, I raced off after you. I had not thought it possible for such a mild mannered wench like you to work out such an elaborate scheme." He laughed and threw back his tousled mane, exposing the strong column of his neck. "You certainly had Sweyn fooled by your story. The man showed such reverence for my battle prowess that I was hard pressed to maintain his admiration. I tried to wheedle the information out of him whence he had taken you, while acting as if I was privy where you had gone. You set me on a merry chase, my love." He leaned closer and whispered softly, "Had I known of the babe, I would have damned my pride and asked Sweyn to come along and show us the way. Instead we raided all along the West coast of the Seine in the hope to find you. We almost did not stop at Honfleur-sur-mer, because we had been there on our previous trip. It was your half-brother's cowardice that lured us back for another visit."

Danielle gasped. She had conveniently forgotten about Jean-Jacques. She raised dazed eyes to Talon. "Oh, dear. I just realized that Honfleur-sur-mer would not survive without Jean-Jacques to see to the lands. Much as I dislike my half-brother I wish I knew if he'd return to take charge. Honfleur-sur-mer was my sire's pride. Apart from the fact that Jean-Jacques was the result of one night's indiscretion between Papa and a chambermaid, he should have inherited at least part of the estate. I wish I could determine why Papa changed his mind in the end to leave it all to me."

Talon shrugged and helped her mount Sundevil. "I'm sorry, love, that we left things unsettled. As for your sire's decision, it's hard to tell what's in another man's heart, Danielle." What more could Talon say?

Darkness fell early, not like the first time when Danielle came along the coast on her way to Dragon's Lair and it was the time of the midnight sun. This night Talon bundled her into the wagon and crept in beside her to keep her warm. And when the wolves howled during the night, he hugged her close and told her not to worry.

When Dragon's Lair came into view, Danielle's heart sank. The stronghold looked even less inviting than the first time she had spied it. She dreaded having to spend the coming winter months within the confines of the thick stonewalls. Talon saw the color drain from her face when they neared the valley and he bit his lip in exasperation. He was unable to understand why Danielle could possibly upset about his stronghold. To him it was paradise with game and fish a-plenty and enough wood to keep the chill from the offshore winds at bay.

As Talon and his party dismounted inside the fortress walls, the servants came running with Myra and Eloise in the lead. The two women watched with round eyes as Talon handed Danielle from her mount and the richness of her dress did not escape their curious gaze.

"She will vent her spleen on us, I wager," Myra said in an aside to Eloise. "Just look at Miss High and Mighty."

Eloise poked a sharp elbow into Myra's ribs. "Give her a chance, Myra. Maybe she'll be nice, since she's shared our lot and knows the hardships. At least she saw to it that her vow came true and she did not return as a slave."

Danielle was tired from the long ride, her back ached fiercely and all she craved was a warm bath and a bed. Remembering the less than friendly way the three of them had parted, she forced a small smile and went to greet them

"Good day, Myra and Eloise." She shrugged ruefully. "I guess when I left I hoped to never return, but here I am."

Before the women had time to say anything, Talon stepped forward. "Danielle will be your mistress henceforth. She is my life mate and I expect you to treat her with respect. Otherwise I will send you back to Herjolfstad."

The two slaves trained shocked eyes on their master and dropped their gazes. Nothing could be worse than to be sent back to Herjolfstad and the degenerate ways of Talon's brother. Quickly, the two women curtsied and let it be known that they were willing to serve Danielle.

The household settled soon enough into a routine. Talon began to spend an inordinate amount of time in the smithy, but refused to let Danielle visit him. She in turn fretted about it, but decided not to make an issue of it. Instead, she selected material from the bolts in Talon's storage shed and set about to sew infant's clothing.

It was some two weeks later, when Talon emerged triumphantly from the smithy and called everyone together. With great ceremony he led Danielle into their midst. Smiling down at her, he held out two elegantly wrought silver armbands in the palm of his huge hand. For her ears only, he whispered, "I made these myself as a token of my sincerity. They are identical to the ones I always wear, down to the runes that will protect you from evil." His gaze briefly touched his two friends before he turned to the assembled servants. "From this day forward let no man deny that Danielle D'Arçenau is my true and sole life-mate," he called. "This is my vow before the great Odin."

Danielle's eyes filled with tears of pride when he slipped the twin bands on her arms. She basked in a glow of happiness for days, content to be at Talon's side and acknowledged as his true mate. And then the babe began to make its presence known and Danielle's thoughts drifted once more across the North Sea and back to Honfleur-sur-mer.

Talon noticed that Danielle was distracted by something. She seemed withdrawn. Concerned he asked her if she was ill.

"Nay, but I have a strong hankering to go back to Honfleur-sur-mer. Your son is stirring inside me and I am afraid that I will not be able to endure the birth in this savage land of yours. I would feel better if I had Lisette with me."

"Bah, you are young and strong and I hear it is only natural to have those misgivings while you are breeding." He kissed her soundly, then teasingly slapped her rump and dismissed her homesickness as just another peculiarity for a woman in her condition. Despite his cavalier treatment of her doubts and fears to her face, he did not leave anything to chance. He gave explicit orders that no one should dare saddle a horse for his wife unless he gave the go ahead himself. He was not about to lose her again, though this time he'd know where to find her.

Danielle did not mention her homesickness again, because she knew she could do nothing about it. Talon watched her like a hawk and tried to keep her spirits high, while her belly expanded. At night Talon would wrap his body around her and cup his hand under the burgeoning mound. It pleased him immensely when the child kicked. Their lovemaking waned considerably until Talon decided one day that it should be curtailed altogether until after the babe's birth. From then on he no longer wrapped his body around Danielle's, lest she notice his constant state of arousal. Instead he always curled his fingers around hers to assure himself of her nearness.

The winter solstice had come and gone. Danielle had grown huge to her own dismay and found it hard to get around. Myra looked at her with barely concealed hatred and muttered beneath her breath to Eloise, "The bitch looks ready to burst. She will scream her lungs raw when this babe makes his entrance, because the Viking is huge and this babe will be big, too. She will be lucky if it doesn't tear her apart," she prophesied.

Eloise cast a sour glance at Myra. "How can you be so bitter toward her, when she always treats us well?"

"Hmph, she thinks herself above us. Don't you remember that she called us twits and the like when she figured she could escape the master? He showed her, though. Serves her right that her belly is bigger than a sow's," Myra sneered and left Eloise standing to gape after her.

Danielle stood in the middle of the room, when her water burst and the pains set in earnestly. She had felt small twinges all day in her lower back, but had dismissed them as nothing to worry about. Eloise happened to walk into the room moments later. Danielle stared at the girl with stricken eyes, unsure what to do.

"Get my husband, Eloise, and be quick about it," she begged hoarsely.

Talon was at her side scant minutes later. One look at her sodden clothes and he swept her up into his arms and carried her to their bed. Eloise trailed behind, uncertain what to do to. Danielle realized that she would have to prod the two if she wanted some help.

"Please get me out of these clothes, Talon, " she begged. Talon obliged, tearing clumsily at the damp garments, driven by her sudden shivering.

When Asgard entered the room some time later, Talon stared at his friend with dull eyes.

"I should have listened to her when she begged to go home. At least she would have Lisette to help her." His lips twisted in a derisive sneer. "I was so sure I had everything in hand that I never bothered to ask if Myra and Eloise had any practice in the ways of birthing. It happens neither ever attended a birth." He slammed his hand against his forehead. "If I hadn't been so damn stubborn she would be in capable hands now," he gritted.

Asgard shrugged and cuffed Talon's shoulder. "It's no great magic really," he bragged. "The woman does most of it herself. I gather it's much like birthing a calf or a goat."

Danielle heard his glib explanation and snorted in the most unladylike manner. "You pompous fool," she hissed. "How dare you compare me to--" She never got to finish her tirade because another sharp pain ripped through her body at that moment and robbed her of breath.

Asgard stayed with Talon through most of the night and Leif checked on the two men now and again. Talon wiped Danielle's brow and held her hand, trying to give her strength, but it did little to ease her pain. As dawn broke on the horizon, Danielle screamed, cursing Talon for his rutting ways and getting her into this horrifying situation. Talon cringed inwardly, condemning himself even worse than she did. Suddenly, Danielle grunted and her eyes grew round with awe.

"I feel the babe's head pressing down," she gritted. Talon stared at her, his heart slamming into his chest. Something welled deep inside him, and brushing aside pride and shame, he stripped the hated gauntlet from his crippled hand. This heralded a new beginning. Past hatred should not touch his newborn. His eyes filled with tears of joy and wonder, when minutes later a perfect little babe slipped into his welcoming hands. And then he laughed a resounding laugh.

"The wench presented me with a healthy daughter," he sputtered between guffaws as Asgard and Leif came running.

"Quit laughing, you jackasses," Danielle screeched. "I feel a second babe coming."

The men stopped and stared in wonder as another babe slid from between Danielle's legs. Talon had only time to hand the astonished Asgard his small daughter in order to catch his son.

"A son," he crowed, "I have a son ...and a daughter." He bent and kissed Danielle. "Thank you my love for making this a perfect day." Danielle nodded weakly and promptly fell asleep.

"She did not even look at her babes," Talon remarked to Asgard as he bade Eloise to bring warm water to bathe the twins.

Then he tenderly wrapped them in furs and laid them next to Danielle.

"Don't hold it against her. It was a rough delivery and she blessed you twice over. A son with the looks of his mother, if you go by that black thatch of hair, yet he has your blue eyes, Talon. Your tiny daughter has your fair locks and her dam's green orbs. What more could any man ask for?"

Talon chuckled, "Looks like my wife has won you over after all this time, huh?"

Asgard's face reddened. "Aye, I must admit that I did not want to like the girl. I thought she would put a strain on our friendship. But seeing as how happy you are, I cannot help but respect her for it."

Talon shook his head and gazed in wonder at his twin babes, fast asleep now like their mother. "Who would have thought that I would be a father by now? I had the same misgivings as you, Asgard. The more I waited to tire of her the deeper my enchantment became for her."

Talon sent word to Herjolfstad that he had been blessed with twins. It was a rarity and the Vikings laid great store by the advent of twins. It was said to be a good omen.

Several days later a small party of horses approached Dragon's Lair. Talon's generous mouth turned downward when he recognized his brother and Arwynna at the head of the group. "I never know how to prepare for my brother, Asgard. One time he is convivial as a brother should be and the next he makes snide remarks as if I were an embarrassment to him."

Asgard shrugged. He knew only too well how Thorson got under Talon's skin. "Take it with a grain of salt. He won't be here for long. Besides, to be kin to a set of twins is a feather in his cap."

As soon as Thorson and Arwynna cleared the stone gate, Talon felt that his sister-in-law was up to no good. Her blue eyes burned hotly into his. There was a challenge in their depths and Talon made a mental note not to get caught alone with her.

Thorson dismounted and clasped his brother's hand warmly and there was a big grin on his ruggedly handsome features. "You have done the family proud, brother. I can't wait to clap eyes on your offspring. I am told that one is the spitting image of his dam and the other resembles his sire. Have you decided upon their names yet?"

Talon met Thorson's gaze. "I have a yen to name my son after his grandsire and my daughter will be Fleurette. It combines our heritage in some way. You see Danielle's home is called Honfleur-sur-mer, so she thought Fleurette would be fitting. It means little flower."

Thorson threw back his head and guffawed loudly. "I never considered that naming a newborn could be such a task." With a sour sideways glance at Arwynna, he muttered, "If she should ever breed and birth, I'll give her that option."

Talon's hackles rose at his brother's remark. So, Thorson and Arwynna were still at odds with each other. He would have to double his efforts in that case to keep Arwynna at arm's length. He made a mental note to ask Asgard and Leif to stay at his side at all times.

CHAPTER TWENTY-SIX

There was much feasting, giving the men an excuse to go on daily hunts to replenish depleted stores. Much to Danielle's chagrin it forced her to spend time with Arwynna. "Arwynna seems too attached to Fleurette," she complained one night to Talon. "She dotes on the child as if it were her own babe."

"Let her have those few days while they are visiting. You will have your daughter for the rest of your life."

Danielle could not entirely reconcile her misgivings with Talon's point of view, but she shrugged, cautioning herself to be more patient.

"I hope this will make her want her own child and that she will be carrying one soon."

Talon shook his head. "I don't think there is much hope for that. Thorson and Arwynna are at each other's throat more times than not, and I have heard that one of his slaves just bore him a child, though it's said that Arwynna does not know it."

Danielle gasped in dismay. "Oh, Talon, but that is terrible. My heart aches for Arwynna, though I must admit that I don't like the woman. What, if she cannot have a babe of her own? I can only imagine how much it would hurt her to see other women have babes."

Talon yawned hugely and patted Danielle's arm. "You have a tender heart, my love, but don't waste your sympathy on those two. Either they will try to work out their problems or they will continue to make each other miserable. Whatever they chose, I don't want any part in it. I am looking forward to the day when they leave for Herjolfstad."

Danielle slapped half playfully at Talon. "You heartless ogre," she hissed into the darkness. "How can you say such things?"

Talon growled softly back. "If you don't quiet your tongue, the rest of me will waken and demand to be fed, though I warn you that I won't stop at suckling at your breast," he threatened.

Danielle tittered into her pillow at his jest. She knew he was but joking because the medicine woman who had come with Thorson's party had cautioned them to hold off on their lovemaking for another month.

Danielle was awakened by a soft shake to her shoulder. Eloise stood next to the bed, a babe in each arm. Smiling down at her mistress she teased, "The majesties are awaiting their breakfast, my lady." As she handed the children down to their mother, she continued, "And I am to give the message that the men have gone bear hunting and won't be back for several days, so not to worry."

Danielle snorted as she sat up to feed her brood. "It's like a man to tell you not to worry, when they leave at the break of dawn and give no inkling where they might be going. Maybe he thinks since we are in the midst of winter, and nearly snowbound, it is of no concern if they go hunting for days on end and bear hunting yet."

Eloise watched her mistress with concern. "You should not fret, my lady, because it will upset the little ones, I am told."

Danielle fixed her with a sour stare. "It's easy for you to say, because you have none but yourself to worry about." How could Talon be so insensitive and leave her alone with Arwynna? He knew she dreaded the woman's company and her obsession with their little daughter.

As if to dispel Danielle's fears, Arwynna breezed into the room, a warm smile curving her mouth. "I have come to take the children and put them down for their nap." She patted Danielle's arm and continued smiling. "You just lay here and rest. What else is there to do, when our men have gone off on a hunt?"

What else indeed, thought Danielle sourly and settled back against her pillow and promptly fell back to sleep.

She was dreaming, she knew she was dreaming because she had never in her life heard such a dreadful scream as that. "Wake up, Danielle. Wake up. The babe is gone."

Danielle forced herself to waken and suppressed the panic that shot through her with icy fingers. She stared at Eloise, who was standing by the bed wringing her hands. Big tears were flowing down the woman's cheeks.

"They have taken her," she wailed. "They have taken her," she repeated and then to Danielle's horror Eloise threw herself on the bed and cried uncontrollably.

Danielle sat up, feeling ill to her stomach, and shook the hysterical woman. First gently, but when she realized that Eloise had lost all reasoning, she beat her fists on the woman's back and screamed for her to stop.

"You must stop this instant, Eloise and tell me what is going on. Who took whom?"

Eloise rolled on her side and stared with tear-reddened eyes at Danielle. "That traitorous Myra. She fair hates you because master Talon brought you back as his wife. Myra hoped he would bring you back in a slave collar and she would get to beat you for the things you said to us the day you were leaving. I told her you did not mean it unkindly--."

"Stop your prattling, Eloise," Danielle interrupted her sharply. "Rather tell me what is going on. I couldn't care less about Myra, if I had to. I have known all along that she bears me a grudge."

"She helped that hateful Arwynna steal your babe."

Danielle sat bolt upright. Her face drained of all color. "What are you talking about, Eloise? Which babe are you speaking of?"

"They stole your little girl, my lady." And with that Eloise started on another bout of sobbing.

Danielle jumped from her bed, frantically snatching at her woolen tunic and fur leggings. "I'll have to go after them," she muttered as she struggled to get dressed. "I cannot let her have my child. God only knows what she might do to Fleurette, and how in the world is she going to feed the poor little mite?"

Eloise suddenly came to her senses. "You can't go by yourself. It is the middle of winter," she pointed out. "You are still not completely recovered and you could catch your death of cold out there. Besides, Talon would have my head if I would let you go."

Danielle stopped and stared. The validity of Eloise's words slowly sank in and with a strangled sob Danielle sat down on the edge of the bed. She had to cling to the hope that Arwynna truly loved the little girl as much as she claimed. If that was the case, and she prayed that it was, then there was time to send someone after Talon and ask him to hurry home.

"Go and fetch one of the stable hands. Tell him I need to speak with him," she finally instructed Eloise.

The stable hand was of English origin and Danielle thanked her lucky stars that he would at least understand her instructions. "Are you any good at tracking, Matthew?" she asked nervously.

The man shrugged and twisted his cap in his work worn hands. "I did some hunting back at my home. 'Twas poaching to be exact, ma'am," he admitted sheepishly. "'Twas the only way we could stay alive." His eyes timidly met hers as he spoke. "I'd try my best to find your husband, mistress. I believe I can read the signs well enough."

Danielle's mouth lifted in a tiny smile and her eyes were warm with gratitude. "That's all I'm asking, Matthew. Put on some warm clothing and take enough provisions for several days. There is no telling how far they might have wandered off or whether they have made camp along the way. God be with you," she whispered at the last.

Danielle barely slept or ate for the next three days. Eloise was worn thin from dashing to the ramparts and looking for any sign of the hunters, because Danielle asked her almost every hour to go and look. Finally, toward the end of the third day she came running, her eyes shining with triumph.

"They are coming. They are coming. I recognize master Talon in the forefront atop Lucifer and the poor horse looks fair exhausted." She did not get any further, because Danielle snatched up a cloak and was running to meet them.

Talon looked haggard beneath a week's growth of beard. He vaulted from Lucifer's back before the horse ever came to a full stop. Danielle was in his arms and clinging to him, savoring the security of his embrace. Tears streamed unheeded down her pale cheeks.

"Oh, Talon," she wailed, her soft mouth trembling. "Arwynna took our babe and she has been gone these past three almost four days."

Thorson rode up, and upon hearing the news, he balled his fist in repressed fury. "This time she has gone too far," he thundered. "When we find her, she will be punished."

Danielle looked aghast at her brother-in-law. She had not thought of the consequences to Arwynna and at sight of Thorson's forbidding face a sliver of dread sliced through her. She lifted a restraining hand toward him and her eyes went soft with pity.

"If we find the babe alive and well, there won't be any need to punish Arwynna. I believe she has a great desire to have a babe of her own and she took Fleurette to ease her longing. I am sure she means her no harm."

Thorson pushed past Danielle as if she were invisible. "Arwynna broke our code of honor. That alone warrants punishment," he gritted, his mouth a thin white line that bespoke his inner fury.

Danielle was hard pressed not to tell him that the kettle should not call the pot black. By getting a slave with child, he had not shown much honor himself, regardless that it was a way of Viking life to keep their female slaves as concubines. She wisely bit back her accusing words in view of Thorson's wrathful visage.

Talon was loath to let go of Danielle, but he knew he had to take action. He pushed her gently from him and stared into her teary eyes. "We'll find the babe and I am sure she will be fine," he soothed as he fought down his own fears. The coastal winds blew bitterly cold at this time of year. It would be a grim struggle for two lone women and worse for a tiny infant.

"We cannot go after them tonight. The horses need their rest, if we plan to push them hard again on the morrow. Nor can we see tracks in the dark." He saw Danielle's doubtful grimace. "Oh, there will be tracks, my love, never fear, even if there was fresh snowfall since." He only hoped that the tracks would not be those of pursuing wolves, but he kept that piece of information to himself as well.

Danielle dug frantic fingers into Talon's woolen tunic. "I want to come along," she begged, her eyes almost black with fear. "The babe will be hungry and--"

Talon cut her short, his golden brows drew together in a forbidding manner, but the look in his aquamarine eyes was tender. "You cannot go, Danielle. We can only hope and pray that Fleurette is strong enough to survive the cold." He smiled teasingly down at his wife. "She is after all our firstborn. And if she survived this far, she will survive by sucking on a pig's bladder full of milk." The finality in his voice told Danielle that further begging would be futile.

That night Danielle turned to Talon despite the warnings of the medicine woman. "I need the feel of you inside me, Talon," she whispered. "I missed you more than life itself and I ache to be loved by you."

"Are you sure?" he questioned as he raised himself on an elbow and tried to see her expression in the gloom of their chamber. He could feel her nod her head and he gasped when her hand wrapped itself around him in eager invitation.

Danielle forgot her troubles for a moment as she chuckled at Talon's immediate response to her ministrations. "I see you are as ready as ever, my lord," she giggled.

"Don't you dare make fun of me, wench," he growled into her ear as his fingers found her. "You are as slippery as an eel and twice as ready as myself." Talon carefully entered Danielle and paced himself lest he would hurt her, but as usual she had a mind of her own and her hips quickly let him know that his pace was less than satisfying.

"You little minx," he chided playfully, "You know we should not make love so soon and here you tempt me to ride you like the wind."

Danielle sighed contentedly, "Aye, like the wind, Talon."

Despite their sorrow they slept afterwards, a healing sleep that would sustain them for the days to come.

The men set off before the break of dawn the next day. Talon and Thorson rode in the lead and Asgard and Leif brought up the rear. It was biting cold outside and a low, dense mist obscured the view of the valley beneath Dragon's Lair. Men and beasts alike blew long banners of gray breaths before them and it gave the small group a ghostly appearance.

Danielle stood on the ramparts and watched them leave, her heart heavy. No sooner than the men passed through the stone gate, the thick fog concealed them from view. Dejectedly, she made her way back to the keep. Though she could warm her chilled hands in front of the cheerfully burning hearth, her heart was filled with dread.

Talon and Thorson set the pace for the group, since both rode stallions. Talon's voice sounded muffled by the density of the swirling mists as he bent to Thorson. "We won't need to look for tracks until we get to the coastline. I doubt that Arwynna would be foolish enough to head North. So the only way left for her is to ride homeward."

Thorson could not meet his brother's gaze as they rode relentlessly away from Dragon's Lair. Guilt weighed heavily on him, knowing he was to blame for much of the misery his wife had caused his brother. He was well aware that she craved a babe of her own, but he had been busy sating his carnal lusts on another. After a long pause, he finally twisted in his saddle and tried to read his brother's emotions. What he saw was utter despair, but not the censure he expected.

Relieved, Thorson shrugged and nodded his head. "Aye, I think Arwynna took the babe to our home. She was beginning to talk of the child as if she had birthed it herself. Looking back I should have seen the signs, but I was too busy anticipating the hunts." There was regret and sorrow in his voice as he added in a harsh aside. "I just hope she made it home safely."

As soon as they reached the coastline, Talon's sharp eyes picked up the tracks of a wolf pack. No one dared to put their fears into word, but worried glances passed between the four men. They whipped their mounts into a faster pace, hoping against hope that their premonition was unfounded.

Several miles down the road, Talon pointed to a double set of hoof prints with wolf tracks overlapping them. "The prints are old, to be sure, and the wolves could have picked up their scent too late." Even as he said it, he did not believe it himself. His heart ached for Danielle for he would be the one who would have to tell her that one of her babes was lost to her forever.

Each time they rounded a bend in the road, they would hold their breath in fear of what they might find. And then their luck ran out. From afar they saw the remains of a horse and a small mound, which could be nothing else than its rider.

Talon spurred Lucifer as raw, unbridled grief threatened to break his heart. He was off his mount before it skidded to a halt. He spared no look at the carcass of the animal, but went straight to the pile of gnawed bones, all of what was left of what once had been a human being.

Talon lifted the torn cloak that shrouded the mangled figure. Had it not been for the shreds left of the tunic, Talon would have been hard pressed to put an identity to the body.

Thorson caught up with his brother in time to hear Talon expel a mournful breath. "Tis one of Arwynna's cloak's," he informed Talon dully as he slipped off his horse. He hunkered down and took a closer look and then he shook his head. "Tis not Arwynna though. This must be the slave who left with her."

Talon nodded dully, "I figured that much by the shreds of the clothing that the wolves left." He shuddered. "Myra must have died a terrible death unless those beasts went for her throat first. There is not much left of her in any case and it makes little sense

to tarry to bury her remains. We will do so on our way back."
The three men agreed. Time was of an essence.

As they rode, the specter of Myra's body was never far from
their minds. Any time around the next bend they knew they
could find Arwynna and the babe. But as the horses' hooves
swallowed mile after mile their hopes rekindled that they would
find the two of them safe.

They arrived late the next day in Herjolfstad, at a time when
most of its inhabitants were at supper. Exhaustion was apparent
in both riders and mounts.

"Leif and Asgard, you take care of the horses. When you get
done met us at Thorson's home."

The two brothers walked rapidly toward Thorson's house, the
snow crunching under the soles of their boots the only sound
between them. As Thorson threw open the door, they found
Arwynna standing by the hearth, cradling Fleurette to her bare
breast in an attempt to suckle her. Arwynna gasped and retreated
a step at sight of her husband and Talon just as the babe twisted
her small head from the empty breast and squalled with
frustration.

Arwynna's eyes were bright with triumph and pride. "Did you
come to see my daughter, Talon?" she questioned eagerly, her
arms tightening protectively around her little bundle.

Talon was shocked and momentarily caught off guard by
Arwynna's action and he stared stupidly at the bared breast,
affronted by its obscenity. He quickly realized that he would
have to approach her with cunning, if he hoped to retrieve his
child.

Out of the corner of his eye, Talon saw his brother move
forward, his repressed fury palpable in the small space. Laying a
restraining hand on the other man's sleeve, he whispered under
his breath, "Let me handle this Thorson. If I need help I will let
you know."

Thorson understood Talon's reasoning and stayed put, though it
pained him to be forced to watch helplessly.

Talon's smile was warm and encouraging as he approached at
his sister-in-law, holding out his arms. "Aye, Arwynna, she is a
lovely babe, I think. Would you let me hold her a moment so I
can have a closer look?"

A cunning light entered Arwynna's eyes and she stepped yet
another step nearer the hearth, the firelight throwing her slim
figure into silhouette, illuminating her flaxen hair with a halo of

gold. She giggled. "You think me daft, Talon? Do you really believe that I will hand her over?" She drew herself up to her full height and her lips drew back in a rictus of hatred. "She is mine," she screeched. "You denied me a child of my own, as did Thorson. So I took her and I will not give her back."

Talon watched anxiously as she stepped ever closer to the hearth. His hand shot out in alarm. "Don't get any nearer the fire, Arwynna," he pleaded. "You are putting yourself and your babe in danger."

Arwynna laughed and it was an eerie sound in the otherwise quiet room. "You'll not trick me that way, Talon." There was a deranged glimmer in her blue eyes as she lifted her chin and leered at the men. "That bitch Myra tried it with me, too. She demanded her reward or the babe." Arwynna cackled. "I gave her a reward all right." Arwynna's eyes took on a faraway look as she continued in a casual tone. "I stuck my dagger in her ribs and left her to the wolves. 'Twas best that way, since the beasts were following us and it was but a matter of time that they would have caught us all."

Talon saw the flicker of a small red ember arching its way toward Arwynna's gown and reached instinctively for his daughter. With an enraged shriek Arwynna drew back. Somehow her heel became stuck in the trailing hem and as she yanked it loose, she lost her balance. To save herself and the child she instinctively flung out her left arm to brace against the wall by the hearth. Talon recognized his opportunity. He swooped down on her like a hawk to snatch his wailing daughter from her grip.

With the grace and agility of a cat, Arwynna pushed away from the wall and launched herself at Talon's retreating back. Thorson saw too late that she had a dagger. He tried desperately to deflect its thrust toward Talon's exposed back. But Arwynna was bent on retrieving what she considered hers. Angrily, she slashed at Thorson to keep him at bay and with a feral snarl she continued on her downward arch and buried the long knife in the muscle just below Talon's shoulder.

Talon howled in pain and went down on his knees. Arwynna's eyes glittered with triumph when she perceived her advantage. She reached to pull the knife from the wound, when the door flew back on its hinges. The broad forms of Asgard and Leif were outlined against the stark winter whiteness in the background. Stunned by the grisly scene before them, the two friends stood in mute horror just inside the room. Arwynna hesitated a fraction of a second to gauge this new source of danger to herself, while Thorson seized the opportunity to spring into action. He made a valiant attempt to take the knife from Arwynna, but she would not allow herself to be parted from her weapon and sliced through the air to keep him away. Thorson tried to dodge. He yelped more in surprise than pain when his wife's blade sliced into his hand.

"Stay away from me, Thorson," she screeched. "Make him give me my babe back." She waved the knife dangerously through the air and took refuge before the fireplace once again, emitting a shrill keening sound that set everyone's nerves on edge.

Aghast, Asgard and Leif pressed cautiously into the room, their eyes never wavering from Arwynna. Her thin form elicited unprecedented menace. Leif, ever the practical thinker, knelt next to Talon and asked him quietly to hand Fleurette over to him. Gratefully, Talon obliged and then held his useless arm in the cradle of the other. Blood flowed copiously from the deep gash in his shoulder.

Asgard crept ever closer to Arwynna with the hope that he and Thorson might corner her and disarm her. Again Arwynna showed how truly cunning she was. She held the knife before her and slashed without pattern first at one man and then the other. Asgard cleared his throat to catch Thorson's attention. Everyone in the room seemed to be caught in suspended animation, even Fleurette was quiet. There were no sounds except the crackle of the fire, Arwynna's eerie wailing and Talon's labored breathing. Suddenly, an ominous whoosh erupted.

It happened so fast that Thorson and Asgard were shocked into immobility. They watched in horror as flames licked a rapid path along the crazed woman's skirt ever upward to her bodice and then her hair turning her into a human torch. Asgard jumped forward, intent to help her douse the flames, but Arwynna could no longer fathom reality. She stabbed at Asgard and then turned the knife on herself.

Her blood-curdling screams gave way to maniacal giggles as she slashed the blade wildly across her wrists. "I'll not give you the pleasure of seeing me die a slow and painful death and I curse you all for the misery you have brought upon me," she wheezed, her eyes bright with menace as she watched her blood spurt from several mortal wounds.

The air inside the room became fraught with the stink of burning flesh and blood. The four men stood mesmerized by the bizarre scene that played before their disbelieving eyes. Arwynna sank slowly to the ground, blackened and charred, a pitiful remnant of the beauty she had once been. She tittered weakly as if she had just heard a witty joke and then she fixed Thorson with a forlorn stare. Her mouth worked, but no words came. With a last mournful sigh her eyes rolled back in her head and she crumpled sideways.

Asgard was by her side in an instant. He looked up at Thorson and shrugged his shoulders. "She is dead, Thorson. I am sorry."

"Don't be, Asgard. She was no longer the same girl I once loved and married. I have been watching her for a long time and I have noticed changes, but it had not prepared me for what just happened. It is I who has to say I am sorry to all of you for all the misery it has brought upon you." He lifted his large hands palm up and his powerful shoulders sagged in defeat.

Fleurette chose that moment to make herself known. It was a lusty wail of protest that left no doubt that the mite was hungry. Leif held the little girl and grinned lopsidedly.

"There is nothing we can do for Arwynna anymore," he said ruefully, "but the babe is hungry and Talon needs tending. Life is after all for the living."

They left the longhouse behind and went to the cottage of the medicine woman. Within minutes the slave girl who had given birth to Thorson's son was summoned to feed Fleurette, while the medicine woman took care of Talon.

The old woman clucked her tongue in dismay as she carefully cut away Talon's tunic. "The wound is deep and jagged, Talon. It is not mortal, mind you, but what I have to tell you will not be to your liking. The blow was meant to kill you. I heard that Thorson deflected her arm, but still the blade cut through sinew and muscle and I fear that you may never swing a two handed sword again."

A pall came over the small room as the woman's words sunk in. "You are telling me that my fighting days are over?" croaked Talon from between parched lips. He buried his massive head in the crook of his powerful arm and his shoulders shook as he allowed himself a silent moment of profound grief.

"You can still fight, Talon. Your right arm can still swing a war ax and a mace as well as wield a knife," Asgard quickly insisted, his voice full of hope and encouragement.

Talon slowly twisted his head and fixed his friend with a weary eye. "Aye, it's true enough what you say, but it's not enough for a Viking warrior. Nay, the witch condemned me for the rest of my life to one of dearth. How can I face Danielle, more a cripple than ever?" he asked bitterly and let his head fall dejectedly back to his forearms again. "May Arwynna reside forever more with Loki," he spat.

Thorson came to stand by his brother's side. "I gave orders to burn the longhouse and all her things with it. From this day forward we will never speak of her again," he said quietly, but there was an underlying vehemence in his composure that bespoke of the pain his wife had caused him.

The next morning dawned in a gray haze, the stench of the smoke from the longhouse still heavy on the air. Thorson had sworn that he would build barns atop the site, but never again a house.

A wagon waited for Talon and his tiny daughter and the slave girl who would provide Fleurette's feedings. Each step Talon took toward the wagon became doubly painful. The walking jarred the torn muscle, but the knowledge that he was forced to ride in the wagon made him cringe. His arm was bound tightly against his ribs and made his movements awkward. Worse yet was Asgard's offer to help him climb into the wagon.

"I am not helpless," he snarled as he jerked angrily away from the helping hand.

It did nothing for his ego to see Lucifer tied to the back and bitterly he turned his face to the wall. They stopped only long enough for the horses to drink and to eat some of the rations they had brought along. Nor did they waste any time at the site of Myra's death, but hurried ever onward with Fleurette's welfare uppermost on their minds.

CHAPTER TWENTY-SEVEN

Danielle's shoulders sagged with fatigue. She had slept little since Talon and his friends had left. Holgar was the only sunshine in her life during those dreary days. Yet even the tiny boy could not always keep up her spirits, since she was sorely reminded that his twin sister was somewhere out there and could well be dead.

Dejected, she turned away from the ramparts. It was getting late. Surely, if they had found her daughter, they would have been back by now? With a last regretful glance, Danielle started to go back inside. And then her heart leapt in her breast, because out of the corner of her eye she spied two riders and a wagon round the bend. It was them. It had to be them. Her heart soared as her gaze searched for her husband.

Danielle braced herself atop the rough stone embrasure and leaned forward for a better look. Dread rushed through her when she spied Lucifer trotting sadly behind the wagon. Her breath clogged in her throat. It could mean but one thing, either Talon was dead or severely wounded.

Danielle had no idea where the keening noise came from until she realized that it was she who wailed so heartbroken into the falling night. She pushed away from the parapet and felt as if the weight of the world had just descended upon her weary shoulders. What would she do without Talon, where would she go? And then she took a deep breath and gave herself a mental shake.

"You twit," she scolded herself loudly. "Don't cry and mourn and carry on until you know for sure that something is awry. If Talon is hurt he does not need to see your face awash in tears. He'll need your encouragement."

Danielle hurried inside and quickly splashed her face with cold water. Determined, she walked back outside and waited patiently for the riders to pass under the stone gate. She searched Asgard's face for a sign, since he was heading the group, but what she saw was a mélange of mixed emotions. She rushed forward, her heart in her eyes.

"Where is Talon?" she demanded on a note of near hysteria.

Asgard pointed toward the wagon. "He is in the wagon. He is hurt, but not to worry. Fleurette is back there with him and she is fine as rain." He forced a grin for Danielle, whose ashen face and huge eyes left little doubt of the agony she had endured in their absence.

Danielle hurried to the rear of the wagon and climbed in. A cursory glance at her child told her that Fleurette was indeed right as rain. But what had happened to Talon? He neither moved from his place in the corner nor gave any indication that he was aware of her presence.

Danielle edged nearer, waving the slave girl from the cart. With a trembling hand, she pulled back the furs only to be greeted by Talon's dull blue eyes staring right through her.

"Talon, my love," she whispered as a great fear gripped her. "Talon, what has happened?"

Talon did not answer, but continued his silent staring. Danielle began to shiver with cold and trepidation. She waited a moment longer, assessing his body with a knowledgeable eye. Finally, she could take his silence no longer and she asked. "Tell me what ails you, Talon. It does neither of us any good to sit out here in the cold."

"I did not ask you to sit by me?" he snapped roughly at her.

The flatness of his voice gave Danielle a small insight into Talon's true pain. She dropped her gaze to the floor and asked quietly, "I know you are hurt, Talon, but you owe me an explanation to the extent of your wounds."

"I am crippled for life," he screamed and the anguish of the two days past escaped in that one agonizing sentence that shook the very walls of the cart.

Danielle sat back on her heels and pondered his answer. He did not look crippled to her, but then she could not see very well in the setting gloom. "How so?" she pressed to know, shaken by the inner rage, which threatened to consume him.

Talon lifted his bandaged arm toward her and there was a hint of tears in his aquamarine gaze. "Arwynna stabbed me in the back when I took our babe from her. The bitch cut through sinew and muscle and the medicine woman told me that I would never swing a broadsword again," he ground out in one continuous sentence and Danielle felt each word slice through her like a knife.

"The medicine woman is not always right, Talon. Give yourself time. You are young and strong, there is a good chance that you will completely recover." Danielle saw the glimmer of hope in the depth of his eyes and her heart soared for that small victory. Later she would point out to him that he beat the odds once before when his hand was disfigured in the smithy accident. One step at a time. "Let's go inside. I would like to see my daughter and I am sure you would like to see your son."

Talon followed her reluctantly. As soon as he walked through the door, Asgard broke into a spontaneous grin. He sensed an air of hope about his friend and he knew he had Danielle to thank for that. "I propose a toast to Talon's health," he offered loudly as he winked broadly at Danielle. "I have a feeling that the love that abodes in this house will do more for him than any medicine could."

Talon did not prove to be a good patient. He was moody to the point of being morose as one week slipped into the next. Finally, Asgard and Leif took pity on Danielle and forcibly dragged Talon with them on a hunt.

"You ask too much of yourself and your waspish tongue fair reminds me of an old hag," lectured Asgard.

"This is one time when I have to agree," Leif nodded. "It's been too long since we heard Danielle giggle in glee at some jest of yours or seen that teasing light in either of your eyes."

"It's easy for you two to find fault with me. Neither of you has ever been crippled and without hope," roared Talon.

Asgard paused and peered at Talon. "You're right, Talon. It is easy to find fault with you, because you have never before let any obstacle stand in your way. Why, when you burnt your hand, your sire turned away from you, sure you would never turn into a warrior. When the children tormented you and called you Talon, did you cringe and hide? Why, no, you took their invective and turned in into your war cry. You were only a boy back then. Look at yourself. You can sit Lucifer as well as ever, who is to say you won't wield a sword by the time the midnight sun shines again?"

"That could be several more months away. How am I to keep my hope alive that long?"

"We'll practice in the courtyard until your arm regains its strength. And then we'll go on a raid and see how well we fare together."

Talon inclined his shaggy head and a ghost of a grin appeared on his generous mouth. "Done! We start tomorrow and I charge the two of you to get me motivated."

The hunt that day went poorly for Talon, but his spirits still soared from the promise the two friends had made him. Danielle was surprised that night at the vigor with which he consummated their lovemaking, but she dared not ask what had changed his mind for fear he would return to his brooding.

At the first signs of Spring the three men became restless and Danielle dreaded to hear their plans. The twins were beginning to sit and although the men helped to entertain the children, it was beginning to wear on Danielle and she craved some time to herself.

"We are planning to ride for Herjolfstad by the end of this week," Talon announced casually that evening over supper. Danielle's head snapped up in surprise and she expected to hear that they all would visit there for a spell. "We intend to ready the Raider for a foray into Paris." Talon grinned sheepishly at her and shrugged. "It proved a good haul the last time we were there."

Danielle allowed his news to sink in while she thoughtfully chewed her food. Finally, she turned to him and there was a challenging glitter in the depth of her green eyes.

"If you intend to raid Paris, then I could take the twins and wait for you back at Honfleur-sur-mer," she announced as her small chin shot upward at that stubborn angle Talon knew so well from their earlier days.

"You'll do no such things," roared Talon, "A woman's place is at home, where she should wait for her mate to come back to from battle."

"And so it is," answered Danielle calmly. "Though in this case it will be my home instead of Dragon's Lair."

Talon glared at her, piqued by the subtle chuckles from Asgard and Leif. "It isn't done," he declared. "I'll not have my wife and babes jostled about on the sea, where dangers abound. Nor would my crew like to be burdened with such nonsense."

"I don't seem to recall one instance where the crew had any say in it when you abducted me first from the nuns and the second time from Honfleur-sur-mer," she replied sweetly, her smile as serene as a Madonna's in church. "Besides, you would not be burdened, as you call it, for long. We'd be out of your hair long before you reach Paris, since it is another day's sail from my childhood home."

Talon fixed Asgard and Leif with a threatening glare of ice blue eyes and then he shrugged his powerful shoulders. "We'll see, Danielle, we'll see."

Danielle quickly lowered her own gaze and paid great attention to the rest of her food on its trencher to hide the triumphant gleam in her soft green orbs.

As Talon and Danielle bade the two men a good night, Asgard turned to Leif. "What are you willing to bet that Talon will lose that fight tonight between the sheets?"

Leif grinned at Asgard and sighed, "There surely could not be a better way to lose, now could there?"

The week went by rapidly. Nothing was said anymore about

Danielle and the twins joining the warrior crew to the mouth of the river Seine, but Danielle was busily planning and packing. As the morning of their departure dawned, Danielle shouldered a fur pack, which held her daughter and handed Talon the other with their son. At his questioning look, she told him calmly that this was a better way for all concerned.

"It won't hamper us as much as a wagon would and the children won't be jolted about as much."

"I'm not some woman, Danielle, to care for and carry about the children," Talon grumbled in a quarrelsome voice.

"I'll take Holgar in front of my mount when we near Herjolfstad, if that will salvage your Viking pride," she snapped.

The trip, despite Danielle's careful planning, took them another half day on top of the normal two, because they had to stop and feed the children. True to her promise Danielle hoisted Holgar in front of her saddle as they approached Herjolfstad.

They stayed the night at Thorson's new house, where he was living freely with the slave girl who had borne him a son. Thorson was less than happy to see them.

"I want no lectures about the merits of wedding slaves, brother," he told Talon bluntly. "I am head of our clan and I am not sure I want this woman for a mate."

Talon cocked his head in Thorson's direction. "I was not about to lecture you, brother, but apparently you must have some qualms over your arrangement or you would not have mentioned it. I came but to ask for shelter for a few days, since I plan to ready the Raider for a raid into France."

"You are welcome to stay, Talon, as are your wife and children and your friends. How the devil are you planning to take Danielle back to your stronghold, once you have mustered your crew?"

Talon grinned wickedly at Thorson, "I want no lectures, brother, but Danielle and the twins are accompanying us as far as her home on the banks of the Seine."

Thorson opened his mouth in protest and then he guffawed loudly. "No lectures received and none given." He still chuckled as he stepped aside to allow Talon entrance.

While Asgard and Leif worked to ready the Viking ship, Talon assembled a crew and Danielle shared her time between the children and seeing to the space in the bow, which would be home to her and the twins for the duration of the trip.

There were many eager warriors to join the crew after the long winter months. Though some turned questioning brows in Danielle's direction, none dared voice any objections. In fact, Talon thought his new crew rather subdued and made a mental note that he needed to fire their spirit once he delivered his wife and children to Honfleur-sur-mer.

CHAPTER TWENTY-EIGHT

The sea remained calm, making the crossing easy. Still, Talon heaved a silent sigh of relief, when the mouth of the Seine came into view. It seemed to him as if years had passed, since he had first come to shore in France or since he had stolen Danielle from the nuns. He grinned at her as the thought of their first meeting entered his mind. She had been such an innocent. The memory stirred his blood and his manhood answered by rising to attention. Suddenly he felt like a kid caught with his hand in the honey jar. He was amazed that his heart still pounded as strong as ever with desire. Reddening he turned abruptly to some contrived task.

Contentedly, he envisioned the coming night. God, he looked forward to sinking into her silky heat. It was as if Danielle could read his thoughts, because she came to stand next to him and allowed her breast to brush against his bare arm. She giggled delightedly, when he jumped as if he had been burned.

"I see you have missed me as much as I have missed you, my love. Wished we could slake our appetites here and now, but that is not what I have come to tell you." She pointed to a dense line of trees, whose branches dipped to the surface of the river. "See those trees, my love? They hide a secret cove. You can drop anchor there and advance on Honfleur-sur-mer from the back."

Talon stared at her in piqued surprise. "Why, you sly little wench, how come you have not told me that before?"

Danielle made a becoming moué and fluttered long lashes provocatively at him. "I did not want you to have undue advantage."

Talon cocked a golden brow in her direction. "You do not mind if I make war on your fellow countrymen?"

Danielle shrugged. "Whether I do or not, would it make a difference to you?"

Talon laughed and threw back his head. "You never fail to surprise and amuse me, wench."

Danielle carefully arranged her face to appear as if she were quite serious, but there was mischief brewing in the back of her mossy green eyes when she wagged her finger at Talon. "You best stay on guard, Viking, because I will make sure you'll never tire of me." Glancing casually about, she whispered through the side of her mouth. "Now hurry and get this ship moored or I vow I will disgrace myself in front of your crew."

Talon's gaze heated with aroused passion and he quickly roared clipped orders at the crew. Once they were anchored, Talon gave Danielle an approving nod. "This spot provides great cover. While the Raider is hidden from curious eyes, we can see all that sail past. Dropping his voice, he whispered, "Why don't you and the children go ahead." He paused eloquently to fix her with a passionate gaze. "I hope you will be ready and waiting for me when I get there."Danielle shouldered the pack with Fleurette and put Holgar on her hip as she made her way toward the manor house. Despite her double load, she felt young and light and there was a big smile on her lovely face.

Lisette was in the garden picking some early vegetables and when she saw the approaching figure, she shaded her old eyes so she could see better. She let loose of a delighted screech the moment she recognized Danielle. Dropping her harvest, she picked up her skirt and ran to meet her.

"*Mademoiselle!*" she cried happily between big salty tears. "We did not dare hope to ever see you again. That formidable Viking was so forbidding. "How did you ever get away from him?"

Danielle laughed and cried and handed Lisette the wiggling Holgar. "That formidable Viking is not far behind me, Lisette." She pointed to the twin armbands, which encircled her upper arms. "I am his wife, Lisette, and you are holding our son." Lisette's eyes grew round with wonder and she held the little boy at arm's length to get a better look at him.

"Sturdy like his sire, I'd say," she mumbled. "But the boy has your hair, *madame*."

Danielle giggled happily and carefully dislodged her bundle from her back. "Here, look what else I have, Lisette. We have a little girl as well. They are twins."

"Ah," sighed Lisette. "The Viking is a powerful man." She slapped her skinny thigh with glee. "I knew it from the moment when you took that nasty tumble off the horse and the babe stayed firmly planted." She giggled some more and led Danielle toward the house, holding both babies as if she would never want to let go of them.

"I need a bath, Lisette, and then I would like a little while alone with my husband." She blushed at Lisette's knowing grin and dropped her eyes.

"It is all right, *petite*, I understand. I once was young, ah yes. I'll see to your bath and then I will see to the *bébés*."

Danielle was luxuriating in the steaming scented bath water, when the door flew open and Talon entered, a huge smile on his handsome face. He turned the key resolutely in the lock. "This way we can be assured that no one will disturb us," he muttered. In three long strides he was by the side of the tub. His hand quickly dipped beneath the warm water, cupping a firm round breast. "Ah, how I have missed the feel of you," he sighed letting his hand roam leisurely over her body.

Danielle's eyes had closed of their own accord as the heat Talon aroused with his touch made her feel faint with heightening desire. They flew open in astonishment a few moments later, when Talon stepped into the tub with her, as naked as the day he was born.

"How did you take off your tunic so fast?" she sputtered in pleased surprise.

Talon chuckled. "I remember once when I could not undo the ties on the damned thing and was laid low by a wily nun and her drugged wine. I never had that problem again since." He leaned across her and beneath the tepid water their bodies touched, eliciting wanton gasps from both lovers. Talon kissed her then and Danielle's hands wound themselves into his tousled mane.

"I will not last long, if you do not hurry my love?" Talon muttered in a pained voice against her questing mouth. Danielle giggled and quickly released him to wash the salt from their skin. They did not take the time to dry, but Talon bore her with great speed to the bed and pressed her into the down feather mattress. He smiled down at her. "You are even more lovely now than when I met you, my love," he whispered. "You have given me more than I ever dared hope for."

Danielle stretched her arms out to him. "You are a beautiful male, Viking, and you have a glib tongue. Let's see if you can surpass your words with the thrust of your manhood."

"You witch," he chuckled happily. "All you want from me is

the pleasure my body can provide for you." And then there was no more conversation, only the heavy breathing of two lovers. Their lips fused in frantic ecstasy as they feverishly strove toward fulfillment.

Talon made love to Danielle twice more during the night. He left her asleep in bed before the sun crested the horizon. Before he walked out the door, he placed a gentle kiss on her forehead. "I will be back two days hence, my love," he murmured, so as not to waken her. "Take care of our babes and don't miss me too much." And then he was gone.

Danielle snuggled deeper into the covers and relished the idea that for once she could stay abed. A short time later she thought she was hearing his war cry and she smiled. Dreamily, she rejoiced in the knowledge that she was home at last.

Lisette bustled in some time later, carrying the squalling twins. "They would like their *petit déjeuner, madame,*" she announced with a happy grin.

The sun was beckoning through the open window, when Danielle finally got up and as was her habit from early youth, she went to look outside and inhale of the fresh breeze wafting in from the North Sea. The twins were sated and napping, leaving Danielle a few precious moments to herself. She bathed her hands and face and quickly rummaged through her wardrobe in search of a riding habit. She sighed with unrestrained pleasure when she found that it still fit even after giving birth to a set of twins.

As Danielle descended the circular staircase, she frowned. Something was not right. Her gaze quickly scanned the large hall, and then she knew. All the paintings and sconces were missing from their brackets, the hall was stripped bare and it had been her footsteps on the stairs reverberating which had called her attention to something being amiss.

"Lisette," she called, annoyance apparent in her tone of voice.

"*Oui, madame?* Is there aught amiss?"

"Yes. Have we been robbed once again, while I was absent?"

Lisette pursed her lips in disapproval. "*Oui,* we've been robbed all right. Not by your usual bands of thieves, but by your very own brother. No sooner than the Viking had carried you off, he came slinking back to the manor and took everything he thought was of any value."

Lisette crooked her finger for Danielle to follow. When she opened the door to the study, Danielle gasped, for it was completely empty. In his haste, Jean-Jacques even forgot to close the intricate secret panel in the fireplace mantel.

"Why did he take everything and left, when it seemed that I would never return?" Danielle wondered aloud.

"Ah, *madame,* the lout was afraid you might just turn up again. I overheard him mutter about how he had not expected you to come back the first time either." Lisette cocked her head in Danielle's direction. "Will you stay this time, *madame?*"

Danielle faced Lisette and there was undisguised regret in her lovely face. She shrugged, "I really don't know. It took all my wiles to coax Talon into bringing the babes and me in the first place. He still has that wanderlust in his bones and I don't know what it would take for him to settle down."

"Ah, *petite,* when the time is right, we'll see. You go and have a nice ride and I will look after the *bébes,*" she offered with a happy smile.

Danielle found that Jean-Jacques had robbed the stables as well and had only left the small mare Minette. It hit her hard that Cinnabar was gone, but she knew there was little she could do about that. "If I knew where you were hiding, brother dear, I'd hunt you down. I was willing to share and share alike, but you had to have it all, didn't you?" Danielle muttered absently as she watched the stable boy saddle the horse for her.

As she rode about the estate, Danielle noted that the crops would need tending and overseeing if they were to flourish for the Fall. She sighed. It would all go to waste eventually, because there would be no firm hand to guide the workers in their duty. The rest of the day she spent with the children, while gossiping with Lisette.

They went to bed early in anticipation of Talon's return by the next day. "Of course, he might like it so much that he might decide to raid some other town or place along the way," Danielle explained wistfully to Lisette as the maid was leaving her room.

Danielle twisted restlessly on her bed. She could not remember ever having missed Talon quite so much. She had come to rely on him to share her dreams and fears and she had so much to get off her chest. She jumped from the bed and went quietly to stand by the window. No wonder, she thought, the moon is waxing and it is almost as light as day outside. On impulse, she snatched a heavy robe and belted it tightly around her slender waist. She would walk to the promontory and watch the sea for a while, she decided.

Danielle sat down on the flat rock and leaned her back against an outcropping behind her. She breathed deeply of the salty air with an acute feeling of homesickness assailing her. If only she could persuade Talon to see the beauty of this land. She sighed quietly.

Below her the waves crashed in mesmerizing rhythm against the barren cliffs, sending a delicate spray of salty spume into the air. Danielle closed her eyes and allowed the peace of her surroundings to seep into her very soul.

"I thought I would find you here." The male voice was full of malice. Startled, Danielle's eyes flew open and the fear in their clear depth was unmistakable.

"How did you know that I was here?" she asked in a panic-stricken voice.

He chuckled derisively. "Is that any way to greet your brother after so long an absence, Danielle?" He moved into her line of vision and hunkered down, so he would be able to better gauge her reaction to his sudden appearance. He picked up a small pebble and idly threw it into the sea. "You have two beautiful children, Danielle. A boy and a girl, by the looks of it?"

Danielle's hand crept to her constricted throat. "You have been to see my children?" she asked in a small voice that sounded utterly terrified even to her own ears. "How did you ever know that I had returned? We only arrived yesterday," she wondered aloud.

Jean-Jacques fleshy lips quirked in an amused smile. "I have my ways, my dear sister." He cocked his head, his hands idly toying with some object Danielle could not identify, since he squatted with his back to the moon. "There are still some treasures in the house and there are still crops to be harvested. So I am keeping an eye out for that which I deem mine."

Danielle sat up straighter. She felt less vulnerable that way. "Why didn't you stay here and take care of the estate, Jean-Jacques? Why did you find it necessary to strip the house of so many valuables and sneak off with them? I agreed to split everything down the middle with you even though I was aware of the stipulation our sire made in his will."

Jean-Jacques rose with an angry snort of disgust, making sure that Danielle saw the wickedly pointed dagger he held in his hand. "Don't play me for the fool, Danielle. Sooner or later you would have found a reason to banish me from Honfleur-sur-mer and I would have had no recourse in the matter. I would be penniless," he gritted from between clenched teeth.

Danielle barely heard him. Her eyes were still trained on the knife. Her heart beat painfully in her chest as she wondered in anguished silence, if Jean-Jacques had hurt her innocent babes. And it shook her to the very core when he answered her as if he could read her thoughts.

"At first I thought about taking revenge on your children, but there would be so little satisfaction in killing them. They would not last long enough." He cackled again. "Don't breathe easy yet, my pet, I have great plans for you. And don't set your hopes on your hulking Viking. He won't come back in time to rescue you."

Jean-Jacques made a sudden lunge for Danielle and snatched her slim wrist in a cruel grip. He jerked her to her feet and brought her within inches of his hate-contorted visage. His breath was sour with wine and it amused him further to see Danielle's nose crinkle with distaste. Out of pure spite he puffed into her face, laughing gleefully at Danielle's disapproving glare.

"Ah, Danielle, what fun we'll have," he promised. With that he brought his arm around her slim waist and pressed the dagger almost playfully against her breast. He shoved her forward. "Let's go. The night is still young, but I have so many ideas that I will have to hurry to see them all through." He pointed toward the shadows of a nearby tree. "Cinnabar is waiting to take us to my hideaway."

Danielle balked. "This is madness, Jean-Jacques. You'll never get away with it."

"Come, come now. Would you rather I'd harm the children?" he chided.

"Why harm anybody? You have taken everything there was of any value. You should have enough to last you a lifetime."

"True enough, my dear sister. Then again I have always wondered what there is to your charms that enticed the Vikings keep you alive." He leered at her and brought one hand up to squeeze her breast. "I aim to find out, my dear ... I aim to find out."

Danielle had the greatest urge to slap his hand away, but the tip of his knife pricked through the material of her robe and reminded her that it would be a futile gesture.

Cinnabar neighed a greeting once he recognized Danielle. Jean-Jacques sneered. "How touching, the horse recognizes you. Hurry up and climb aboard, unless you'd rather have me throw you across the saddle."

Danielle acquiesced. She had no desire to put herself in greater jeopardy. Knowing her children were safe allowed her to concentrate on her own plight. "Where are you taking me?" she asked with quiet dignity.

"It doesn't matter. You'll see when you get there."

Agilely, he swung up behind her and kicked Cinnabar into a fast canter. After they had ridden almost to the Western boundary of the estate, Jean-Jacques reached suddenly around and tied a silken scarf over Danielle's eyes.

"No need for you to know where we are going, my pet. Just consider this the last trip of your life." He snickered evilly behind her as Danielle's heart plummeted to her slippers.

"You mean to kill me, Jean-Jacques?" she questioned in a toneless voice. "But why?"

"But why?" he mimicked sarcastically. "You are so full of questions, you stupid chit. Had you left well enough alone, you could be spending the rest of your life within the safety of the walls of the abbey." He leaned close to her ear. "The time will come soon enough, when you will *beg* me to end your life," he hissed sadistically.

Danielle could not refrain from shivering at his threat and Jean-Jacques chuckled with glee. "I will warm you posthaste, *ma petite*," he offered, and to back up his promise, he reached beneath her robe and crudely fondled her sex.

Danielle gasped at his temerity and slapped at his hand. "How dare you, brother?" she spat emphasizing the word brother in hopes to bring him to his senses.

"Oh, I dare all right, Danielle. Just wait when we get where we are going and see what I will dare."

Dread threatened to rob Danielle of breath and she fervently prayed that Talon was on his way back and would come to rescue her.

CHAPTER TWENTY-NINE

Talon took the stairs two at a time. The soles of his fur boots whispered across the marble steps. There was an expectant grin on his handsome face. Ah, how he had missed that wench, he thought lovingly. It was barely past midnight and she would not expect him home at this time, but the wind had been kind and the voyage from Paris had gone faster than he had anticipated. But not fast enough for a man who wanted to share his inner revelation with the woman he had come to treasure.

Talon was so eager to go to Danielle that he had not waited to see the Raider moored. Instead he jumped from her gunwale as soon as they came close enough to land. Asgard and Leif kidded him about it, when he told them of his plan, and Asgard vowed once again that love was too tasking and that he would give it a wide berth.

Talon stopped short at the door to Danielle's chamber, listening if she might be walking about with one of the babes or be in the middle of feeding them. He grimaced. The little critters did have a way of taking their toll on their parents' independence. They no longer could make love when they chose, he thought wryly, but just as quickly his smile returned when he remembered the joy the twins had brought into their lives.

He depressed the door handle with all the stealth born of long habit. His eyes, already accustomed to the dark, cut straight to the bed. It was empty. A small stab of disappointment slashed through him. Where could she be at this time of night? And then it dawned on him that Danielle might have gone to the kitchens for a snack. He chuckled into the darkness and tiptoed over to the crib, where his two babes were sleeping. He smiled down at them, hoping that they would not waken any time soon. His eyes alight with mischief he quickly chucked his tunic and boots and climbed into bed. Now all he had to figure out was how he would surprise her without scaring her out of her wits.

Talon relaxed against the goose down pillows. With a pleased grin he leered at the tented sheet, proof of just how much he'd missed Danielle. He lay there for what he presumed a considerable time and still Danielle did not show up. He frowned. Even if Danielle were hungry as a bear, she would have curbed that appetite by now, he thought grumpily.

Finally, Talon could wait no longer. His desire had taken a down turn and he was beginning to worry about her whereabouts. Muttering softly, he rummaged for the breeches Danielle had loaned him once and upon finding them he slipped them on. Barefoot, he padded downstairs and went to the kitchen. It was dark. Nothing was amiss, no dirty dishes, nothing.

The cliffs! Danielle had a penchant for those cliffs. She loved to go up there and let the wind blow through her hair. Blow the cobwebs from her brain she'd teased once. It was like a soothing balm to her when she watched the sea, though he could not recall that she ever went there in the middle of the night. However, his good mood was restored again, now that he'd figured out where to look for her. He raced for the plateau, love lending his feet wings.

He knew she was not there before he even topped the hill, but his keen sense of smell had picked up a scent that took but a moment to manifest itself in his brain. Horse droppings! Not too long ago, a horse had been near the tree to his left. But Danielle would not ride carelessly through the night, or would she? Talon walked cautiously toward the tree and within seconds he found an almost fresh pile of horse manure.

Upon looking closer Talon found hoof prints in the soft ground as well. Only the skilled eyes of a born hunter would notice that the prints coming were not quite as deep as the ones leaving. Talon sucked his breath in. No, he shook his massive head. It couldn't be. It was too far fetched, but the idea had taken root in his mind. Back in the Norseland it was common that warring clans would come in a man's absence and steal his wife. Talon turned abruptly and sped back to the manor.

He knocked at Lisette's door, his voice booming through the stillness of the house. "Lisette, wake up! Where is Danielle?"

Lisette opened her door, staring owlishly at Talon. "You might check in her chamber," she answered peevishly. "We did not expect you back until tomorrow, if then."

Talon reigned in his temper. "I have been upstairs. Danielle was not there. I even checked in the kitchens. Where could she be? Is it a habit of hers to wander about at night?"

Lisette sniffed. "How am I supposed to know?" And then her eyes clouded with worry. "The *bébés*! Oh, my, it is almost their feeding time."

"You take care of the babes. Feed them as well as you can. Tell her I'll be down at the cove if she comes back in the next few minutes. I am going for Asgard and Leif, just in case. If I were in my homeland I would worry about those horse tracks up by the plateau, but this is civilized country. No one would think to steal Danielle." Talon was already sprinting out the door, anxious to get to the cove, when he heard Lisette calling behind him.

"Jean-Jacques! *Oui*, he is a bad seed. I would not put it past him to come here and take revenge on Danielle." She wrung her hands in despair. Talon heard her, but never broke his easy lope.

Jean-Jacques held a tight grip on Danielle's arm as he tethered Cinnabar. He led her into a deserted hut, built by some farm hand years ago. Jean-Jacques pulled off her blindfold with a flourish and bowed mockingly. "We have arrived," he tittered.

Danielle tossed her head and wrinkled her nose in distaste. "It stinks in here. I don't want to come in." The single room was bare of furniture, except for a raised wooden platform, which must have served as a bedstead at one time. Animal droppings proclaimed that it had been uninhabited for some time.

Jean-Jacques laughed, but there was no humor in the sound as he shoved her roughly into the room. "You have no choice. You can scream all you want to ... and you will want to shortly. There is no one to hear you."

"Talon will be back soon. He will find you and slice your black heart from your skinny chest," Danielle spat out with bravado.

"He will not come in time, *petite*. If he is lucky, the buzzards will leave him a keepsake." His eyes narrowed as he began to stalk her.

Danielle backed away from him and circled slowly around the small room. She had to play for time. Had to think how she might thwart his plans.

Jean-Jacques cocked a brow her way. "I know what you are thinking, but there is no way out. If you give in gracefully, I just might allow you to die quicker."

Talon led Asgard and Leif back to the tree, where Cinnabar had been tethered not too long ago. "Let's fan out. If her brother has her, there is no telling what he might do." Talon's chest erupted with an anxious groan. "The bastard was too cowardly to come after me. I know that he took Danielle to revenge himself on me."

"Don't blame yourself, Talon. The man is more evil than you can imagine, if he kidnaps his own sister." Asgard and Leif exchanged glances of sympathy behind Talon's broad back.

"The coward is mine, when we catch up with him," Talon growled. He set off at a loping pace, one he employed when hunting wolves, his aquamarine eyes as turbulent as the churning sea riveted to the dew wet ground. He knew which way the horse had gone. Now it remained to be seen whether he would get there in time. Asgard and Leif jogged alongside their friend, grimly watching for signs.

Jean-Jacques quickly succeeded in cornering Danielle. His pale hand shot out, grabbing the belt of her robe. The knot untied easily enough and he jerked the belt from its loops. Despite her valiant effort to retain her composure Danielle cried out. Indignant green eyes flashed at her brother as she fumbled to hold the edges of the garment together.

"Take the robe off" he ordered hoarsely. Aghast, Danielle hesitated. "Take it off or by God I will rip it off you," he threatened.

Biting her lip Danielle did as he bade her. Her night shift underneath was of gossamer thin linen and left nothing to the imagination. Mutely, her eyes hot with shame, she watched, as Jean-Jacques looked her up and down like a choice morsel of food. She swallowed with difficulty when she saw him lick his fleshy lips in anticipation of what was to come.

In a last ditch effort Danielle stretched her hands out in front of her, begging. "Please, Jean-Jacques, don't do this to me. You are my brother." She loathed herself for the obvious quaver in her voice, but she did not want to die and there seemed no way out for her.

Jean-Jacques leered at her and broke out in another gale of laughter. "And you don't think that siblings copulate or kill each other, you stupid, coddled chit?" Leaning slightly forward, he jeered, "Normally I would not tell you this, but you see, you don't know everything, Miss High and Mighty. As it turns out, our sire had serious doubts whether I was really his offspring. He never could prove anything either way, but my mother told me before she died." He giggled, slashing his dagger playfully through the air. "Of course, I will let you speculate about that, *ma cherie*. I am through with the preliminaries. We will begin the fun part now." He shuttered his eyes to mere slits and before Danielle could ward him off, he neatly slashed the front of her night shift.

Her scream was one of pain and outrage. She stared incredulous at the thin red line, which ran from her collarbone to her navel. "You cut me, Jean-Jacques," she whispered in alarm. She traced the wound with trembling fingers, and despite all her resolve, tears rolled down her pale cheeks. She lifted her gaze once more to her brother's face, but her heart sank when she saw the vacuity in his eyes and the trickle of spittle running unheeded from the corner of his mouth. There would be no mercy from this man. This was no longer her brother but a stranger. Suddenly, she prayed that he might not be related to her.

Jean-Jacques advanced on her, knife in hand. His free arm
snaked about her slender waist and he pulled her into the circle
of his surprisingly strong embrace. He brought his fleshy mouth
to hers in an attempt to kiss her, but Danielle could not bear the
idea. She screamed her outrage and with all her might she
pushed against him and brought her knee up hard between his
legs.

Jean-Jacques cursed. His eyes narrowing with malice, he
slapped her with the open palm of his hand, making Danielle's
head snap backward upon impact. His pale eyes glazed over
with agony as he reached for his crotch. "You'll suffer for this,
you bitch," he hissed.

Talon stopped in his tracks. Years of living by his wits in the
wilds of the Norseland had attuned his hearing to the slightest
noises. Apparently, Asgard and Leif had heard it, too.
Communicating with hand signals they converged on the small
hut, half hidden behind a stand of trees.

Even from the distance Talon recognized Cinnabar. He
motioned for his friends to wait at either side of the door.
Roaring, Talon crashed his powerful shoulder against the rickety
door. It splintered off its hinges and propelled Talon to the
middle of the room.

Panting with fury, he took a quick look at Danielle to assure
himself that she was all right before his icy gaze encompassed
Jean-Jacques. It did not matter to him that he held no weapon
and that the other man had a long-bladed dagger. The moment
Talon saw the slowly oozing line of blood along his wife's torso,
he knew she had suffered. It spiraled his fury to new heights.

Danielle had never seen Talon in such a towering rage. Her
gaze glued to Talon's angry visage, she slowly backed against
the wall, giving him more room to maneuver. Jean-Jacques saw
his chances dwindling before his eyes. He darted after Danielle
in hopes of using her for a shield. Too late. Talon's long sinewy
arm grabbed hold of his jacket and hauled him up short.

Jean-Jacques slashed his dagger across Talon's forearm. Talon
paid it no more heed than he would have an insect bite. With
deadly determination, he intercepted his opponent's knife-
wielding arm on the next downward arch and neatly broke it at
the wrist. Before Jean-Jacques could cry out his pain, Talon's
huge fist smashed into his face, followed quickly by a muscular
knee ramming into his middle. Jean-Jacques was barely aware,
when the side of Talon's solid hand sliced across his nape to

complete his collapse.

Without another glance at the crumpled bloody form on the ground, Talon swooped toward Danielle. He lifted her gently into his powerful embrace, burying his face in the soft fall of her hair. Closing his eyes, he breathed of her scent.

"Ah, love, you have no idea the torture I endured when I found you missing," he rasped against her ear. "The thought of losing you was almost more than I could bear." He rained tender kisses on her pale face, grazed her mouth with feathery laps of his tongue and pressed her against his hard form as if he meant to never let go of her again. Holding her tightly, he walked out of the stinking hut and at a nod of his head, Asgard and Leif quickly prepared the place for burning.

Talon lifted Danielle onto Cinnabar and then mounted the gelding behind her. With great tenderness he pulled her into his lap and turned the horse toward Honfleur-sur-mer. Behind them the first wisps of smoke curled lazily into the dawning sky.

Snuggling against Talon, Danielle savored his warmth, the security of his embrace and the knowledge that she was truly loved. Squinting coyly up at him, she whispered, "Tell me again how it was almost too much to bear when you thought of losing me."

Talon's broad chest rose with unbridled mirth, his generous mouth stretched across the strong white line of teeth and the skin around his aquamarine eyes crinkled as he let go of a loud guffaw. "You little minx," he growled playfully. "You know full well that you have captured my heart and that I am smitten by you." He leaned forward and kissed her softly. "I came back to tell you that life without you has no longer any meaning. As we fought our way through the streets of Paris, it suddenly dawned on me that all the plunder and gold in the world could not replace you. I have decided to stay at Honfleur-sur-mer and raise our family here, if that is still what you wish."

Danielle pulled out of his embrace to stare dumbfounded at the powerful Viking. Talon's face reflected the love he felt for her. He chuckled, then raised a golden eyebrow in mock derision. "I see, I have at last succeeded this once in stilling your waspish tongue," he teased and then he captured her mouth in a tender kiss full of promise.

Printed in the United Kingdom
by Lightning Source UK Ltd.
107009UKS00001BA/21